• • •

E. M. FORSTER

HOWARDS END
AND OTHER STORIES

· · ·

E. M. FORSTER

HOWARDS END
AND OTHER STORIES

an imprint of
RUNNING PRESS
Philadelphia • London

Howards End is reprinted from the first edition, published in 1910 by Edward
Arnold, London, and made available through the courtesy of Van Pelt Library,
University of Pennsylvania. *The Celestial Omnibus and Other Stories* is reprinted
from the first edition, published in 1911 by Sidgwick and Jackson Ltd., London,
and made available through the courtesy of Bartle Library, State University of
New York at Binghamton. All spellings and punctuation are preserved as they
appeared in the original editions, except for obvious typographical errors.

The review 'The Season's Great Novel' is reprinted from
the London *Daily Mail*, 17 November, 1910.

Cover photograph reproduced with permission from
the King's College Library, Cambridge.

9 8 7 6 5 4 3 2 1
Digit on the right indicates the number of this printing.

Library of Congress Cataloging-in-Publication Number 96-71143

ISBN 0-7624-0176-1

Cover design by Diane Miljat
Set in ITC Berkeley Oldstyle

Published by Courage Books, an imprint of
Running Press Book Publishers
125 South Twenty-second Street
Philadelphia, Pennsylvania 19103-4399

. . .

CONTENTS

. . .

Howards End

By E. M. Forster

"Only connect . . ."

CHAPTER I

One may as well begin with Helen's letters to her sister.

"HOWARDS END,
"Tuesday.

"DEAREST MEG,

"It isn't going to be what we expected. It is old and little, and altogether delightful—red brick. We can scarcely pack in as it is, and the dear knows what will happen when Paul (younger son) arrives to-morrow. From hall you go right or left into dining-room or drawing-room. Hall itself is practically a room. You open another door in it, and there are the stairs going up in a sort of tunnel to the first-floor. Three bedrooms in a row there, and three attics in a row above. That isn't all the house really, but it's all that one notices—nine windows as you look up from the front garden.

"Then there's a very big wych-elm—to the left as you look up—leaning a little over the house, and standing on the boundary between the garden and meadow. I quite love that tree already. Also ordinary elms, oaks—no nastier than ordinary oaks—pear-trees, apple-trees, and a vine. No silver birches, though. However, I must get on to my host and hostess. I only wanted to show that it isn't the least what we expected. Why did we settle that their house would be all gables and wiggles, and their garden all gamboge-coloured paths? I believe simply because we associate them with expensive hotels—Mrs. Wilcox trailing in beautiful dresses down long corridors, Mr. Wilcox bullying porters, etc. We females are that unjust.

"I shall be back Saturday; will let you know train later. They are as angry as I am that you did not come too; really Tibby is too tiresome, he starts a new mortal disease every month. How could he have got hay fever in London? and even if he could, it seems hard that you should give up a visit to hear a schoolboy sneeze. Tell him that Charles Wilcox (the son who is here) has hay fever too, but he's brave, and gets quite cross when we inquire after it. Men like the Wilcoxes would do Tibby a power of good. But you won't agree, and I'd better change the subject.

"This long letter is because I'm writing before breakfast. Oh, the beautiful vine leaves! The house is covered with a vine. I looked out earlier, and Mrs. Wilcox was already in the garden. She evidently loves it. No wonder she sometimes looks tired. She was watching the large red poppies come out. Then she walked off the lawn to the meadow, whose corner to the right I can just see. Trail, trail, went her long dress over the sopping grass, and she came back with her hands full of the hay that was cut yesterday—I suppose for rabbits or something, as she kept on smelling it. The air here is delicious. Later on I heard the noise of croquet balls, and looked out again, and it was Charles Wilcox practising; they are keen on all games. Presently he started sneezing and had to stop. Then I hear more clicketing, and it is Mr. Wilcox practising, and then, 'a-tissue, a-tissue': he has to stop too. Then Evie comes out, and does some calisthenic exercises on a machine that is tacked on to a greengage-tree—they put everything to use—and then she says 'a-tissue,' and in she goes. And finally Mrs. Wilcox reappears, trail, trail, still smelling hay and looking at the flowers. I inflict all this on you because once you said that life is sometimes life and sometimes only a drama, and one must learn to distinguish tother from which, and up to now I have always put that down as 'Meg's clever nonsense.' But this morning, it really does seem not life but a play, and it did amuse me enormously to watch the W's. Now Mrs. Wilcox has come in.

"I am going to wear [omission]. Last night Mrs. Wilcox wore an [omission], and Evie [omission]. So it isn't exactly a go-as-you-please place, and if you shut your eyes it still seems the wiggly hotel that we expected. Not if you open them. The dog-roses are too sweet. There is a great hedge of them over the lawn—magnificently tall, so that they fall down in garlands, and nice and thin at the bottom, so that you can see ducks through it and a cow. These belong to the farm, which is the only house near us. There goes the breakfast gong. Much love. Modified love to Tibby. Love to Aunt Juley; how good of her to come and keep you company, but what a bore. Burn this. Will write again Thursday.

"HELEN."

"HOWARDS END,
"Friday.

"DEAREST MEG,

"I am having a glorious time. I like them all. Mrs. Wilcox, if quieter than in Germany, is sweeter than ever, and I never saw anything like her steady unselfishness, and the best of it is that the others do not take advantage of her. They are the very happiest, jolliest family that you can imagine. I do really feel that we are making friends. The fun of it is that they think me a noodle, and say so—at least, Mr. Wilcox does—and when that happens, and one doesn't mind, it's a pretty sure test, isn't it? He says the most horrid things about women's suffrage so nicely, and when I said I believed in equality he just folded his arms and gave me such a setting down as I've never had. Meg, shall we ever learn to talk less? I never felt so ashamed of myself in my life. I couldn't point to a time when men had been equal, nor even to a time when the wish to be equal had made them happier in other ways. I couldn't say a word. I had just picked up the notion that equality is good from some book—probably from poetry, or you. Anyhow, it's been knocked into pieces, and, like all people who are really strong, Mr. Wilcox did it without hurting me. On the other hand, I laugh at them for catching hay fever. We live like fighting-cocks, and Charles takes us out every day in the motor—a tomb with trees in it, a hermit's house, a wonderful road that was made by the Kings of Mercia—tennis—a cricket match—bridge—and at night we squeeze up in this lovely house. The whole clan's here now—it's like a rabbit warren. Evie is a dear. They want me to stop over Sunday—I suppose it won't matter if I do. Marvellous weather and the views marvellous—views westward to the high ground. Thank you for your letter. Burn this.

"Your affectionate
"HELEN."

"HOWARDS END,
"Sunday.

"Dearest dearest Meg,—I do not know what you will say: Paul and I are in love—the younger son who only came here Wednesday."

CHAPTER II

Margaret glanced at her sister's note and pushed it over the breakfast-table to her aunt. There was a moment's hush, and then the flood-gates opened.

"I can tell you nothing, Aunt Juley. I know no more than you do. We met—we only met the father and mother abroad last spring. I know so little that I didn't even know their son's name. It's all so——" She waved her hand and laughed a little.

"In that case it is far too sudden."

"Who knows, Aunt Juley, who knows?"

"But, Margaret dear, I mean, we mustn't be unpractical now that we've come to facts. It is too sudden, surely."

"Who knows!"

"But Margaret dear——"

"I'll go for her other letters," said Margaret. "No, I won't, I'll finish my breakfast. In fact, I haven't them. We met the Wilcoxes on an awful expedition that we made from Heidelberg to Speyer. Helen and I had got it into our heads that there was a grand old cathedral at Speyer—the Archbishop of Speyer was one of the seven electors—you know—'Speyer, Maintz, and Köln.' Those three sees once commanded the Rhine Valley and got it the name of Priest Street."

"I still feel quite uneasy about this business, Margaret."

"The train crossed by a bridge of boats, and at first sight it looked quite fine. But oh, in five minutes we had seen the whole thing. The cathedral had been ruined, absolutely ruined, by restoration; not an inch left of the original structure. We wasted a whole day, and came across the Wilcoxes as we were eating our sandwiches in the public gardens. They too, poor things, had been taken in—they were actually stopping at Speyer—and they rather liked Helen insisting that they must fly with us to Heidelberg. As a matter of fact, they did come on next day. We all took some drives together. They knew us well enough to ask Helen to come and see them—at least, I was asked too, but Tibby's illness prevented me, so last Monday she went alone. That's all. You know as much as I do now. It's a young man out the unknown. She was to have come back Saturday, but put off till Monday, perhaps on account of—I don't know."

She broke off, and listened to the sounds of a London morning. Their house was in Wickham Place, and fairly quiet, for a lofty promontory of buildings separated it from the main thoroughfare. One had the sense of a backwater, or rather of an estuary, whose waters flowed in from the invisible sea, and ebbed into a profound silence while the waves without were still beating. Though the promontory consisted of flats—expensive, with cavernous entrance halls, full of concierges and palms—it fulfilled its purpose, and gained for the older houses opposite a certain measure of peace. These, too, would be swept away in time, and another promontory would arise upon their site, as humanity piled itself higher and higher on the precious soil of London.

Mrs. Munt had her own method of interpreting her nieces. She decided that Margaret was a little hysterical, and was trying to gain time by a torrent of talk. Feeling very diplomatic, she lamented the fate of Speyer, and declared that never, never should she be so misguided as to visit it, and added of her own accord that the principles of restoration were ill understood in Germany. "The Germans," she said, "are too thorough, and this is all very well sometimes, but at other times it does not do."

"Exactly," said Margaret; "Germans are too thorough." And her eyes began to shine.

"Of course I regard you Schlegels as English," said Mrs. Munt hastily—"English to the backbone."

Margaret leaned forward and stroked her hand.

"And that reminds me—Helen's letter——"

"Oh yes, Aunt Juley, I am thinking all right about Helen's letter. I know—I must go down and see her. I am thinking about her all right. I am meaning to go down."

"But go with some plan," said Mrs. Munt, admitting into her kindly voice a note of exasperation. "Margaret, if I may interfere, don't be taken by surprise. What do you think of the Wilcoxes? Are they our sort? Are they likely people? Could they appreciate Helen, who is to my mind a very special sort of person? Do they care about Literature and Art? That is most important when you come to think of it. Literature and Art. Most important. How old would the son be? She says 'younger son.' Would he be in a position to marry? Is he likely to make Helen happy? Did you gather——"

"I gathered nothing."

They began to talk at once.

"Then in that case——"

"In that case I can make no plans, don't you see."

"On the contrary——"

"I hate plans. I hate lines of action. Helen isn't a baby."

"Then in that case, my dear, why go down?"

Margaret was silent. If her aunt could not see why she must go down, she was not going to tell her. She was not going to say "I love my dear sister; I must be near her at this crisis of her life." The affections are more reticent than the passions, and their expression more subtle. If she herself should ever fall in love with a man, she, like Helen, would proclaim it from the house-tops, but as she only loved a sister she used the voiceless language of sympathy.

"I consider you odd girls," continued Mrs. Munt, "and very wonderful girls, and in many ways far older than your years. But—you won't be offended?—frankly, I feel you are not up to this business. It requires an older person. Dear, I have nothing to call me back to Swanage." She spread out her plump arms. "I am all at your disposal. Let me go down to this house whose name I forget instead of you."

"Aunt Juley"—she jumped up and kissed her—"I must, must go to Howards End myself. You don't exactly understand, though I can never thank you properly for offering."

"I do understand," retorted Mrs. Munt, with immense confidence. "I go down in no spirit of interference, but to make inquiries. Inquiries are necessary. Now, I am going to be rude. You would say the wrong thing; to a certainty you would. In your anxiety for Helen's happiness you would offend the whole of these Wilcoxes by asking one of your impetuous questions—not that one minds offending them."

"I shall ask no questions. I have it in Helen's writing that she and a man are in love. There is no question to ask as long as she keeps to that. All the rest isn't worth a straw. A long engagement if you like, but inquiries, questions, plans, lines of action—no, Aunt Juley, no."

Away she hurried, not beautiful, not supremely brilliant, but filled with something that took the place of both qualities—something best described as a profound vivacity, a continual and sincere response to all that she encountered in her path through life.

"If Helen had written the same to me about a shop-assistant or a penniless clerk——"

"Dear Margaret, do come into the library and shut the door. Your good maids are dusting the banisters."

"—or if she had wanted to marry the man who calls for Carter Paterson, I should have said the same." Then, with one of those turns that convinced her aunt that she was not mad really, and convinced observers of another type that she was not a barren theorist, she added: "Though in the case of Carter Paterson I should want it to be a very long engagement indeed, I must say."

"I should think so," said Mrs. Munt; "and, indeed, I can scarcely follow you. Now, just imagine if you said anything of that sort to the Wilcoxes. I understand it, but most good people would think you mad. Imagine how disconcerting for Helen! What is wanted is a person who will go slowly, slowly in this business, and see how things are and where they are likely to lead to."

Margaret was down on this.

"But you implied just now that the engagement must be broken off."

"I think probably it must; but slowly."

"Can you break an engagement off slowly?" Her eyes lit up. "What's an engagement made of, do you suppose? I think it's made of some hard stuff, that may snap, but can't break. It is different to the other ties of life. They stretch or bend. They admit of degree. They're different."

"Exactly so. But won't you let me just run down to Howards House, and save you all the discomfort? I will really not interfere, but I do so thoroughly understand the kind of thing you Schlegels want that one quiet look round will be enough for me."

Margaret again thanked her, and again kissed her, and then ran upstairs to see her brother.

He was not so well.

The hay fever had worried him a good deal all night. His head ached, his eyes were wet, his mucous membrane, he informed her, in a most unsatisfactory condition. The only thing that made life worth living was the thought of Walter Savage Landor, from whose "Imaginary Conversations" she had promised to read at frequent intervals during the day.

It was rather difficult. Something must be done about Helen. She must be assured that it is not a criminal offence to love at first sight. A telegram to this effect would be cold and cryptic, a personal visit seemed each moment more impossible. Now the doctor arrived, and said that Tibby was quite bad. Might it really be best to accept Aunt Juley's kind offer, and to send her down to Howards End with a note?

Certainly Margaret was impulsive. She did swing rapidly from one decision to another. Running downstairs into the library, she cried: "Yes, I have changed my mind; I do wish that you would go."

There was a train from King's Cross at eleven. At half-past ten Tibby, with rare self-effacement, fell asleep, and Margaret was able to drive her aunt to the station.

"You will remember, Aunt Juley, not to be drawn into discussing the engagement. Give my letter to Helen, and say whatever you feel yourself, but do keep clear of the relatives. We have scarcely got their names straight yet, and, besides, that sort of thing is so uncivilized and wrong."

"So uncivilized?" queried Mrs. Munt, fearing that she was losing the point of some brilliant remark.

"Oh, I used an affected word. I only meant would you please only talk the thing over with Helen."

"Only with Helen."

"Because——" But it was no moment to expound the personal nature of love. Even Margaret shrank from it, and contented herself with stroking her good aunt's hand, and with meditating, half sensibly and half poetically, on the journey that was about to begin from King's Cross.

Like many others who have lived long in a great capital, she had strong feelings about the various railway termini. They are our gates to the glorious and the unknown. Through them we pass out into adventure and sunshine, to them, alas! we return. In Paddington all Cornwall is latent and the remoter west; down the inclines of Liverpool Street lie fenlands and the illimitable Broads; Scotland is through the pylons of Euston; Wessex behind the poised chaos of Waterloo. Italians realize this, as is natural; those of them who are so unfortunate as to serve as waiters in Berlin call the Anhalt Bahnhof the Stazione d'Italia, because by it they must return to their homes. And he is a chilly Londoner who does not endow his stations with some personality, and extend to them, however shyly, the emotions of fear and love.

To Margaret—I hope that it will not set the reader against her—the station of King's Cross had always suggested Infinity. Its very situation—withdrawn a little behind the facile splendours of St. Pancras—implied a comment on the materialism of life. Those two great arches, colourless, indifferent, shouldering between them an unlovely clock, were fit portals for some eternal adventure, whose issue might be prosperous, but would certainly not be expressed in the ordinary language of prosperity. If you think this ridiculous, remember that it is not Margaret who is telling you about it; and let me hasten to add that they were in plenty of time for the train; that Mrs. Munt, though she took a second-class ticket, was put by the guard into a first (only two seconds on the train, one smoking and the other babies—one cannot be expected to travel with babies); and that Margaret, on her return to Wickham Place, was confronted with the following telegram:

"All over. Wish I had never written. Tell no one.—HELEN."

But Aunt Juley was gone—gone irrevocably, and no power on earth could stop her.

CHAPTER III

Most complacently did Mrs. Munt rehearse her mission. Her nieces were independent young women, and it was not often that she was able to help them. Emily's daughters had never been quite like other girls. They had been left motherless when Tibby was born, when Helen was five and Margaret herself but thirteen. It was before the passing of the Deceased Wife's Sister Bill, so Mrs. Munt could without impropriety offer to go and keep house at Wickham Place. But her brother-in-law, who was peculiar and a

German, had referred the question to Margaret, who with the crudity of youth had answered, 'No, they could manage much better alone.' Five years later Mr. Schlegel had died too, and Mrs. Munt had repeated her offer. Margaret, crude no longer, had been grateful and extremely nice, but the substance of her answer had been the same. "I must not interfere a third time," thought Mrs. Munt. However, of course she did. She learnt, to her horror, that Margaret, now of age, was taking her money out of the old safe investments and putting it into Foreign Things, which always smash. Silence would have been criminal. Her own fortune was invested in Home Rails, and most ardently did she beg her niece to imitate her. "Then we should be together, dear." Margaret, out of politeness, invested a few hundreds in the Nottingham and Derby Railway, and though the Foreign Things did admirably and the Nottingham and Derby declined with the steady dignity of which only Home Rails are capable, Mrs. Munt never ceased to rejoice, and to say, "I did manage that, at all events. When the smash comes poor Margaret will have a nest-egg to fall back upon." This year Helen came of age, and exactly the same thing happened in Helen's case; she also would shift her money out of Consols, but she, too, almost without being pressed, consecrated a fraction of it to the Nottingham and Derby Railway. So far so good, but in social matters their aunt had accomplished nothing. Sooner or later the girls would enter on the process known as throwing themselves away, and if they had delayed hitherto, it was only that they might throw themselves more vehemently in the future. They saw too many people at Wickham Place—unshaven musicians, an actress even, German cousins (one knows what foreigners are), acquaintances picked up at Continental hotels (one knows what they are too). It was interesting, and down at Swanage no one appreciated culture more than Mrs. Munt; but it was dangerous, and disaster was bound to come. How right she was, and how lucky to be on the spot when the disaster came!

The train sped northward, under innumerable tunnels. It was

only an hour's journey, but Mrs. Munt had to raise and lower the window again and again. She passed through the South Welwyn Tunnel, saw light for a moment, and entered the North Welwyn Tunnel, of tragic fame. She traversed the immense viaduct, whose arches span untroubled meadows and the dreamy flow of Tewin Water. She skirted the parks of politicians. At times the Great North Road accompanied her, more suggestive of infinity than any railway, awakening, after a nap of a hundred years, to such life as is conferred by the stench of motor-cars, and to such culture as is implied by the advertisements of antibilious pills. To history, to tragedy, to the past, to the future, Mrs. Munt remained equally indifferent; hers but to concentrate on the end of her journey, and to rescue poor Helen from this dreadful mess.

The station for Howards End was at Hilton, one of the large villages that are strung so frequently along the North Road, and that owe their size to the traffic of coaching and pre-coaching days. Being near London, it had not shared in the rural decay, and its long High Street had budded out right and left into residential estates. For about a mile a series of tiled and slated houses passed before Mrs. Munt's inattentive eyes, a series broken at one point by six Danish tumuli that stood shoulder to shoulder along the highroad, tombs of soldiers. Beyond these tumuli habitations thickened, and the train came to a standstill in a tangle that was almost a town.

The station, like the scenery, like Helen's letters, struck an indeterminate note. Into which country will it lead, England or Suburbia? It was new, it had island platforms and a subway, and the superficial comfort exacted by business men. But it held hints of local life, personal intercourse, as even Mrs. Munt was to discover.

"I want a house," she confided to the ticket boy. "Its name is Howards Lodge. Do you know where it is?"

"Mr. Wilcox!" the boy called.

A young man in front of them turned round.

"She's wanting Howards End."

There was nothing for it but to go forward, though Mrs. Munt was too much agitated even to stare at the stranger. But remembering that there were two brothers, she had the sense to say to him, "Excuse me asking, but are you the younger Mr. Wilcox or the elder?"

"The younger. Can I do anything for you?"

"Oh, well"—she controlled herself with difficulty. "Really. Are you? I——" She moved away from the ticket boy and lowered her voice. "I am Miss Schlegel's aunt. I ought to introduce myself, oughtn't I? My name is Mrs. Munt."

She was conscious that he raised his cap and said quite coolly, "Oh, rather; Miss Schlegel is stopping with us. Did you want to see her?"

"Possibly——"

"I'll call you a cab. No; wait a mo." He thought. "Our motor's here. I'll run you up in it."

"That is very kind——"

"Not at all, if you'll just wait till they bring out a parcel from the office. This way."

"My niece is not with you by any chance?"

"No; I came over with my father. He has gone on north in your train. You'll see Miss Schlegel at lunch. You're coming up to lunch, I hope?"

"I should like to come up," said Mrs. Munt, not committing herself to nourishment until she had studied Helen's lover a little more. He seemed a gentleman, but had so rattled her round that her powers of observation were numbed. She glanced at him stealthily. To a feminine eye there was nothing amiss in the sharp depressions at the corners of his mouth, nor in the rather box-like construction of his forehead. He was dark, clean-shaven, and seemed accustomed to command.

"In front or behind? Which do you prefer? It may be windy in front."

"In front if I may; then we can talk."

"But excuse me one moment—I can't think what they're doing with that parcel." He strode into the booking-office, and called with a new voice: "Hi! hi, you there! Are you going to keep me waiting all day? Parcel for Wilcox, Howards End. Just look sharp!" Emerging, he said in quieter tones: "This station's abominably organized; if I had my way, the whole lot of 'em should get the sack. May I help you in?"

"This is very good of you," said Mrs. Munt, as she settled herself into a luxurious cavern of red leather, and suffered her person to be padded with rugs and shawls. She was more civil than she had intended, but really this young man was very kind. Moreover, she was a little afraid of him: his self-possession was extraordinary. "Very good indeed," she repeated, adding: "It is just what I should have wished."

"Very good of you to say so," he replied, with a slight look of surprise, which, like most slight looks, escaped Mrs. Munt's attention. "I was just tooling my father over to catch the down train."

"You see, we heard from Helen this morning."

Young Wilcox was pouring in petrol, starting his engine, and performing other actions with which this story has no concern. The great car began to rock, and the form of Mrs. Munt, trying to explain things, sprang agreeably up and down among the red cushions. "The mater will be very glad to see you," he mumbled. "Hi! I say. Parcel. Parcel for Howards End. Bring it out. Hi!"

A bearded porter emerged with the parcel in one hand and an entry book in the other. With the gathering whir of the motor these ejaculations mingled: "Sign, must I? Why the —— should I sign after all this bother? Not even got a pencil on you? Remember next time I report you to the station-master. My time's of value, though yours mayn't be. Here"—here being a tip.

"Extremely sorry, Mrs. Munt."

"Not at all, Mr. Wilcox."

"And do you object to going through the village? It is rather a longer spin, but I have one or two commissions."

"I should love going through the village. Naturally I am very anxious to talk things over with you."

As she said this she felt ashamed, for she was disobeying

Margaret's instructions. Only disobeying them in the letter, surely. Margaret had only warned her against discussing the incident with outsiders. Surely it was not 'uncivilized or wrong' to discuss it with the young man himself, since chance had thrown them together.

A reticent fellow, he made no reply. Mounting by her side, he put on gloves and spectacles, and off they drove, the bearded porter—life is a mysterious business—looking after them with admiration.

The wind was in their faces down the station road, blowing the dust into Mrs. Munt's eyes. But as soon as they turned into the Great North Road she opened fire. "You can well imagine," she said, "that the news was a great shock to us."

"What news?"

"Mr. Wilcox," she said frankly, "Margaret has told me everything—everything. I have seen Helen's letter."

He could not look her in the face, as his eyes were fixed on his work; he was travelling as quickly as he dared down the High Street. But he inclined his head in her direction, and said, "I beg your pardon; I didn't catch."

"About Helen. Helen, of course. Helen is a very exceptional person—I am sure you will let me say this, feeling towards her as you do—indeed, all the Schlegels are exceptional. I come in no spirit of interference, but it was a great shock."

They drew up opposite a draper's. Without replying, he turned round in his seat, and contemplated the cloud of dust that they had raised in their passage through the village. It was settling again, but not all into the road from which he had taken it. Some of it had percolated through the open windows, some had whitened the roses and gooseberries of the wayside gardens, while a certain proportion had entered the lungs of the villagers. "I wonder when they'll learn wisdom and tar the roads," was his comment. Then a man ran out of the draper's with a roll of oilcloth, and off they went again.

"Margaret could not come herself, on account of poor Tibby, so I am here to represent her and to have a good talk."

"I'm sorry to be so dense," said the young man, again drawing up outside a shop. "But I still haven't quite understood."

"Helen, Mr. Wilcox—my niece and you."

He pushed up his goggles and gazed at her, absolutely bewildered. Horror smote her to the heart, for even she began to suspect that they were at cross-purposes, and that she had commenced her mission by some hideous blunder.

"Miss Schlegel and myself?" he asked, compressing his lips.

"I trust there has been no misunderstanding," quavered Mrs. Munt. "Her letter certainly read that way."

"What way?"

"That you and she——" She paused, then drooped her eyelids.

"I think I catch your meaning," he said stickily. "What an extraordinary mistake!"

"Then you didn't the least——" she stammered, getting blood-red in the face, and wishing she had never been born.

"Scarcely, as I am already engaged to another lady." There was a moment's silence, and then he caught his breath and exploded with, "Oh, good God! Don't tell me it's some silliness of Paul's."

"But you are Paul."

"I'm not."

"Then why did you say so at the station?"

"I said nothing of the sort."

"I beg your pardon, you did."

"I beg your pardon, I did not. My name is Charles."

"Younger" may mean son as opposed to father, or second brother as opposed to first. There is much to be said for either view, and later on they said it. But they had other questions before them now.

"Do you mean to tell me that Paul——"

But she did not like his voice. He sounded as if he was talking to a porter, and, certain that he had deceived her at the station, she too grew angry.

"Do you mean to tell me that Paul and your niece——"

Mrs. Munt—such is human nature—determined that she would champion the lovers. She was not going to be bullied by a severe young man. "Yes, they care for one another very much indeed," she said. "I dare say they will tell you about it by-and-by. We heard this morning."

And Charles clenched his fist and cried, "The idiot, the idiot, the little fool!"

Mrs. Munt tried to divest herself of her rugs. "If that is your attitude, Mr. Wilcox, I prefer to walk."

"I beg you will do no such thing. I take you up this moment to the house. Let me tell you the thing's impossible, and must be stopped."

Mrs. Munt did not often lose her temper, and when she did it was only to protect those whom she loved. On this occasion she blazed out. "I quite agree, sir. The thing is impossible, and I will come up and stop it. My niece is a very exceptional person, and I am not inclined to sit still while she throws herself away on those who will not appreciate her."

Charles worked his jaws.

"Considering she has only known your brother since Wednesday, and only met your father and mother at a stray hotel——"

"Could you possibly lower your voice? The shopman will overhear."

"Esprit de classe"—if one may coin the phrase—was strong in Mrs. Munt. She sat quivering while a member of the lower orders deposited a metal funnel, a saucepan, and a garden squirt beside the roll of oilcloth.

"Right behind?"

"Yes, sir." And the lower orders vanished in a cloud of dust.

"I warn you: Paul hasn't a penny; it's useless."

"No need to warn us, Mr. Wilcox, I assure you. The warning is all the other way. My niece has been very foolish, and I shall give her a good scolding and take her back to London with me."

"He has to make his way out in Nigeria. He couldn't think of marrying for years, and when he does it must be a woman who can stand the climate, and is in other ways—— Why hasn't he told us? Of course he's ashamed. He knows he's been a fool. And so he has—a damned fool."

She grew furious.

"Whereas Miss Schlegel has lost no time in publishing the news."

"If I were a man, Mr. Wilcox, for that last remark I'd box your ears. You're not fit to clean my niece's boots, to sit in the same room with her, and you dare—you actually dare—— I decline to argue with such a person."

"All I know is, she's spread the thing and he hasn't, and my father's away and I——"

"And all I know is——"

"Might I finish my sentence, please?"

"No."

Charles clenched his teeth and sent the motor swerving all over the lane.

She screamed.

So they played the game of Capping Families, a round of which is always played when love would unite two members of our race. But they played it with unusual vigour, stating in so many words that Schlegels were better than Wilcoxes, Wilcoxes better than Schlegels. They flung decency aside. The man was young, the woman deeply stirred; in both a vein of coarseness was latent. Their quarrel was no more surprising than are most quarrels—inevitable at the time, incredible afterwards. But it was more than usually futile. A few minutes, and they were enlightened. The motor drew up at Howards End, and Helen, looking very pale, ran out to meet her aunt.

"Aunt Juley, I have just had a telegram from Margaret; I—I meant to stop your coming. It isn't—it's over."

The climax was too much for Mrs. Munt. She burst into tears.

"Aunt Juley dear, don't. Don't let them know I've been so silly. It wasn't anything. Do bear up for my sake."

"Paul," cried Charles Wilcox, pulling his gloves off.

"Don't let them know. They are never to know."

"Oh, my darling Helen——"

"Paul! Paul!"

A very young man came out of the house.

"Paul, is there any truth in this?"

"I didn't—I don't——"

"Yes or no, man; plain question, plain answer. Did or didn't Miss Schlegel——"

"Charles dear," said a voice from the garden. "Charles, dear Charles, one doesn't ask plain questions. There aren't such things."

They were all silent. It was Mrs. Wilcox.

She approached just as Helen's letter had described her, trailing noiselessly over the lawn, and there was actually a wisp of hay in her hands. She seemed to belong not to the young people and their motor, but to the house, and to the tree that overshadowed it. One knew that she worshipped the past, and that the instinctive wisdom the past can alone bestow had descended upon her—that wisdom to which we give the clumsy name of aristocracy. High born she might not be. But assuredly she cared about her ancestors, and let them help her. When she saw Charles angry, Paul frightened, and Mrs. Munt in tears, she heard her ancestors say, "Separate those human beings who will hurt each other most. The rest can wait." So she did not ask questions. Still less did she pretend that nothing had happened, as a competent society hostess would have done. She said, "Miss Schlegel, would you take your aunt up to your room or to my room, whichever you think best. Paul, do find Evie, and tell her lunch for six, but I'm not sure whether we shall all be downstairs for it." And when they had obeyed her, she turned to her elder son, who still stood in the throbbing, stinking car, and smiled at him with tenderness, and without saying a word, turned away from him towards her flowers.

"Mother," he called, "are you aware that Paul has been playing the fool again?"

"It is all right, dear. They have broken off the engagement."

"Engagement———!"

"They do not love any longer, if you prefer it put that way," said Mrs. Wilcox, stooping down to smell a rose.

CHAPTER IV

Helen and her aunt returned to Wickham Place in a state of collapse, and for a little time Margaret had three invalids on her hands. Mrs. Munt soon recovered. She possessed to a remarkable degree the power of distorting the past, and before many days were over she had forgotten the part played by her own imprudence in the catastrophe. Even at the crisis she had cried, "Thank goodness, poor Margaret is saved this!" which during the journey to London evolved into, "It had to be gone through by someone," which in its turn ripened into the permanent form of "The one time I really did help Emily's girls was over the Wilcox business." But Helen was a more serious patient. New ideas had burst upon her like a thunder clap, and by them and their reverberations she had been stunned.

The truth was that she had fallen in love, not with an individual, but with a family.

Before Paul arrived she had, as it were, been tuned up into his key. The energy of the Wilcoxes had fascinated her, had created new images of beauty in her responsive mind. To be all day with them in the open air, to sleep at night under their roof, had seemed the supreme joy of life, and had led to that abandonment of personality that is a possible prelude to love. She had liked giving in to Mr. Wilcox, or Evie, or Charles; she had liked being told that her notions of life were sheltered or academic; that Equality was nonsense, Votes for Women nonsense, Socialism nonsense, Art and Literature, except when conducive to strengthening the character, nonsense. One by one the Schlegel fetiches had been overthrown, and, though professing to defend them, she had rejoiced. When Mr. Wilcox said that one sound man of business did more good to the world than a dozen of your social reformers, she had swallowed the curious assertion without a gasp, and had leant back luxuriously among the cushions of his motor-car. When Charles said, "Why be so polite to servants? they don't understand it," she had not given the Schlegel retort of, "If they don't understand it, I do." No; she had vowed to be less polite to servants in the future. "I am swathed in cant," she thought, "and it is good for me to be stripped of it." And all that she thought or did or breathed was a quiet preparation for Paul. Paul was inevitable. Charles was taken up with another girl, Mr. Wilcox was so old, Evie so young, Mrs. Wilcox so different. Round the absent brother she began to throw the halo of Romance, to irradiate him with all the splendour of those happy days, to feel that in him she should draw nearest to the robust ideal. He and she were about the same age, Evie said. Most people thought Paul handsomer than his brother. He was certainly a better shot, though not so good at golf. And when Paul appeared, flushed with the triumph of getting through an examination, and ready to flirt with any pretty girl, Helen met him halfway, or more than halfway, and turned towards him on the Sunday evening.

He had been talking of his approaching exile in Nigeria, and he should have continued to talk of it, and allowed their guest to recover. But the heave of her bosom flattered him. Passion was possible, and he became passionate. Deep down in him something whispered, "This girl would let you kiss her; you might not have such a chance again."

That was "how it happened," or, rather, how Helen described it to her sister, using words even more unsympathetic than my own. But the poetry of that kiss, the wonder of it, the magic that there was in life for hours after it—who can describe that? It is so easy for an Englishman to sneer at these chance collisions of human beings. To the insular cynic and the insular moralist they offer an equal opportunity. It is so easy to talk of "passing emotion," and to forget how vivid the emotion was ere it passed. Our impulse to sneer, to forget, is at root a good one. We recognize

that emotion is not enough, and that men and women are person-
alities capable of sustained relations, not mere opportunities for
an electrical discharge. Yet we rate the impulse too highly. We do
not admit that by collisions of this trivial sort the doors of heaven
may be shaken open. To Helen, at all events, her life was to bring
nothing more intense than the embrace of this boy who played no
part in it. He had drawn her out of the house, where there was
danger of surprise and light; he had led her by a path he knew,
until they stood under the column of the vast wych-elm. A man
in the darkness, he had whispered "I love you" when she was
desiring love. In time his slender personality faded, the scene that
he had evoked endured. In all the variable years that followed she
never saw the like of it again.

"I understand," said Margaret—"at least, I understand as
much as ever is understood of these things. Tell me now what
happened on the Monday morning."

"It was over at once."

"How, Helen?"

"I was still happy while I dressed, but as I came downstairs I
got nervous, and when I went into the dining-room I knew it was
no good. There was Evie—I can't explain—managing the tea-urn,
and Mr. Wilcox reading the 'Times.'"

"Was Paul there?"

"Yes; and Charles was talking to him about Stocks and Shares,
and he looked frightened."

By slight indications the sisters could convey much to each
other. Margaret saw horror latent in the scene, and Helen's next
remark did not surprise her.

"Somehow, when that kind of man looks frightened it is too
awful. It is all right for us to be frightened, or for men of another
sort—father, for instance; but for men like that! When I saw all the
others so placid, and Paul mad with terror in case I said the wrong
thing, I felt for a moment that the whole Wilcox family was a fraud,
just a wall of newspapers and motor-cars and golf-clubs, and that if
it fell I should find nothing behind it but panic and emptiness."

"I don't think that. The Wilcoxes struck me as being genuine people, particularly the wife."

"No, I don't really think that. But Paul was so broad-shouldered; all kinds of extraordinary things made it worse, and I knew that it would never do—never. I said to him after breakfast, when the others were practising strokes, 'We rather lost our heads,' and he looked better at once, though frightfully ashamed. He began a speech about having no money to marry on, but it hurt him to make it, and I stopped him. Then he said, 'I must beg your pardon over this, Miss Schlegel; I can't think what came over me last night.' And I said, 'Nor what over me; never mind.' And then we parted—at least, until I remembered that I had written straight off to tell you the night before, and that frightened him again. I asked him to send a telegram for me, for he knew you would be coming or something; and he tried to get hold of the motor, but Charles and Mr. Wilcox wanted it to go to the station; and Charles offered to send the telegram for me, and then I had to say that the telegram was of no consequence, for Paul said Charles might read it, and though I wrote it out several times, he always said people would suspect something. He took it himself at last, pretending that he must walk down to get cartridges, and, what with one thing and the other, it was not handed in at the Post Office until too late. It was the most terrible morning. Paul disliked me more and more, and Evie talked cricket averages till I nearly screamed. I cannot think how I stood her all the other days. At last Charles and his father started for the station, and then came your telegram warning me that Aunt Juley was coming by that train, and Paul—oh, rather horrible—said that I had muddled it. But Mrs. Wilcox knew."

"Knew what?"

"Everything; though we neither of us told her a word, and had known all along, I think."

"Oh, she must have overheard you."

"I suppose so, but it seemed wonderful. When Charles and Aunt Juley drove up, calling each other names, Mrs. Wilcox stepped in from the garden and made everything less terrible. Ugh! but it has been a disgusting business. To think that——" She sighed.

"To think that because you and a young man meet for a moment, there must be all these telegrams and anger," supplied Margaret.

Helen nodded.

"I've often thought about it, Helen. It's one of the most interesting things in the world. The truth is that there is a great outer life that you and I have never touched—a life in which telegrams and anger count. Personal relations, that we think supreme, are not supreme there. There love means marriage settlements, death, death duties. So far I'm clear. But here my difficulty. This outer life, though obviously horrid, often seems the real one—there's grit in it. It does breed character. Do personal relations lead to sloppiness in the end?"

"Oh, Meg, that's what I felt, only not so clearly, when the Wilcoxes were so competent, and seemed to have their hands on all the ropes."

"Don't you feel it now?"

"I remember Paul at breakfast," said Helen quietly. "I shall never forget him. He had nothing to fall back upon. I know that personal relations are the real life, for ever and ever."

"Amen!"

So the Wilcox episode fell into the background, leaving behind it memories of sweetness and horror that mingled, and the sisters pursued the life that Helen had commended. They talked to each other and to other people, they filled the tall thin house at Wickham Place with those whom they liked or could befriend. They even attended public meetings. In their own fashion they cared deeply about politics, though not as politicians would have us care; they desired that public life should mirror whatever is good in the life within. Temperance, tolerance, and sexual equality were intelligible cries to them; whereas they did not follow our Forward Policy in Thibet with the keen attention that it merits,

and would at times dismiss the whole British Empire with a puzzled, if reverent, sigh. Not out of them are the shows of history
erected: the world would be a grey, bloodless place were it entirely
composed of Miss Schlegels. But the world being what it is, perhaps they shine out in it like stars.

A word on their origin. They were not "English to the backbone," as their aunt had piously asserted. But, on the other hand,
they were not "Germans of the dreadful sort." Their father had
belonged to a type that was more prominent in Germany fifty
years ago than now. He was not the aggressive German, so dear to
the English journalist, nor the domestic German, so dear to the
English wit. If one classed him at all it would be as the country-
man of Hegel and Kant, as the idealist, inclined to be dreamy,
whose Imperialism was the Imperialism of the air. Not that his life
had been inactive. He had fought like blazes against Denmark,
Austria, France. But he had fought without visualizing the results
of victory. A hint of the truth broke on him after Sedan, when he
saw the dyed moustaches of Napoleon going grey; another when
he entered Paris, and saw the smashed windows of the Tuileries.
Peace came—it was all very immense, one had turned into an
Empire—but he knew that some quality had vanished for which
not all Alsace-Lorraine could compensate him. Germany a commercial Power, Germany a naval Power, Germany with colonies
here and a Forward Policy there, and legitimate aspirations in the
other place, might appeal to others, and be fitly served by them;
for his own part, he abstained from the fruits of victory, and natu-
ralized himself in England. The more earnest members of his
family never forgave him, and knew that his children, though
scarcely English of the dreadful sort, would never be German to
the backbone. He had obtained work in one of our provincial
Universities, and there married Poor Emily (or Die Engländerin,
as the case may be), and as she had money, they proceeded to
London, and came to know a good many people. But his gaze was
always fixed beyond the sea. It was his hope that the clouds of
materialism obscuring the Fatherland would part in time, and the

mild intellectual light re-emerge. "Do you imply that we Germans are stupid, Uncle Ernst?" exclaimed a haughty and magnificent nephew. Uncle Ernst replied, "To my mind. You use the intellect, but you no longer care about it. That I call stupidity." As the haughty nephew did not follow, he continued, "You only care about the things that you can use, and therefore arrange them in the following order: Money, supremely useful; intellect, rather useful; imagination, of no use at all. No"—for the other had protested—"your Pan-Germanism is no more imaginative than is our Imperialism over here. It is the vice of a vulgar mind to be thrilled by bigness, to think that a thousand square miles are a thousand times more wonderful than one square mile, and that a million square miles are almost the same as heaven. That is not imagination. No, it kills it. When their poets over here try to celebrate bigness they are dead at once, and naturally. Your poets too are dying, your philosophers, your musicians, to whom Europe has listened for two hundred years. Gone. Gone with the little courts that nurtured them—gone with Esterhaz and Weimar. What? What's that? Your Universities? Oh yes, you have learned men, who collect more facts than do the learned men of England. They collect facts, and facts, and empires of facts. But which of them will rekindle the light within?"

To all this Margaret listened, sitting on the haughty nephew's knee.

It was a unique education for the little girls. The haughty nephew would be at Wickham Place one day, bringing with him an even haughtier wife, both convinced that Germany was appointed by God to govern the world. Aunt Juley would come the next day, convinced that Great Britain had been appointed to the same post by the same authority. Were both these loud-voiced parties right? On one occasion they had met, and Margaret with clasped hands had implored them to argue the subject out in her presence. Whereat they blushed, and began to talk about the weather. "Papa," she cried—she was a most offensive child—"why will they not discuss this most clear question?" Her father, surveying the parties grimly, replied that he did not know. Putting her head on one side, Margaret then remarked, "To me one of two things is very clear; either God does not know his own mind about England and Germany, or else these do not know the mind of God." A hateful little girl, but at thirteen she had grasped a dilemma that most people travel through life without perceiving. Her brain darted up and down; it grew pliant and strong. Her conclusion was, that any human being lies nearer to the unseen than any organization, and from this she never varied.

Helen advanced along the same lines, though with a more irresponsible tread. In character she resembled her sister, but she was pretty, and so apt to have a more amusing time. People gathered round her more readily, especially when they were new acquaintances, and she did enjoy a little homage very much. When their father died and they ruled alone at Wickham Place, she often absorbed the whole of the company, while Margaret—both were tremendous talkers—fell flat. Neither sister bothered about this. Helen never apologized afterwards, Margaret did not feel the slightest rancour. But looks have their influence upon character. The sisters were alike as little girls, but at the time of the Wilcox episode their methods were beginning to diverge; the younger was rather apt to entice people, and, in enticing them, to be herself enticed; the elder went straight ahead, and accepted an occasional failure as part of the game.

Little need be premised about Tibby. He was now an intelligent man of sixteen, but dyspeptic and difficile.

CHAPTER V

It will be generally admitted that Beethoven's Fifth Symphony is the most sublime noise that has ever penetrated into the ear of man. All sorts and conditions are satisfied by it. Whether you are like Mrs. Munt, and tap surreptitiously when the tunes come—of course, not so as to disturb the others—or like Helen, who can

see heroes and shipwrecks in the music's flood; or like Margaret,
who can only see the music; or like Tibby, who is profoundly
versed in counterpoint, and holds the full score open on his knee;
or like their cousin, Fräulein Mosebach, who remembers all the
time that Beethoven is "echt Deutsch"; or like Fräulein Mosebach's young man, who can remember nothing but Fräulein
Mosebach: in any case, the passion of your life becomes more
vivid, and you are bound to admit that such noise is cheap at two
shillings. It is cheap, even if you hear it in the Queen's Hall, drea-
riest music-room in London, though not as dreary as the Free
Trade Hall, Manchester; and even if you sit on the extreme left of
that hall, so that the brass bumps at you before the rest of the
orchestra arrives, it is still cheap.

"Who is Margaret talking to?" said Mrs. Munt, at the conclusion of the first movement. She was again in London on a visit to
Wickham Place.

Helen looked down the long line of their party, and said that
she did not know.

"Would it be some young man or other whom she takes an
interest in?"

"I expect so," Helen replied. Music enwrapped her, and she
could not enter into the distinction that divides young men whom
one takes an interest in from young men whom one knows.

"You girls are so wonderful in always having—— Oh dear!
one mustn't talk."

For the Andante had begun—very beautiful, but bearing a
family likeness to all the other beautiful Andantes that Beethoven
had written, and, to Helen's mind, rather disconnecting the heroes
and shipwrecks of the first movement from the heroes and goblins of the third. She heard the tune through once, and then her
attention wandered, and she gazed at the audience, or the organ,
or the architecture. Much did she censure the attenuated Cupids
who encircle the ceiling of the Queen's Hall, inclining each to
each with vapid gesture, and clad in sallow pantaloons, on which
the October sunlight struck. "How awful to marry a man like

those Cupids!" thought Helen. Here Beethoven started decorating his tune, so she heard him through once more, and then she smiled at her cousin Frieda. But Frieda, listening to Classical Music, could not respond. Herr Liesecke, too, looked as if wild horses could not make him inattentive; there were lines across his forehead, his lips were parted, his pince-nez at right angles to his nose, and he had laid a thick, white hand on either knee. And next to her was Aunt Juley, so British, and wanting to tap. How interesting that row of people was! What diverse influences had gone to the making! Here Beethoven, after humming and hawing with great sweetness, said "Heigho," and the Andante came to an end. Applause, and a round of "wunderschöning" and "pracht" volleying from the German contingent. Margaret started talking to her new young man; Helen said to her aunt: "Now comes the wonderful movement: first of all the goblins, and then a trio of elephants dancing;" and Tibby implored the company generally to look out for the transitional passage on the drum.

"On the what, dear?"

"On the *drum*, Aunt Juley."

"No; look out for the part where you think you have done with the goblins and they come back," breathed Helen, as the music started with a goblin walking quietly over the universe, from end to end. Others followed him. They were not aggressive creatures; it was that that made them so terrible to Helen. They merely observed in passing that there was no such thing as splendour or heroism in the world. After the interlude of elephants dancing, they returned and made the observation for the second time. Helen could not contradict them, for, once at all events, she had felt the same, and had seen the reliable walls of youth collapse. Panic and emptiness! Panic and emptiness! The goblins were right.

Her brother raised his finger: it was the transitional passage on the drum.

For, as if things were going too far, Beethoven took hold of the goblins and made them do what he wanted. He appeared in person. He gave them a little push, and they began to walk in major key instead of in a minor, and then—he blew with his mouth and they were scattered! Gusts of splendour, gods and demi-gods contending with vast swords, colour and fragrance broadcast on the field of battle, magnificent victory, magnificent death! Oh, it all burst before the girl, and she even stretched out her gloved hands as if it was tangible. Any fate was titanic; any contest desirable; conqueror and conquered would alike be applauded by the angels of the utmost stars.

And the goblins—they had not really been there at all? They were only the phantoms of cowardice and unbelief? One healthy human impulse would dispel them? Men like the Wilcoxes, or President Roosevelt, would say yes. Beethoven knew better. The goblins really had been there. They might return—and they did. It was as if the splendour of life might boil over and waste to steam and froth. In its dissolution one heard the terrible, ominous note, and a goblin, with increased malignity, walked quietly over the universe from end to end. Panic and emptiness! Panic and emptiness! Even the flaming ramparts of the world might fall.

Beethoven chose to make all right in the end. He built the ramparts up. He blew with his mouth for the second time, and again the goblins were scattered. He brought back the gusts of splendour, the heroism, the youth, the magnificence of life and of death, and, amid vast roarings of a superhuman joy, he led his Fifth Symphony to its conclusion. But the goblins were there. They could return. He had said so bravely, and that is why one can trust Beethoven when he says other things.

Helen pushed her way out during the applause. She desired to be alone. The music had summed up to her all that had happened or could happen in her career. She read it as a tangible statement, which could never be superseded. The notes meant this and that to her, and they could have no other meaning, and life could have no other meaning. She pushed right out of the building, and walked slowly down the outside staircase, breathing the autumnal air, and then she strolled home.

"Margaret," called Mrs. Munt, "is Helen all right?"

"Oh yes."

"She is always going away in the middle of a programme," said Tibby.

"The music has evidently moved her deeply," said Fräulein Mosebach.

"Excuse me," said Margaret's young man, who had for some time been preparing a sentence, "but that lady has, quite inadvertently, taken my umbrella."

"Oh, good gracious me!—I am so sorry. Tibby, run after Helen."

"I shall miss the Four Serious Songs if I do."

"Tibby love, you must go."

"It isn't of any consequence," said the young man, in truth a little uneasy about his umbrella.

"But of course it is. Tibby! Tibby!"

Tibby rose to his feet, and wilfully caught his person on the backs of the chairs. By the time he had tipped up the seat and found his hat, and had deposited his full score in safety, it was "too late" to go after Helen. The Four Serious Songs had begun, and one could not move during their performance.

"My sister is so careless," whispered Margaret.

"Not at all," replied the young man; but his voice was dead and cold.

"If you would give me your address——"

"Oh, not at all, not at all;" and he wrapped his greatcoat over his knees.

Then the Four Serious Songs rang shallow in Margaret's ears. Brahms, for all his grumbling and grizzling, had never guessed what it felt like to be suspected of stealing an umbrella. For this fool of a young man thought that she and Helen and Tibby had been playing the confidence trick on him, and that if he gave his address they would break into his rooms some midnight or other and steal his walking-stick too. Most ladies would have laughed, but Margaret really minded, for it gave her a glimpse into squalor. To trust people is a luxury in which only the wealthy can indulge;

the poor cannot afford it. As soon as Brahms had grunted himself
out, she gave him her card and said, "That is where we live; if you
preferred, you could call for the umbrella after the concert, but I
didn't like to trouble you when it has all been our fault."

His face brightened a little when he saw that Wickham Place
was W. It was sad to see him corroded with suspicion, and yet not
daring to be impolite, in case these well-dressed people were honest after all. She took it as a good sign that he said to her, "It's a fine
programme this afternoon, is it not?" for this was the remark with
which he had originally opened, before the umbrella intervened.

"The Beethoven's fine," said Margaret, who was not a female of
the encouraging type. "I don't like the Brahms, though, nor the
Mendelssohn that came first—and ugh! I don't like this Elgar
that's coming."

"What, what?" called Herr Liesecke, overhearing. "The 'Pomp
and Circumstance' will not be fine?"

"Oh, Margaret, you tiresome girl!" cried her aunt. "Here have I
been persuading Herr Liesecke to stop for 'Pomp and Circumstance,' and you are undoing all my work. I am so anxious for
him to hear what we are doing in music. Oh, you mustn't run
down our English composers, Margaret."

"For my part, I have heard the composition at Stettin," said
Fräulein Mosebach. "On two occasions. It is dramatic, a little."

"Frieda, you despise English music. You know you do. And
English art. And English literature, except Shakespeare, and he's a
German. Very well, Frieda, you may go."

The lovers laughed and glanced at each other. Moved by a
common impulse, they rose to their feet and fled from "Pomp and
Circumstance."

"We have this call to pay in Finsbury Circus, it is true," said
Herr Liesecke, as he edged past her and reached the gangway just
as the music started.

"Margaret——" loudly whispered by Aunt Juley. "Margaret,
Margaret! Fräulein Mosebach has left her beautiful little bag behind her on the seat."

Sure enough, there was Frieda's reticule, containing her address book, her pocket dictionary, her map of London, and her money.

"Oh, what a bother—what a family we are! Fr—Frieda!"

"Hush!" said all those who thought the music fine.

"But it's the number they want in Finsbury Circus——"

"Might I—couldn't I——" said the suspicious young man, and got very red.

"Oh, I would be so grateful."

He took the bag—money clinking inside it—and slipped up the gangway with it. He was just in time to catch them at the swing-door, and he received a pretty smile from the German girl and a fine bow from her cavalier. He returned to his seat upsides with the world. The trust that they had reposed in him was trivial, but he felt that it cancelled his mistrust for them, and that probably he would not be "had" over his umbrella. This young man had been "had" in the past—badly, perhaps overwhelmingly— and now most of his energies went in defending himself against the unknown. But this afternoon—perhaps on account of music —he perceived that one must slack off occasionally, or what is the good of being alive? Wickham Place, W., though a risk, was as safe as most things, and he would risk it.

So when the concert was over and Margaret said, "We live quite near; I am going there now. Could you walk round with me, and we'll find your umbrella?" he said, "Thank you," peaceably, and followed her out of the Queen's Hall. She wished that he was not so anxious to hand a lady downstairs, or to carry a lady's programme for her—his class was near enough her own for its manners to vex her. But she found him interesting on the whole—everyone interested the Schlegels on the whole at that time—and while her lips talked culture, her heart was planning to invite him to tea.

"How tired one gets after music!" she began.

"Do you find the atmosphere of Queen's Hall oppressive?"

"Yes, horribly."

"But surely the atmosphere of Covent Garden is even more oppressive."

"Do you go there much?"

"When my work permits, I attend the gallery for the Royal Opera."

Helen would have exclaimed, "So do I. I love the gallery," and thus have endeared herself to the young man. Helen could do these things. But Margaret had an almost morbid horror of "drawing people out," of "making things go." She had been to the gallery at Covent Garden, but she did not "attend" it, preferring the more expensive seats; still less did she love it. So she made no reply.

"This year I have been three times—to 'Faust,' 'Tosca,' and ——" Was it 'Tannhouser' or 'Tannhoyser'? Better not risk the word.

Margaret disliked "Tosca" and "Faust." And so, for one reason and another, they walked on in silence, chaperoned by the voice of Mrs. Munt, who was getting into difficulties with her nephew.

"I do in a *way* remember the passage, Tibby, but when every instrument is so beautiful, it is difficult to pick out one thing rather than another. I am sure that you and Helen take me to the very nicest concerts. Not a dull note from beginning to end. I only wish that our German friends would have stayed till it finished."

"But surely you haven't forgotten the drum steadily beating on the low C, Aunt Juley?" came Tibby's voice. "No one could. It's unmistakable."

"A specially loud part?" hazarded Mrs. Munt. "Of course I do not go in for being musical," she added, the shot failing. "I only care for music—a very different thing. But still I will say this for myself—I do know when I like a thing and when I don't. Some people are the same about pictures. They can go into a picture gallery—Miss Conder can—and say straight off what they feel, all round the wall. I never could do that. But music is so different to pictures, to my mind. When it comes to music I am as safe as houses, and I assure you, Tibby, I am by no means pleased by everything. There was a thing—something about a faun in French

—which Helen went into ecstasies over, but I thought it most tinkling and superficial, and said so, and I held to my opinion too."

"Do you agree?" asked Margaret. "Do you think music is so different to pictures?"

"I—I should have thought so, kind of," he said.

"So should I. Now, my sister declares they're just the same. We have great arguments over it. She says I'm dense; I say she's sloppy." Getting under way, she cried: "Now, doesn't it seem absurd to you? What *is* the good of the Arts if they're interchangeable? What *is* the good of the ear if it tells you the same as the eye? Helen's one aim is to translate tunes into the language of painting, and pictures into the language of music. It's very ingenious, and she says several pretty things in the process, but what's gained, I'd like to know? Oh, it's all rubbish, radically false. If Monet's really Debussy, and Debussy's really Monet, neither gentleman is worth his salt—that's my opinion."

Evidently these sisters quarrelled.

"Now, this very symphony that we've just been having—she won't let it alone. She labels it with meanings from start to finish; turns it into literature. I wonder if the day will ever return when music will be treated as music. Yet I don't know. There's my brother—behind us. He treats music as music, and oh, my goodness! He makes me angrier than anyone, simply furious. With him I daren't even argue."

An unhappy family, if talented.

"But, of course, the real villain is Wagner. He has done more than any man in the nineteenth century towards the muddling of the arts. I do feel that music is in a very serious state just now, though extraordinarily interesting. Every now and then in history there do come these terrible geniuses, like Wagner, who stir up all the wells of thought at once. For a moment it's splendid. Such a splash as never was. But afterwards—such a lot of mud; and the wells—as it were, they communicate with each other too easily now, and not one of them will run quite clear. That's what Wagner's done."

Her speeches fluttered away from the young man like birds. If only he could talk like this, he would have caught the world. Oh, to acquire culture! Oh, to pronounce foreign names correctly! Oh, to be well informed, discoursing at ease on every subject that a lady started! But it would take one years. With an hour at lunch and a few shattered hours in the evening, how was it possible to catch up with leisured women, who had been reading steadily from childhood? His brain might be full of names, he might have even heard of Monet and Debussy; the trouble was that he could not string them together into a sentence, he could not make them "tell," he could not quite forget about his stolen umbrella. Yes, the umbrella was the real trouble. Behind Monet and Debussy the umbrella persisted, with the steady beat of a drum. "I suppose my umbrella will be all right," he was thinking. "I don't really mind about it. I will think about music instead. I suppose my umbrella will be all right." Earlier in the afternoon he had worried about seats. Ought he to have paid as much as two shillings? Earlier still he had wondered, "Shall I try to do without a programme?" There had always been something to worry him ever since he could remember, always something that distracted him in the pursuit of beauty. For he did pursue beauty, and, therefore, Margaret's speeches did flutter away from him like birds.

Margaret talked ahead, occasionally saying, "Don't you think so? don't you feel the same?" And once she stopped, and said, "Oh, do interrupt me!" which terrified him. She did not attract him, though she filled him with awe. Her figure was meagre, her face seemed all teeth and eyes, her references to her sister and her brother were uncharitable. For all her cleverness and culture, she was probably one of those soulless, atheistical women who have been so shown up by Miss Corelli. It was surprising (and alarming) that she should suddenly say, "I do hope that you'll come in and have some tea."

"I do hope that you'll come in and have some tea. We should be so glad. I have dragged you so far out of your way."

They had arrived at Wickham Place. The sun had set, and the

backwater, in deep shadow, was filling with a gentle haze. To the right the fantastic sky-line of the flats towered black against the hues of evening; to the left the older houses raised a square-cut, irregular parapet against the grey. Margaret fumbled for her latchkey. Of course she had forgotten it. So, grasping her umbrella by its ferrule, she leant over the area and tapped at the dining-room window.

"Helen! Let us in!"

"All right," said a voice.

"You've been taking this gentleman's umbrella."

"Taken a what?" said Helen, opening the door. "Oh, what's that? Do come in! How do you do?"

"Helen, you must not be so ramshackly. You took this gentleman's umbrella away from Queen's Hall, and he has had the trouble of coming round for it."

"Oh, I am so sorry!" cried Helen, all her hair flying. She had pulled off her hat as soon as she returned, and had flung herself into the big dining-room chair. "I do nothing but steal umbrellas. I am so very sorry! Do come in and choose one. Is yours a hooky or a nobbly? Mine's a nobbly—at least, I *think* it is."

The light was turned on, and they began to search the hall, Helen, who had abruptly parted with the Fifth Symphony, commenting with shrill little cries.

"Don't you talk, Meg! You stole an old gentleman's silk top-hat. Yes, she did, Aunt Juley. It is a positive fact. She thought it was a muff. Oh, heavens! I've knocked the In and Out card down. Where's Frieda? Tibby, why don't you ever—— No, I can't remember what I was going to say. That wasn't it, but do tell the maids to hurry tea up. What about this umbrella?" she opened it. "No, it's all gone along the seams. It's an appalling umbrella. It must be mine."

But it was not.

He took it from her, murmured a few words of thanks, and then fled, with the lilting step of the clerk.

"But if you will stop——" cried Margaret. "Now, Helen, how stupid you've been!"

"Whatever have I done?"

"Don't you see that you've frightened him away? I meant him to stop to tea. You oughtn't to talk about stealing or holes in an umbrella. I saw his nice eyes getting so miserable. No, it's not a bit of good now." For Helen had darted out into the street, shouting, "Oh, do stop!"

"I dare say it is all for the best," opined Mrs. Munt. "We know nothing about the young man, Margaret, and your drawing-room is full of very tempting little things."

But Helen cried: "Aunt Juley, how can you! You make me more and more ashamed. I'd rather he *had* been a thief and taken all the apostle spoons than that I—— Well, I must shut the front-door, I suppose. One more failure for Helen."

"Yes, I think the apostle spoons could have gone as rent," said Margaret. Seeing that her aunt did not understand, she added: "You remember 'rent'? It was one of father's words—Rent to the ideal, to his own faith in human nature. You remember how he would trust strangers, and if they fooled him he would say, 'It's better to be fooled than to be suspicious'—that the confidence trick is the work of man, but the want-of-confidence-trick is the work of the devil."

"I remember something of the sort now," said Mrs. Munt, rather tartly, for she longed to add, "It was lucky that your father married a wife with money." But this was unkind, and she contented herself with, "Why, he might have stolen the little Ricketts picture as well."

"Better that he had," said Helen stoutly.

"No, I agree with Aunt Juley," said Margaret. "I'd rather mistrust people than lose my little Ricketts. There are limits."

Their brother, finding the incident commonplace, had stolen upstairs to see whether there were scones for tea. He warmed the teapot—almost too deftly—rejected the Orange Pekoe that the parlour-maid had provided, poured in five spoonfuls of a superior blend, filled up with really boiling water, and now called to the ladies to be quick or they would lose the aroma.

"All right, Auntie Tibby," called Helen, while Margaret, thoughtful again, said: "In a way, I wish we had a real boy in the house—the kind of boy who cares for men. It would make entertaining so much easier."

"So do I," said her sister. "Tibby only cares for cultured females singing Brahms." And when they joined him she said rather sharply: "Why didn't you make that young man welcome, Tibby? You must do the host a little, you know. You ought to have taken his hat and coaxed him into stopping, instead of letting him be swamped by screaming women."

Tibby sighed, and drew a long strand of hair over his forehead.

"Oh, it's no good looking superior. I mean what I say."

"Leave Tibby alone!" said Margaret, who could not bear her brother to be scolded.

"Here's the house a regular hen-coop!" grumbled Helen.

"Oh, my dear!" protested Mrs. Munt. "How can you say such dreadful things! The number of men you get here has always astonished me. If there is any danger it's the other way round."

"Yes, but it's the wrong sort of men, Helen means."

"No, I don't," corrected Helen. "We get the right sort of man, but the wrong side of him, and I say that's Tibby's fault. There ought to be a something about the house—an—I don't know what."

"A touch of the W.'s, perhaps?"

Helen put out her tongue.

"Who are the W.'s?" asked Tibby.

"The W.'s are things I and Meg and Aunt Juley know about and you don't, so there!"

"I suppose that ours is a female house," said Margaret, "and one must just accept it. No, Aunt Juley, I don't mean that this house is full of women. I am trying to say something much more clever. I mean that it was irrevocably feminine, even in father's time. Now I'm sure you understand! Well, I'll give you another example. It'll shock you, but I don't care. Suppose Queen Victoria gave a dinner-party, and that the guests had been Leighton, Millais, Swinburne, Rossetti, Meredith, Fitzgerald, etc. Do you suppose that the atmosphere of that dinner would have been artistic? Heavens, no! The very chairs on which they sat would have seen to that. So with our house—it must be feminine, and all we can do is to see that it isn't effeminate. Just as another house that I can mention, but won't, sounded irrevocably masculine, and all its inmates can do is to see that it isn't brutal."

"That house being the W.s' house, I presume," said Tibby.

"Your're not going to be told about the W.'s, my child," Helen cried, "so don't you think it. And on the other hand, I don't the least mind if you find out, so don't you think you've done anything clever, in either case. Give me a cigarette."

"You do what you can for the house," said Margaret. "The drawing-room reeks of smoke."

"If you smoked too, the house might suddenly turn masculine. Atmosphere is probably a question of touch and go. Even at Queen Victoria's dinner-party—if something had been just a little different—perhaps if she'd worn a clinging Liberty tea-gown instead of a magenta satin——"

"With an Indian shawl over her shoulders——"

"Fastened at the bosom with a Cairngorm-pin——"

Bursts of disloyal laughter—you must remember that they are half German—greeted these suggestions, and Margaret said pensively, "How inconceivable it would be if the Royal Family cared about Art." And the conversation drifted away and away, and Helen's cigarette turned to a spot in the darkness, and the great flats opposite were sown with lighted windows, which vanished and were relit again, and vanished incessantly. Beyond them the thoroughfare roared gently—a tide that could never be quiet, while in the east, invisible behind the smokes of Wapping, the moon was rising.

"That reminds me, Margaret. We might have taken that young man into the dining-room, at all events. Only the majolica plate—and that is so firmly set in the wall. I am really distressed that he had no tea."

For that little incident had impressed the three women more

than might be supposed. It remained as a goblin footfall, as a hint that all is not for the best in the best of all possible worlds, and that beneath these superstructures of wealth and art there wanders an ill-fed boy, who has recovered his umbrella indeed, but who has left no address behind him, and no name.

CHAPTER VI

We are not concerned with the very poor. They are unthinkable, and only to be approached by the statistician or the poet. This story deals with gentlefolk, or with those who are obliged to pretend that they are gentlefolk.

The boy, Leonard Bast, stood at the extreme verge of gentility. He was not in the abyss, but he could see it, and at times people whom he knew had dropped in, and counted no more. He knew that he was poor, and would admit it: he would have died sooner than confess any inferiority to the rich. This may be splendid of him. But he was inferior to most rich people, there is not the least doubt of it. He was not as courteous as the average rich man, nor as intelligent, nor as healthy, nor as lovable. His mind and his body had been alike underfed, because he was poor, and because he was modern they were always craving better food. Had he lived some centuries ago, in the brightly coloured civilizations of the past, he would have had a definite status, his rank and his income would have corresponded. But in his day the angel of Democracy had arisen, enshadowing the classes with leathern wings, and proclaiming, "All men are equal—all men, that is to say, who possess umbrellas," and so he was obliged to assert gentility, lest he slipped into the abyss where nothing counts, and the statements of Democracy are inaudible.

As he walked away from Wickham Place, his first care was to prove that he was as good as the Miss Schlegels. Obscurely wounded in his pride, he tried to wound them in return. They were probably not ladies. Would real ladies have asked him to tea? They were certainly ill-natured and cold. At each step his feeling of superiority increased. Would a real lady have talked about stealing an umbrella? Perhaps they were thieves after all, and if he had gone into the house they would have clapped a chloroformed handkerchief over his face. He walked on complacently as far as the Houses of Parliament. There an empty stomach asserted itself, and told him that he was a fool.

"Evening, Mr. Bast."

"Evening, Mr. Dealtry."

"Nice evening."

"Evening."

Mr. Dealtry, a fellow clerk, passed on, and Leonard stood wondering whether he would take the tram as far as a penny would take him, or whether he would walk. He decided to walk—it is no good giving in, and he had spent money enough at Queen's Hall—and he walked over Westminster Bridge, in front of St. Thomas's Hospital, and through the immense tunnel that passes under the South-Western main line at Vauxhall. In the tunnel he paused and listened to the roar of the trains. A sharp pain darted through his head, and he was conscious of the exact form of his eye sockets. He pushed on for another mile, and did not slacken speed until he stood at the entrance of a road called Camelia Road, which was at present his home.

Here he stopped again, and glanced suspiciously to right and left, like a rabbit that is going to bolt into its hole. A block of flats, constructed with extreme cheapness, towered on either hand. Farther down the road two more blocks were being built, and beyond these an old house was being demolished to accommodate another pair. It was the kind of scene that may be observed all over London, whatever the locality—bricks and mortar rising and falling with the restlessness of the water in a fountain, as the city receives more and more men upon her soil. Camelia Road would soon stand out like a fortress, and command, for a little, an extensive view. Only for a little. Plans were out for the erection of flats in Magnolia Road also. And again a few years, and all the flats in

either road might be pulled down, and new buildings, of a vast-
ness at present unimaginable, might arise where they had fallen.

"Evening, Mr. Bast."

"Evening, Mr. Cunningham."

"Very serious thing this decline of the birth-rate in Manchester."

"I beg your pardon?"

"Very serious thing this decline of the birth-rate in Manchester," repeated Mr. Cunningham, tapping the Sunday paper, in
which the calamity in question had just been announced to him.

"Ah, yes," said Leonard, who was not going to let on that he
had not bought a Sunday paper.

"If this kind of thing goes on the population of England will
be stationary in 1960."

"You don't say so."

"I call it a very serious thing, eh?"

"Good-evening, Mr. Cunningham."

"Good-evening, Mr. Bast."

Then Leonard entered Block B of the flats, and turned, not
upstairs, but down, into what is known to house agents as a semi-
basement, and to other men as a cellar. He opened the door, and
cried "Hullo!" with the pseudo-geniality of the Cockney. There
was no reply. "Hullo!" he repeated. The sitting-room was empty,
though the electric light had been left burning. A look of relief
came over his face, and he flung himself into the armchair.

The sitting-room contained, besides the armchair, two other
chairs, a piano, a three-legged table, and a cosy corner. Of the
walls, one was occupied by the window, the other by a draped
mantleshelf bristling with Cupids. Opposite the window was the
door, and beside the door a bookcase, while over the piano there
extended one of the masterpieces of Maud Goodman. It was an
amorous and not unpleasant little hole when the curtains were
drawn, and the lights turned on, and the gas-stove unlit. But it
struck that shallow makeshift note that is so often heard in the
modern dwelling-place. It had been too easily gained, and could
be relinquished too easily.

As Leonard was kicking off his boots he jarred the three-legged table, and a photograph frame, honourably poised upon it, slid sideways, fell off into the fireplace, and smashed. He swore in a colourless sort of way, and picked the photograph up. It represented a young lady called Jacky, and had been taken at the time when young ladies called Jacky were often photographed with their mouths open. Teeth of dazzling whiteness extended along either of Jacky's jaws, and positively weighed her head sideways, so large were they and so numerous. Take my word for it, that smile was simply stunning, and it is only you and I who will be fastidious, and complain that true joy begins in the eyes, and that the eyes of Jacky did not accord with her smile, but were anxious and hungry.

Leonard tried to pull out the fragments of glass, and cut his fingers and swore again. A drop of blood fell on the frame, another followed, spilling over onto the exposed photograph. He swore more vigorously, and dashed into the kitchen, where he bathed his hands. The kitchen was the same size as the sitting-room: through it was a bedroom. This completed his home. He was renting the flat furnished: of all the objects that encumbered it none were his own except the photograph frame, the Cupids, and the books.

"Damn, damn, damnation!" he murmured, together with such other words as he had learnt from older men. Then he raised his hand to his forehead and said, "Oh, damn it all——" which meant something different. He pulled himself together. He drank a little tea, black and silent, that still survived upon an upper shelf. He swallowed some dusty crumbs of a cake. Then he went back to the sitting-room, settled himself anew, and began to read a volume of Ruskin.

'Seven miles to the north of Venice——'

How perfectly the famous chapter opens! How supreme its command of admonition and of poetry! The rich man is speaking to us from his gondola.

'Seven miles to the north of Venice the banks of sand which

nearer the city rise little above low-water mark attain by degrees a
higher level, and knit themselves at last into fields of salt morass,
raised here and there into shapeless mounds, and intercepted by
narrow creeks of sea.'

Leonard was trying to form his style on Ruskin: he understood
him to be the greatest master of English Prose. He read forward
steadily, occasionally making a few notes.

'Let us consider a little each of these characters in succession,
and first (for of the shafts enough has been said already), what is
very peculiar to this church—its luminousness.'

Was there anything to be learnt from this fine sentence? Could
he adapt it to the needs of daily life? Could he introduce it, with
modifications, when he next wrote a letter to his brother, the lay-
reader? For example—

'Let us consider a little each of these characters in succession,
and first (for of the absence of ventilation enough has been said
already), what is very peculiar to this flat—its obscurity.'

Something told him that the modifications would not do; and
that something, had he known it, was the spirit of English Prose.
'My flat is dark as well as stuffy.' Those were the words for him.

And the voice in the gondola rolled on, piping melodiously of
Effort and Self-Sacrifice, full of high purpose, full of beauty, full
even of sympathy and the love of men, yet somehow eluding all
that was actual and insistent in Leonard's life. For it was the voice
of one who had never been dirty or hungry, and had not guessed
successfully what dirt and hunger are.

Leonard listened to it with reverence. He felt that he was being
done good to, and that if he kept on with Ruskin, and the Queen's
Hall Concerts, and some pictures by Watts, he would one day
push his head out of the grey waters and see the universe. He
believed in sudden conversion, a belief which may be right, but
which is peculiarly attractive to a half-baked mind. It is the basis
of much popular religion: in the domain of business it dominates
the Stock Exchange, and becomes that "bit of luck" by which all
successes and failures are explained. "If only I had a bit of luck,

the whole thing would come straight. . . . He's got a most magnificent place down at Streatham and a 20 h.-p. Fiat, but then, mind you, he's had luck. . . . I'm sorry the wife's so late, but she never has any luck over catching trains." Leonard was superior to these people; he did believe in effort and in a steady preparation for the change that he desired. But of a heritage that may expand gradually, he had no conception: he hoped to come to Culture suddenly, much as the Revivalist hopes to come to Jesus. Those Miss Schlegels had come to it; they had done the trick; their hands were upon the ropes, once and for all. And meanwhile, his flat was dark, as well as stuffy.

Presently there was a noise on the staircase. He shut up Margaret's card in the pages of Ruskin, and opened the door. A woman entered, of whom it is simplest to say that she was not respectable. Her appearance was awesome. She seemed all strings and bell-pulls—ribbons, chains, bead necklaces that clinked and caught—and a boa of azure feathers hung round her neck, with the ends uneven. Her throat was bare, wound with a double row of pearls, her arms were bare to the elbows, and might again be detected at the shoulder, through cheap lace. Her hat, which was flowery, resembled those punnets, covered with flannel, which we sowed with mustard and cress in our childhood, and which germinated here yes, and there no. She wore it on the back of her head. As for her hair, or rather hairs, they were too complicated to describe, but one system went down her back, lying in a thick pad there, while another, created for a lighter destiny, rippled around her forehead. The face—the face does not signify. It was the face of the photograph, but older, and the teeth were not so numerous as the photographer had suggested, and certainly not so white. Yes, Jacky was past her prime, whatever that prime may have been. She was descending quicker than most women into the colourless years, and the look in her eyes confessed it.

"What ho!" said Leonard, greeting the apparition with much spirit, and helping it off with its boa.

Jacky, in husky tones, replied, "What ho!"

"Been out?" he asked. The question sounds superfluous, but it cannot have been really, for the lady answered, "No," adding, "Oh, I am so tired."

"You tired?"

"Eh?"

"I'm tired," said he, hanging the boa up.

"Oh, Len, I am so tired."

"I've been to that classical concert I told you about," said Leonard.

"What's that?"

"I came back as soon as it was over."

"Anyone been round to our place?" asked Jacky.

"Not that I've seen. I met Mr. Cunningham outside, and we passed a few remarks."

"What, not Mr. Cunningham?"

"Yes."

"Oh, you mean Mr. Cunningham."

"Yes. Mr. Cunningham."

"I've been out to tea at a lady friend's."

Her secret being at last given to the world, and the name of the lady-friend being even adumbrated, Jacky made no further experiments in the difficult and tiring art of conversation. She never had been a great talker. Even in her photographic days she had relied upon her smile and her figure to attract, and now that she was—

> "On the shelf,
> On the shelf,
> Boys, boys, I'm on the shelf,"

she was not likely to find her tongue. Occasional bursts of song (of which the above is an example) still issued from her lips, but the spoken word was rare.

She sat down on Leonard's knee, and began to fondle him. She was now a massive woman of thirty-three, and her weight hurt him, but he could not very well say anything. Then she said, "Is that a book you're reading?" and he said, "That's a book," and

drew it from her unreluctant grasp. Margaret's card fell out of it. It
fell face downwards, and he murmured, "Bookmarker."

"Len——"

"What is it?" he asked, a little wearily, for she only had one
topic of conversation when she sat upon his knee.

"You do love me?"

"Jacky, you know that I do. How can you ask such questions!"

"But you do love me, Len, don't you?"

"Of course I do."

A pause. The other remark was still due.

"Len——"

"Well? What is it?"

"Len, you will make it all right?"

"I can't have you ask me that again," said the boy, flaring up
into a sudden passion. "I've promised to marry you when I'm of
age, and that's enough. My word's my word. I've promised to
marry you as soon as ever I'm twenty-one, and I can't keep on
being worried. I've worries enough. It isn't likely I'd throw you
over, let alone my word, when I've spent all this money. Besides,
I'm an Englishman, and I never go back on my word. Jacky, do be
reasonable. Of course I'll marry you. Only do stop badgering me."

"When's your birthday, Len?"

"I've told you again and again, the eleventh of November next.
Now get off my knee a bit; someone must get supper, I suppose."

Jacky went through to the bedroom, and began to see to her
hat. This meant blowing at it with short sharp puffs. Leonard
tidied up the sitting-room, and began to prepare their evening
meal. He put a penny into the slot of the gas-meter, and soon the
flat was reeking with metallic fumes. Somehow he could not
recover his temper, and all the time he was cooking he continued
to complain bitterly.

"It really is too bad when a fellow isn't trusted. It makes one
feel so wild, when I've pretended to the people here that you're
my wife—all right, all right, you *shall* be my wife—and I've
bought you the ring to wear, and I've taken this flat furnished,

and it's far more than I can afford, and yet you aren't content, and I've also not told the truth when I've written home." He lowered his voice. "He'd stop it." In a tone of horror, that was a little luxurious, he repeated: "My brother 'd stop it. I'm going against the whole world, Jacky.

"That's what I am, Jacky. I don't take any heed of what anyone says. I just go straight forward, I do. That's always been my way. I'm not one of your weak knock-kneed chaps. If a woman's in trouble, I don't leave her in the lurch. That's not my street. No, thank you.

"I'll tell you another thing too. I care a good deal about improving myself by means of Literature and Art, and so getting a wider outlook. For instance, when you came in I was reading Ruskin's 'Stones of Venice.' I don't say this to boast, but just to show you the kind of man I am. I can tell you, I enjoyed that classical concert this afternoon."

To all his moods Jacky remained equally indifferent. When supper was ready—and not before—she emerged from the bedroom, saying: "But you do love me, don't you?"

They began with a soup square, which Leonard had just dissolved in some hot water. It was followed by the tongue—a freckled cylinder of meat, with a little jelly at the top, and a great deal of yellow fat at the bottom—ending with another square dissolved in water (jelly: pineapple), which Leonard had prepared earlier in the day. Jacky ate contentedly enough, occasionally looking at her man with those anxious eyes, to which nothing else in her appearance corresponded, and which yet seemed to mirror her soul. And Leonard managed to convince his stomach that it was having a nourishing meal.

After supper they smoked cigarettes and exchanged a few statements. She observed that her 'likeness' had been broken. He found occasion to remark, for the second time, that he had come straight back home after the concert at Queen's Hall. Presently she sat upon his knee. The inhabitants of Camelia Road tramped to and fro outside the window, just on a level with their heads, and the family in the flat on the ground-floor began to sing, "Hark, my soul, it is the Lord."

"That tune fairly gives me the hump," said Leonard.

Jacky followed this, and said that, for her part, she thought it a lovely tune.

"No; I'll play you something lovely. Get up, dear, for a minute."

He went to the piano and jingled out a little Grieg. He played badly and vulgarly, but the performance was not without its effect, for Jacky said she thought she'd be going to bed. As she receded, a new set of interests possessed the boy, and he began to think of what had been said about music by that odd Miss Schlegel—the one that twisted her face about so when she spoke. Then the thoughts grew sad and envious. There was the girl named Helen, who had pinched his umbrella, and the German girl who had smiled at him pleasantly, and Herr someone, and Aunt someone, and the brother—all, all with their hands on the ropes. They had all passed up that narrow, rich staircase at Wickham Place, to some ample room, whither he could never follow them, not if he read for ten hours a day. Oh, it was no good, this continual aspiration. Some are born cultured; the rest had better go in for whatever comes easy. To see life steadily and to see it whole was not for the likes of him.

From the darkness beyond the kitchen a voice called, "Len?"

"You in bed?" he asked, his forehead twitching.

"M'm."

"All right."

Presently she called him again.

"I must clean my boots ready for the morning," he answered.

Presently she called him again.

"I rather want to get this chapter done."

"What?"

He closed his ears against her.

"What's that?"

"All right, Jacky, nothing; I'm reading a book."

"What?"

"What?" he answered, catching her degraded deafness.

Presently she called him again.

Ruskin had visited Torcello by this time, and was ordering his gondoliers to take him to Murano. It occurred to him, as he glided over the whispering lagoons, that the power of Nature could not be shortened by the folly, nor her beauty altogether saddened by the misery, of such as Leonard.

CHAPTER VII

"Oh, Margaret," cried her aunt next morning, "such a most unfortunate thing has happened. I could not get you alone."

The most unfortunate thing was not very serious. One of the flats in the ornate block opposite had been taken furnished by the Wilcox family, "coming up, no doubt, in the hope of getting into London society." That Mrs. Munt should be the first to discover the misfortune was not remarkable, for she was so interested in the flats, that she watched their every mutation with unwearying care. In theory she despised them—they took away that old-world look—they cut off the sun—flats house a flashy type of person. But if the truth had been known, she found her visits to Wickham Place twice as amusing since the Wickham Mansions had arisen, and would in a couple of days learn more about them than her nieces in a couple of months, or her nephew in a couple of years. She would stroll across and make friends with the porters, and inquire what the rents were, exclaiming for example: "What! a hundred and twenty for a basement? You'll never get it!" And they would answer: "One can but try, madam." The passenger lifts, the provision lifts, the arrangement for coals (a great temptation for a dishonest porter), were all familiar matters to her, and perhaps a relief from the politico-economical-æsthetic atmosphere that reigned at the Schlegels'.

Margaret received the information calmly, and did not agree that it would throw a cloud over poor Helen's life.

"Oh, but Helen isn't a girl with no interests," she explained. "She has plenty of other things and other people to think about. She made a false start with the Wilcoxes, and she'll be as willing as we are to have nothing more to do with them."

"For a clever girl, dear, how very oddly you do talk. Helen 'll *have* to have something more to do with them, now that they're all opposite. She may meet that Paul in the street. She cannot very well not bow."

"Of course she must bow. But look here; let's do the flowers. I was going to say, the will to be interested in him has died, and what else matters? I look on that disastrous episode (over which you were so kind) as the killing of a nerve in Helen. It's dead, and she'll never be troubled with it again. The only things that matter are the things that interest one. Bowing, even calling and leaving cards, even a dinner-party—we can do all those things to the Wilcoxes, if they find it agreeable; but the other thing, the one important thing—never again. Don't you see?"

Mrs. Munt did not see, and indeed Margaret was making a most questionable statement—that any emotion, any interest once vividly aroused, can wholly die.

"I also have the honour to inform you that the Wilcoxes are bored with us. I didn't tell you at the time—it might have made you angry, and you had enough to worry you—but I wrote a letter to Mrs. W., and apologized for the trouble that Helen had given them. She didn't answer it."

"How very rude!"

"I wonder. Or was it sensible?"

"No, Margaret, most rude."

"In either case one can class it as reassuring."

Mrs. Munt sighed. She was going back to Swanage on the morrow, just as her nieces were wanting her most. Other regrets crowded upon her: for instance, how magnificently she would have cut Charles if she had met him face to face. She had already seen him, giving an order to the porter—and very common he looked in a tall hat. But unfortunately his back was turned to her, and though she had cut his back, she could not regard this as a telling snub.

"But you will be careful, won't you?" she exhorted.

"Oh, certainly. Fiendishly careful."

"And Helen must be careful, too."

"Careful over what?" cried Helen, at that moment coming into the room with her cousin.

"Nothing," said Margaret, seized with a momentary awkwardness.

"Careful over what, Aunt Juley?"

Mrs. Munt assumed a cryptic air. "It is only that a certain family, whom we know by name but do not mention, as you said yourself last night after the concert, have taken the flat opposite from the Mathesons—where the plants are in the balcony."

Helen began some laughing reply, and then disconcerted them all by blushing. Mrs. Munt was so disconcerted that she exclaimed, "What, Helen, you don't mind them coming, do you?" and deepened the blush to crimson.

"Of course I don't mind," said Helen a little crossly. "It is that you and Meg are both so absurdly grave about it, when there's nothing to be grave about at all."

"I'm not grave," protested Margaret, a little cross in her turn.

"Well, you look grave; doesn't she, Frieda?"

"I don't feel grave, that's all I can say; you're going quite on the wrong tack."

"No, she does not feel grave," echoed Mrs. Munt. "I can bear witness to that. She disagrees——"

"Hark!" interrupted Fräulein Mosebach. "I hear Bruno entering the hall."

For Herr Liesecke was due at Wickham Place to call for the two younger girls. He was not entering the hall—in fact, he did not enter it for quite five minutes. But Frieda detected a delicate situation, and said that she and Helen had much better wait for Bruno down below, and leave Margaret and Mrs. Munt to finish arranging the flowers. Helen acquiesced. But, as if to prove that

the situation was not delicate really, she stopped in the doorway
and said:

"Did you say the Mathesons' flat, Aunt Juley? How wonderful
you are! I never knew that the woman who laced too tightly's
name was Matheson."

"Come, Helen," said her cousin.

"Go, Helen," said her aunt; and continued to Margaret almost
in the same breath: "Helen cannot deceive me. She does mind."

"Oh, hush!" breathed Margaret. "Frieda 'll hear you, and she
can be so tiresome."

"She minds," persisted Mrs. Munt, moving thoughtfully about
the room, and pulling the dead chrysanthemums out of the vases.
"I knew she'd mind—and I'm sure a girl ought to! Such an experience! Such awful coarse-grained people! I know more about
them than you do, which you forget, and if Charles had taken
you that motor drive—well, you'd have reached the house a perfect wreck. Oh, Margaret, you don't know what you are in for.
They're all bottled up against the drawing-room window. There's
Mrs. Wilcox—I've seen her. There's Paul. There's Evie, who is a
minx. There's Charles—I saw him to start with. And who would
an elderly man with a moustache and a copper-coloured face be?"

"Mr. Wilcox, possibly."

"I knew it. And there's Mr. Wilcox."

"It's a shame to call his face copper colour," complained
Margaret. "He has a remarkably good complexion for a man of
his age."

Mrs. Munt, triumphant elsewhere, could afford to concede Mr.
Wilcox his complexion. She passed on from it to the plan of campaign that her nieces should pursue in the future. Margaret tried
to stop her.

"Helen did not take the news quite as I expected, but the
Wilcox nerve is dead in her really, so there's no need for plans."

"It's as well to be prepared."

"No—it's as well not to be prepared."

"Why?"

"Because——"

Her thought drew being from the obscure borderland. She could not explain in so many words, but she felt that those who prepare for all the emergencies of life beforehand may equip themselves at the expense of joy. It is necessary to prepare for an examination, or a dinner-party, or a possible fall in the price of stock: those who attempt human relations must adopt another method, or fail. "Because I'd sooner risk it," was her lame conclusion.

"But imagine the evenings," exclaimed her aunt, pointing to the Mansions with the spout of the watering-can. "Turn the electric light on here or there, and it's almost the same room. One evening they may forget to draw their blinds down, and you'll see them; and the next, you yours, and they'll see you. Impossible to sit out on the balconies. Impossible to water the plants, or even speak. Imagine going out of the front-door, and they come out opposite at the same moment. And yet you tell me that plans are unnecessary, and you'd rather risk it."

"I hope to risk things all my life."

"Oh, Margaret, most dangerous."

"But after all," she continued with a smile, "there's never any great risk as long as you have money."

"Oh, shame! What a shocking speech!"

"Money pads the edges of things," said Miss Schlegel. "God help those who have none."

"But this is something quite new!" said Mrs. Munt, who collected new ideas as a squirrel collects nuts, and was especially attracted by those that are portable.

"New for me; sensible people have acknowledged it for years. You and I and the Wilcoxes stand upon money as upon islands. It is so firm beneath our feet that we forget its very existence. It's only when we see someone near us tottering that we realize all that an independent income means. Last night, when we were talking up here round the fire, I began to think that the very soul of the world is economic, and that the lowest abyss is not the absence of love, but the absence of coin."

"I call that rather cynical."

"So do I. But Helen and I, we ought to remember, when we are tempted to criticize others, that we are standing on these islands, and that most of the others are down below the surface of the sea. The poor cannot always reach those whom they want to love, and they can hardly ever escape from those whom they love no longer. We rich can. Imagine the tragedy last June, if Helen and Paul Wilcox had been poor people, and couldn't invoke railways and motor-cars to part them."

"That's more like Socialism," said Mrs. Munt suspiciously.

"Call it what you like. I call it going through life with one's hand spread open on the table. I'm tired of these rich people who pretend to be poor, and think it shows a nice mind to ignore the piles of money that keep their feet above the waves. I stand each year upon six hundred pounds, and Helen upon the same, and Tibby will stand upon eight, and as fast as our pounds crumble away into the sea they are renewed—from the sea, yes, from the sea. And all our thoughts are the thoughts of six-hundred-pounders, and all our speeches; and because we don't want to steal umbrellas ourselves, we forget that below the sea people do want to steal them, and do steal them sometimes, and that what's a joke up here is down there reality——"

"There they go—there goes Fräulein Mosebach. Really, for a German she does dress charmingly. Oh——"

"What is it?"

"Helen was looking up at the Wilcoxes' flat."

"Why shouldn't she?"

"I beg your pardon, I interrupted you. What was it you were saying about reality?"

"I had worked round to myself, as usual," answered Margaret in tones that were suddenly preoccupied.

"Do tell me this, at all events. Are you for the rich or for the poor?"

"Too difficult. Ask me another. Am I for poverty or for riches? For riches. Hurrah for riches!"

"For riches!" echoed Mrs. Munt, having, as it were, at last secured her nut.

"Yes. For riches. Money for ever!"

"So am I, and so, I am afraid, are most of my acquaintances at Swanage, but I am surprised that you agree with us."

"Thank you so much, Aunt Juley. While I have talked theories, you have done the flowers."

"Not at all, dear. I wish you would let me help you in more important things."

"Well, would you be very kind? Would you come round with me to the registry office? There's a housemaid who won't say yes but doesn't say no."

On their way thither they too looked up at the Wilcoxes' flat. Evie was in the balcony, "staring most rudely," according to Mrs. Munt. Oh, yes, it was a nuisance, there was no doubt of it. Helen was proof against a passing encounter, but—— Margaret began to lose confidence. Might it reawake the dying nerve if the family were living close against her eyes? And Frieda Mosebach was stopping with them for another fortnight, and Frieda was sharp, abominably sharp, and quite capable of remarking, "You love one of the young gentlemen opposite, yes?" The remark would be untrue, but of the kind which, if stated often enough, may become true; just as the remark, 'England and Germany are bound to fight,' renders war a little more likely each time that it is made, and is therefore made the more readily by the gutter press of either nation. Have the private emotions also their gutter press? Margaret thought so, and feared that good Aunt Juley and Frieda were typical specimens of it. They might, by continual chatter, lead Helen into a repetition of the desires of June. Into a repetition—they could not do more; they could not lead her into lasting love. They were—she saw it clearly—Journalism; her father, with all his defects and wrong-headedness, had been Literature, and had he lived, he would have persuaded his daughter rightly.

The registry office was holding its morning reception. A string

of carriages filled the street. Miss Schlegel waited her turn, and
finally had to be content with an insidious "temporary," being
rejected by genuine housemaids on the ground of her numerous
stairs. Her failure depressed her, and though she forgot the failure,
the depression remained. On her way home she again glanced up
at the Wilcoxes' flat, and took the rather matronly step of speaking about the matter to Helen.

"Helen, you must tell me whether this thing worries you."

"If what?" said Helen, who was washing her hands for lunch.

"The W.s' coming."

"No, of course not."

"Really?"

"Really." Then she admitted that she was a little worried on
Mrs. Wilcox's account; she implied that Mrs. Wilcox might reach
backward into deep feelings, and be pained by things that never
touched the other members of that clan. "I shan't mind if Paul
points at our house and says, 'There lives the girl who tried to
catch me.' But she might."

"If even that worries you, we could arrange something. There's
no reason we should be near people who displease us or whom
we displease, thanks to our money. We might even go away for
a little."

"Well, I am going away. Frieda's just asked me to Stettin, and I
shan't be back till after the New Year. Will that do? Or must I fly
the country altogether? Really, Meg, what has come over you to
make such a fuss?"

"Oh, I'm getting an old maid, I suppose. I thought I minded
nothing, but really I—I should be bored if you fell in love with
the same man twice and"—she cleared her throat—"you did go
red, you know, when Aunt Juley attacked you this morning. I
shouldn't have referred to it otherwise."

But Helen's laugh rang true, as she raised a soapy hand to
heaven and swore that never, nowhere and nohow, would she
again fall in love with any of the Wilcox family, down to its
remotest collaterals.

CHAPTER VIII

The friendship between Margaret and Mrs. Wilcox, which was to develop so quickly and with such strange results, may perhaps have had its beginnings at Speyer, in the spring. Perhaps the elder lady, as she gazed at the vulgar, ruddy cathedral, and listened to the talk of Helen and her husband, may have detected in the other and less charming of the sisters a deeper sympathy, a sounder judgment. She was capable of detecting such things. Perhaps it was she who had desired the Miss Schlegels to be invited to Howards End, and Margaret whose presence she had particularly desired. All this is speculation: Mrs. Wilcox has left few clear indications behind her. It is certain that she came to call at Wickham Place a fortnight later, the very day that Helen was going with her cousin to Stettin.

"Helen!" cried Fräulein Mosebach in awestruck tones (she was now in her cousin's confidence)—"his mother has forgiven you!" And then, remembering that in England the new-comer ought not to call before she is called upon, she changed her tone from awe to disapproval, and opined that Mrs. Wilcox was "keine Dame."

"Bother the whole family!" snapped Margaret. "Helen, stop giggling and pirouetting, and go and finish your packing. Why can't the woman leave us alone?"

"I don't know what I shall do with Meg," Helen retorted, collapsing upon the stairs. "She's got Wilcox and Box upon the brain. Meg, Meg, I don't love the young gentleman; I don't love the young gentleman, Meg, Meg. Can a body speak plainer?"

"Most certainly her love has died," asserted Fräulein Mosebach.

"Most certainly it has, Frieda, but that will not prevent me from being bored with the Wilcoxes if I return the call."

Then Helen simulated tears, and Fräulein Mosebach, who thought her extremely amusing, did the same. "Oh, boo hoo! boo hoo hoo! Meg's going to return the call, and I can't. 'Cos why? 'Cos I'm going to German-eye."

"If you are going to Germany, go and pack; if you aren't, go and call on the Wilcoxes instead of me."

"But Meg, Meg, I don't love the young gentleman; I don't love the young—O lud, who's that coming down the stairs: I vow 'tis my brother. O crimini!"

A male—even such a male as Tibby—was enough to stop the foolery. The barrier of sex, though decreasing among the civilized, is still high, and higher on the side of women. Helen could tell her sister all, and her cousin much about Paul; she told her brother nothing. It was not prudishness, for she now spoke of "the Wilcox ideal" with laughter, and even with a growing brutality. Nor was it precaution, for Tibby seldom repeated any news that did not concern himself. It was rather the feeling that she betrayed a secret into the camp of men, and that, however trivial it was on this side of the barrier, it would become important on that. So she stopped, or rather began to fool on other subjects, until her long-suffering relatives drove her upstairs. Fräulein Mosebach followed her, but lingered to say heavily over the banisters to Margaret, "It is all right—she does not love the young man—he has not been worthy of her."

"Yes, I know; thanks very much."

"I thought I did right to tell you."

"Ever so many thanks."

"What's that?" asked Tibby. No one told him, and he proceeded into the dining-room, to eat Elvas plums.

That evening Margaret took decisive action. The house was very quiet, and the fog—we are in November now—pressed against the windows like an excluded ghost. Frieda and Helen and all their luggages had gone. Tibby, who was not feeling well, lay stretched on a sofa by the fire. Margaret sat by him, thinking. Her mind darted from impulse to impulse, and finally marshalled them all in review. The practical person, who knows what he wants at once, and generally knows nothing else, will excuse her of indecision. But this was the way her mind worked. And when she did act, no one could accuse her of indecision then. She hit out as lustily as if she had not considered the matter at all. The letter that she wrote Mrs. Wilcox glowed with the native hue of resolution. The pale cast of thought was with her a breath rather than a tarnish, a breath that leaves the colours all the more vivid when it has been wiped away.

"DEAR MRS. WILCOX,

"I have to write something discourteous. It would be better if we did not meet. Both my sister and my aunt have given displeasure to your family, and, in my sister's case, the grounds for displeasure might recur. As far as I know, she no longer occupies her thoughts with your son. But it would not be fair, either to her or to you, if they met, and it is therefore right that our acquaintance, which began so pleasantly, should end.

"I fear that you will not agree with this; indeed, I know that you will not, since you have been good enough to call on us. It is only an instinct on my part, and no doubt the instinct is wrong. My sister would, undoubtedly, say that it is wrong. I write without her knowledge, and I hope that you will not associate her with my discourtesy.

"Believe me,
"Yours truly,
"M.J. SCHLEGEL."

Margaret sent this letter round by the post. Next morning she received the following reply by hand:

"DEAR MISS SCHLEGEL,

"You should not have written me such a letter. I called to tell you that Paul has gone abroad.

"RUTH WILCOX."

Margaret's cheeks burnt. She could not finish her breakfast. She was on fire with shame. Helen had told her that the youth was leaving England, but other things had seemed more important, and she had forgotten. All her absurd anxieties fell to the ground, and in their place arose the certainty that she had been rude to Mrs. Wilcox. Rudeness affected Margaret like a bitter taste in the mouth. It poisoned life. At times it is necessary, but woe to those who employ it without due need. She flung on a hat and shawl, just like a poor woman, and plunged into the fog, which still continued. Her lips were compressed, the letter remained in her hand, and in this state she crossed the street, entered the marble vestibule of the flats, eluded the concierges, and ran up the stairs till she reached the second-floor.

She sent in her name, and to her surprise was shown straight into Mrs. Wilcox's bedroom.

"Oh, Mrs. Wilcox, I have made the baddest blunder. I am more, more ashamed and sorry than I can say."

Mrs. Wilcox bowed gravely. She was offended, and did not pretend to the contrary. She was sitting up in bed, writing letters on an invalid table that spanned her knees. A breakfast tray was on another table beside her. The light of the fire, the light from the window, and the light of a candle-lamp, which threw a quivering halo round her hands, combined to create a strange atmosphere of dissolution.

"I knew he was going to India in November, but I forgot."

"He sailed on the 17th for Nigeria, in Africa."

"I knew—I know. I have been too absurd all through. I am very much ashamed."

Mrs. Wilcox did not answer.

"I am more sorry than I can say, and I hope that you will forgive me."

"It doesn't matter, Miss Schlegel. It is good of you to have come round so promptly."

"It does matter," cried Margaret. "I have been rude to you; and my sister is not even at home, so there was not even that excuse."

"Indeed?"

"She has just gone to Germany."

"She gone as well," murmured the other. "Yes, certainly, it is quite safe—safe, absolutely, now."

"You've been worrying too!" exclaimed Margaret, getting more and more excited, and taking a chair without invitation. "How perfectly extraordinary! I can see that you have. You felt as I do; Helen mustn't meet him again."

"I did think it best."

"Now why?"

"That's a most difficult question," said Mrs. Wilcox, smiling, and a little losing her expression of annoyance. "I think you put it best in your letter—it was an instinct, which may be wrong."

"It wasn't that your son still——"

"Oh no; he often—my Paul is very young, you see."

"Then what was it?"

She repeated: "An instinct which may be wrong."

"In other words, they belong to types that can fall in love, but couldn't live together. That's dreadfully probable. I'm afraid that in nine cases out of ten Nature pulls one way and human nature another."

"These are indeed 'other words,'" said Mrs. Wilcox. "I had nothing so coherent in my head. I was merely alarmed when I knew that my boy cared for your sister."

"Ah, I have always been wanting to ask you. How *did* you know? Helen was so surprised when our aunt drove up, and you stepped forward and arranged things. Did Paul tell you?"

"There is nothing to be gained by discussing that," said Mrs. Wilcox after a moment's pause.

"Mrs. Wilcox, were you very angry with us last June?" I wrote you a letter and you didn't answer it."

"I was certainly against taking Mrs. Matheson's flat. I knew it was opposite your house."

"But it's all right now?"

"I think so."

"You only think? You aren't sure? I do love these little muddles tidied up?"

"Oh yes, I'm sure," said Mrs. Wilcox, moving with uneasiness beneath the clothes. "I always sound uncertain over things. It is my way of speaking."

"That's all right, and I'm sure too."

Here the maid came in to remove the breakfast-tray. They were interrupted, and when they resumed conversation it was on more normal lines.

"I must say good-bye now—you will be getting up."

"No—please stop a little longer—I am taking a day in bed. Now and then I do."

"I thought of you as one of the early risers."

"At Howards End—yes; there is nothing to get up for in London."

"Nothing to get up for?" cried the scandalized Margaret. "When there are all the autumn exhibitions, and Ysaye playing in the afternoon! Not to mention people."

"The truth is, I am a little tired. First came the wedding, and then Paul went off, and, instead of resting yesterday, I paid a round of calls."

"A wedding?"

"Yes; Charles, my elder son, is married."

"Indeed!"

"We took the flat chiefly on that account, and also that Paul could get his African outfit. The flat belongs to a cousin of my husband's, and she most kindly offered it to us. So before the day came we were able to make the acquaintance of Dolly's people, which we had not yet done."

Margaret asked who Dolly's people were.

"Fussell. The father is in the Indian army—retired; the brother is in the army. The mother is dead."

So perhaps these were the "chinless sunburnt men" whom Helen had espied one afternoon through the window. Margaret felt mildly interested in the fortunes of the Wilcox family. She had acquired the habit on Helen's account, and it still clung to her. She asked for more information about Miss Dolly Fussell that was, and was given it in even, unemotional tones. Mrs. Wilcox's voice, though sweet and compelling, had little range of expression. It suggested that pictures, concerts, and people are all of small and equal value. Only once had it quickened—when speaking of Howards End.

"Charles and Albert Fussell have known one another some time. They belong to the same club, and are both devoted to golf. Dolly plays golf too, though I believe not so well, and they first met in a mixed foursome. We all like her, and are very much pleased. They were married on the 11th, a few days before Paul sailed. Charles was very anxious to have his brother as best man, so he made a great point of having it on the 11th. The Fussells would have preferred it after Christmas, but they were very nice about it. There is Dolly's photograph—in that double frame."

"Are you quite certain that I'm not interrupting, Mrs. Wilcox?"

"Yes, quite."

"Then I will stay. I'm enjoying this."

Dolly's photograph was now examined. It was signed "For dear Mims," which Mrs. Wilcox interpreted as "the name she and Charles had settled that she should call me." Dolly looked silly, and had one of those triangular faces that so often prove attractive to a robust man. She was very pretty. From her Margaret passed to Charles, whose features prevailed opposite. She speculated on the forces that had drawn the two together till God parted them. She found time to hope that they would be happy.

"They have gone to Naples for their honeymoon."

"Lucky people!"

"I can hardly imagine Charles in Italy."

"Doesn't he care for travelling?"

"He likes travel, but he does see through foreigners so. What he enjoys most is a motor tour in England, and I think that would have carried the day if the weather had not been so abominable. His father gave him a car of his own for a wedding present, which for the present is being stored at Howards End."

"I suppose you have a garage there?"

"Yes. My husband built a little one only last month, to the west of the house, not far from the wych-elm, in what used to be the paddock for the pony."

The last words had an indescribable ring about them.

"Where's the pony gone?" asked Margaret after a pause.

"The pony? Oh, dead, ever so long ago."

"The wych-elm I remember. Helen spoke of it as a very splendid tree."

"It is the finest wych-elm in Hertfordshire. Did your sister tell you about the teeth?

"No."

"Oh, it might interest you. There are pigs' teeth stuck into the trunk, about four feet from the ground. The country people put them in long ago, and they think that if they chew a piece of the bark, it will cure the toothache. The teeth are almost grown over now, and no one comes to the tree."

"I should. I love folklore and all festering superstitions."

"Do you think that the tree really did cure toothache, if one believed in it?"

"Of course it did. It would cure anything—once."

"Certainly I remember cases—you see I lived at Howards End long, long before Mr. Wilcox knew it. I was born there."

The conversation again shifted. At the time it seemed little more than aimless chatter. She was interested when her hostess explained that Howards End was her own property. She was bored when too minute an account was given of the Fussell family, of the anxieties of Charles concerning Naples, of the movements of Mr. Wilcox and Evie, who were motoring in Yorkshire. Margaret could not bear being bored. She grew inattentive, played with the photograph frame, dropped it, smashed Dolly's glass, apologized, was pardoned, cut her finger thereon, was pitied, and finally said she must be going—there was all the housekeeping to do, and she had to interview Tibby's riding-master.

Then the curious note was struck again.

"Good-bye, Miss Schlegel, good-bye. Thank you for coming. You have cheered me up."

"I'm so glad!"

"I—I wonder whether you ever think about yourself?"

"I think of nothing else," said Margaret, blushing, but letting her hand remain in that of the invalid.

"I wonder. I wondered at Heidelberg."

"*I'm* sure!"

"I almost think——"

"Yes?" asked Margaret, for there was a long pause—a pause that was somehow akin to the flicker of the fire, the quiver of the reading-lamp upon their hands, the white blur from the window; a pause of shifting and eternal shadows.

"I almost think you forget you're a girl."

Margaret was startled and a little annoyed. "I'm twenty-nine," she remarked. "That's not so wildly girlish."

Mrs. Wilcox smiled.

"What makes you say that? Do you mean that I have been gauche and rude?"

A shake of the head. "I only meant that I am fifty-one, and that to me, both of you—— Read it all in some book or other; I cannot put things clearly."

"Oh, I've got it—inexperience. I'm no better than Helen, you mean, and yet I presume to advise her."

"Yes. You have got it. Inexperience is the word."

"Inexperience," repeated Margaret, in serious yet buoyant tones. "Of course, I have everything to learn—absolutely everything—just as much as Helen. Life's very difficult and full of surprises. At all events, I've got as far as that. To be humble and kind, to go straight ahead, to love people rather than pity them, to remember the submerged—well, one can't do all these things at once, worse luck, because they're so contradictory. It's then that proportion comes in—to live by proportion. Don't *begin* with proportion. Only prigs do that. Let proportion come in as a last resource, when the better things have failed, and a deadlock—— Gracious me, I've started preaching!"

"Indeed, you put the difficulties of life splendidly," said Mrs. Wilcox, withdrawing her hand into the deeper shadows. "It is just what I should have liked to say about them myself."

CHAPTER IX

Mrs. Wilcox cannot be accused of giving Margaret much information about life. And Margaret, on the other hand, has made a fair
show of modesty, and has pretended to an inexperience that she
certainly did not feel. She had kept house for over ten years; she
had entertained, almost with distinction; she had brought up a
charming sister, and was bringing up a brother. Surely, if experience is attainable, she had attained it.

Yet the little luncheon-party that she gave in Mrs. Wilcox's
honour was not a success. The new friend did not blend with the
"one or two delightful people" who had been asked to meet her,
and the atmosphere was one of polite bewilderment. Her tastes
were simple, her knowledge of culture slight, and she was not
interested in the New English Art Club, nor in the dividing-line
between Journalism and Literature, which was started as a con-
versational hare. The delightful people darted after it with cries of
joy, Margaret leading them, and not till the meal was half over did
they realize that the principal guest had taken no part in the
chase. There was no common topic. Mrs. Wilcox, whose life had
been spent in the service of husband and sons, had little to say to
strangers who had never shared it, and whose age was half her
own. Clever talk alarmed her, and withered her delicate imagin-
ings; it was the social counterpart of a motor-car, all jerks, and she
was a wisp of hay, a flower. Twice she deplored the weather, twice
criticized the train service on the Great Northern Railway. They
vigorously assented, and rushed on, and when she inquired
whether there was any news of Helen, her hostess was too much
occupied in placing Rothenstein to answer. The question was
repeated: "I hope that your sister is safe in Germany by now."
Margaret checked herself and said "Yes, thank you; I heard on
Tuesday." But the demon of vociferation was in her, and the next
moment she was off again.

"Only on Tuesday, for they live right away at Stettin. Did you
ever know anyone living at Stettin?"

"Never," said Mrs. Wilcox gravely, while her neighbour, a young man low down in the Education Office, began to discuss what people who lived at Stettin ought to look like. Was there such a thing as Stettininity? Margaret swept on.

"People at Stettin drop things into boats out of overhanging warehouses. At least, our cousins do, but aren't particularly rich. The town isn't interesting, except for a clock that rolls its eyes, and the view of the Oder, which truly is something special. Oh, Mrs. Wilcox, you would love the Oder! The river, or rather rivers—there seem to be dozens of them—are intense blue, and the plain they run through an intensest green."

"Indeed! That sounds like a most beautiful view, Miss Schlegel."

"So I say, but Helen, who will muddle things, says no, it's like music. The course of the Oder is to be like music. It's obliged to remind her of a symphonic poem. The part by the landing-stage is in B minor, if I remember rightly, but lower down things get extremely mixed. There is a slodgy theme in several keys at once, meaning mud banks, and another for the navigable canal, and the exit into the Baltic is in C sharp major, pianissimo."

"What do the overhanging warehouses make of that?" asked the man, laughing.

"They make a great deal of it," replied Margaret, unexpectedly rushing off on a new track. "I think it's affectation to compare the Oder to music, and so do you, but the overhanging warehouses of Stettin take beauty seriously, which we don't, and the average Englishman doesn't, and despises all who do. Now don't say 'Germans have no taste,' or I shall scream. They haven't. But—but—such a tremendous but!—they take poetry seriously. They do take poetry seriously."

"Is anything gained by that?"

"Yes, yes. The German is always on the lookout for beauty. He may miss it through stupidity, or misinterpret it, but he is always asking beauty to enter his life, and I believe that in the end it will come. At Heidelberg I met a fat veterinary surgeon whose voice broke with sobs as he repeated some mawkish poetry. So easy for me to laugh—I, who never repeat poetry, good or bad, and cannot remember one fragment of verse to thrill myself with. My blood boils—well, I'm half German, so put it down to patriotism—when I listen to the tasteful contempt of the average islander for things Teutonic, whether they're Böcklin or my veterinary surgeon. "Oh, Böcklin,' they say; 'he strains after beauty, he peoples Nature with gods too consciously.' Of course Böcklin strains, because he wants something—beauty and all the other intangible gifts that are floating about the world. So his landscapes don't come off, and Leader's do."

"I am not sure that I agree. Do you?" said he, turning to Mrs. Wilcox.

She replied: "I think Miss Schlegel puts everything splendidly"; and a chill fell on the conversation.

"Oh, Mrs. Wilcox, say something nicer than that. It's such a snub to be told you put things splendidly."

"I do not mean it as a snub. Your last speech interested me so much. Generally people do not seem quite to like Germany. I have long wanted to hear what is said on the other side."

"The other side? Then you do disagree. Oh, good! Give us your side."

"I have no side. But my husband"—her voice softened, and the chill increased—"has very little faith in the Continent, and our children have all taken after him."

"On what grounds? Do they feel that the Continent is in bad form?"

Mrs. Wilcox had no idea; she paid little attention to grounds. She was not intellectual, nor even alert, and it was odd that, all the same, she should give the idea of greatness. Margaret, zigzagging with her friends over Thought and Art, was conscious of a personality that transcended their own and dwarfed their activities. There was no bitterness in Mrs. Wilcox; there was not even criticism; she was lovable, and no ungracious or uncharitable word had passed her lips. Yet she and daily life were out of focus: one or the other must show blurred. And at lunch she seemed more out of focus than usual, and nearer the line that divides daily life from a life that may be of greater importance.

"You will admit, though, that the Continent—it seems silly to speak of 'the Continent,' but really it is all more like itself than any part of it is like England. England is unique. Do have another jelly first. I was going to say that the Continent, for good or for evil, is interested in ideas. Its Literature and Art have what one might call the kink of the unseen about them, and this persists even through decadence and affectation. There is more liberty of action in England, but for liberty of thought go to bureaucratic Prussia. People will there discuss with humility vital questions that we here think ourselves too good to touch with tongs.

"I do not want to go to Prussia," said Mrs. Wilcox—"not even to see that interesting view that you were describing. And for discussing with humility I am too old. We never discuss anything at Howards End."

"Then you ought to!" said Margaret. "Discussion keeps a house alive. It cannot stand by bricks and mortar alone."

"It cannot stand without them," said Mrs. Wilcox, unexpectedly catching on to the thought, and rousing, for the first and last time, a faint hope in the breasts of the delightful people. "It cannot stand without them, and I sometimes think—— But I cannot expect your generation to agree, for even my daughter disagrees with me here."

"Never mind us or her. Do say!"

"I sometimes think that it is wiser to leave action and discussion to men."

There was a little silence.

"One admits that the arguments against the suffrage *are* extraordinarily strong," said a girl opposite, leaning forward and crumbling her bread.

"Are they? I never follow any arguments. I am only too thankful not to have a vote myself."

"We didn't mean the vote, though, did we?" supplied Margaret.

"Aren't we differing on something much wider, Mrs. Wilcox? Whether women are to remain what they have been since the dawn of history; or whether, since men have moved forward so far, they too may move forward a little now. I say they may. I would even admit a biological change."

"I don't know, I don't know."

"I must be getting back to my overhanging warehouse," said the man. "They've turned disgracefully strict."

Mrs. Wilcox also rose.

"Oh, but come upstairs for a little. Miss Quested plays. Do you like MacDowell? Do you mind him only having two noises? If you must really go, I'll see you out. Won't you even have coffee?"

They left the dining-room, closing the door behind them, and as Mrs. Wilcox buttoned up her jacket, she said: "What an interesting life you all lead in London!"

"No, we don't," said Margaret, with a sudden revulsion. "We lead the lives of gibbering monkeys. Mrs. Wilcox—really—— We have something quiet and stable at the bottom. We really have. All my friends have. Don't pretend you enjoyed lunch, for you loathed it, but forgive me by coming again, alone, or by asking me to you."

"I am used to young people," said Mrs. Wilcox, and with each word she spoke the outlines of known things grew dim. "I hear a great deal of chatter at home, for we, like you, entertain a great deal. With us it is more sport and politics, but—I enjoyed my lunch very much, Miss Schlegel, dear, and am not pretending, and only wish I could have joined in more. For one thing, I'm not particularly well just to-day. For another, you younger people move so quickly that it dazes me. Charles is the same, Dolly the same. But we are all in the same boat, old and young. I never forget that."

They were silent for a moment. Then, with a newborn emotion, they shook hands. The conversation ceased suddenly when Margaret re-entered the dining-room: her friends had been talking over her new friend, and had dismissed her as interesting.

CHAPTER X

Several days passed.

Was Mrs. Wilcox one of the unsatisfactory people—there are many of them—who dangle intimacy and then withdraw it? They evoke our interests and affections, and keep the life of the spirit dawdling round them. Then they withdraw. When physical passion is involved, there is a definite name for such behaviour— flirting—and if carried far enough it is punishable by law. But no law—not public opinion even—punishes those who coquette with friendship, though the dull ache that they inflict, the sense of misdirected effort and exhaustion, may be as intolerable. Was she one of these?

Margaret feared so at first, for, with a Londoner's impatience, she wanted everything to be settled up immediately. She mistrusted the periods of quiet that are essential to true growth. Desiring to book Mrs. Wilcox as a friend, she pressed on the ceremony, pencil, as it were, in hand, pressing the more because the rest of the family were away, and the opportunity seemed favourable. But the elder woman would not be hurried. She refused to fit in with the Wickham Place set, or to reopen discussion of Helen and Paul, whom Margaret would have utilized as a short-cut. She took her time, or perhaps let time take her, and when the crisis did come all was ready.

The crisis opened with a message: would Miss Schlegel come shopping? Christmas was nearing, and Mrs. Wilcox felt behindhand with the presents. She had taken some more days in bed, and must make up for lost time. Margaret accepted, and at eleven o'clock one cheerless morning they started out in a brougham.

"First of all," began Margaret, "we must make a list and tick off the people's names. My aunt always does, and this fog may thicken up any moment. Have you any ideas?"

"I thought we would go to Harrod's or the Haymarket Stores," said Mrs. Wilcox rather hopelessly. "Everything is sure to be there. I am not a good shopper. The din is so confusing, and your aunt is quite right—one ought to make a list. Take my note-book, then, and write your own name at the top of the page."

"Oh, hooray!" said Margaret, writing it. "How very kind of you to start with me!" But she did not want to receive anything expensive. Their acquaintance was singular rather than intimate, and she divined that the Wilcox clan would resent any expenditure on outsiders; the more compact families do. She did not want to be thought a second Helen, who would snatch presents since she could not snatch young men, nor to be exposed, like a second Aunt Juley, to the insults of Charles. A certain austerity of demeanour was best, and she added: "I don't really want a Yuletide gift, though. In fact, I'd rather not."

"Why?"

"Because I've odd ideas about Christmas. Because I have all that money can buy. I want more people, but no more things."

"I should like to give you something worth your acquaintance, Miss Schlegel, in memory of your kindness to me during my lonely fortnight. It has so happened that I have been left alone, and you have stopped me from brooding. I am too apt to brood."

"If that is so," said Margaret, "if I have happened to be of use to you, which I didn't know, you cannot pay me back with anything tangible."

"I suppose not, but one would like to. Perhaps I shall think of something as we go about."

Her name remained at the head of the list, but nothing was written opposite it. They drove from shop to shop. The air was white, and when they alighted it tasted like cold pennies. At times they passed through a clot of grey. Mrs. Wilcox's vitality was low that morning, and it was Margaret who decided on a horse for this little girl, a golliwog for that, for the rector's wife a copper warming-tray. "We always give the servants money." "Yes, do you, yes, much easier," replied Margaret, but felt the grotesque impact of the unseen upon the seen, and saw issuing from a forgotten manger at Bethlehem this torrent of coins and toys. Vulgarity reigned. Public-houses, besides their usual exhortation against temperance reform, invited men to "Join our Christmas goose club"—one bottle of gin, etc., or two, according to subscription. A poster of a woman in tights heralded the Christmas pantomime, and little red devils, who had come in again that year, were prevalent upon the Christmas-cards. Margaret was no morbid idealist. She did not wish this spate of business and self-advertisement checked. It was only the occasion of it that struck her with amazement annually. How many of these vacillating shoppers and tired shop-assistants realized that it was a divine event that drew them together? She realized it, though standing outside in the matter. She was not a Christian in the accepted sense; she did not believe that God had ever worked among us as a young artisan. These people, or most of them, believed it, and if pressed, would affirm it in words. But the visible signs of their belief were Regent Street or Drury Lane, a little mud displaced, a little money spent, a little food cooked, eaten, and forgotten. Inadequate. But in public who shall express the unseen adequately? It is private life that holds out the mirror to infinity; personal intercourse, and that alone, that ever hints at a personality beyond our daily vision.

"No, I do like Christmas on the whole," she announced. "In its clumsy way, it does approach Peace and Goodwill. But oh, it is clumsier every year."

"Is it? I am only used to country Christmases."

"We are usually in London, and play the game with vigour—carols at the Abbey, clumsy midday meal, clumsy dinner for the maids, followed by Christmas-tree and dancing of poor children, with songs from Helen. The drawing-room does very well for that. We put the tree in the powder-closet, and draw a curtain when the candles are lighted, and with the looking-glass behind it looks quite pretty. I wish we might have a powder-closet in our next house. Of course, the tree has to be very small, and the presents don't hang on it. No; the presents reside in a sort of rocky landscape made of crumpled brown paper."

"You spoke of your 'next house,' Miss Schlegel. Then are you leaving Wickham Place?"

"Yes, in two or three years, when the lease expires. We must."

"Have you been there long?"

"All our lives."

"You will be very sorry to leave it."

"I suppose so. We scarcely realize it yet. My father——" She broke off, for they had reached the stationery department of the Haymarket Stores, and Mrs. Wilcox wanted to order some private greeting cards.

"If possible, something distinctive," she sighed. At the counter she found a friend, bent on the same errand, and conversed with her insipidly, wasting much time. "My husband and our daughter are motoring." "Bertha too?" Oh, fancy, what a coincidence!" Margaret, though not practical, could shine in such company as this. While they talked, she went through a volume of specimen cards, and submitted one for Mrs. Wilcox's inspection. Mrs. Wilcox was delighted—so original, words so sweet; she would order a hundred like that, and could never be sufficiently grateful. Then, just as the assistant was booking the order, she said: "Do you know, I'll wait. On second thoughts, I'll wait. There's plenty of time still, isn't there, and I shall be able to get Evie's opinion."

They returned to the carriage by devious paths; when they were in, she said, "But couldn't you get it renewed?"

"I beg your pardon?" asked Margaret.

"The lease, I mean."

"Oh, the lease! Have you been thinking of that all the time! How very kind of you!"

"Surely something could be done."

"No; values have risen too enormously. They mean to pull down Wickham Place, and build flats like yours."

"But how horrible!"

"Landlords are horrible."

Then she said vehemently: "It is monstrous, Miss Schlegel; it isn't right. I had no idea that this was hanging over you. I do pity you from the bottom of my heart. To be parted from your house, your father's house—it oughtn't to be allowed. It is worse than dying. I would rather die than—— Oh, poor girls! Can what they call civilization be right, if people mayn't die in the room where they were born? My dear, I am so sorry——"

Margaret did not know what to say. Mrs. Wilcox had been overtired by the shopping, and was inclined to hysteria.

"Howards End was nearly pulled down once. I would have killed me."

"Howards End must be a very different house to ours. We are fond of ours, but there is nothing distinctive about it. As you saw, it is an ordinary London house. We shall easily find another."

"So you think."

"Again my lack of experience, I suppose!" said Margaret, easing away from the subject. "I can't say anything when you take up that line, Mrs. Wilcox. I wish I could see myself as you see me—foreshortened into a backfisch. Quite the ingénue. Very charming—wonderfully well read for my age, but incapable——"

Mrs. Wilcox would not be deterred. "Come down with me to Howards End now," she said, more vehemently than ever. "I want you to see it. You have never seen it. I want to hear what you say about it, for you do put things so wonderfully."

Margaret glanced at the pitiless air and then at the tired face of her companion. "Later on I should love it," she continued, "but it's hardly the weather for such an expedition, and we ought to start when we're fresh. Isn't the house shut up, too?"

She received no answer. Mrs. Wilcox appeared to be annoyed.

"Might I come some other day?"

Mrs. Wilcox bent forward and tapped the glass. "Back to Wickham Place, please!" was her order to the coachman. Margaret had been snubbed.

"A thousand thanks, Miss Schlegel, for all your help."

"Not at all."

"It is such a comfort to get the presents off my mind—the Christmas-cards especially. I do admire your choice."

It was her turn to receive no answer. In her turn Margaret became annoyed.

"My husband and Evie will be back the day after to-morrow. That is why I dragged you out shopping to-day. I stayed in town chiefly to shop, but got through nothing, and now he writes that they must cut their tour short, the weather is so bad, and the police-traps have been so bad—nearly as bad as in Surrey. Ours is such a careful chauffeur, and my husband feels it particularly hard that they should be treated like road-hogs."

"Why?"

"Well, naturally he—he isn't a road-hog."

"He was exceeding the speed-limit, I conclude. He must expect to suffer with the lower animals."

Mrs. Wilcox was silenced. In growing discomfort they drove homewards. The city seemed Satanic, the narrower streets oppressing like the galleries of a mine. No harm was done by the fog to trade, for it lay high, and the lighted windows of the shops were thronged with customers. It was rather a darkening of the spirit which fell back upon itself, to find a more grievous darkness within. Margaret nearly spoke a dozen times, but something throttled her. She felt petty and awkward, and her meditations on Christmas grew more cynical. Peace? It may bring other gifts, but is there a single Londoner to whom Christmas is peaceful? The craving for excitement and for elaboration has ruined that blessing. Goodwill? Had she seen any example of it in the hordes of purchasers? Or in herself? She had failed to respond to this invitation merely because it was a little queer and imaginative—she, whose birthright it was to nourish imagination! Better to have accepted, to have tired themselves a little by the journey, than coldly to reply, "Might I come some other day?" Her cynicism left her. There would be no other day. This shadowy woman would never ask her again.

They parted at the Mansions. Mrs. Wilcox went in after due civilities, and Margaret watched the tall, lonely figure sweep up the hall to the lift. As the glass doors closed on it she had the sense of an imprisonment. The beautiful head disappeared first, still buried in the muff; the long trailing skirt followed. A woman of undefinable rarity was going up heavenward, like a specimen in a bottle. And into what a heaven—a vault as of hell, sooty black, from which soots descended!

At lunch her brother, seeing her inclined for silence, insisted on talking. Tibby was not ill-natured, but from babyhood something drove him to do the unwelcome and the unexpected. Now he gave her a long account of the day-school that he sometimes patronized. The account was interesting, and she had often pressed him for it before, but she could not attend now, for her mind was focussed on the invisible. She discerned that Mrs. Wilcox, though a loving wife and mother, had only one passion in life—her house—and that the moment was solemn when she invited a friend to share this passion with her. To answer "another day" was to answer as a fool. "Another day" will do for brick and mortar, but not for the Holy of Holies into which Howards End had been transfigured. Her own curiosity was slight. She had heard more than enough about it in the summer. The nine windows, the vine, and the wych-elm had no pleasant connections for her, and she would have preferred to spend the afternoon at a concert. But imagination triumphed. While her brother held forth she determined to go, at whatever cost, and to compel Mrs. Wilcox to go, too. When lunch was over she stepped over to the flats.

Mrs. Wilcox had just gone away for the night.

Margaret said that it was of no consequence, hurried downstairs, and took a hansom to King's Cross. She was convinced that the escapade was important, though it would have puzzled her to say why. There was question of imprisonment and escape, though she did not know the time of the train, she strained her eyes for St. Pancras' clock.

Then the clock of King's Cross swung into sight, a second moon in that infernal sky, and her cab drew up at the station. There was a train for Hilton in five minutes. She took a ticket, asking in her agitation for a single. As she did so, a grave and happy voice saluted her and thanked her.

"I will come if I still may," said Margaret, laughing nervously.

"You are coming to sleep, dear, too. It is in the morning that my house is most beautiful. You are coming to stop. I cannot show you my meadow properly except at sunrise. These fogs"— she pointed at the station roof—"never spread far. I dare say they are sitting in the sun in Hertfordshire, and you will never repent joining them."

"I shall never repent joining you."

"It is the same."

They began the walk up the long platform. Far at its end stood the train, breasting the darkness without. They never reached it. Before imagination could triumph, there were cries of "Mother! mother!" and a heavy-browed girl darted out of the cloak-room and seized Mrs. Wilcox by the arm.

"Evie!" she gasped—"Evie, my pet——"

The girl called, "Father! I say! look who's here."

"Evie, dearest girl, why aren't you in Yorkshire?"

"No—motor smash—changed plans—father's coming."

"Why, Ruth!" cried Mr. Wilcox, joining them. "What in the name of all that's wonderful are you doing here, Ruth?"

Mrs. Wilcox had recovered herself.

"Oh, Henry dear!—here's a lovely surprise—but let me introduce—but I think you know Miss Schlegel."

"Oh yes," he replied, not greatly interested. "But how's yourself, Ruth?"

"Fit as a fiddle," she answered gaily.

"So are we, and so was our car, which ran A1 as far as Ripon, but there a wretched horse and cart which a fool of a driver——"

"Miss Schlegel, our little outing must be for another day."

"I was saying that this fool of a driver, as the policeman himself admits——"

"Another day, Mrs. Wilcox. Of course."

"—But as we've insured against third party risks, it won't so much matter——"

"—Cart and car being practically at right angles——"

The voices of the happy family rose high. Margaret was left alone. No one wanted her. Mrs. Wilcox walked out of King's Cross between her husband and her daughter, listening to both of them.

CHAPTER XI

The funeral was over. The carriages had rolled away through the soft mud, and only the poor remained. They approached the newly-dug shaft and looked their last at the coffin, now almost hidden beneath the spadefuls of clay. It was their moment. Most of them were women from the dead woman's district, to whom black garments had been served out by Mr. Wilcox's orders. Pure curiosity had brought others. They thrilled with the excitement of a death, and of a rapid death, and stood in groups or moved between the graves, like drops of ink. The son of one of them, a wood-cutter, was perched high above their heads, pollarding one of the churchyard elms. From where he sat he could see the village of Hilton, strung upon the North Road, with its accreting suburbs; the sunset beyond, scarlet and orange, winking at him beneath brows of grey; the church; the plantations; and behind him an unspoilt country of fields and farms. But he, too, was rolling the event luxuriously in his mouth. He tried to tell his mother down below all that he had felt when he saw the coffin approaching: how he could not leave his work, and yet did not like to go on with it; how he had almost slipped out of the tree, he was so upset; the rooks had cawed, and no wonder—it was as if rooks knew too. His mother claimed the prophetic power herself—she had seen a strange look about Mrs. Wilcox for some time. London had done the mischief, said others. She had been a kind lady; her grandmother had been kind, too—a plainer person, but very kind. Ah, the old sort was dying out! Mr. Wilcox, he was a kind gentleman. They advanced to the topic again and again, dully, but with exaltation. The funeral of a rich person was to them what the funeral of Alcestis or Ophelia is to the educated. It was Art; though remote from life, it enhanced life's values, and they witnessed it avidly.

The grave-diggers, who had kept up an undercurrent of disapproval—they disliked Charles; it was not a moment to speak of such things, but they did not like Charles Wilcox—the grave-diggers finished their work and piled up the wreaths and crosses above it. The sun set over Hilton: the grey brows of the evening flushed a little, and were cleft with one scarlet frown. Chattering sadly to each other, the mourners passed through the lych-gate and traversed the chestnut avenues that led down to the village. The young wood-cutter stayed a little longer, poised above the silence and swaying rhythmically. At last the bough fell beneath his saw. With a grunt, he descended, his thoughts dwelling no longer on death, but on love, for he was mating. He stopped as he passed the new grave; a sheaf of tawny chrysanthemums had caught his eye. "They didn't ought to have coloured flowers at buryings," he reflected. Trudging on a few steps, he stopped again, looked furtively at the dusk, turned back, wrenched a chrysanthemum from the sheaf, and hid it in his pocket.

After him came silence absolute. The cottage that abutted on the churchyard was empty, and no other house stood near. Hour after hour the scene of the interment remained without an eye to witness it. Clouds drifted over it from the west; or the church may have been a ship, high-prowed, steering with all its company towards infinity. Towards morning the air grew colder, the sky clearer, the surface of the earth hard and sparkling above the prostrate dead. The wood-cutter, returning after a night of joy, reflected: "They lilies, they chrysants; it's a pity I didn't take them all."

Up at Howards End they were attempting breakfast. Charles and Evie sat in the dining-room, with Mrs. Charles. Their father, who could not bear to see a face, breakfasted upstairs. He suffered acutely. Pain came over him in spasms, as if it was physical, and even while he was about to eat, his eyes would fill with tears, and he would lay down the morsel untasted.

He remembered his wife's even goodness during thirty years. Not anything in detail—not courtship or early raptures—but just the unvarying virtue, that seemed to him a woman's noblest quality. So many women are capricious, breaking into odd flaws of passion or frivolity. Not so his wife. Year after year, summer and winter, as bride and mother, she had been the same, he had always trusted her. Her tenderness! Her innocence! The wonderful innocence that was hers by the gift of God. Ruth knew no more of worldly wickedness and wisdom than did the flowers in her garden, or the grass in her field. Her idea of business— "Henry, why do people who have enough money try to get more money?" Her idea of politics—"I am sure that if the mothers of various nations could meet, there would be no more wars." Her idea of religion—ah, this had been a cloud, but a cloud that passed. She came of Quaker stock, and he and his family, formerly Dissenters, were now members of the Church of England. The rector's sermons had at first repelled her, and she had expressed a desire for "a more inward light," adding, "not so much for myself as for baby" (Charles). Inward light must have been granted, for he heard no complaints in later years. They brought up their three children without dispute. They had never disputed.

She lay under the earth now. She had gone, and as if to make her going the more bitter, had gone with a touch of mystery that was all unlike her. "Why didn't you tell me you knew of it?" he had moaned, and her faint voice had answered: "I didn't want to, Henry—I might have been wrong—and everyone hates illnesses." He had been told of the horror by a strange doctor, whom she had consulted during his absence from town. Was this altogether just? Without fully explaining, she had died. It was a fault on her part, and—tears rushed into his eyes—what a little fault! It was the only time she had deceived him in those thirty years.

He rose to his feet and looked out of the window, for Evie had come in with the letters, and he could meet no one's eye. Ah yes—she had been a good woman—she had been steady. He chose the word deliberately. To him steadiness included all praise.

He himself, gazing at the wintry garden, is in appearance a steady man. His face was not as square as his son's, and, indeed, the chin, though firm enough in outline, retreated a little, and the lips, ambiguous, were curtained by a moustache. But there was no external hint of weakness. The eyes, if capable of kindness and good-fellowship, if ruddy for the moment with tears, were the eyes of one who could not be driven. The forehead, too, was like Charles's. High and straight, brown and polished, merging abruptly into temples and skull, it had the effect of a bastion that protected his head from the world. At times it had the effect of a blank wall. He had dwelt behind it, intact and happy, for fifty years.

"The post's come, father," said Evie awkwardly.

"Thanks. Put it down."

"Has the breakfast been all right?"

"Yes, thanks."

The girl glanced at him and at it with constraint. She did not know what to do.

"Charles says do you want the 'Times'?"

"No, I'll read it later."

"Ring if you want anything, father, won't you?"

"I've all I want."

Having sorted the letters from the circulars, she went back to the dining-room.

"Father's eaten nothing," she announced, sitting down with wrinkled brows behind the tea-urn.

Charles did not answer, but after a moment he ran quickly upstairs, opened the door, and said: "Look here, father, you must eat, you know;" and having paused for a reply that did not come, stole down again. "He's going to read his letters first, I think," he said evasively; "I dare say he will go on with his breakfast afterwards." Then he took up the 'Times,' and for some time there was no sound except the clink of cup against saucer and of knife on plate.

Poor Mrs. Charles sat between her silent companions, terrified at the course of events, and a little bored. She was a rubbishy little creature, and she knew it. A telegram had dragged her from Naples to the death-bed of a woman whom she had scarcely known. A word from her husband had plunged her into mourning. She desired to mourn inwardly as well, but she wished that Mrs. Wilcox, since fated to die, could have died before the marriage, for then less would have been expected of her. Crumbling her toast, and too nervous to ask for the butter, she remained almost motionless, thankful only for this, that her father-in-law was having his breakfast upstairs.

At last Charles spoke. "They had no business to be pollarding those elms yesterday," he said to his sister.

"No indeed."

"I must make a note of that," he continued. "I am surprised that the rector allowed it."

"Perhaps it may not be the rector's affair."

"Whose else could it be?"

"The lord of the manor."

"Impossible."

"Butter, Dolly?"

"Thank you, Evie dear. Charles——"

"Yes, dear?"

"I didn't know one could pollard elms. I thought one only pollarded willows."

"Oh no, one can pollard elms."

"Then why oughtn't the elms in the churchyard to be pollarded?" Charles frowned a little, and turned again to his sister.

"Another point. I must speak to Chalkeley."

"Yes, rather; you must complain to Chalkeley."

"It's no good him saying he is not responsible for those men. He is responsible."

"Yes, rather."

Brother and sister were not callous. They spoke thus, partly because they desired to keep Chalkeley up to the mark—a healthy desire in its way—partly because they avoided the personal note in life. All Wilcoxes did. It did not seem to them of

supreme importance. Or it may be as Helen supposed: they realized its importance, but were afraid of it. Panic and emptiness,
could one glance behind. They were not callous, and they left the
breakfast-table with aching hearts. Their mother never had come
in to breakfast. It was in the other rooms, and especially in the
garden, that they felt her loss most. As Charles went out to the
garage, he was reminded at every step of the woman who had
loved him and whom he could never replace. What battles he had
fought against her gentle conservatism! How she had disliked
improvements, yet how loyally she had accepted them when
made! He and his father—what trouble they had had to get this
very garage! With what difficulty had they persuaded her to yield
them the paddock for it—the paddock that she loved more dearly
than the garden itself! The vine—she had got her way about the
vine. It still encumbered the south wall with its unproductive
branches. And so with Evie, as she stood talking to the cook.
Though she could take up her mother's work inside the house,
just as the man could take it up without, she felt that something
unique had fallen out of her life. Their grief, though less poignant
than their father's, grew from deeper roots, for a wife may be
replaced; a mother never.

Charles would go back to the office. There was little to do at
Howards End. The contents of his mother's will had been long
known to them. There were no legacies, no annuities, none of the
posthumous bustle with which some of the dead prolong their
activities. Trusting her husband, she had left him everything without reserve. She was quite a poor woman—the house had been all
her dowry, and the house would come to Charles in time. Her
watercolours Mr. Wilcox intended to reserve for Paul, while Evie
would take the jewellery and lace. How easily she slipped out of
life! Charles thought the habit laudable, though he did not intend
to adopt it himself, whereas Margaret would have seen in it an
almost culpable indifference to earthly fame. Cynicism—not the
superficial cynicism that snarls and sneers, but the cynicism that
can go with courtesy and tenderness—that was the note of Mrs.

Wilcox's will. She wanted not to vex people. That accomplished, the earth might freeze over her for ever.

No, there was nothing for Charles to wait for. He could not go on with his honeymoon, so he would go up to London and work— he felt too miserable hanging about. He and Dolly would have the furnished flat while his father rested quietly in the country with Evie. He could also keep an eye on his own little house, which was being painted and decorated for him in one of the Surrey suburbs, and in which he hoped to instal himself soon after Christmas. Yes, he would go up after lunch in his new motor, and the town servants, who had come down for the funeral, would go up by train.

He found his father's chauffeur in the garage, said "Morning" without looking at the man's face, and, bending over the car, continued: "Hullo! my new car's been driven!"

"Has it, sir?"

"Yes," said Charles, getting rather red; "and whoever's driven it hasn't cleaned it properly, for there's mud on the axle. Take it off."

The man went for the cloths without a word. He was a chauffeur as ugly as sin—not that this did him disservice with Charles, who thought charm in a man rather rot, and had soon got rid of the little Italian beast with whom they had started.

"Charles——" His bride was tripping after him over the hoarfrost, a dainty black column, her little face and elaborate mourning hat forming the capital thereof.

"One minute, I'm busy. Well, Crane, who's been driving it, do you suppose?"

"Don't know, I'm sure, sir. No one's driven it since I've been back, but, of course, there's the fortnight I've been away with the other car in Yorkshire."

The mud came off easily.

"Charles, your father's down. Something's happened. He wants you in the house at once. Oh, Charles!"

"Wait, dear, wait a minute. Who had the key of the garage while you were away, Crane?"

"The gardener, sir."

"Do you mean to tell me that old Penny can drive a motor?"

"No, sir; no one's had the motor out, sir."

"Then how do you account for the mud on the axle?"

"I can't, of course, say for the time I've been in Yorkshire. No more mud now, sir."

Charles was vexed. The man was treating him as a fool, and if his heart had not been so heavy he would have reported him to his father. But it was not a morning for complaints. Ordering the motor to be round after lunch, he joined his wife, who had all the while been pouring out some incoherent story about a letter and a Miss Schlegel.

"Now, Dolly, I can attend to you. Miss Schlegel? What does she want?"

When people wrote a letter Charles always asked what they wanted. Want was to him the only cause of action. And the question in this case was correct, for his wife replied, "She wants Howards End."

"Howards End? Now, Crane, just don't forget to put on the Stepney wheel."

"No, sir."

"Now, mind you don't forget, for I—— Come, little woman." When they were out of the chauffeur's sight he put his arm round her waist and pressed her against him. All his affection and half his attention—it was what he granted her throughout their happy married life.

"But you haven't listened, Charles——"

"What's wrong."

"I keep on telling you—Howards End. Miss Schlegel's got it."

"Got what?" said Charles, unclasping her. "What the dickens are you talking about?"

"Now, Charles, you promised not to say those naughty——"

"Look here, I'm in no mood for foolery. It's no morning for it either."

"I tell you—I keep on telling you—Miss Schlegel—she's got it—your mother's left it to her—and you've all got to move out!"

"*Howards End?*"

"*Howards End!*" she screamed, mimicking him, and as she did so Evie came dashing out of the shrubbery.

"Dolly, go back at once! My father's much annoyed with you. Charles"—she hit herself wildly—"come in at once to father. He's had a letter that's too awful."

Charles began to run, but checked himself, and stepped heavily across the gravel path. There the house was—the nine windows, the unprolific vine. He exclaimed, "Schlegels again!" and as if to complete chaos, Dolly said, "Oh no, the matron of the nursing home has written instead of her."

"Come in, all three of you!" cried his father, no longer inert. "Dolly, why have you disobeyed me?"

"Oh, Mr. Wilcox——"

"I told you not to go out to the garage. I've heard you all shouting in the garden. I won't have it. Come in."

He stood in the porch, transformed, letters in his hand.

"Into the dining-room, every one of you. We can't discuss private matters in the middle of all the servants. Here, Charles, here; read these. See what you make."

Charles took two letters, and read them as he followed the procession. The first was a covering note from the matron. Mrs. Wilcox had desired her, when the funeral should be over, to forward the enclosed. The enclosed—it was from his mother herself. She had written: "To my husband: I should like Miss Schlegel (Margaret) to have Howards End."

"I suppose we're going to have a talk about this?" he remarked ominously calm.

"Certainly. I was coming out to you when Dolly——"

"Well, let's sit down."

"Come, Evie, don't waste time, sit down."

In silence they drew to up the breakfast-table. The events of yesterday—indeed, of this morning—suddenly receded into a past so remote that they seemed scarcely to have lived in it. Heavy breathings were heard. They were calming themselves. Charles, to steady them further, read the enclosure out loud: "A note in my mother's handwriting, in an envelope addressed to my father, sealed. Inside: 'I should like Miss Schlegel (Margaret) to have Howards End.' No date, no signature. Forwarded through the matron of that nursing home. Now, the question is——"

Dolly interrupted him. "But I say that note isn't legal. Houses ought to be done by a lawyer, Charles, surely."

Her husband worked his jaw severely. Little lumps appeared in front of either ear—a symptom that she had not yet learnt to respect, and she asked whether she might see the note. Charles looked at his father for permission, who said abstractedly, "Give it her." She seized it, and at once exclaimed: "Why, it's only in pencil! I said so. Pencil never counts."

"We know that it is not legally binding, Dolly," said Mr. Wilcox, speaking from out of his fortress. "We are aware of that. Legally, I should be justified in tearing it up and throwing it into the fire. Of course, my dear, we consider you as one of the family, but it will be better if you do not interfere with what you do not understand."

Charles, vexed both with his father and his wife, then repeated: "The question is——" He had cleared a space of the breakfast-table from plates and knives, so that he could draw patterns on the tablecloth. "The question is whether Miss Schlegel, during the fortnight we were all away, whether she unduly——" he stopped.

"I don't think that," said his father, whose nature was nobler than his son's.

"Don't think what?"

"That she would have—that it is a case of undue influence. No, to my mind the question is the—the invalid's condition at the time she wrote."

"My dear father, consult an expert if you like, but I don't admit it is my mother's writing."

"Why, you just said it was!" cried Dolly.

"Never mind if I did," he blazed out; "and hold your tongue."

The poor little wife coloured at this, and, drawing her

handkerchief from her pocket, shed a few tears. No one noticed
her. Evie was scowling like an angry boy. The two men were gradually assuming the manner of the committee-room. They were
both at their best when serving on committees. They did not
make the mistake of handling human affairs in the bulk, but disposed of them item by item, sharply. Caligraphy was the item
before them now, and on it they turned their well-trained brains.
Charles, after a little demur, accepted the writing as genuine, and
they passed on to the next point. It is the best—perhaps the
only—way of dodging emotion. They were the average human
article, and had they considered the note as a whole it would have
driven them miserable or mad. Considered item by item, the
emotional content was minimized, and all went forward
smoothly. The clock ticked, the coals blazed higher, and contended with the white radiance that poured in through the
windows. Unnoticed, the sun occupied his sky, and the shadows
of the tree stems, extraordinarily solid, fell like trenches of purple
across the frosted lawn. It was a glorious winter morning. Evie's
fox terrier, who had passed for white, was only a dirty grey dog
now, so intense was the purity that surrounded him. He was dis-
credited, but the blackbirds that he was chasing glowed with
Arabian darkness, for all the conventional colouring of life had
been altered. Inside, the clock struck ten with a rich and confident note. Other clocks confirmed it, and the discussion moved
towards its close.

To follow it is unnecessary. It is rather a moment when the
commentator should step forward. Ought the Wilcoxes to have
offered their home to Margaret? I think not. The appeal was too
flimsy. It was not legal; it had been written in illness, and under
the spell of a sudden friendship; it was contrary to the dead
woman's intentions in the past, contrary to her very nature, so far
as that nature was understood by them. To them Howards End
was a house: they could not know that to her it had been a spirit,
for which she sought a spiritual heir. And—pushing one step farther in these mists—may they not have decided even better than

they supposed? Is it credible that the possessions of the spirit can be bequeathed at all? Has the soul offspring? A wych-elm tree, a vine, a wisp of hay with dew on it—can passion for such things be transmitted where there is no bond of blood? No; the Wilcoxes are not to be blamed. The problem is too terrific, and they could not even perceive a problem. No; it is natural and fitting that after due debate they should tear the note up and throw it on to their dining-room fire. The practical moralist may acquit them absolutely. He sho strives to look deeper may acquit them—almost. For one hard fact remains. They did neglect a personal appeal. The woman who had died did say to them, "Do this," and they answered, "We will not."

The incident made a most painful impression on them. Grief mounted into the brain and worked there disquietingly. Yesterday they had lamented: "She was a dear mother, a true wife: in our absence she neglected her health and died." To-day they thought: "She was not as true, as dear, as we supposed." The desire for a more inward light had found expression at last, the unseen had impacted on the seen, and all that they could say was "Treachery." Mrs. Wilcox had been treacherous to the family, to the laws of property, to her own written word. How did she expect Howards End to be conveyed to Miss Schlegel? Was her husband, to whom it legally belonged, to make it over to her as a free gift? Was the said Miss Schlegel to have a life interest in it, or to own it absolutely? Was there to be no compensation for the garage and other improvements that they had made under the assumption that all would be theirs some day? Treacherous! treacherous and absurd! When we think the dead both treacherous and absurd, we have gone far towards reconciling ourselves to their departure. That note, scribbled in pencil, sent through the matron, was un-businesslike as well as cruel, and decreased at once the value of the woman who had written it.

"Ah, well!" said Mr. Wilcox, rising from the table. "I shouldn't have thought it possible."

"Mother couldn't have meant it," said Evie, still frowning.

"No, my girl, of course not."

"Mother believed so in ancestors too—it isn't like her to leave anything to an outsider, who'd never appreciate."

"The whole thing is unlike her," he announced. "If Miss Schlegel had been poor, if she had wanted a house, I could understand it a little. But she has a house of her own. Why should she want another? She wouldn't have any use for Howards End."

"That time may prove," murmured Charles.

"How?" asked his sister.

"Presumably she knows—mother will have told her. She got twice or three times into the nursing home. Presumably she is awaiting developments."

"What a horrid woman!" And Dolly, who had recovered, cried, "Why, she may be coming down to turn us out now!"

Charles put her right. "I wish she would," he said ominously. "I could then deal with her."

"So could I," echoed his father, who was feeling rather in the cold. Charles had been kind in undertaking the funeral arrangements and in telling him to eat his breakfast, but the boy as he grew up was a little dictatorial, and assumed the post of chairman too readily. "I could deal with her, if she comes, but she won't come. You're all a bit hard on Miss Schlegel."

"That Paul business was pretty scandalous, though."

"I want no more of the Paul business, Charles, as I said at the time, and besides, it is quite apart from this business. Margaret Schlegel has been officious and tiresome during this terrible week, and we have all suffered under her, but upon my soul she's honest. She's *not* in collusion with the matron. I'm absolutely certain of it. Nor was she with the doctor, I'm equally certain of that. She did not hide anything from us, for up to that very afternoon she was as ignorant as we are. She, like ourselves, was a dupe——" He stopped for a moment. "You see, Charles, in her terrible pain your poor mother put us all in false positions. Paul would not have left England, you would not have gone to Italy, nor Evie and I into Yorkshire, if only we had known. Well, Miss Schlegel's position has been equally false. Take all in all, she has not come out of it badly."

Evie said: "But those chrysanthemums——"

"Or coming down to the funeral at all——" echoed Dolly.

"Why shouldn't she come down? She had the right to, and she stood far back among the Hilton women. The flowers—certainly we should not have sent such flowers, but they may have seemed the right thing to her, Evie, and for all you know they may be the custom in Germany."

"Oh, I forget she isn't really English," cried Evie. "That would explain a lot."

"She's a cosmopolitan," said Charles, looking at his watch. "I admit I'm rather down on cosmopolitans. My fault, doubtless. I cannot stand them, and a German cosmopolitan is the limit. I think that's about all, isn't it? I want to run down and see Chalkeley. A bicycle will do. And, by the way, I wish you'd speak to Crane some time. I'm certain he's had my new car out."

"Has he done it any harm?"

"No."

"In that case I shall let it pass. It's not worth while having a row."

Charles and his father sometimes disagreed. But they always parted with an increased regard for one another, and each desired no doughtier comrade when it was necessary to voyage for a little past the emotions. So the sailors of Ulysses voyaged past the Sirens, having first stopped one another's ears with wool.

CHAPTER XII

Charles need not have been anxious. Miss Schlegel had never heard of his mother's strange request. She was to hear of it in after years, when she had built up her life differently, and it was to fit into position as the headstone of the corner. Her mind was bent on other questions now, and by her also it would have been rejected as the fantasy of an invalid.

She was parting from these Wilcoxes for the second time. Paul and his mother, ripple and great wave, had flowed into her life and ebbed out of it for ever. The ripple had left no traces behind: the wave had strewn at her feet fragments torn from the unknown. A curious seeker, she stood for a while at the verge of the sea that tells so little, but tells a little, and watched the outgoing of this last tremendous tide. Her friend had vanished in agony, but not, she believed, in degradation. Her withdrawal had hinted at other things besides disease and pain. Some leave our life with tears, others with an insane frigidity; Mrs. Wilcox had taken the middle course, which only rarer natures can pursue. She had kept proportion. She had told a little of her grim secret to her friends, but not too much; she had shut up her heart—almost, but not entirely. It is thus, if there is any rule, that we ought to die—neither as victim nor as fanatic, but as the seafarer who can greet with an equal eye the deep that he is entering, and the shore that he must leave.

The last word—whatever it would be—had certainly not been said in Hilton churchyard. She had not died there. A funeral is not death, any more than baptism is birth or marriage union. All three are the clumsy devices, coming now too late, now too early, by which Society would register the quick motions of man. In Margaret's eyes Mrs. Wilcox had escaped registration. She had gone out of life vividly, her own way, and no dust was so truly dust as the contents of that heavy coffin, lowered with ceremonial until it rested on the dust of the earth, no flowers so utterly wasted as the chrysanthemums that the frost must have withered before morning. Margaret had once said she "loved superstition." It was not true. Few women had tried more earnestly to pierce the accretions in which body and soul are enwrapped. The death of Mrs. Wilcox had helped her in her work. She saw a little more clearly than hitherto what a human being is, and to what he may aspire. Truer relationships gleamed. Perhaps the last word would be hope—hope even on this side of the grave.

Meanwhile, she could take an interest in the survivors. In spite

of her Christmas duties, in spite of her brother, the Wilcoxes continued to play a considerable part in her thoughts. She had seen
so much of them in the final week. They were not "her sort," they
were often suspicious and stupid, and deficient where she
excelled; but collision with them stimulated her, and she felt an
interest that verged into liking, even for Charles. She desired to
protect them, and often felt that they could protect her, excelling
where she was deficient. Once past the rocks of emotion, they
knew so well what to do, whom to send for; their hands were on
all the ropes, they had grit as well as grittiness, and she valued grit
enormously. They led a life that she could not attain to—the outer
life of "telegrams and anger," which had detonated when Helen
and Paul had touched in June, and had detonated again the other
week. To Margaret this life was to remain a real force. She could
not despise it, as Helen and Tibby affected to do. It fostered such
virtues as neatness, decision, and obedience, virtues of the second
rank, no doubt, but they have formed our civilization. They form
character, too; Margaret could not doubt it: they keep the soul
from becoming sloppy. How dare Schlegels despise Wilcoxes,
when it takes all sorts to make a world?

"Don't brood too much," she wrote to Helen, "on the superiority of the unseen to the seen. It's true, but to brood on it is medieval.
Our business is not to contrast the two, but to reconcile them."

Helen replied that she had no intention of brooding on such a
dull subject. What did her sister take her for? The weather was
magnificent. She and the Mosebachs had gone tobogganing on
the only hill that Pomerania boasted. It was fun, but over-
crowded, for the rest of Pomerania had gone there too. Helen
loved the country, and her letter glowed with physical exercise
and poetry. She spoke of the scenery, quiet, yet august; of the
snow-clad fields, with their scampering herds of deer; of the river
and its quaint entrance into the Baltic Sea; of the Oderberge, only
three hundred feet high, from which one slid all too quickly back
into the Pomeranian plains, and yet these Oderberge were real
mountains, with pine-forests, streams, and views complete. "It

isn't size that counts so much as the way things are arranged." In another paragraph she referred to Mrs. Wilcox sympathetically, but the news had not bitten into her. She had not realized the accessories of death, which are in a sense more memorable than death itself. The atmosphere of precautions and recriminations, and in the midst a human body growing more vivid because it was in pain; the end of that body in Hilton churchyard; the survival of something that suggested hope, vivid in its turn against life's workaday cheerfulness;—all these were lost to Helen, who only felt that a pleasant lady could now be pleasant no longer. She returned to Wickham Place full of her own affairs—she had had another proposal—and Margaret, after a moment's hesitation, was content that this should be so.

The proposal had not been a serious matter. It was the work of Fräulein Mosebach, who had conceived the large and patriotic notion of winning back her cousins to the Fatherland by matrimony. England had played Paul Wilcox, and lost; Germany played Herr Förstmeister someone—Helen could not remember his name. Herr Förstmeister lived in a wood, and, standing on the summit of the Oderberge, he had pointed out his house to Helen, or rather, had pointed out the wedge of pines in which it lay. She had exclaimed, "Oh, how lovely! That's the place for me!" and in the evening Frieda appeared in her bedroom. "I have a message, dear Helen," etc., and so she had, but had been very nice when Helen laughed; quite understood—a forest too solitary and damp—quite agreed, but Herr Förstmeister believed he had assurance to the contrary. Germany had lost, but with good-humour; holding the manhood of the world, she felt bound to win. "And there will even be someone for Tibby," concluded Helen. "There now, Tibby, think of that; Frieda is saving up a little girl for you, in pig-tails and white worsted stockings, but the feet of the stockings are pink, as if the little girl had trodden in strawberries. I've talked too much. My head aches. Now you talk."

Tibby consented to talk. He too was full of his own affairs, for he had just been up to try for a scholarship at Oxford. The men

were down, and the candidates had been housed in various colleges, and had dined in hall. Tibby was sensitive to beauty, the
experience was new, and he gave a description of his visit that was
almost glowing. The august and mellow University, soaked with
the richness of the western counties that it has served for a thousand years, appealed at once to the boy's taste: it was the kind of
thing he could understand, and he understood it all the better
because it was empty. Oxford is—Oxford: not a mere receptacle for
youth, like Cambridge. Perhaps it wants its inmates to love
it rather than to love one another: such at all events was to be
its effect on Tibby. His sisters sent him there that he might make
friends, for they knew that his education had been cranky, and had
severed him from other boys and men. He made no friends. His
Oxford remained Oxford empty, and he took into life with him, not
the memory of a radiance, but the memory of a colour scheme.

It pleased Margaret to hear her brother and sister talking. They
did not get on overwell as a rule. For a few moments she listened
to them, feeling elderly and benign. Then something occurred to
her, and she interrupted:

"Helen, I told you about poor Mrs. Wilcox; that sad business?"

"Yes."

"I have had a correspondence with her son. He was winding up
the estate, and wrote to ask me whether his mother had wanted
me to have anything. I thought it good of him, considering I knew
her for so little. I said that she had once spoken of giving me a
Christmas present, but we both forgot about it afterwards."

"I hope Charles took the hint."

"Yes—that is to say, her husband wrote later on, and thanked
me for being a little kind to her, and actually gave me her silver
vinaigrette. Don't you think that is extraordinarily generous? It
has made me like him very much. He hopes that this will not be
the end of our acquaintance, but that you and I will go and stop
with Evie some time in the future. I like Mr. Wilcox. He is taking
up his work—rubber—it is a big business. I gather he is launch-
ing out rather. Charles is in it, too. Charles is married—a pretty

little creature, but she doesn't seem wise. They took on the flat, but now they have gone off to a house of their own."

Helen, after a decent pause, continued her account of Stettin. How quickly a situation changes! In June she had been in a crisis; even in November she could blush and be unnatural; now it was January, and the whole affair lay forgotten. Looking back on the past six months, Margaret realized the chaotic nature of our daily life, and its difference from the orderly sequence that has been fabricated by historians. Actual life is full of false clues and signposts that lead nowhere. With infinite effort we nerve ourselves for a crisis that never comes. The most successful career must show a waste of strength that might have removed mountains, and the most unsuccessful is not that of the man who is taken unprepared, but of him who has prepared and is never taken. On a tragedy of that kind our national morality is duly silent. It assumes that preparation against danger is in itself a good, and that men, like nations, are the better for staggering through life fully armed. The tragedy of preparedness has scarcely been handled, save by the Greeks. Life is indeed dangerous, but not in the way morality would have us believe. It is indeed unmanageable, but the essence of it is not a battle. It is unmanageable because it is a romance, and its essence is romantic beauty.

Margaret hoped that for the future she would be less cautious, not more cautious, than she had been in the past.

CHAPTER XIII

Over two years passed, and the Schlegel household continued to lead its life of cultured, but not ignoble, ease, still swimming gracefully on the grey tides of London. Concerts and plays swept past them, money had been spent and renewed, reputations won and lost, and the city herself, emblematic of their lives, rose and fell in a continual flux, while her shallows washed more widely against the hills of Surrey and over the fields of Hertfordshire. This famous building had arisen, that was doomed. To-day Whitehall had been transformed: it would be the turn of Regent Street to-morrow. And month by month the roads smelt more strongly of petrol, and were more difficult to cross, and human beings heard each other speak with greater difficulty, breathed less of the air, and saw less of the sky. Nature withdrew: the leaves were falling by midsummer; the sun shone through dirt with an admired obscurity.

To speak against London is no longer fashionable. The Earth as an artistic cult has had its day, and the literature of the rear future will probably ignore the country and seek inspiration from the town. One can understand the reaction. Of Pan and the ele-mental forces, the public has heard a little too much—they seem Victorian, while London is Georgian—and those who care for the earth with sincerity may wait long ere the pendulum swings back to her again. Certainly London fascinates. One visualizes it as a tract of quivering grey, intelligent without purpose, and excitable without love; as a spirit that has altered before it can be chroni-cled; as a heart that certainly beats, but with no pulsation of humanity. It lies beyond everything: Nature, with all her cruelty, comes nearer to us than do these crowds of men. A friend ex-plains himself: the earth is explicable—from her we came, and we must return to her. But who can explain Westminster Bridge Road or Liverpool Street in the morning—the city inhaling—or the same thoroughfares in the evening—the city exhaling her exhausted air? We reach in desperation beyond the fog, beyond the very stars, the voids of the universe are ransacked to justify the monster, and stamped with a human face. London is religion's opportunity—not the decorous religion of theologians, but anthropomorphic, crude. Yes, the continuous flow would be tolerable if a man of our own sort—not anyone pompous or tear-ful—were caring for us up in the sky.

The Londoner seldom understands his city until it sweeps him, too, away from his moorings, and Margaret's eyes were not opened until the lease of Wickham Place expired. She had always known that it must expire, but the knowledge only became vivid about nine months before the event. Then the house was suddenly ringed with pathos. It had seen so much happiness. Why had it to be swept away? In the streets of the city she noted for the first time the architecture of hurry, and heard the language of hurry on the mouths of its inhabitants—clipped words, formless sentences, potted expressions of approval or disgust. Month by month things were stepping livelier, but to what goal? The population still rose, but what was the quality of the men born? The particular million-aire who owned the freehold of Wickham Place, and desired to erect Babylonian flats upon it—what right had he to stir so large a portion of the quivering jelly? He was not a fool—she had heard him expose Socialism—but true insight began just where his intelligence ended, and one gathered that this was the case with most millionaires. What right had such men—— But Margaret checked herself. That way lies madness. Thank goodness she, too, had some money, and could purchase a new home.

Tibby, now in his second year at Oxford, was down for the Easter vacation, and Margaret took the opportunity of having a serious talk with him. Did he at all know where he wanted to live? Tibby didn't know that he did know. Did he at all know what he wanted to do? He was equally uncertain, but when pressed remarked that he should prefer to be quite free of any profession. Margaret was not shocked, but went on sewing for a few minutes before she replied:

"I was thinking of Mr. Vyse. He never strikes me as particu-larly happy."

"Ye-es," said Tibby, and then held his mouth open in a curious quiver, as if he, too, had thought of Mr. Vyse, had seen round, through, over, and beyond Mr. Vyse, had weighed Mr. Vyse, grouped him, and finally dismissed him as having no possible bearing on the subject under discussion. That bleat of Tibby's infuriated Helen. But Helen was now down in the dining-room preparing a speech about political economy. At times her voice could be heard declaiming through the floor.

"But Mr. Vyse is rather a wretched, weedy man, don't you think?

Then there's Guy. That was a pitiful business. Besides"—shifting
to the general—"everyone is the better for some regular work."
   Groans.
   "I shall stick to it," she continued, smiling. "I am not saying it
to educate you; it is what I really think. I believe that in the last
century men have developed the desire for work, and they must
not starve it. It's a new desire. It goes with a great deal that's bad,
but in itself it's good, and I hope that for women, too, 'not to
work' will soon become as shocking as 'not to be married' was a
hundred years ago."
   "I have no experience of this profound desire to which you
allude," enunciated Tibby.
   "Then we'll leave the subject till you do. I'm not going to rattle
you round. Take your time. Only do think over the lives of the
men you like most, and see how they've arranged them."
   "I like Guy and Mr. Vyse most," said Tibby faintly, and leant so
far back in his chair that he extended in a horizontal line from
knees to throat.
   "And don't think I'm not serious because I don't use the tradi-
tional arguments—making money, a sphere awaiting you, and so
on—all of which are, for various reasons, cant." She sewed on.
"I'm only your sister. I haven't any authority over you, and I don't
want to have any. Just to put before you what I think the truth.
You see"—she shook off the pince-nez to which she had recently
taken—"in a few years we shall be the same age practically, and I
shall want you to help me. Men are so much nicer than women."
   "Labouring under such a delusion, why do you not marry?"
   "I sometimes jolly well think I would if I got the chance."
   "Has no body arst you?"
   "Only ninnies."
   "Do people ask Helen?"
   "Plentifully."
   "Tell me about them."
   "No."
   "Tell me about your ninnies, then."

"They were men who had nothing better to do," said his sister, feeling that she was entitled to score this point. "So take warning: you must work, or else you must pretend to work, which is what I do. Work, work, work if you'd save your soul and your body. It is honestly a necessity, dear boy. Look at the Wilcoxes, look at Mr. Pembroke. With all their defects of temper and understanding, such men give me more pleasure than many who are better equipped, and I think it is because they have worked regularly and honestly."

"Spare me the Wilcoxes," he moaned.

"I shall not. They are the right sort."

"Oh, goodness me, Meg!" he protested, suddenly sitting up, alert and angry. Tibby, for all his defects, had a genuine personality.

"Well, they're as near the right sort as you can imagine."

"No, no—oh, no!"

"I was thinking of the younger son, whom I once classed as a ninny, but who came back so ill from Nigeria. He's gone out there again, Evie Wilcox tells me—out to his duty."

'Duty' always elicited a groan.

"He doesn't want the money, it is work he wants, though it is beastly work—dull country, dishonest natives, an eternal fidget over fresh water and food. A nation who can produce men of that sort may well be proud. No wonder England has become an Empire."

"*Empire!*"

"I can't bother over results," said Margaret, a little sadly. "They are too difficult for me. I can only look at the men. An Empire bores me, so far, but I can appreciate the heroism that builds it up. London bores me, but what thousands of splendid people are labouring to make London——"

"What it is," he sneered.

"What it is, worse luck. I want activity without civilization. How paradoxical! Yet I expect that is what we shall find in heaven."

"And I," said Tibby, "want civilization without activity, which, I expect, is what we shall find in the other place."

"You needn't go as far as the other place, Tibbikins, if you want that. You can find it at Oxford."

"Stupid——"

"If I'm stupid, get me back to the house-hunting. I'll even live in Oxford if you like—North Oxford. I'll live anywhere except Bournemouth, Torquay, and Cheltenham. Oh yes, or Ilfracombe and Swanage and Tunbridge Wells and Surbiton and Bedford. There on no account."

"London, then."

"I agree, but Helen rather wants to get away from London. However, there's no reason we shouldn't have a house in the country and also a flat in town, provided we all stick together and contribute. Though of course—— Oh, how one does maunder on, and to think, to think of the people who are really poor. How do they live? Not to move about the world would kill me."

As she spoke, the door was flung open, and Helen burst in in a state of extreme excitement.

"Oh, my dears, what do you think? You'll never guess. A woman's been here asking me for her husband. Her *what*?" (Helen was fond of supplying her own surprise.) "Yes, for her husband, and it really is so."

"Not anything to do with Bracknell?" cried Margaret, who had lately taken on an unemployed of that name to clean the knives and boots.

"I offered Bracknell, and he was rejected. So was Tibby. (Cheer up, Tibby!) It's no one we know. I said 'Hunt, my good woman; have a good look round, hunt under the tables, poke up the chimney, shake out the antimacassars. Husband? husband?' Oh, and she so magnificently dressed and tinkling like a chandelier."

"Now, Helen, what did happen really?"

"What I say. I was, as it were, orating my speech. Annie opens the door like a fool, and shows a female straight in on me, with my mouth open. Then we began—very civilly. 'I want my husband, what I have reason to believe is here.' No—how unjust one

is. She said 'whom,' not 'what.' She got it perfectly. So I said,
'Name, please?' and she said, 'Lan, Miss,' and there we were."

"Lan?"

"Lan or Len. We were not nice about our vowels. Lanoline."

"But what an extraordinary——"

"I said, 'My good Mrs. Lanoline, we have some grave misunderstanding here. Beautiful as I am, my modesty is even more
remarkable than my beauty, and never, never has Mr. Lanoline
rested his eyes on mine.'"

"I hope you were pleased," said Tibby.

"Of course," Helen squeaked. "A perfectly delightful experience. Oh, Mrs. Lanoline's a dear—she asked for a husband
as if he was an umbrella. She mislaid him Saturday afternoon—
and for a long time suffered no inconvenience. But all night, and
all this morning her apprehensions grew. Breakfast didn't
seem the same—no, no more did lunch, and so she strolled up
to 2, Wickham Place as being the most likely place for the missing article."

"But how on earth——"

"Don't begin how on earthing. 'I know what I know,' she kept
repeating, not uncivilly, but with extreme gloom. In vain I asked
her what she did know. Some knew what others knew, and others
didn't, and if they didn't, then others again had better be careful.
Oh dear, she was incompetent! She had a face like a silkworm,
and the dining-room reeks of orris-root. We chatted pleasantly a
little about husbands, and I wondered where hers was too, and
advised her to go to the police. She thanked me. We agreed that
Mr. Lanoline's a notty, notty man, and hasn't no business to go on
the lardy-da. But I think she suspected me up to the last. Bags I
writing to Aunt Juley about this. Now, Meg, remember—bags I."

"Bag it by all means," murmured Margaret, putting down her
work. "I'm not sure that this is so funny, Helen. It means some
horrible volcano smoking somewhere, doesn't it?"

"I don't think so—she doesn't really mind. The admirable creature isn't capable of tragedy."

"Her husband may be, though," said Margaret, moving to the window.

"Oh no, not likely. No one capable of tragedy could have married Mrs. Lanoline."

"Was she pretty?"

"Her figure may have been good once."

The flats, their only outlook, hung like an ornate curtain between Margaret and the welter of London. Her thoughts turned sadly to house-hunting. Wickham Place had been so safe. She feared, fantastically, that her own little flock might be moving into turmoil and squalor, into nearer contact with such episodes as these.

"Tibby and I have again been wondering where we'll live next September," she said at last.

"Tibby had better first wonder what he'll do," retorted Helen; and that topic was resumed, but with acrimony. Then tea came, and after tea Helen went on preparing her speech, and Margaret prepared one, too, for they were going out to a discussion society on the morrow. But her thoughts were poisoned. Mrs. Lanoline had risen out of the abyss, like a faint smell, a goblin football, telling of a life where love and hatred had both decayed.

CHAPTER XIV

The mystery, like so many mysteries, was explained. Next day, just as they were dressed to go out to dinner, a Mr. Bast called. He was a clerk in the employment of the Porphyrion Fire Insurance Company. Thus much from his card. He had come "about the lady yesterday." Thus much from Annie, who had shown him into the dining-room.

"Cheers, children!" cried Helen. "It's Mrs. Lanoline."

Tibby was interested. The three hurried downstairs, to find, not the gay dog they expected, but a young man, colourless, toneless, who had already the mournful eyes above a drooping

moustache that are so common in London, and that haunt some
streets of the city like accusing presences. One guessed him as the
third generation, grandson to the shepherd or ploughboy whom
civilization had sucked into the town; as one of the thousands
who have lost the life of the body and failed to reach the life of the
spirit. Hints of robustness survived in him, some than a hint of
primitive good looks, and Margaret, noting the spine that might
have been straight, and the chest that might have broadened,
wondered whether it paid to give up the glory of the animal for a
tail coat and a couple of ideas. Culture had worked in her own
case, but during the last few weeks she had doubted whether it
humanized the majority, so wide and so widening is the gulf that
stretches between the natural and the philosophic man, so many
the good chaps who are wrecked in trying to cross it. She knew
this type very well—the vague aspirations, the mental dishonesty,
the familiarity with the outsides of books. She knew the very
tones in which he would address her. She was only unprepared
for an example of her own visiting-card.

"You wouldn't remember giving me this, Miss Schlegel?" said
he, uneasily familiar.

"No; I can't say I do."

"Well, that was how it happened, you see."

"Where did we meet, Mr. Bast? For the minute I don't remember."

"It was a concert at the Queen's Hall. I think you will recollect," he added pretentiously, "when I tell you that it included a
performance of the Fifth Symphony of Beethoven."

"We hear the Fifth practically every time it's done, so I'm not
sure—do you remember, Helen?"

"Was it the time the sandy cat walked round the balustrade?"

He thought not.

"Then I don't remember. That's the only Beethoven I ever
remember specially."

"And you, if I may say so, took away my umbrella, inadvertently of course."

"Likely enough," Helen laughed, "for I steal umbrellas even oftener than I hear Beethoven. Did you get it back?"

"Yes, thank you, Miss Schlegel."

"The mistake arose out of my card, did it?" interposed Margaret.

"Yes, the mistake arose—it was a mistake."

"The lady who called here yesterday thought that you were calling too, and that she could find you?" she continued, pushing him forward, for, though he had promised an explanation, he seemed unable to give one.

"That's so, calling too—a mistake."

"Then why——?" began Helen, but Margaret laid a hand on her arm.

"I said to my wife," he continued more rapidly—"I said to Mrs. Bast, 'I have to pay a call on some friends,' and Mrs. Bast said to me, 'Do go.' While I was gone, however, she wanted me on important business, and thought I had come here, owing to the card, and so came after me, and I beg to tender my apologies, and hers as well, for any inconvenience we may have inadvertently caused you."

"No inconvenience," said Helen; "but I still don't understand."

An air of evasion characterized Mr. Bast. He explained again, but was obviously lying and Helen didn't see why he should get off. She had the cruelty of youth. Neglecting his sister's pressure, she said, "I still don't understand. When did you say you paid this call?"

"Call? What call?" said he, staring as if her question had been a foolish one, a favourite device of those in mid-stream.

"This afternoon call."

"In the afternoon, of course!" he replied, and looked at Tibby to see how the repartee went. But Tibby, himself a repartee, was unsympathetic, and said, "Saturday or Sunday afternoon?"

"S—Saturday."

"Really!" said Helen; "and you were still calling on Sunday, when your wife came here. A long visit."

"I don't call that fair," said Mr. Bast, going scarlet and hand-some. There was fight in his eyes. "I know what you mean, and it isn't so."

"Oh, don't let us mind," said Margaret, distressed again by odours from the abyss.

"It was something else," he asserted, his elaborate man-ner breaking down. "I was somewhere else to what you think, so there!"

"It was good of you to come and explain," she said. "The rest is naturally no concern of ours."

"Yes, but I want—I wanted—have you ever read 'The Ordeal of Richard Feverel'?"

Margaret nodded.

"It's a beautiful book. I wanted to get back to the Earth, don't you see, like Richard does in the end. Or have you ever read Stevenson's 'Prince Otto'?"

Helen and Tibby groaned gently.

"That's another beautiful book. You get back to the Earth in that. I wanted——" He mouthed affectedly. Then through the mists of his culture came a hard fact, hard as a pebble. "I walked all the Saturday night," said Leonard. "I walked." A thrill of approval ran through the sisters. But culture closed in again. He asked whether they had ever read E. V. Lucas's "Open Road."

Said Helen, "No doubt it's another beautiful book, but I'd rather hear about your road."

"Oh, I walked."

"How far?"

"I don't know, nor for how long. It got too dark to see my watch."

"Were you walking alone, may I ask?"

"Yes," he said, straightening himself; "but we'd been talking it over at the office. There's been a lot of talk at the office lately about these things. The fellows there said one steers by the Pole Star, and I looked it up in the celestial atlas, but once out of doors everything gets so mixed——"

"Don't talk to me about the Pole Star," interrupted Helen, who was becoming interested. "I know its little ways. It goes round and round, and you go round after it."

"Well, I lost it entirely. First of all the street lamps, then the trees, and towards morning it got cloudy."

Tibby, who preferred his comedy undiluted, slipped from the room. He knew that this fellow would never attain to poetry, and did not want to hear him trying. Margaret and Helen remained. Their brother influenced them more than they knew: in his absence they were stirred to enthusiasm more easily.

"Where did you start from?" cried Margaret. "Do tell us more."

"I took the Underground to Wimbledon. As I came out of the office I said to myself, 'I must have a walk once in a way. If I don't take this walk now, I shall never take it.' I had a bit of dinner at Wimbledon, and then——"

"But not good country there, is it?"

"It was gas-lamps for hours. Still, I had all the night, and being out was the great thing. I did get into woods, too, presently."

"Yes, go on," said Helen.

"You've no idea how difficult uneven ground is when it's dark."

"Did you actually go off the roads?"

"Oh yes. I always meant to go off the roads, but the worst of it is that it's more difficult to find one's way."

"Mr. Bast, you're a born adventurer," laughed Margaret. "No professional athlete would have attempted what you've done. It's a wonder your walk didn't end in a broken neck. Whatever did your wife say?"

"Professional athletes never move without lanterns and compasses," said Helen. "Besides, they can't walk. It tires them. Go on."

"I felt like R.L.S. You probably remember how in 'Virgini-bus——'"

"Yes, but the wood. This 'ere wood. How did you get out of it?"

"I managed one wood, and found a road the other side which went a good bit uphill. I rather fancy it was those North Downs, for the road went off into grass, and I got into another wood. That was awful, with gorse bushes. I did wish I'd never come, but suddenly it got light—just while I seemed going under one tree. Then I found a road down to a station, and took the first train I could back to London."

"But was the dawn wonderful?" asked Helen.

With unforgettable sincerity he replied, "No." The word flew again like a pebble from the sling. Down toppled all that had seemed ignoble or literary in his talk, down toppled tiresome R.L.S. and the "love of the earth" and his silk top-hat. In the presence of these women Leonard had arrived, and he spoke with a flow, an exultation, that he had seldom known.

"The dawn was only grey, it was nothing to mention——"

"Just a grey evening turned upside down. I know."

"—and I was too tired to lift up my head to look at it, and so cold too. I'm glad I did it, and yet at the time it bored me more than I can say. And besides—you can believe me or not as you choose—I was very hungry. That dinner at Wimbledon—I meant it to last me all night like other dinners. I never thought that walking would make such a difference. Why, when you're walking you want, as it were, a breakfast and luncheon and tea during the night as well, and I'd nothing but a packet of Woodbines. Lord, I did feel bad! Looking back, it wasn't what you may call enjoyment. It was more a case of sticking to it. I did stick. I—I was determined. Oh, hang it all! what's the good—I mean, the good of living in a room for ever? There one goes on day after day, same old game, same up and down to town, until you forget there is any other game. You ought to see once in a way what's going on outside, if it's only nothing particular after all."

"I should just think you ought," said Helen, sitting on the edge of the table.

The sound of a lady's voice recalled him from sincerity, and he said: "Curious it should all come about from reading something of Richard Jefferies."

"Excuse me, Mr. Bast, but you're wrong there. It didn't. It came from something far greater."

But she could not stop him. Borrow was imminent after Jef-feries—Borrow, Thoreau, and sorrow. R.L.S. brought up the rear, and the outburst ended in a swamp of books. No disrespect to these great names. The fault is ours, not theirs. They mean us to use them for sign-posts, and are not to blame if, in our weakness, we mistake the sign-post for the destination. And Leonard had reached the destination. He had visited the county of Surrey when darkness covered its amenities, and its cosy villas had re-entered ancient night. Every twelve hours this miracle happens, but he had troubled to go and see for himself. Within his cramped little mind dwelt something that was greater than Jefferies' books—the spirit that led Jefferies to write them; and his dawn, though revealing nothing but monotones, was part of the eternal sunrise that shows George Borrow Stonehenge.

"Then you don't think I was foolish?" he asked, becoming again the naïve and sweet-tempered boy for whom Nature had intended him.

"Heavens, no!" replied Margaret.

"Heaven help us if we do!" replied Helen.

"I'm very glad you say that. Now, my wife would never under-stand—not if I explained for days."

"No, it wasn't foolish!" cried Helen, her eyes aflame. "You've pushed back the boundaries; I think it splendid of you."

"You've not been content to dream as we have——"

"Though we have walked, too——"

"I must show you a picture upstairs——"

Here the door-bell rang. The hansom had come to take them to their evening party.

"Oh, bother, not to say dash—I had forgotten we were dining out; but do, do, come round again and have a talk."

"Yes, you must—do," echoed Margaret.

Leonard, with extreme sentiment, replied: "No, I shall not. It's better like this."

"Why better?" asked Margaret.

"No, it is better not to risk a second interview. I shall always look back on this talk with you as one of the finest things in my life. Really. I mean this. We can never repeat. It has done me real good, and there we had better leave it."

"That's rather a sad view of life, surely."

"Things so often get spoiled."

"I know," flashed Helen, "but people don't."

He could not understand this. He continued in a vein which mingled true imagination and false. What he said wasn't wrong, but it wasn't right, and a false note jarred. One little twist, they felt, and the instrument might be in tune. One little strain, and it might be silent for ever. He thanked the ladies very much, but he would not call again. There was a moment's awkwardness, and then Helen said: "Go, then; perhaps you know best; but never forget you're better than Jefferies." And he went. Their hansom caught him up at the corner, passed with a waving of hands, and vanished with its accomplished load into the evening.

London was beginning to illuminate herself against the night. Electric lights sizzled and jagged in the main thorough-fares, gas-lamps in the side streets glimmered a canary gold or green. The sky was a crimson battlefield of spring, but London was not afraid. Her smoke mitigated the splendour, and the clouds down Oxford Street were a delicately painted ceiling, which adorned while it did not distract. She has never known the clear-cut armies of the purer air. Leonard hurried through her tinted wonders, very much part of the picture. His was a grey life, and to brighten it he had ruled off a few corners for romance. The Miss Schlegels—or, to speak more accurately, his interview with them—were to fill such a corner, nor was it by any means the first time that he had talked intimately to strangers. The habit was analogous to a debauch, an outlet, though the worst of outlets, for instincts that would not be denied. Terrifying him, it would beat down his suspicions and prudence until he was confiding secrets to people whom he had scarcely seen. It brought him many fears and some pleasant memories. Perhaps the keenest happiness he had ever known was during a railway journey to Cambridge, where a decent-mannered undergraduate had spoken to him. They had got into conversation, and gradually Leonard flung reticence aside, told some of his domestic troubles, and hinted at the rest. The undergraduate, supposing they could start a friendship, asked him to "coffee after hall," which he accepted, but afterwards grew shy, and took care not to stir from the commercial hotel where he lodged. He did not want Romance to collide with the Porphyrion, still less with Jacky, and people with fuller, happier lives are slow to understand this. To the Schlegels, as to the undergraduate, he was an interesting creature, of whom they wanted to see more. But they to him were denizens of Romance, who must keep to the corner he had assigned them, pictures that must not walk out of their frames.

His behaviour over Margaret's visiting-card had been typical. His had scarcely been a tragic marriage. Where there is no money and no inclination to violence tragedy cannot be generated. He could not leave his wife, and he did not want to hit her. Petulance and squalor was enough. Here "that card" had come in. Leonard, though furtive, was untidy, and left it lying about. Jacky found it, and then began, "What's that card, eh?" "Yes, don't you wish you knew what that card was?" "Len, who's Miss Schlegel?" etc. Months passed, and the card, now as a joke, now as a grievance, was handed about, getting dirtier and dirtier. It followed them when they moved from Camelia Road to Tulse Hill. It was submitted to third parties. A few inches of pasteboard, it became the battlefield on which the souls of Leonard and his wife contended. Why did he not say, "A lady took my umbrella, another gave me this that I might call for my umbrella"? Because Jacky would have disbelieved him? Partly, but chiefly because he was sentimental. No affection gathered round the card, but it symbolized the life of culture, that Jacky should never spoil. At night he would say to himself, "Well, at all events, she doesn't know about that card. Yah! done her there!"

Poor Jacky! she was not a bad sort, and had a great deal to bear. She drew her own conclusion—she was only capable of drawing one conclusion—and in the fulness of time she acted upon it. All the Friday Leonard had refused to speak to her, and had spent the evening observing the stars. On the Saturday he went up, as usual, to town, but he came not back Saturday night, nor Sunday morning, nor Sunday afternoon. The inconvenience grew intolerable, and though she was now of a retiring habit, and shy of women, she went up to Wickham Place. Leonard returned in her absence. The card, the fatal card, was gone from the pages of Ruskin, and he guessed what had happened.

"Well?" he had exclaimed, greeting her with peals of laughter. "I know where you've been, but you don't know where I've been."

Jacky sighed, said, "Len, I do think you might explain," and resumed domesticity.

Explanations were difficult at this stage, and Leonard was too silly—or it is tempting to write, too sound a chap to attempt them. His reticence was not entirely the shoddy article that a business life promotes, the reticence that pretends that nothing is something, and hides behind the 'Daily Telegraph.' The adventurer, also, is reticent, and it is an adventure for a clerk to walk for a few hours in darkness. You may laugh at him, you who have slept nights out on the veldt, with your rifle beside you and all the atmosphere of adventure pat. And you also may laugh who think adventures silly. But do not be surprised if Leonard is shy whenever he meets you, and if the Schlegels rather than Jacky hear about the dawn.

That the Schlegels had not thought him foolish became a permanent joy. He was at his best when he thought of them. It buoyed him as he journeyed home beneath fading heavens. Somehow the barriers of wealth had fallen, and there had been— he could not phrase it—a general assertion of the wonder of the world. "My conviction," says the mystic, "gains infinitely the moment another soul will believe in it," and they had agreed that there was something beyond life's daily grey. He took off his top-hat and smoothed it thoughtfully. He had hitherto supposed the unknown to books, literature, clever conversation, culture. One raised oneself by study, and got upsides with the world. But in that quick interchange a new light dawned. Was that "something" walking in the dark among the suburban hills?

He discovered that he was going bareheaded down Regent Street. London came back with a rush. Few were about at this hour, but all whom he passed looked at him with a hostility that was the more impressive because it was unconscious. He put his hat on. It was too big; his head disappeared like a pudding into a basin, the ears bending outwards at the touch of the curly brim. He wore it a little backwards, and its effect was greatly to elongate the face and to bring out the distance between the eyes and the moustache. Thus equipped, he escaped criticism. No one felt uneasy as he titupped along the pavements, the heart of a man ticking fast in his chest.

CHAPTER XV

The sisters went out to dinner full of their adventure, and when they were both full of the same subject, there were few dinner-parties that could stand up against them. This particular one, which was all ladies, had more kick in it than most, but succumbed after a struggle. Helen at one part of the table, Margaret at the other, would talk of Mr. Bast and of no one else, and somewhere about the entrée their monologues collided, fell ruining, and became common property. Nor was this all. The dinner-party was really an informal discussion club; there was a paper after it, read amid coffee-cups and laughter in the drawing-room, but dealing more or less thoughtfully with some topic of general interest. After the paper came a debate, and in this debate Mr. Bast also figured, appearing now as a bright spot in civilization, now as a dark spot, according to the temperament of the speaker. The subject of the paper had been, "How ought I to dispose of my money?" the reader professing to be a millionaire on the point of death, inclined to bequeath her fortune for the foundation of local art galleries, but open to conviction from other sources. The various parts had been assigned beforehand, and some of the speeches were amusing. The hostess assumed the ungrateful rôle of 'the millionaire's eldest son,' and implored her expiring parent not to dislocate Society by allowing such vast sums to pass out of the family. Money was the fruit of self-denial, and the second generation had a right to profit by the self-denial of the first. What right had 'Mr. Bast' to profit? The National Gallery was good enough for the likes of him. After property had had its say—a saying that is necessarily ungracious—the various philanthropists stepped forward. Something must be done for 'Mr. Bast'; his conditions must be improved without impairing his independence; he must have a free library, or free tennis-courts; his rent must be paid in such a way that he did not know it was being paid; it must be made worth his while to join the Territorials; he must be forcibly parted from his uninspiring wife, the money going to her as compensation; he must be assigned a Twin Star, some member of the leisured classes who would watch over him ceaselessly (groans from Helen); he must be given food but no clothes, clothes but no food, a third-return ticket to Venice, without either food or clothes when he arrived there. In short, he might be given anything and everything so long as it was not the money itself.

And here Margaret interrupted.

"Order, order, Miss Schlegel!" said the reader of the paper. "You are here, I understand, to advise me in the interests of the Society for the Preservation of Places of Historic Interest or Natural Beauty. I cannot have you speaking out of your rôle. It makes my poor head go round, and I think you forget that I am very ill."

"Your head won't go round if only you'll listen to my argument," said Margaret. "Why not give him the money itself? You're supposed to have about thirty thousand a year."

"Have I? I thought I had a million."

"Wasn't a million your capital? Dear me! we ought to have settled that. Still, it doesn't matter. Whatever you've got, I order you to give as many poor men as you can three hundred a year each."

"But that would be pauperizing them," said an earnest girl, who liked the Schlegels, but thought them a little unspiritual at times.

"Not if you gave them so much. A big windfall would not pauperize a man. It is these little driblets, distributed among too many, that do the harm. Money's educational. It's far more educational than the things it buys." There was a protest. "In a sense," added Margaret, but the protest continued. "Well, isn't the most civilized thing going, the man who has learnt to wear his income properly?"

"Exactly what your Mr. Bast won't do."

"Give them a chance. Give them money. Don't dole them out poetry-books and railway-tickets like babies. Give them the wherewithal to buy these things. When your Socialism comes it may be different, and we may think in terms of commodities instead of cash. Till it comes give people cash, for it is the warp of civilization, whatever the woof may be. The imagination ought to play upon money and realize it vividly, for it's the—the second most important thing in the world. It is so slurred over and hushed up, there is so little clear thinking—oh, political economy, of course, but so few of us think clearly about our own private incomes, and admit that independent thoughts are in nine cases out of ten the result of independent means. Money: give Mr. Bast money, and don't bother about his ideals. He'll pick up those for himself."

She leant back while the more earnest members of the club began to misconstrue her. The female mind, though cruelly practical in daily life, cannot bear to hear ideals belittled in conversation, and Miss Schlegel was asked however she could say such dreadful things, and what it would profit Mr. Bast if he gained the whole world and lost his own soul. She answered, "Nothing, but he would not gain his soul until he had gained a little of the world." Then they said, "No, they did not believe it," and she admitted that an overworked clerk may save his soul in the superterrestrial sense, where the effort will be taken for the deed, but she denied that he will ever explore the spiritual resources of this world, will ever know the rarer joys of the body, or attain to clear and passionate intercourse with his fellows. Others had attacked the fabric of Society—Property, Interest, etc.; she only fixed her eyes on a few human beings, to see how, under present conditions, they could be made happier. Doing good to humanity was useless: the many-coloured efforts thereto spreading over the vast area like films and resulting in an universal grey. To do good to one, or, as in this case, to a few, was the utmost she dare hope for.

Between the idealists, and the political economists, Margaret had a bad time. Disagreeing elsewhere, they agreed in disowning her, and in keeping the administration of the millionaire's money in their own hands. The earnest girl brought forward a scheme of "personal supervision and mutual help," the effect of which was to alter poor people until they became exactly like people who were not so poor. The hostess pertinently remarked that she, as eldest son, might surely rank among the millionaire's legatees. Margaret weakly admitted the claim, and another claim was at once set up by Helen, who declared that she had been the millionaire's housemaid for over forty years, overfed and underpaid; was nothing to be done for her, so corpulent and poor? The millionaire then read out her last will and testament, in which she left the whole of her fortune to the Chancellor of the Exchequer. Then she died. The serious parts of the discussion had been of higher merit than the playful—in a men's debate is the reverse more general?—but the meeting broke up hilariously enough, and a dozen happy ladies dispersed to their homes.

Helen and Margaret walked the earnest girl as far as Battersea Bridge Station, arguing copiously all the way. When she had gone they were conscious of an alleviation, and of the great beauty of the evening. They turned back towards Oakley Street. The lamps and the plane-trees, following the line of the embankment, struck a note of dignity that is rare in English cities. The seats, almost deserted, were here and there occupied by gentlefolk in evening dress, who had strolled out from the houses behind to enjoy fresh air and the whisper of the rising tide. There is something continental about Chelsea Embankment. It is an open space used rightly, a blessing more frequent in Germany than here. As Margaret and Helen sat down, the city behind them seemed to be a vast theatre, an opera-house in which some endless trilogy was performing, and they themselves a pair of satisfied subscribers, who did not mind losing a little of the second act.

"Cold?"

"No."

"Tired?"

"Doesn't matter."

The earnest girl's train rumbled away over the bridge.

"I say, Helen——"

"Well?"

"Are we really going to follow up Mr. Bast?"

"I don't know."

"I think we won't."

"As you like."

"It's no good, I think, unless you really mean to know people. The discussion brought that home to me. We got on well enough with him in a spirit of excitement, but think of rational intercourse. We mustn't play at friendship. No, it's no good."

"There's Mrs. Lanoline, too," Helen yawned. "So dull."

"Just so, and possibly worse than dull."

"I should like to know how he got hold of your card."

"But he said—something about a concert and an umbrella——"

"Then did the card see the wife——"

"Helen, come to bed."

"No, just a little longer, it is so beautiful. Tell me; oh yes; did you say money is the warp of the world?"

"Yes."

"Then what's the woof?"

"Very much what one chooses," said Margaret. "It's something that isn't money—one can't say more."

"Walking at night?"

"Probably."

"For Tibby, Oxford?"

"It seems so."

"For you?"

"Now that we have to leave Wickham Place, I begin to think it's that. For Mrs. Wilcox it was certainly Howards End."

One's own name will carry immense distances. Mr. Wilcox, who was sitting with friends many seats away, heard his, rose to his feet, and strolled along towards the speakers.

"It is sad to suppose that places may ever be more important than people," continued Margaret.

"Why, Meg? They're so much nicer generally. I'd rather think of that forester's house in Pomerania than of the fat Herr Förstmeister who lived in it."

"I believe we shall come to care about people less and less, Helen. The more people one knows the easier it becomes to replace them. It's one of the curses of London. I quite expect to end my life caring most for a place."

Here Mr. Wilcox reached them. It was several weeks since they had met.

"How do you do?" he cried. "I thought I recognized your voices. Whatever are you both doing down here?"

His tones were protective. He implied that one ought not to sit out on Chelsea Embankment without a male escort. Helen resented this, but Margaret accepted it as part of the good man's equipment.

"What an age it is since I've seen you, Mr. Wilcox. I met Evie in the Tube, though, lately. I hope you have good news of your son."

"Paul?" said Mr. Wilcox, extinguishing his cigarette, and sitting down between them. "Oh, Paul's all right. We had a line from Madeira. He'll be at work again by now."

"Ugh——" said Helen, shuddering from complex causes.

"I beg your pardon?"

"Isn't the climate of Nigeria too horrible?"

"Someone's got to go," he said simply. "England will never keep her trade overseas unless she is prepared to make sacrifices.

Unless we get firm in West Africa, Ger—— untold complications may follow. Now tell me all your news."

"Oh, we've had a splendid evening," cried Helen, who always woke up at the advent of a visitor. "We belong to a kind of club that reads papers, Margaret and I—all women, but there is a discussion after. This evening it was on how one ought to leave one's money—whether to one's family, or to the poor, and if so how—oh, most interesting."

The man of business smiled. Since his wife's death he had almost doubled his income. He was an important figure at last, a reassuring name on company prospectuses, and life had treated him very well. The world seemed in his grasp as he listened to the River Thames, which still flowed inland from the sea. So wonderful to the girls, it held no mysteries for him. He had helped to shorten its long tidal trough by taking shares in the lock at Teddington, and if he and other capitalists thought good, some day it could be shortened again. With a good dinner inside him and an amiable but academic woman on either flank, he felt that his hands were on all the ropes of life, and that what he did not know could not be worth knowing.

"Sounds a most original entertainment!" he exclaimed, and laughed in his pleasant way. "I wish Evie would go to that sort of thing. But she hasn't the time. She's taken to breed Aberdeen terriers—jolly little dogs."

"I expect we'd better be doing the same, really."

"We pretend we're improving ourselves, you see," said Helen a little sharply, for the Wilcox glamour is not of the kind that returns, and she had bitter memories of the days when a speech such as he had just made would have impressed her favourably. "We suppose it a good thing to waste an evening once a fortnight over a debate, but, as my sister says, it may be better to breed dogs."

"Not at all. I don't agree with your sister. There's nothing like a debate to teach one quickness. I often wish I had gone in for them when I was a youngster. It would have helped me no end."

"Quickness——?"

"Yes. Quickness in argument. Time after time I've missed scoring a point because the other man has had the gift of the gab and I haven't. Oh, I believe in these discussions."

The patronizing tone, thought Margaret, came well enough from a man who was old enough to be their father. She had always maintained that Mr. Wilcox had a charm. In times of sorrow or emotion his inadequacy had pained her, but it was pleasant to listen to him now, and to watch his thick brown moustache and high forehead confronting the stars. But Helen was nettled. The aim of *their* debates she implied was Truth.

"Oh yes, it doesn't much matter what subject you take," said he.

Margaret laughed and said, "But this is going to be far better than the debate itself." Helen recovered herself and laughed too. "No, I won't go on," she declared. "I'll just put our special case to Mr. Wilcox."

"About Mr. Bast? Yes, do. He'll be more lenient to a special case."

"But, Mr. Wilcox, do first light another cigarette. It's this. We've just come across a young fellow, who's evidently very poor, and who seems interest——"

"What's his profession?"

"Clerk."

"What in?"

"Do you remember, Margaret?"

"Porphyrion Fire Insurance Company."

"Oh, yes; the nice people who gave Aunt Juley a new hearthrug. He seems interesting, in some ways very, and one wishes one could help him. He is married to a wife whom he doesn't seem to care for much. He likes books, and what one may roughly call adventure, and if he had a chance—— But he is so poor. He lives a life where all the money is apt to go on nonsense and clothes. One is so afraid that circumstances will be too strong for him and that he will sink. Well, he got mixed up in our debate. He wasn't the subject of it, but it seemed to bear on his point. Suppose a millionaire died, and desired to leave money to help such a man.

How should he be helped? Should he be given three hundred pounds a year direct, which was Margaret's plan? Most of them thought this would pauperize him. Should he and those like him be given free libraries? I said 'No!' He doesn't want more books to read, but to read books rightly. My suggestion was he should be given something every year towards a summer holiday, but then there is his wife, and they said she would have to go too. Nothing seemed quite right! Now what do you think? Imagine that you were a millionaire, and wanted to help the poor. What would you do?"

Mr. Wilcox, whose fortune was not so very far below the standard indicated, laughed exuberantly. "My dear Miss Schlegel, I will not rush in where your sex has been unable to tread. I will not add another plan to the numerous excellent ones that have been already suggested. My only contribution is this: let your young friend clear out of the Porphyrion Fire Insurance Company with all possible speed."

"Why?" said Margaret.

He lowered his voice. "This is between friends. It'll be in the Receiver's hands before Christmas. It'll smash," he added, thinking that she had not understood.

"Dear me, Helen, listen to that. And he'll have to get another place!"

"*Will* have? Let him leave the ship before it sinks. Let him get one now."

"Rather than wait, to make sure?"

"Decidedly."

"Why's that?"

Again the Olympian laugh, and the lowered voice. "Naturally the man who's in a situation when he applies stands a better chance, is in a stronger position, than the man who isn't. It looks as if he's worth something. I know by myself—(this is letting you into the State secrets)—it affects an employer greatly. Human nature, I'm afraid."

"I hadn't thought of that," murmured Margaret, while Helen

said, "Our human nature appears to be the other way round. We employ people because they're unemployed. The boot man, for instance."

"And how does he clean the boots?"

"Not well," confessed Margaret.

"There you are!"

"Then do you really advise us to tell this youth——?"

"I advise nothing," he interrupted, glancing up and down the Embankment, in case his indiscretion had been overheard. "I oughtn't to have spoken—but I happen to know, being more or less behind the scenes. The Porphyrion's a bad, bad concern—— Now, don't say I said so. It's outside the Tariff Ring."

"Certainly I won't say. In fact, I don't know what that means."

"I thought an insurance company never smashed," was Helen's contribution. "Don't the others always run in and save them?"

"You're thinking of reinsurance," said Mr. Wilcox mildly. "It is exactly there that the Porphyrion is weak. It has tried to undercut, has been badly hit by a long series of small fires, and it hasn't been able to reinsure. I'm afraid that public companies don't save one another for love."

"'Human nature,' I suppose," quoted Helen, and he laughed and agreed that it was. When Margaret said that she supposed that clerks, like everyone else, found it extremely difficult to get situations in these days, he replied, "Yes, extremely," and rose to rejoin his friends. He knew by his own office—seldom a vacant post, and hundreds of applicants for it; at present no vacant post.

"And how's Howards End looking?" said Margaret, wishing to change the subject before they parted. Mr. Wilcox was a little apt to think one wanted to get something out of him.

"It's let."

"Really. And you wandering homeless in long-haired Chelsea? How strange are the ways of Fate!"

"No; it's let unfurnished. We've moved."

"Why, I thought of you both as anchored there for ever. Evie never told me."

"I dare say when you met Evie the thing wasn't settled. We only moved a week ago. Paul has rather a feeling for the old place, and we held on for him to have his holiday there; but, really, it is impossibly small. Endless drawbacks. I forget whether you've been up to it?"

"As far as the house, never."

"Well, Howards End is one of those converted farms. They don't really do, spend what you will on them. We messed away with a garage all among the wych-elm roots, and last year we enclosed a bit of the meadow and attempted a rockery. Evie got rather keen on Alpine plants. But it didn't do—no, it didn't do. You remember, or your sister will remember, the farm with those abominable guinea-fowls, and the hedge that the old woman never would cut properly, so that it all went thin at the bottom. And, inside the house, the beams—and the staircase through a door—picturesque enough, but not a place to live in." He glanced over the parapet cheerfully. "Full tide. And the position wasn't right either. The neighbourhood's getting suburban. Either be in London or out of it, I say; so we've taken a house in Ducie Street, close to Sloane Street, and a place right down in Shropshire—Oniton Grange. Ever heard of Oniton? Do come and see us—right away from everywhere, up towards Wales."

"What a change!" said Margaret. But the change was in her own voice, which had become most sad. "I can't imagine Howards End or Hilton without you."

"Hilton isn't without us," he replied. "Charles is there still."

"Still?" said Margaret, who had not kept up with the Charles'. "But I thought he was still at Epsom. They were furnishing that Christmas—one Christmas. How everything alters! I used to admire Mrs. Charles from our windows very often. Wasn't it Epsom?"

"Yes, but they moved eighteen months ago. Charles, the good chap"—his voice dropped—"thought I should be lonely. I didn't want him to move, but he would, and took a house at the other end of Hilton, down by the Six Hills. He had a motor, too. There they all are, a very jolly party—he and she and the two grandchildren."

"I manage other people's affairs so much better than they manage them themselves," said Margaret as they shook hands. "When you moved out of Howards End, I should have moved Mr. Charles Wilcox into it. I should have kept so remarkable a place in the family."

"So it is," he replied. "I haven't sold it, and don't mean to."

"No; but none of you are there."

"Oh, we've got a splendid tenant—Hamar Bryce, an invalid. If Charles ever wanted it—but he won't. Dolly is so dependent on modern conveniences. No, we have all decided against Howards End. We like it in a way, but now we feel that it is neither one thing nor the other. One must have one thing or the other."

"And some people are lucky enough to have both. You're doing yourself proud, Mr. Wilcox. My congratulations."

"And mine," said Helen.

"Do remind Evie to come and see us—two, Wickham Place. We shan't be there very long, either."

"You, too, on the move?"

"Next September," Margaret sighed.

"Everyone moving! Good-bye."

The tide had begun to ebb. Margaret leant over the parapet and watched it sadly. Mr. Wilcox had forgotten his wife, Helen her lover; she herself was probably forgetting. Everyone moving. Is it worth while attempting the past when there is this continual flux even in the hearts of men?

Helen roused her by saying: "What a prosperous vulgarian Mr. Wilcox has grown! I have very little use for him in these days. However, he did tell us about the Porphyrion. Let us write to Mr. Bast as soon as ever we get home, and tell him to clear out of it at once."

"Do; yes, that's worth doing. Let us."

"Let's ask him to tea."

CHAPTER XVI

Leonard accepted the invitation to tea next Saturday. But he was right; the visit proved a conspicuous failure.

"Sugar?" said Margaret.

"Cake?" said Helen. "The big cake or the little deadlies? I'm afraid you thought my letter rather odd, but we'll explain—we aren't odd, really—nor affected, really. We're over-expressive: that's all."

As a lady's lap-dog Leonard did not excel. He was not an Italian, still less a Frenchman, in whose blood there runs the very spirit of persiflage and of gracious repartee. His wit was the Cockney's; it opened no doors into imagination, and Helen was drawn up short by "The more a lady has to say, the better," administered waggishly.

"Oh yes," she said.

"Ladies brighten——"

"Yes, I know. The darlings are regular sunbeams. Let me give you a plate."

"How do you like your work?" interposed Margaret.

He, too, was drawn up short. He would not have these women prying into his work. They were Romance, and so was the room to which he had at last penetrated, with the queer sketches of people bathing upon its walls, and so were the very tea-cups, with their delicate borders of wild strawberries. But he would not let Romance interfere with his life. There is the devil to pay then.

"Oh, well enough," he answered.

"Your company is the Porphyrion, isn't it?"

"Yes, that's so"—becoming rather offended. "It's funny how things get round."

"Why funny?" asked Helen, who did not follow the workings of his mind. "It was written as large as life on your card, and considering we wrote to you there, and that you replied on the stamped paper——"

"Would you call the Porphyrion one of the big Insurance Companies?" pursued Margaret.

"It depends what you call big."

"I mean by big, a solid, well-established concern, that offers a reasonably good career to its employés."

"I couldn't say—some would tell you one thing and others another," said the employé uneasily. "For my own part"—he shook his head—"I only believe half I hear. Not that even; it's safer. Those clever ones come to the worse grief, I've often noticed. Ah, you can't be too careful."

He drank, and wiped his moustache, which was going to be one of those moustaches that always droop into tea-cups—more bother than they're worth, surely, and not fashionable either.

"I quite agree, and that's why I was curious to know: is it a solid, well-established concern?"

Leonard had no idea. He understood his own corner of the machine, but nothing beyond it. He desired to confess neither knowledge nor ignorance, and under these circumstances, another motion of the head seemed safest. To him, as to the British public, the Porphyrion was the Porphyrion of the advertisement—a giant, in the classical style, but draped sufficiently, who held in one hand a burning torch, and pointed with the other to St. Paul's and Windsor Castle. A large sum of money was inscribed below, and you drew your own conclusions. This giant caused Leonard to do arithmetic and write letters, to explain the regulations to new clients, and re-explain them to old ones. A giant was of an impulsive morality—one knew that much. He would pay for Mrs. Munt's hearth-rug with ostentatious haste, a large claim he would repudiate quietly, and fight court by court. But his true fighting weight, his antecedents, his amours with other members of the commercial Pantheon—all these were as uncertain to ordinary mortals as were the escapades of Zeus. While the gods are powerful, we learn little about them. It is only in the days of their decadence that a strong light beats into heaven.

"We were told the Porphyrion's no go," blurted Helen. "We wanted to tell you; that's why we wrote."

"A friend of ours did think that it is insufficiently reinsured,"
said Margaret.

Now Leonard had his clue. He must praise the Porphyrion.
"You can tell your friend," he said, "that he's quite wrong."

"Oh, good!"

The young man coloured a little. In his circle to be wrong was
fatal. The Miss Schlegels did not mind being wrong. They were
genuinely glad that they had been misinformed. To them nothing
was fatal but evil.

"Wrong, so to speak," he added.

"How 'so to speak'?"

"I mean I wouldn't say he's right altogether."

But this was a blunder. "Then he is right partly," said the elder
woman, quick as lightning.

Leonard replied that everyone was right partly, if it came to that.

"Mr. Bast, I don't understand business, and I dare say my questions are stupid, but can you tell me what makes a concern 'right'
or 'wrong'?"

Leonard sat back with a sigh.

"Our friend, who is also a business man, was so positive. He
said before Christmas——"

"And advised you to clear out of it," concluded Helen. "But I
don't see why he should know better than you do."

Leonard rubbed his hands. He was tempted to say that he
knew nothing about the thing at all. But a commercial training
was too strong for him. Nor could he say it was a bad thing, for
this would be giving it away; nor yet that it was good, for this
would be giving it away equally. He attempted to suggest that it
was something between the two, with vast possibilities in either
direction, but broke down under the gaze of four sincere eyes.
And yet he scarcely distinguished between the two sisters. One
was more beautiful and more lively, but "the Miss Schlegels" still
remained a composite Indian god, whose waving arms and contradictory speeches were the product of a single mind.

"One can but see," he remarked, adding, "as Ibsen says, 'things happen.'" He was itching to talk about books and make the most of his romantic hour. Minute after minute slipped away, while the ladies, with imperfect skill, discussed the subject of reinsurance or praised their anonymous friend. Leonard grew annoyed—perhaps rightly. He made vague remarks about not being one of those who minded their affairs being talked over by others, but they did not take the hint. Men might have shown more tact. Women, however tactful elsewhere, are heavy-handed here. They cannot see why we should shroud our incomes and our prospects in a veil. "How much exactly have you, and how much do you expect to have next June?" And these were women with a theory, who held that reticence about money matters is absurd, and that life would be truer if each would state the exact size of the golden island upon which he stands, the exact stretch of warp over which he throws the woof that is not money. How can we do justice to the pattern otherwise?

And the precious minutes slipped away, and Jacky and squalor came nearer. At last he could bear it no longer, and broke in, reciting the names of books feverishly. There was a moment of piercing joy when Margaret said, "So *you* like Carlyle," and then the door opened, and "Mr. Wilcox, Miss Wilcox" entered, preceded by two prancing puppies.

"Oh, the dears! Oh, Evie, how too impossibly sweet!" screamed Helen, falling on her hands and knees.

"We brought the little fellows round," said Mr. Wilcox.

"I bred 'em myself."

"Oh, really! Mr. Bast, come and play with puppies."

"I've got to be going now," said Leonard sourly.

"But play with puppies a little first."

"This is Ahab, that's Jezebel," said Evie, who was one of those who name animals after the less successful characters of Old Testament history.

"I've got to be going."

Helen was too much occupied with puppies to notice him.

"Mr. Wilcox, Mr. Ba—— Must you be really? Good-bye!"

"Come again," said Helen from the floor.

Then Leonard's gorge arose. Why should he come again? What was the good of it? He said roundly: "No, I shan't; I knew it would be a failure."

Most people would have let him go. "A little mistake. We tried knowing another class—impossible." But the Schlegels had never played with life. They had attempted friendship, and they would take the consequences. Helen retorted, "I call that a very rude remark. What do you want to turn on me like that for?" and suddenly the drawing-room re-echoed to a vulgar row.

"You ask me why I turn on you?"

"Yes."

"What do you want to have me here for?"

"To help you, you silly boy!" cried Helen. "And don't shout."

"*I* don't want your patronage. *I* don't want your tea. I was quite happy. What do you want to unsettle me for?" He turned to Mr. Wilcox. "I put it to this gentleman. I ask you, sir, am I to have my brain picked?"

Mr. Wilcox turned to Margaret with the air of humorous strength that he could so well command. "Are we intruding, Miss Schlegel? Can we be of any use, or shall we go?"

But Margaret ignored him.

"I'm connected with a leading insurance company, sir. I receive what I take to be an invitation from these—ladies" (he drawled the word). "I come, and it's to have my brain picked. I ask you, is it fair?"

"Highly unfair," said Mr. Wilcox, drawing a gasp from Evie, who knew that her father was becoming dangerous.

"There, you hear that? Most unfair, the gentleman says. There! Not content with"—pointing at Margaret—"you can't deny it." His voice rose: he was falling into the rhythm of a scene with Jacky. "But as soon as I'm useful it's a very different thing. 'Oh yes, send for him. Cross-question him. Pick his brains.' Oh yes. Now, take me on the whole, I'm a quiet fellow: I'm law-abiding, I don't wish any unpleasantness; but I—I——"

"You," said Margaret—"you—you——"

Laughter from Evie, as at a repartee.

"You are the man who tried to walk by the Pole star."

More laughter.

"You saw the sunrise."

Laughter.

"You tried to get away from the fogs that are stifling us all—away past books and houses to the truth. You were looking for a real home."

"I fail to see the connection," said Leonard, hot with stupid anger.

"So do I." There was a pause. "You were that last Sunday—you are this to-day. Mr. Bast! I and my sister have talked you over. We wanted to help you; we also supposed you might help us. We did not have you here out of charity—which bores us—but because we hoped there would be a connection between last Sunday and other days. What is the good of your stars and trees, your sunrise and the wind, if they do not enter into our daily lives? They have never entered into mine, but into yours, we thought—— Haven't we all to struggle against life's daily greyness, against pettiness, against mechanical cheerfulness, against suspicion? I struggle by remembering my friends; others I have known by remembering some place—some beloved place or tree—we thought you were one of these."

"Of course, if there's been any misunderstanding," mumbled Leonard, "all I can do is to go. But I beg to state——" He paused. Ahab and Jezebel danced at his boots and made him look ridiculous. "You were picking my brain for official information—I can prove it—I——" He blew his nose and left them.

"Can I help you now?" said Mr. Wilcox, turning to Margaret. "May I have one quiet word with him in the hall?"

"Helen, go after him—do anything—*anything*—to make the noodle understand."

Helen hesitated.

"But really——" said their visitor. "Ought she to?"

At once she went.

He resumed. "I would have chimed in, but I felt that you could polish him off for yourselves—I didn't interfere. You were splendid, Miss Schlegel—absolutely splendid. You can take my word for it, but there are very few women who could have managed him."

"Oh yes," said Margaret distractedly.

"Bowling him over with those long sentences was what fetched me," cried Evie.

"Yes, indeed," chuckled her father; "all that part about 'mechanical cheerfulness'—oh, fine!"

"I'm very sorry," said Margaret, collecting herself. "He's a nice creature really. I cannot think what set him off. It has been most unpleasant for you."

"Oh, *I* didn't mind." Then he changed his mood. He asked if he might speak as an old friend, and, permission given, said: "Oughtn't you really to be more careful?"

Margaret laughed, though her thoughts still strayed after Helen. "Do you realize that it's all your fault?" she said. "You're responsible."

"I?"

"This is the young man whom we were to warn against the Porphyrion. We warn him, and—look!"

Mr. Wilcox was annoyed. "I hardly consider that a fair deduction," he said.

"Obviously unfair," said Margaret. "I was only thinking how tangled things are. It's our fault mostly—neither yours nor his."

"Not his?"

"No."

"Miss Schlegel, you are too kind."

"Yes, indeed," nodded Evie, a little contemptuously.

"You behave much too well to people, and then they impose on you. I know the world and that type of man, and as soon as I entered the room I saw you had not been treating him properly. You must keep that type at a distance. Otherwise they forget themselves. Sad, but true. They aren't our sort, and one must face the fact."

"Ye-es."

"Do admit that we should never have had the outburst if he was a gentleman."

"I admit it willingly," said Margaret, who was pacing up and down the room. "A gentleman would have kept his suspicions to himself."

Mr. Wilcox watched her with a vague uneasiness.

"What did he suspect you of?"

"Of wanting to make money out of him."

"Intolerable brute! But how were you to benefit?"

"Exactly. How indeed! Just horrible, corroding suspicion. One touch of thought or of goodwill would have brushed it away. Just the senseless fear that does make men intolerable brutes."

"I come back to my original point. You ought to be more careful, Miss Schlegel. Your servants ought to have orders not to let such people in."

She turned to him frankly. "Let me explain exactly why we like this man, and want to see him again."

"That's your clever way of talking. I shall never believe you like him."

"I do. Firstly, because he cares for physical adventure, just as you do. Yes, you go motoring and shooting; he would like to go camping out. Secondly, he cares for something special *in* adventure. It is quickest to call that special something poetry——"

"Oh, he's one of that writer sort."

"No—oh no! I mean he may be, but it would be loathsome stuff. His brain is filled with the husks of books, culture—horrible; we want him to wash out his brain and go to the real thing. We want to show him how he may get upsides with life. As I said, either friends or the country, some"—she hesitated—"either some very dear person or some very dear place seems necessary to relieve life's daily grey, and to show that it is grey. If possible, one should have both."

Some of her words ran past Mr. Wilcox. He let them run past. Others he caught and criticized with admirable lucidity.

"Your mistake is this, and it is a very common mistake. This young bounder has a life of his own. What right have you to conclude it is an unsuccessful life, or, as you call it, 'grey'?"

"Because——"

"One minute. You know nothing about him. He probably has his own joys and interests—wife, children, snug little home. That's where we practical fellows"—he smiled—"are more tolerant than you intellectuals. We live and let live, and assume that things are jogging on fairly well elsewhere, and that the ordinary plain man may be trusted to look after his own affairs. I quite grant—I look at the faces of the clerks in my own office, and observe them to be dull, but I don't know what's going on beneath. So, by the way, with London. I have heard you rail against London, Miss Schlegel, and it seems a funny thing to say but I was very angry with you. What do you know about London? You only see civilization from the outside. I don't say in your case, but in too many cases that attitude leads to morbidity, discontent, and Socialism."

She admitted the strength of his position, though it undermined imagination. As he spoke, some outposts of poetry and perhaps of sympathy fell ruining, and she retreated to what she called her "second line"—to the special facts of the case.

"His wife is an old bore," she said simply. "He never came home last Saturday night because he wanted to be alone, and she thought he was with us."

"With *you*?"

"Yes." Evie tittered. "He hasn't got the cosy home that you assumed. He needs outside interests."

"Naughty young man!" cried the girl.

"Naughty?" said Margaret, who hated naughtiness more than sin. "When you're married, Miss Wilcox, won't you want outside interests?"

"He has apparently got them," put in Mr. Wilcox slyly.

"Yes, indeed, father."

"He was tramping in Surrey, if you mean that," said Margaret, pacing away rather crossly.

"Oh, I dare say!"

"Miss Wilcox, he was!"

"M-m-m-m!" from Mr. Wilcox, who thought the episode amusing, if risqué. With most ladies he would not have discussed it, but he was trading on Margaret's reputation as an emancipated woman.

"He said so, and about such a thing he wouldn't lie."

They both began to laugh.

"That's where I differ from you. Men lie about their positions and prospects, but not about a thing of that sort."

He shook his head. "Miss Schlegel, excuse me, but I know the type."

"I said before—he isn't a type. He cares about adventures rightly. He's certain that our smug existence isn't all. He's vulgar and hysterical and bookish, but don't think that sums him up. There's manhood in him as well. Yes, that's what I'm trying to say. He's a real man."

As she spoke their eyes met, and it was as if Mr. Wilcox's defences fell. She saw back to the real man in him. Unwittingly she had touched his emotions. A woman and two men—they had formed the magic triangle of sex, and the male was thrilled to jealousy, in case the female was attracted by another male. Love, say the ascetics, reveals our shameful kinship with the beasts. Be it so: one can bear that; jealousy is the real shame. It is jealousy, not love, that connects us with the farmyard intolerably, and calls up visions of two angry cocks and a complacent hen. Margaret crushed complacency down because she was civilized. Mr. Wilcox, uncivilized, continued to feel anger long after he had rebuilt his defences, and was again presenting a bastion to the world.

"Miss Schlegel, you're a pair of dear creatures, but you really *must* be careful in this uncharitable world. What does your brother say?"

"I forget."

"Surely he has some opinion?"

"He laughs, if I remember correctly."

"He's very clever, isn't he?" said Evie, who had met and detested Tibby at Oxford.

"Yes, pretty well—but I wonder what Helen's doing."

"She is very young to undertake this sort of thing," said Mr. Wilcox.

Margaret went out into the landing. She heard no sound, and Mr. Bast's topper was missing from the hall.

"Helen!" she called.

"Yes!" replied a voice from the library.

"You in there?"

"Yes—he's gone some time."

Margaret went to her. "Why, you're all alone," she said.

"Yes—it's all right, Meg. Poor, poor creature——"

"Come back to the Wilcoxes and tell me later—Mr. W. much concerned, and slightly titillated."

"Oh, I've no patience with him. I hate him. Poor dear Mr. Bast! he wanted to talk literature, and we would talk business. Such a muddle of a man, and yet so worth pulling through. I like him extraordinarily."

"Well done," said Margaret, kissing her, "but come into the drawing-room now, and don't talk about him to the Wilcoxes. Make light of the whole thing."

Helen came and behaved with a cheerfulness that reassured their visitor—this hen at all events was fancy-free.

"He's gone with my blessing," she cried, "and now for puppies."

As they drove away, Mr. Wilcox said to his daughter:

"I am really concerned at the way those girls go on. They are as clever as you make 'em, but unpractical—God bless me! One of these days they'll go too far. Girls like that oughtn't to live alone in London. Until they marry, they ought to have someone to look after them. We must look in more often—we're better than no one. You like them, don't you, Evie?"

Evie replied: "Helen's right enough, but I can't stand the toothy one. And I shouldn't have called either of them girls."

Evie had grown up handsome. Dark-eyed, with the glow of youth under sunburn, built firmly and firm-lipped, she was the best the Wilcoxes could do in the way of feminine beauty. For the present, puppies and her father were the only things she loved, but the net of matrimony was being prepared for her, and a few days later she was attracted to a Mr. Percy Cahill, an uncle of Mrs. Charles', and he was attracted to her.

CHAPTER XVII

The Age of Property holds bitter moments even for a proprietor. When a move is imminent, furniture becomes ridiculous, and Margaret now lay awake at nights wondering where, where on earth they and all their belongings would be deposited in September next. Chairs, tables, pictures, books, that had rumbled down to them through the generations, must rumble forward again like a slide of rubbish to which she longed to give the final push, and send toppling into the sea. But there were all their father's books— they never read them, but they were their father's, and must be kept. There was the marble-topped cheffonier—their mother had set store by it, they could not remember why. Round every knob and cushion in the house sentiment gathered, a sentiment that was at times personal, but more often a faint piety to the dead, a prolongation of rites that might have ended at the grave.

It was absurd, if you came to think of it; Helen and Tibby came to think of it: Margaret was too busy with the house-agents. The feudal ownership of land did bring dignity, whereas the modern ownership of movables is reducing us again to a nomadic horde. We are reverting to the civilization of luggage, and historians of the future will note how the middle classes accreted possessions without taking root in the earth, and may find in this the secret of their imaginative poverty. The Schlegels were

certainly the poorer for the loss of Wickham Place. It had helped
to balance their lives, and almost to counsel them. Nor is their
ground-landlord spiritually the richer. He has built flats on its
site, his motor-cars grow swifter, his exposures of Socialism more
trenchant. But he has spilt the precious distillation of the years,
and no chemistry of his can give it back to society again.

Margaret grew depressed; she was anxious to settle on a house
before they left town to pay their annual visit to Mrs. Munt. She
enjoyed this visit, and wanted to have her mind at ease for it.
Swanage, though dull, was stable, and this year she longed more
than usual for its fresh air and for the magnificent downs that
guard it on the north. But London thwarted her; in its atmosphere
she could not concentrate. London only stimulates, it cannot sus-
tain; and Margaret, hurrying over its surface for a house without
knowing what sort of a house she wanted, was paying for many a
thrilling sensation in the past. She could not even break loose
from culture, and her time was wasted by concerts which it
would be a sin to miss, and invitations which it would never do
to refuse. At last she grew desperate; she resolved that she would
go nowhere and be at home to no one until she found a house,
and broke the resolution in half an hour.

Once she had humorously lamented that she had never been
to Simpson's restaurant in the Strand. Now a note arrived from
Miss Wilcox, asking her to lunch there. Mr. Cahill was coming,
and the three would have such a jolly chat, and perhaps end up at
the Hippodrome. Margaret had no strong regard for Evie, and no
desire to meet her fiancé, and she was surprised that Helen, who
had been far funnier about Simpson's, had not been asked instead.
But the invitation touched her by its intimate tone. She must
know Evie Wilson better than she supposed, and declaring that
she "simply must," she accepted.

But when she saw Evie at the entrance of the restaurant, staring
fiercely at nothing after the fashion of athletic women, her heart
failed her anew. Miss Wilcox had changed perceptibly since her
engagement. Her voice was gruffer, her manner more downright,

and she was inclined to patronize the more foolish virgin. Margaret was silly enough to be pained at this. Depressed at her isolation, she saw not only houses and furniture, but the vessel of life itself slipping past her, with people like Evie and Mr. Cahill on board.

There are moments when virtue and wisdom fail us, and one of them came to her at Simpson's in the Strand. As she trod the staircase, narrow, but carpeted thickly, as she entered the eating-room, where saddles of mutton were being trundled up to expectant clergymen, she had a strong, if erroneous, conviction of her own futility, and wished she had never come out of her back-water, where nothing happened except art and literature, and where no one ever got married or succeeded in remaining engaged. Then came a little surprise. 'Father might be of the party—yes, father was.' With a smile of pleasure she moved forward to greet him, and her feeling of loneliness vanished.

"I thought I'd get round if I could," said he. "Evie told me of her little plan, so I just slipped in and secured a table. Always secure a table first. Evie, don't pretend you want to sit by your old father, because you don't. Miss Schlegel, come in my side, out of pity. My goodness, but you look tired! Been worrying round after your young clerks?"

"No, after houses," said Margaret, edging past him into the box. "I'm hungry, not tired; I want to eat heaps."

"That's good. What'll you have?"

"Fish pie," said she, with a glance at the menu.

"Fish pie! Fancy coming for fish pie to Simpson's. It's not a bit the thing to go for here."

"Go for something for me, then," said Margaret, pulling off her gloves. Her spirits were rising, and his reference to Leonard Bast had warmed her curiously.

"Saddle of mutton," said he after profound reflection; "and cider to drink. That's the type of thing. I like this place, for a joke, once in a way. It is so thoroughly Old English. Don't you agree?"

"Yes," said Margaret, who didn't. The order was given, the joint rolled up, and the carver, under Mr. Wilcox's direction, cut the meat where it was succulent, and piled their plates high. Mr. Cahill insisted on sirloin, but admitted that he had made a mistake later on. He and Evie soon fell into a conversation of the 'No, I didn't; yes, you did' type—conversation which, though fascinating to those who are engaged in it, neither desires nor deserves the attention of others.

"It's a golden rule to tip the carver. Tip everywhere's my motto."

"Perhaps it does make life more human."

"Then the fellows know one again. Especially in the East, if you tip, they remember you from year's end to year's end."

"Have you been in the East?"

"Oh, Greece and the Levant. I used to go out for sport and business to Cyprus; some military society of a sort there. A few piastres, properly distributed, help to keep one's memory green. But you, of course, think this shockingly cynical. How's your discussion society getting on? Any new Utopias lately?"

"No, I'm house-hunting, Mr. Wilcox, as I've already told you once. Do you know of any houses?"

"Afraid I don't."

"Well, what's the point of being practical if you can't find two distressed females a house? We merely want a small house with large rooms, and plenty of them."

"Evie, I like that! Miss Schlegel expects me to turn house agent for her!"

"What's that, father?"

"I want a new home in September, and someone must find it. I can't."

"Percy, do you know of anything?"

"I can't say I do," said Mr. Cahill.

"How like you! You're never any good."

"Never any good. Just listen to her! Never any good. Oh, come!"

"Well, you aren't. Miss Schlegel, is he?"

The torrent of their love, having splashed these drops at Margaret, swept away on its habitual course. She sympathized with it

now, for a little comfort had restored her geniality. Speech and
silence pleased her equally, and while Mr. Wilcox made some pre-
liminary inquiries about cheese, her eyes surveyed the restaurant,
and admired its well-calculated tributes to the solidity of our past.
Though no more Old English than the works of Kipling, it had
selected its reminiscences so adroitly that her criticism was lulled,
and the guests whom it was nourishing for imperial purposes
bore the outer semblance of Parson Adams or Tom Jones. Scraps
of their talk jarred oddly on the ear. "Right you are! I'll cable out
to Uganda this evening," came from the table behind. "Their
Emperor wants war; well, let him have it," was the opinion of a
clergyman. She smiled at such incongruities. "Next time," she
said to Mr. Wilcox, "you shall come to lunch with me at Mr.
Eustace Miles's."

"With pleasure."

"No, you'd hate it," she said, pushing her glass towards him
for some more cider. "It's all proteids and body buildings, and
people come up to you and beg your pardon, but you have such a
beautiful aura."

"A what?"

"Never heard of an aura? Oh, happy, happy man! I scrub at
mine for hours. Nor of an astral plane?"

He had heard of astral planes, and censured them.

"Just so. Luckily it was Helen's aura, not mine, and she had to
chaperone it and do the politenesses. I just sat with my handkerchief in my mouth till the man went."

"Funny experiences seem to come to you two girls. No
one's ever asked me about my—what d'ye call it? Perhaps I've not
got one."

"You're bound to have one, but it may be such a terrible colour
that no one dares mention it."

"Tell me, though, Miss Schlegel, do you really believe in the
supernatural and all that?"

"Too difficult a question."

"Why's that? Gruyère or Stilton?"

"Gruyère, please."

"Better have Stilton."

"Stilton. Because, though I don't believe in auras, and think Theosophy's only a halfway-house——"

"—Yet there may be something in it all the same," he concluded, with a frown.

"Not even that. It may be halfway in the wrong direction. I can't explain. I don't believe in all these fads, and yet I don't like saying that I don't believe in them."

He seemed unsatisfied, and said: "So you wouldn't give me your word that you *don't* hold with astral bodies and all the rest of it?"

"I could," said Margaret, surprised that the point was of any importance to him. "Indeed, I will. When I talked about scrubbing my aura, I was only trying to be funny. But why do you want this settled?"

"I don't know."

"Now, Mr. Wilcox, you do know."

"Yes, I am," "No, you're not," burst from the lovers opposite. Margaret was silent for a moment, and then changed the subject.

"How's your house?"

"Much the same as when you honoured it last week."

"I don't mean Ducie Street. Howards End, of course."

"Why 'of course'?"

"Can't you turn out your tenant and let it to us? We're nearly demented."

"Let me think. I wish I could help you. But I thought you wanted to be in town. One bit of advice: fix your district, then fix your price, and then don't budge. That's how I got both Ducie Street and Oniton. I said to myself, 'I mean to be exactly here,' and I was, and Oniton's a place in a thousand."

"But I do budge. Gentlemen seem to mesmerize houses—cow them with an eye, and up they come, trembling. Ladies can't. It's the houses that are mesmerizing me. I've no control over the saucy things. Houses are alive. No?"

"I'm out of my depth," he said, and added: "Didn't you talk rather like that to your office boy?"

"Did I?—I mean I did, more or less. I talk the same way to everyone—or try to."

"Yes, I know. And how much do you suppose that he understood of it?"

"That's his lookout. I don't believe in suiting my conversation to my company. One can doubtless hit upon some medium of exchange that seems to do well enough, but it's no more like the real thing than money is like food. There's no nourishment in it. You pass it to the lower classes, and they pass it back to you, and this you call 'social intercourse' or 'mutual endeavour,' when it's mutual priggishness if it's anything. Our friends at Chelsea don't see this. They say one ought to be at all costs intelligible, and sacrifice——"

"Lower classes," interrupted Mr. Wilcox, as it were thrusting his hand into her speech. "Well, you do admit that there are rich and poor. That's something."

Margaret could not reply. Was he incredibly stupid, or did he understand her better than she understood herself?

"You do admit that, if wealth was divided up equally, in a few years there would be rich and poor again just the same. The hard-working man would come to the top, the wastrel sink to the bottom."

"Everyone admits that."

"Your Socialists don't."

"My Socialists do. Yours mayn't; but I strongly suspect yours of being not Socialists, but ninepins, which you have constructed for your own amusement. I can't imagine any living creature who would bowl over quite so easily."

He would have resented this had she not been a woman. But women may say anything—it was one of his holiest beliefs—and he only retorted, with a gay smile: "I don't care. You've made two damaging admissions, and I'm heartily with you in both."

In time they finished lunch, and Margaret, who had excused

herself from the Hippodrome, took her leave. Evie had scarcely addressed her, and she suspected that the entertainment had been planned by the father. He and she were advancing out of their respective families towards a more intimate acquaintance. It had begun long ago. She had been his wife's friend, and, as such, he had given her that silver vinaigrette as a memento. It was pretty of him to have given that vinaigrette, and he had always preferred her to Helen—unlike most men. But the advance had been astonishing lately. They had done more in a week than in two years, and were really beginning to know each other.

She did not forget his promise to sample Eustace Miles, and asked him as soon as she could secure Tibby as his chaperon. He came, and partook of body-building dishes with humility.

Next morning the Schlegels left for Swanage. They had not succeeded in finding a new home.

CHAPTER XVIII

As they were seated at Aunt Juley's breakfast-table at The Bays, parrying her excessive hospitality and enjoying the view of the bay, a letter came for Margaret and threw her into perturbation. It was from Mr. Wilcox. It announced an "important change" in his plans. Owing to Evie's marriage, he had decided to give up his house in Ducie Street, and was willing to let it on a yearly tenancy. It was a businesslike letter, and stated frankly what he would do for them and what he would not do. Also the rent. If they approved, Margaret was to come up *at once*—the words were underlined, as is necessary when dealing with women—and to go over the house with him. If they disapproved, a wire would oblige, as he should put it into the hands of an agent.

The letter perturbed, because she was not sure what it meant. If he liked her, if he had manœuvred to get her to Simpson's, might this be a manœuvre to get her to London, and result in an offer of marriage? She put it to herself as indelicately as possible, in the hope that her brain would cry, "Rubbish, you're a self-conscious fool!" But her brain only tingled a little and was silent, and for a time she sat gazing at the mincing waves, and wondering whether the news would seem strange to the others.

As soon as she began speaking, the sound of her own voice reassured her. There could be nothing in it. The replies also were typical, and in the burr of conversation her fears vanished.

"You needn't go though——" began her hostess.

"I needn't, but hadn't I better? It's really getting rather serious. We let chance after chance slip, and the end of it is we shall be bundled out bag and baggage into the street. We don't know what we *want*, that's the mischief with us——"

"No, we have no real ties," said Helen, helping herself to toast.

"Shan't I go up to town to-day, take the house if it's the least possible, and then come down by the afternoon train to-morrow, and start enjoying myself. I shall be no fun to myself or to others until this business is off my mind."

"But you won't do anything rash, Margaret?"

"There's nothing rash to do."

"Who *are* the Wilcoxes?" said Tibby, a question that sounds silly, but was really extremely subtle, as his aunt found to her cost when she tried to answer it. "I don't *manage* the Wilcoxes; I don't see where they come *in*."

"No more do I," agreed Helen. "It's funny that we just don't lose sight of them. Out of all our hotel acquaintances, Mr. Wilcox is the only one who has stuck. It is now over three years, and we have drifted away from far more interesting people in that time."

"Interesting people don't get one houses."

"Meg, if you start in your honest-English vein, I shall throw the treacle at you."

"It's a better vein than the cosmopolitan," said Margaret, getting up. Now, children, which is it to be? You know the Ducie Street house. Shall I say yes or shall I say no? Tibby love—which? I'm specially anxious to pin you both."

"It all depends what meaning you attach to the word 'possi——'"

"It depends on nothing of the sort. Say 'yes.'"

"Say 'no.'"

Then Margaret spoke rather seriously. "I think," she said, "that our race is degenerating. We cannot settle even this little thing; what will it be like when we have to settle a big one?"

"It will be as easy as eating," returned Helen.

"I was thinking of father. How could he settle to leave Germany as he did, when he had fought for it as a young man, and all his feelings and friends were Prussian? How could he break loose with Patriotism and begin aiming at something else? It would have killed me. When he was nearly forty he could change countries and ideals—and we, at our age, can't change houses. It's humiliating."

"Your father may have been able to change countries," said Mrs. Munt with asperity, "and that may or may not be a good thing. But he could change houses no better than you can, in fact, much worse. Never shall I forget what poor Emily suffered in the move from Manchester."

"I knew it," cried Helen. "I told you so. It is the little things one bungles at. The big, real ones are nothing when they come."

"Bungle, my dear! You are too little to recollect—in fact, you weren't there. But the furniture was actually in the vans and on the move before the lease for Wickham Place was signed, and Emily took train with baby—who was Margaret then—and the smaller luggage for London, without so much as knowing where her new home would be. Getting away from that house may be hard, but it is nothing to the misery that we all went through getting you into it."

Helen, with her mouth full, cried:

"And that's the man who beat the Austrians, and the Danes, and the French, and who beat the Germans that were inside himself. And we're like him."

"Speak for yourself," said Tibby. "Remember that I am cosmopolitan, please."

"Helen may be right."

"Of course she's right," said Helen.

Helen might be right, but she did not go up to London. Margaret did that. An interrupted holiday is the worst of the minor worries, and one may be pardoned for feeling morbid when a business letter snatches one away from the sea and friends. She could not believe that her father had ever felt the same. Her eyes had been troubling her lately, so that she could not read in the train, and it bored her to look at the landscape, which she had seen but yesterday. At Southampton she "waved" to Frieda: Frieda was on her way down to join them at Swanage, and Mrs. Munt had calculated that their trains would cross. But Frieda was looking the other way, and Margaret travelled on to town feeling solitary and old-maidish. How like an old maid to fancy that Mr. Wilcox was courting her! She had once visited a spinster—poor, silly, and unattractive—whose mania it was that every man who approached her fell in love. How Margaret's heart had bled for the deluded thing! How she had lectured, reasoned, and in despair acquiesced! "I may have been deceived by the curate, my dear, but the young fellow who brings the midday post really is fond of me, and has, as a matter of fact——" It had always seemed to her the most hideous corner of old age, yet she might be driven into it herself by the mere pressure of virginity.

Mr. Wilcox met her at Waterloo himself. She felt certain that he was not the same as usual; for one thing, he took offence at everything she said.

"This is awfully kind of you," she began, "but I'm afraid it's not going to do. The house has not been built that suits the Schlegel family."

"What! Have you come up determined not to deal?"

"Not exactly."

"Not exactly? In that case let's be starting."

She lingered to admire the motor, which was new, and a fairer creature than the vermilion giant that had borne Aunt Juley to her doom three years before.

"Presumably it's very beautiful," she said. "How do you like it, Crane?"

"Come, let's be starting," repeated her host. "How on earth did you know that my chauffeur was called Crane?"

"Why, I know Crane: I've been for a drive with Evie once. I know that you've got a parlourmaid called Milton. I know all sorts of things."

"Evie!" he echoed in injured tones. "You won't see her. She's gone out with Cahill. It's no fun, I can tell you, being left so much alone. I've got my work all day—indeed, a great deal too much of it—but when I come home in the evening, I tell you, I can't stand the house."

"In my absurd way, I'm lonely too," Margaret replied. "It's heart-breaking to leave one's old home. I scarcely remember anything before Wickham Place, and Helen and Tibby were born there. Helen says——"

"You, too, feel lonely?"

"Horribly. Hullo, Parliament's back!"

Mr. Wilcox glanced at Parliament contemptuously. The more important ropes of life lay elsewhere. "Yes, they are talking again," said he. "But you were going to say——"

"Only some rubbish about furniture. Helen says it alone endures while men and houses perish, and that in the end the world will be a desert of chairs and sofas—just imagine it!—rolling through infinity with no one to sit upon them."

"Your sister always likes her little joke."

"She says 'Yes,' my brother says 'No,' to Ducie Street. It's no fun helping us, Mr. Wilcox, I assure you."

"You are not as unpractical as you pretend. I shall never believe it."

Margaret laughed. But she was—quite as unpractical. She could not concentrate on details. Parliament, the Thames, the irresponsive chauffeur, would flash into the field of house-hunting, and all demand some comment or response. It is impossible to see modern life steadily and see it whole, and she had chosen to see it whole. Mr. Wilcox saw steadily. He never bothered over the mysterious or the private. The Thames might run inland from the sea, the chauffeur might conceal all passion and philosophy beneath his unhealthy skin. They knew their own business, and he knew his.

Yet she liked being with him. He was not a rebuke, but a stimulus, and banished morbidity. Some twenty years her senior, he preserved a gift that she supposed herself to have already lost—not youth's creative power, but its self-confidence and optimism. He was so sure that it was a very pleasant world. His complexion was robust, his hair had receded but not thinned, the thick moustache and the eyes that Helen had compared to brandy-balls had an agreeable menace in them, whether they were turned towards the slums or towards the stars. Some day—in the millennium—there may be no need for his type. At present, homage is due to it from those who think themselves superior, and who possibly are.

"At all events you responded to my telegram promptly," he remarked.

"Oh, even I know a good thing when I see it."

"I'm glad you don't despise the goods of this world."

"Heavens, no! Only idiots and prigs do that."

"I am glad, very glad," he repeated, suddenly softening and turning to her, as if the remark had pleased him. "There is so much cant talked in would-be intellectual circles. I am glad you don't share it. Self-denial is all very well as a means of strengthening the character. But I can't stand those people who run down comforts. They have usually some axe to grind. Can you?"

"Comforts are of two kinds," said Margaret, who was keeping herself in hand—"those we can share with others, like fire, weather, or music; and those we can't—food, for instance. It depends."

"I mean reasonable comforts, of course. I shouldn't like to think that you——" He bent nearer; the sentence died unfinished. Margaret's head turned very stupid, and the inside of it seemed to revolve like the beacon in a lighthouse. He did not kiss her, for the hour was half-past twelve, and the car was passing by the stables of Buckingham Palace. But the atmosphere was so charged with emotion that people only seemed to exist on her account, and she was surprised that Crane did not realize this, and turn round. Idiot though she might be, surely Mr. Wilcox was more—how should one put it?—more psychological than usual. Always a good judge of character for business purposes, he seemed this afternoon to enlarge his field, and to note qualities outside neatness, obedience, and decision.

"I want to go over the whole house," she announced when they arrived. "As soon as I get back to Swanage, which will be to-morrow afternoon, I'll talk it over once more with Helen and Tibby, and wire you 'yes' or 'no.'"

"Right. The dining-room." and they began their survey.

The dining-room was big, but over-furnished. Chelsea would have moaned aloud. Mr. Wilcox had eschewed those decorative schemes that wince, and relent, and refrain, and achieve beauty by sacrificing comfort and pluck. After so much self-colour and self-denial, Margaret viewed with relief the sumptuous dado, the frieze, the gilded wall-paper, amid whose foliage parrots sang. It would never do with her own furniture, but those heavy chairs, that immense sideboard loaded with presentation plate, stood up against its pressure like men. The room suggested men, and Margaret, keen to derive the modern capitalist from the warriors and hunters of the past, saw it as an ancient guest-hall, where the lord sat at meat among his thanes. Even the Bible—the Dutch Bible that Charles had brought back from the Boer War—fell into position. Such a room admitted loot.

"Now the entrance-hall."

The entrance-hall was paved.

"Here we fellows smoke."

We fellows smoked in chairs of maroon leather. It was as if a motor-car had spawned. "Oh, jolly!" said Margaret, sinking into one of them.

"You do like it?" he said, fixing his eyes on her upturned face, and surely betraying an almost intimate note. "It's all rubbish not making oneself comfortable. Isn't it?"

"Ye-es. Semi-rubbish. Are those Cruikshanks?"

"Gillrays. Shall we go on upstairs?"

"Does all this furniture come from Howards End?"

"The Howards End furniture has all gone to Oniton."

"Does—— However, I'm concerned with the house, not the furniture. How big is this smoking-room?"

"Thirty by fifteen. No, wait a minute. Fifteen and a half."

"Ah, well. Mr. Wilcox, aren't you ever amused at the solemnity with which we middle classes approach the subject of houses?"

They proceeded to the drawing-room. Chelsea managed better here. It was sallow and ineffective. One could visualize the ladies withdrawing to it, while their lords discussed life's realities below, to the accompaniment of cigars. Had Mrs. Wilcox's drawing-room looked thus at Howards End? Just as this thought entered Margaret's brain, Mr. Wilcox did ask her to be his wife, and the knowledge that she had been right so overcame her that she nearly fainted.

But the proposal was not to rank among the world's great love scenes.

"Miss Schlegel"—his voice was firm—"I have had you up on false pretences. I want to speak about a much more serious matter than a house."

Margaret almost answered: "I know——"

"Could you be induced to share my—is it probable——"

"Oh, Mr. Wilcox!" she interrupted, holding the piano and averting her eyes. "I see, I see. I will write to you afterwards if I may."

He began to stammer. "Miss Schlegel—Margaret—you don't understand."

"Oh yes! Indeed, yes!" said Margaret.

"I am asking you to be my wife."

So deep already was her sympathy, that when he said, "I am asking you to be my wife," she made herself give a little start. She must show surprise if he expected it. An immense joy came over her. It was indescribable. It had nothing to do with humanity, and most resembled the all-pervading happiness of fine weather. Fine weather is due to the sun, but Margaret could think of no central radiance here. She stood in his drawing-room happy, and longing to give happiness. On leaving him she realized that the central radiance had been love.

"You aren't offended, Miss Schlegel?"

"How could I be offended?"

There was a moment's pause. He was anxious to get rid of her, and she knew it. She had too much intuition to look at him as he struggled for possessions that money cannot buy. He desired comradeship and affection, but he feared them, and she, who had taught herself only to desire, and could have clothed the struggle with beauty, held back, and hesitated with him.

"Good-bye," she continued. "You will have a letter from me—I am going back to Swanage to-morrow."

"Thank you."

"Good-bye, and it's you I thank."

"I may order the motor round, mayn't I?"

"That would be most kind."

"I wish I had written instead. Ought I to have written?"

"Not at all."

"There's just one question———"

She shook her head. He looked a little bewildered, and they parted.

They parted without shaking hands: she had kept the interview, for his sake, in tints of the quietest grey. Yet she thrilled with happiness ere she reached her own house. Others had loved her in the past, if one may apply to their brief desires so grave a word, but those others had been "ninnies"—young men who had nothing to do, old men who could find nobody better. And she had often "loved," too, but only so far as the facts of sex demanded: mere yearnings for the masculine, to be dismissed for what they were worth, with a smile. Never before had her personality been touched. She was not young or very rich, and it amazed her that a man of any standing should take her seriously. As she sat trying to do accounts in her empty house, amidst beautiful pictures and noble books, waves of emotion broke, as if a tide of passion was flowing through the night air. She shook her head, tried to concentrate her attention, and failed. In vain did she repeat: "But I've been through this sort of thing before." She had never been through it; the big machinery, as opposed to the little, had been set in motion, and the idea that Mr. Wilcox loved, obsessed her before she came to love him in return.

She would come to no decision yet. "Oh, sir, this is so sudden"—that prudish phrase exactly expressed her when her time came. Premonitions are not preparation. She must examine more closely her own nature and his; she must talk it over judicially with Helen. It had been a strange love-scene—the central radiance unacknowledged from first to last. She, in his place, would have said "Ich liebe dich," but perhaps it was not his habit to open the heart. He might have done it if she had pressed him—as a matter of duty, perhaps; England expects every man to open his heart once; but the effort would have jarred him, and never, if she could avoid it, should he lose those defences that he had chosen to raise against the world. He must never be bothered with emotional talk, or with a display of sympathy. He was an elderly man now, and it would be futile and impudent to correct him.

Mrs. Wilcox strayed in and out, ever a welcome ghost; surveying the scene, thought Margaret, without one hint of bitterness.

CHAPTER XIX

If one wanted to show a foreigner England, perhaps the wisest course would be to take him to the final section of the Purbeck Hills, and stand him on their summit, a few miles to the east of Corfe. Then system after system of our island would roll together under his feet. Beneath him is the valley of the Frome, and all the wild lands that come tossing down from Dorchester, black and gold, to mirror their gorse in the expanses of Poole. The valley of the Stour is beyond, unaccountable stream, dirty at Blandford,

pure at Wimborne—the Stour, sliding out of fat fields, to marry
the Avon beneath the tower of Christchurch. The valley of the
Avon—invisible, but far to the north the trained eye may see
Clearbury Ring that guards it, and the imagination may leap
beyond that on to Salisbury Plain itself, and beyond the Plain to
all the glorious downs of Central England. Nor is Suburbia
absent. Bournemouth's ignoble coast cowers to the right, herald-
ing the pine-trees that mean, for all their beauty, red houses, and
the Stock Exchange, and extend to the gates of London itself. So
tremendous is the City's trail! But the cliffs of Freshwater it shall
never touch, and the island will guard the Island's purity till the
end of time. Seen from the west, the Wight is beautiful beyond all
laws of beauty. It is as if a fragment of England floated forward to
greet the foreigner—chalk of our chalk, turf of our turf, epitome
of what will follow. And behind the fragment lies Southampton,
hostess to the nations, and Portsmouth, a latent fire, and all
around it, with double and treble collision of tides, swirls the sea.
How many villages appear in this view! How many castles! How
many churches, vanished or triumphant! How many ships, railways, and roads! What incredible variety of men working beneath
that lucent sky to what final end! The reason fails, like a wave on
the Swanage beach; the imagination swells, spreads, and deepens,
until it becomes geographic and encircles England.

So Frieda Mosebach, now Frau Architect Liesecke, and mother
to her husband's baby, was brought up to these heights to be
impressed, and, after a prolonged gaze, she said that the hills were
more swelling here than in Pomerania, which was true, but did
not seem to Mrs. Munt apposite. Poole Harbour was dry, which
led her to praise the absence of muddy foreshore at Friedrich Wil-
helms Bar, Rügen, where beech-trees hang over the tideless Baltic,
and cows may contemplate the brine. Rather unhealthy Mrs.
Munt thought this would be, water being safer when it moved
about.

"And your English lakes—Vindermere, Grasmere—are they,
then, unhealthy?"

"No, Frau Liesecke; but that is because they are fresh water, and different. Salt water ought to have tides, and go up and down a great deal, or else it smells. Look, for instance, at an aquarium."

"An aquarium? Oh, *Meesis* Munt, you mean to tell me that fresh aquariums stink less than salt? Why, then Victor, my brother-in-law, collected many tadpoles——"

"You are not to say 'stink,'" interrupted Helen; "at least, you may say it, but you must pretend you are being funny while you say it."

"Then 'smell.' And the mud of your Poole down there—does it not smell, or may I say 'stink, ha, ha'?"

"There always has been mud in Poole Harbour," said Mrs. Munt, with a slight frown. "The rivers bring it down, and a most valuable oyster-fishery depends upon it."

"Yes, that is so," conceded Frieda; and another international incident was closed.

"'Bournemouth is,'" resumed their hostess, quoting a local rhyme to which she was much attached—"'Bournemouth is, Poole was, and Swanage is to be the most important town of all and biggest of the three.' Now, Frau Liesecke, I have shown you Bournemouth, and I have shown you Poole, so let us walk backward a little, and look down again at Swanage."

"Aunt Juley, wouldn't that be Meg's train?"

A tiny puff of smoke had been circling the harbour, and now was bearing southwards towards them over the black and the gold.

"Oh, dearest Margaret, I do hope she won't be overtired."

"Oh, I do wonder—I do wonder whether she's taken the house."

"I hope she hasn't been hasty."

"So do I—oh, *so* do I."

"Will it be as beautiful as Wickham Place?" Frieda asked.

"I should think it would. Trust Mr. Wilcox for doing himself proud. All those Ducie Street houses are beautiful in their modern way, and I can't think why he doesn't keep on with it. But it's really for Evie that he went there, and now that Evie's going to be married——"

"Ah!"

"You've never seen Miss Wilcox, Frieda. How absurdly matrimonial you are!"

"But sister to that Paul?"

"Yes."

"And to that Charles," said Mrs. Munt with feeling. "Oh, Helen, Helen, what a time that was!"

Helen laughed. "Meg and I haven't got such tender hearts. If there's a chance of a cheap house, we go for it."

"Now look, Frau Liesecke, at my niece's train. You see, it is coming towards us—coming, coming; and, when it gets to Corfe, it will actually go *through* the downs, on which we are standing, so that, if we walk over, as I suggested, and look down on Swanage, we shall see it coming on the other side. Shall we?"

Frieda assented, and in a few minutes they had crossed the ridge and exchanged the greater view for the lesser. Rather a dull valley lay below, backed by the slope of the coastward downs. They were looking across the Isle of Purbeck and on to Swanage, soon to be the most important town of all, and ugliest of the three. Margaret's train reappeared as promised, and was greeted with approval by her aunt. It came to a standstill in the middle distance, and there it had been planned that Tibby should meet her, and drive her, and a tea-basket, up to join them.

"You see," continued Helen to her cousin, "the Wilcoxes collect houses as your Victor collects tadpoles. They have, one, Ducie Street; two, Howards End, where my great rumpus was; three, a country seat in Shropshire; four, Charles has a house in Hilton; and five, another near Epsom; and six, Evie will have a house when she marries, and probably a pied-à-terre in the country—which makes seven. Oh yes, and Paul a hut in Africa makes eight. I wish we could get Howards End. That was something like a dear little house! Didn't you think so, Aunt Juley?"

"I had too much to do, dear, to look at it," said Mrs. Munt, with a gracious dignity. "I had everything to settle and explain, and Charles Wilcox to keep in his place besides. It isn't likely

I should remember much. I just remember having lunch in your bedroom."

"Yes, so do I. But, oh dear, dear, how dreadful it all seems! And in the autumn there began that anti-Pauline movement—you, and Frieda, and Meg, and Mrs. Wilcox, all obsessed with the idea that I might yet marry Paul."

"You yet may," said Frieda despondently.

Helen shook her head. "The Great Wilcox Peril will never return. If I'm certain of anything it's of that."

"One is certain of nothing but the truth of one's own emotions."

The remark fell damply on the conversation. But Helen slipped her arm round her cousin, somehow liking her the better for making it. It was not an original remark, nor had Frieda appropriated it passionately, for she had a patriotic rather than a philosophic mind. Yet it betrayed that interest in the universal which the average Teuton possesses and the average Englishman does not. It was, however illogically, the good, the beautiful, the true, as opposed to the respectable, the pretty, the adequate. It was a landscape of Böcklin's beside a landscape of Leader's, strident and ill-considered, but quivering into supernatural life. It sharpened idealism, stirred the soul. It may have been a bad preparation for what followed.

"Look!" cried Aunt Juley, hurrying away from generalities over the narrow summit of the down. "Stand where I stand, and you will see the pony-cart coming. I see the pony-cart coming."

They stood and saw the pony-cart coming. Margaret and Tibby were presently seen coming in it. Leaving the outskirts of Swanage, it drove for a little through the budding lanes, and then began the ascent.

"Have you got the house?" they shouted, long before she could possibly hear.

Helen ran down to meet her. The highroad passed over a saddle, and a track went thence at right angles along the ridge of the down.

"Have you got the house?"

Margaret shook her head.

"Oh, what a nuisance! So we're as we were?"

"Not exactly."

She got out, looking tired.

"Some mystery," said Tibby. "We are to be enlightened presently."

Margaret came close up to her and whispered that she had had a proposal of marriage from Mr. Wilcox.

Helen was amused. She opened the gate on to the downs so that her brother might lead the pony through. "It's just like a widower," she remarked. "They've cheek enough for anything, and invariably select one of their first wife's friends."

Margaret's face flashed despair.

"That type——" She broke off with a cry. "Meg, not anything wrong with you?"

"Wait one minute," said Margaret, whispering always.

"But you've never conceivably—you've never——" She pulled herself together. "Tibby, hurry up through; I can't hold this gate indefinitely. Aunt Juley! I say, Aunt Juley, make the tea, will you, and Frieda; we've got to talk houses, and 'll come on afterwards." And then, turning her face to her sister's, she burst into tears.

Margaret was stupefied. She heard herself saying, "Oh, really——" She felt herself touched with a hand that trembled.

"Don't," sobbed Helen, "don't, don't, Meg, don't!" She seemed incapable of saying any other word. Margaret, trembling herself, led her forward up the road, till they strayed through another gate on to the down.

"Don't, don't do such a thing! I tell you not to—don't! I know —don't!"

"What do you know?"

"Panic and emptiness," sobbed Helen. "Don't!"

Then Margaret thought, "Helen is a little selfish. I have never behaved like this when there has seemed a chance of her marrying," She said: "But we would still see each other very often, and you——"

"It's not a thing like that," sobbed Helen. And she broke right away and wandered distractedly upwards, stretching her hands towards the view and crying.

"What's happened to you?" called Margaret, following through the wind that gathers at sundown on the northern slopes of hills. "But it's stupid!" And suddenly stupidity seized her, and the immense landscape was blurred. But Helen turned back.

"Meg——"

"I don't know what's happened to either of us," said Margaret, wiping her eyes. "We must both have gone mad." Then Helen wiped hers, and they even laughed a little.

"Look here, sit down."

"All right; I'll sit down if you'll sit down."

"There. (One kiss.) Now, whatever, whatever is the matter?"

"I do mean what I said. Don't; it wouldn't do."

"Oh, Helen, stop saying 'don't'! It's ignorant. It's as if your head wasn't out of the slime. 'Don't' is probably what Mrs. Bast says all day to Mr. Bast."

Helen was silent.

"Well?"

"Tell me about it first, and meanwhile perhaps I'll have got my head out of the slime."

"That's better. Well, where shall I begin? When I arrived at Waterloo—no, I'll go back before that, because I'm anxious you should know everything from the first. The 'first' was about ten days ago. It was the day Mr. Bast came to tea and lost his temper. I was defending him, and Mr. Wilcox became jealous about me, however slightly. I thought it was the involuntary thing, which men can't help any more than we can. You know—at least, I know in my own case—when a man has said to me, 'So-and-so's a pretty girl,' I am seized with a momentary sourness against So-and-so, and long to tweak her ear. It's a tiresome feeling, but not an important one, and one easily manages it. But it wasn't only this in Mr. Wilcox's case, I gather now."

"Then you love him?"

Margaret considered. "It is wonderful knowing that a real man cares for you," she said. "The mere fact of that grows more tremendous. Remember, I've known and liked him steadily for nearly three years."

"But loved him?"

Margaret peered into her past. It is pleasant to analyze feelings while they are still only feelings, and unembodied in the social fabric. With her arm round Helen, and her eyes shifting over the view, as if this country or that could reveal the secret of her own heart, she meditated honestly, and said, "No."

"But you will?"

"Yes," said Margaret, "of that I'm pretty sure. Indeed, I began the moment he spoke to me."

"And have settled to marry him?"

"I had, but am wanting a long talk about it now. What *is* it against him, Helen? You must try and say."

Helen, in her turn, looked outwards. "It is ever since Paul," she said finally.

"But what has Mr. Wilcox to do with Paul?"

"But he was there, they were all there that morning when I came down to breakfast, and saw that Paul was frightened—the man who loved me frightened and all his paraphernalia fallen, so that I knew it was impossible, because personal relations are the important thing for ever and ever, and not this outer life of telegrams and anger."

She poured the sentence forth in one breath, but her sister understood it, because it touched on thoughts that were familiar between them.

"That's foolish. In the first place, I disagree about the outer life. Well, we've often argued that. The real point is that there is the widest gulf between my love-making and yours. Yours was romance; mine will be prose. I'm not running it down—a very good kind of prose, but well considered, well thought out. For instance, I know all Mr. Wilcox's faults. He's afraid of emotion. He cares too much about success, too little about the past. His sympathy lacks poetry, and so isn't sympathy really. I'd even say"—she looked at the shining lagoons—"that, spiritually, he's not as honest as I am. Doesn't that satisfy you?"

"No, it doesn't," said Helen. "It makes me feel worse and worse. You must be mad."

Margaret made a movement of irritation.

"I don't intend him, or any man or any woman, to be all my life—good heavens, no! There are heaps of things in me that he doesn't, and shall never, understand."

Thus she spoke before the wedding ceremony and the physical union, before the astonishing glass shade had fallen that interposes between married couples and the world. She was to keep her independence more than do most women as yet. Marriage was to alter her fortunes rather than her character, and she was not far wrong in boasting that she understood her future husband. Yet he did alter her character—a little. There was an unforeseen surprise, a cessation of the winds and odours of life, a social pressure that would have her think conjugally.

"So with him," she continued. "There are heaps of things in him—more especially things that he does—that will always be hidden from me. He has all those public qualities which you so despise and enable all this——" She waved her hand at the landscape, which confirmed anything. "If Wilcoxes hadn't worked and died in England for thousands of years, you and I couldn't sit here without having our throats cut. There would be no trains, no ships to carry us literary people about in, no fields even. Just savagery. No—perhaps not even that. Without their spirit life might never have moved out of protoplasm. More and more do I refuse to draw my income and sneer at those who guarantee it. There are times when it seems to me——"

"And to me, and to all women. So one kissed Paul."

"That's brutal," said Margaret. "Mine is an absolutely different case. I've thought things out."

"It makes no difference thinking things out. They come to the same."

"Rubbish!"

There was a long silence, during which the tide returned into Poole Harbour. "One would lose something," murmured Helen, apparently to herself. The water crept over the mud-flats towards the gorse and the blackened heather. Branksea Island lost its immense foreshores, and became a sombre episode of trees. Frome was forced inward towards Dorchester, Stour against Wimborne, Avon towards Salisbury, and over the immense displacement the sun presided, leading it to triumph ere he sank to rest. England was alive, throbbing through all her estuaries, crying for joy through the mouths of all her gulls, and the north wind, with contrary motion, blew stronger against her rising seas. What did it mean? For what end are her fair complexities, her changes of soil, her sinuous coast? Does she belong to those who have moulded her and made her feared by other lands, or to those who have added nothing to her power, but have somehow seen her, seen the whole island at once, lying as a jewel in a silver sea, sailing as a ship of souls, with all the brave world's fleet accompanying her towards eternity?

CHAPTER XX

Margaret had often wondered at the disturbance that takes place in the world's waters, when Love, who seems so tiny a pebble, slips in. Whom does Love concern beyond the beloved and the lover? Yet his impact deluges a hundred shores. No doubt the disturbance is really the spirit of the generations, welcoming the new generation, and chafing against the ultimate Fate, who holds all the seas in the palm of her hand. But Love cannot understand this. He cannot comprehend another's infinity; he is conscious only of his own—flying sunbeam, falling rose, pebble that asks for one quiet plunge below the fretting interplay of space and time. He knows that he will survive at the end of things, and be gathered by Fate as a jewel from the slime, and be handed with admiration round the assembly of the gods. "Men did produce this," they will say, and, saying, they will give men immortality. But meanwhile—what agitations meanwhile! The foundations of Property and Propriety are laid bare, twin rocks; Family Pride flounders to the surface, puffing and blowing, and refusing to be comforted; Theology, vaguely ascetic, gets up a nasty ground swell. Then the lawyers are aroused—cold brood—and creep out of their holes. They do what they can; they tidy up Property and Propriety, reassure Theology and Family Pride. Half-guineas are poured on the troubled waters, the lawyers creep back, and, if all has gone well, Love joins one man and woman together in Matrimony.

Margaret had expected the disturbance, and was not irritated by it. For a sensitive woman she had steady nerves, and could bear with the incongruous and the grotesque; and, besides, there was nothing excessive about her love-affair. Good-humour was the dominant note of her relations with Mr. Wilcox, or, as I must now call him, Henry. Henry did not encourage romance, and she was no girl to fidget for it. An acquaintance had become a lover, might become a husband, but would retain all that she had noted in the acquaintance; and love must confirm an old relation rather than reveal a new one.

In this spirit she promised to marry him.

He was in Swanage on the morrow, bearing the engagement-ring. They greeted one another with a hearty cordiality that impressed Aunt Juley. Henry dined at The Bays, but had engaged a bedroom in the principal hotel: he was one of those men who know the principal hotel by instinct. After dinner he asked Margaret if she wouldn't care for a turn on the Parade. She accepted, and could not repress a little tremor; it would be her first real love scene. But as she put on her hat she burst out laughing. Love was so unlike the article served up in books: the joy, though genuine, was different; the mystery an unexpected mystery. For one thing, Mr. Wilcox still seemed a stranger.

For a time they talked about the ring; then she said:

"Do you remember the Embankment at Chelsea? It can't be ten days ago."

"Yes," he said, laughing. "And you and your sister were head and ears deep in some Quixotic scheme. Ah well!"

"I little thought then, certainly. Did you?"

"I don't know about that; I shouldn't like to say."

"Why, was it earlier?" she cried. "Did you think of me this way earlier! How extraordinarily interesting, Henry! Tell me."

But Henry had no intention of telling. Perhaps he could not have told, for his mental states became obscure as soon as he had passed through them. He misliked the very word "interesting," connoting it with wasted energy and even with morbidity. Hard facts were enough for him.

"I didn't think of it," she pursued. "No; when you spoke to me in the drawing-room, that was practically the first. It was all so different from what it's supposed to be. On the stage, or in books, a proposal is—how shall I put it?—a full-blown affair, a kind of bouquet; it loses its literal meaning. But in life a proposal really is a proposal——"

"By the way——"

"—a suggestion, a seed," she concluded; and the thought flew away into darkness.

"I was thinking, if you didn't mind, that we ought to spend this evening in a business talk; there will be so much to settle."

"I think so too. Tell me, in the first place, how did you get on with Tibby?"

"With your brother?"

"Yes, during cigarettes."

"Oh, very well."

"I am so glad," she answered, a little surprised. "What did you talk about? Me, presumably."

"About Greece too."

"Greece was a very good card, Henry. Tibby's only a boy still, and one has to pick and choose subjects a little. Well done."

"I was telling him I have shares in a currant-farm near Calamata."

"What a delightful thing to have shares in! Can't we go there for our honeymoon?"

"What to do?"

"To eat the currants. And isn't there marvellous scenery?"

"Moderately, but it's not the kind of place one could possibly go to with a lady."

"Why not?"

"No hotels."

"Some ladies do without hotels. Are you aware that Helen and I have walked alone over the Apennines, with our luggage on our backs?"

"I wasn't aware, and, if I can manage it, you will never do such a thing again."

She said more gravely: "You haven't found time for a talk with Helen yet, I suppose?"

"No."

"Do, before you go. I am so anxious you two should be friends."

"Your sister and I have always hit it off," he said negligently. "But we're drifting away from our business. Let me begin at the beginning. You know that Evie is going to marry Percy Cahill."

"Dolly's uncle."

"Exactly. The girl's madly in love with him. A very good sort of fellow, but he demands—and rightly—a suitable provision with her. And in the second place, you will naturally understand, there is Charles. Before leaving town, I wrote Charles a very careful letter. You see, he has an increasing family and increasing expenses, and the I. and W.A. is nothing particular just now, though capable of development."

"Poor fellow!" murmured Margaret, looking out to sea, and not understanding.

"Charles being the elder son, some day Charles will have Howards End; but I am anxious, in my own happiness, not to be unjust to others."

"Of course not," she began, and then gave a little cry. "You mean money. How stupid I am! Of course not!"

Oddly enough, he winced a little at the word. "Yes. Money, since you put it so frankly. I am determined to be just to all—just to you, just to them. I am determined that my children shall have no case against me."

"Be generous to them," she said sharply. "Bother justice!"

"I am determined—and have already written to Charles to that effect——"

"But how much have you got?"

"What?"

"How much have you a year? I've six hundred."

"My income?"

"Yes. We must begin with how much you have, before we can settle how much you can give Charles. Justice, and even generosity, depend on that."

"I must say you're a downright young woman," he observed, patting her arm and laughing a little. "What a question to spring on a fellow!"

"Don't you know your income? Or don't you want to tell it me?"

"I——"

"That's all right"—now she patted him—"don't tell me. I don't want to know. I can do the sum just as well by proportion. Divide your income into ten parts. How many parts would you give to Evie, how many to Charles, how many to Paul?"

"The fact is, my dear, I hadn't any intention of bothering you with details. I only wanted to let you know that—well, that something must be done for the others, and you've understood me perfectly, so let's pass on to the next point."

"Yes, we've settled that," said Margaret, undisturbed by his strategic blunderings. "Go ahead; give away all you can, bearing in mind. I've a clear six hundred. What a mercy it is to have all this money about one."

"We've none too much, I assure you; you're marrying a poor man."

"Helen wouldn't agree with me here," she continued. "Helen daren't slang the rich, being rich herself, but she would like to. There's an odd notion, that I haven't yet got hold of, running about at the back of her brain, that poverty is somehow 'real.'

She dislikes all organization, and probably confuses wealth with the technique of wealth. Sovereigns in a stocking wouldn't bother her; cheques do. Helen is too relentless. One can't deal in her high-handed manner with the world."

"There's this other point, and then I must go back to my hotel and write some letters. What's to be done now about the house in Ducie Street?"

"Keep it on—at least, it depends. When do you want to marry me?"

She raised her voice, as too often, and some youths, who were also taking the evening air, overheard her. "Getting a bit hot, eh?" said one. Mr. Wilcox turned on them, and said sharply, "I say!" There was silence. "Take care I don't report you to the police." They moved away quietly enough, but were only biding their time, and the rest of the conversation was punctuated by peals of ungovernable laughter.

Lowering his voice and infusing a hint of reproof into it, he said: "Evie will probably be married in September. We could scarcely think of anything before then."

"The earlier the nicer, Henry. Females are not supposed to say such things, but the earlier the nicer."

"How about September for us too?" he asked, rather dryly.

"Right. Shall we go to Ducie Street ourselves in September? Or shall we try to bounce Helen and Tibby into it? That's rather an idea. They are so unbusinesslike, we could make them do anything by judicious management. Look here—yes. We'll do that. And we ourselves could live at Howards End or Shropshire."

He blew out his cheeks. "Heavens! how you women do fly round! My head's in a whirl. Point by point, Margaret. Howards End's impossible. I let it to Hamar Bryce on a three years' agreement last March. Don't you remember? Oniton. Well, that is much, much too far away to rely on entirely. You will be able to be down there entertaining a certain amount, but we must have a house within easy reach of Town. Only Ducie Street has huge drawbacks. There's a mews behind."

Margaret could not help laughing. It was the first she had heard of the mews behind Ducie Street. When she was a possible tenant it had suppressed itself, not consciously, but automatically. The breezy Wilcox manner, though genuine, lacked the clearness of vision that is imperative for truth. When Henry lived in Ducie Street he remembered the mews; when he tried to let he forgot it; and if anyone had remarked that the mews must be either there or not, he would have felt annoyed, and afterwards have found some opportunity of stigmatizing the speaker as academic. So does my grocer stigmatize me when I complain of the quality of his sultanas, and he answers in one breath that they are the best sultanas, and how can I expect the best sultanas at that price? It is a flaw inherent in the business mind, and Margaret may do well to be tender to it, considering all that the business mind has done for England.

"Yes, in summer especially, the mews is a serious nuisance. The smoking-room, too, is an abominable little den. The house opposite has been taken by operatic people. Ducie Street's going down, it's my private opinion."

"How sad! It's only a few years since they built those pretty houses."

"Shows things are moving. Good for trade."

"I hate this continual flux of London. It is an epitome of us at our worst—eternal formlessness; all the qualities, good, bad, and indifferent, streaming away—streaming, streaming for ever. That's why I dread it so. I mistrust rivers, even in scenery. Now, the sea——"

"High tide, yes."

"Hoy toid"—from the promenading youths.

"And these are the men to whom we give the vote," observed Mr. Wilcox, omitting to add that they were also the men to whom he gave work as clerks—work that scarcely encouraged them to grow into other men. "However, they have their own lives and interests. Let's get on."

He turned as he spoke, and prepared to see her back to The

Bays. The business was over. His hotel was in the opposite direction, and if he accompanied her his letters would be late for the post. She implored him not to come, but he was obdurate.

"A nice beginning, if your aunt saw you slip in alone!"

"But I always do go about alone. Considering I've walked over the Apennines, it's common sense. You will make me so angry. I don't the least take it as a compliment."

He laughed, and lit a cigar. "It isn't meant as a compliment, my dear. I just won't have you going about in the dark. Such people about too! It's dangerous."

"Can't I look after myself? I do wish——"

"Come along, Margaret; no wheedling."

A younger woman might have resented his masterly ways, but Margaret had too firm a grip of life to make a fuss. She was, in her own way, as masterly. If he was a fortress she was a mountain peak, whom all might tread, but whom the snows made nightly virginal. Disdaining the heroic outfit, excitable in her methods, garrulous, episodical, shrill, she misled her lover much as she had misled her aunt. He mistook her fertility for weakness. He supposed her "as clever as they make 'em," but no more, not realizing that she was penetrating to the depths of his soul, and approving of what she found there.

And if insight were sufficient, if the inner life were the whole of life, their happiness had been assured.

They walked ahead briskly. The parade and the road after it were well lighted, but it was darker in Aunt Juley's garden. As they were going up by the side-paths, through some rhododendrons, Mr. Wilcox, who was in front, said "Margaret" rather huskily, turned, dropped his cigar, and took her in his arms.

She was startled, and nearly screamed, but recovered herself at once, and kissed with genuine love the lips that were pressed against her own. It was their first kiss, and when it was over he saw her safely to the door and rang the bell for her, but disappeared into the night before the maid answered it. On looking back, the incident displeased her. It was so isolated. Nothing in their previous

conversation had heralded it, and, worse still, no tenderness had
ensued. If a man cannot lead up to passion he can at all events lead
down from it, and she had hoped, after her complaisance, for some
interchange of gentle words. But he had hurried away as if
ashamed, and for an instant she was reminded of Helen and Paul.

CHAPTER XXI

Charles had just been scolding his Dolly. She deserved the scolding, and had bent before it, but her head, though bloody, was
unsubdued, and her chirrupings began to mingle with his retreating thunder.

"You've woken the baby. I knew you would. (Rum-ti-foo, Rack-
ety-tackety-Tompkin!) I'm not responsible for what Uncle Percy
does, nor for anybody else or anything, so there!"

"Who asked him while I was away? Who asked my sister down
to meet him? Who sent them out in the motor day after day?"

"Charles, that reminds me of some poem."

"Does it indeed? We shall all be dancing to a very different
music presently. Miss Schlegel has fairly got us on toast."

"I could simply scratch that woman's eyes out, and to say it's
my fault is most unfair."

"It's your fault, and five months ago you admitted it."

"I didn't."

"You did."

"Tootle, tootle, playing on the pootle!" exclaimed Dolly, suddenly devoting herself to the child.

"It's all very well to turn the conversation, but father would
have never dreamt of marrying as long as Evie was there to make
him comfortable. But you must needs start match-making.
Besides, Cahill's too old."

"Of course, if you're going to be rude to Uncle Percy——"

"Miss Schlegel always meant to get hold of Howards End, and
thanks to you, she's got it."

"I call the way you twist things round and make them hang together most unfair. You couldn't have been nastier if you'd caught me flirting. Could he, diddums?"

"We're in a bad hole, and must make the best of it. I shall answer the pater's letter civilly. He's evidently anxious to do the decent thing. But I do not intend to forget these Schlegels in a hurry. As long as they're on their best behaviour—Dolly, are you listening?—we'll behave, too. But if I find them giving themselves airs, or monopolizing my father, or at all ill-treating him, or worrying him with their artistic beastliness, I intend to put my foot down, yes, firmly. Taking my mother's place! Heaven knows what poor old Paul will say when the news reaches him."

The interlude closes. It has taken place in Charles's garden at Hilton. He and Dolly are sitting in deck-chairs, and their motor is regarding them placidly from its garage across the lawn. A short-frocked edition of Charles also regards them placidly; a perambulator edition is squeaking; a third edition is expected shortly. Nature is turning out Wilcoxes in this peaceful abode, so that they may inherit the earth.

CHAPTER XXII

Margaret greeted her lord with peculiar tenderness on the morrow. Mature as he was, she might yet be able to help him to the building of the rainbow bridge that should connect the prose in us with the passion. Without it we are meaningless fragments, half monks, half beasts, unconnected arches that have never joined into a man. With it love is born, and alights on the highest curve, glowing against the grey, sober against the fire. Happy the man who sees from either aspect the glory of these outspread wings. The roads of his soul lie clear, and he and his friends shall find easy-going.

It was hard-going in the roads of Mr. Wilcox's soul. From boyhood he had neglected them. "I am not a fellow who bothers about my own inside." Outwardly he was cheerful, reliable, and brave; but within, all had reverted to chaos, ruled, so far as it was ruled at all, by an incomplete asceticism. Whether as boy, husband, or widower, he had always the sneaking belief that bodily passion is bad, a belief that is desirable only when held passionately. Religion had confirmed him. The words that were read aloud on Sunday to him and to other respectable men were the words that had once kindled the souls of St. Catharine and St. Francis into a white-hot hatred of the carnal. He could not be as the saints and love the Infinite with a seraphic ardour, but he could be a little ashamed of loving a wife. 'Amabat, amare timebat.' And it was here that Margaret hoped to help him.

It did not seem so difficult. She need trouble him with no gift of her own. She would only point out the salvation that was latent in his own soul, and in the soul of every man. Only connect! That was the whole of her sermon. Only connect the prose and the passion, and both will be exalted, and human love will be seen at its height. Live in fragments no longer. Only connect, and the beast and the monk, robbed of the isolation that is life to either, will die.

Nor was the message difficult to give. It need not take the form of a good "talking." By quiet indications the bridge would be built and span their lives with beauty.

But she failed. For there was one quality in Henry for which she was never prepared, however much she reminded herself of it: his obtuseness. He simply did not notice things, and there was no more to be said. He never noticed that Helen and Frieda were hostile, or that Tibby was not interested in currant plantations; he never noticed the lights and shades that exist in the greyest conversation, the finger-posts, the milestones, the collisions, the illimitable views. Once—on another occasion—she scolded him about it. He was puzzled, but replied with a laugh: "My motto is Concentrate. I've no intention of frittering away my strength on that sort of thing." "It isn't frittering away the strength," she protested. "It's enlarging the space in which you may be strong." He answered: "You're a clever little woman, but my motto's Concentrate." And this morning he concentrated with a vengeance.

They met in the rhododendrons of yesterday. In the daylight the bushes were inconsiderable and the path was bright in the morning sun. She was with Helen, who had been ominously quiet since the affair was settled. "Here we all are!" she cried, and took him by one hand, retaining her sister's in the other.

"Here we are. Good-morning, Helen."

Helen replied, "Good-morning, Mr. Wilcox."

"Henry, she has had such a nice letter from the queer, cross boy. Do you remember him? He had a sad moustache, but the back of his head was young."

"I have had a letter too. Not a nice one—I want to talk it over with you;" for Leonard Bast was nothing to him now that she had given him her word; the triangle of sex was broken for ever.

"Thanks to your hint, he's clearing out of the Porphyrion."

"Not a bad business that Porphyrion," he said absently, as he took his own letter out of his pocket.

"Not a *bad*——" she exclaimed, dropping his hand. "Surely, on Chelsea Embankment——"

"Here's our hostess. Good-morning, Mrs. Munt. Fine rhododendrons. Good-morning, Frau Liesecke; we manage to grow flowers in England, don't we?"

"Not a *bad* business?"

"No. My letter's about Howards End. Bryce has been ordered abroad, and wants to sublet it. I am far from sure that I shall give him permission. There was no clause in the agreement. In my opinion, subletting is a mistake. If he can find me another tenant, whom I consider suitable, I may cancel the agreement. Morning, Schlegel. Don't you think that's better than subletting?"

Helen had dropped her hand now, and he had steered her past the whole party to the seaward side of the house. Beneath them was the bourgeois little bay, which must have yearned all through the centuries for just such a watering-place as Swanage to be built on its margin. The waves were colourless, and the Bournemouth steamer gave a further touch of insipidity, drawn up against the pier and hooting wildly for excursionists.

"When there is a sublet I find that damage——"

"Do excuse me, but about the Porphyrion. I don't feel easy—might I just bother you, Henry?"

Her manner was so serious that he stopped, and asked her a little sharply what she wanted.

"You said on Chelsea Embankment, surely, that it was a bad concern, so we advised this clerk to clear out. He writes this morning that he's taken our advice, and now you say it's not a bad concern."

"A clerk who clears out of any concern, good or bad, without securing a berth somewhere else first, is a fool, and I've no pity for him."

"He has not done that. He's going into a bank in Camden Town, he says. The salary's much lower, but he hopes to manage —a branch of Dempster's Bank. Is that all right?"

"Dempster! My goodness me, yes."

"More right than the Porphyrion?"

"Yes, yes, yes; safe as houses—safer."

"Very many thanks. I'm sorry—if you sublet——?"

"If he sublets, I shan't have the same control. In theory there should be no more damage done at Howards End; in practice there will be. Things may be done for which no money can compensate. For instance, I shouldn't want that fine wych-elm spoilt. It hangs ——Margaret, we must go and see the old place some time. It's pretty in its way. We'll motor down and have lunch with Charles."

"I should enjoy that," said Margaret bravely.

"What about next Wednesday?"

"Wednesday? No, I couldn't well do that. Aunt Juley expects us to stop here another week at least."

"But you can give that up now."

"Er—no," said Margaret, after a moment's thought.

"Oh, that'll be all right. I'll speak to her."

"This visit is a high solemnity. My aunt counts on it year after year. She turns the house upside down for us; she invites our special friends—she scarcely knows Frieda, and we can't leave her on her hands. I missed one day, and she would be so hurt if I didn't stay the full ten."

"But I'll say a word to her. Don't you bother."

"Henry, I won't go. Don't bully me."

"You want to see the house, though?"

"Very much—I've heard so much about it, one way or the other. Aren't there pigs' teeth in the wych-elm?"

"*Pigs' teeth?*"

"And you chew the bark for toothache."

"What a rum notion! Of course not!"

"Perhaps I have confused it with some other tree. There are still a great number of sacred trees in England, it seems."

But he left her to intercept Mrs. Munt, whose voice could be heard in the distance: to be intercepted himself by Helen.

"Oh, Mr. Wilcox, about the Porphyrion——" she began, and went scarlet all over her face.

"It's all right," called Margaret, catching them up. "Dempster's Bank's better."

"But I think you told us the Porphyrion was bad, and would smash before Christmas."

"Did I? It was still outside the Tariff Ring, and had to take rotten policies. Lately it came in—safe as houses now."

"In other words, Mr. Bast need never have left it."

"No, the fellow needn't."

"—and needn't have started life elsewhere at a greatly reduced salary."

"He only says 'reduced,'" corrected Margaret, seeing trouble ahead.

"With a man so poor, every reduction must be great. I consider it a deplorable misfortune."

Mr. Wilcox, intent on his business with Mrs. Munt, was going steadily on, but the last remark made him say: "What? What's that? Do you mean that I'm responsible?"

"You're ridiculous, Helen."

"You seem to think——" He looked at his watch. "Let me explain the point to you. It is like this. You seem to assume, when a business concern is conducting a delicate negotiation, it ought to keep the public informed stage by stage. The Porphyrion, according to you, was bound to say, 'I am trying all I can to get into the Tariff Ring. I am not sure that I shall succeed, but it is the only thing that will save me from insolvency, and I am trying.' My dear Helen——"

"Is that your point? A man who had little money has less—that's mine."

"I am grieved for your clerk. But it is all in the day's work. It's part of the battle of life."

"A man who had little money," she repeated, "has less, owing to us. Under these circumstances I do not consider 'the battle of life' a happy expression."

"Oh come, come!" he protested pleasantly. "You're not to blame. No one's to blame."

"Is no one to blame for anything?"

"I wouldn't say that, but you're taking it far too seriously. Who is this fellow?"

"We have told you about the fellow twice already," said Helen. "You have even met the fellow. He is very poor and his wife is an extravagant imbecile. He is capable of better things. We—we, the upper classes—thought we would help him from the height of our superior knowledge—and here's the result!"

He raised his finger. "Now, a word of advice."

"I require no more advice."

"A word of advice. Don't take up that sentimental attitude over the poor. See that she doesn't, Margaret. The poor are poor, and one's sorry for them, but there it is. As civilization moves forward, the shoe is bound to pinch in places, and it's absurd to pretend that anyone is responsible personally. Neither you, nor I, nor my informant, nor the man who informed him, nor the directors of the Porphyrion, are to blame for this clerk's loss of salary. It's just the shoe pinching—no one can help it; and it might easily have been worse."

Helen quivered with indignation.

"By all means subscribe to charities—subscribe to them largely—but don't get carried away by absurd schemes of Social Reform. I see a good deal behind the scenes, and you can take it from me that there is no Social Question—except for a few journalists who try to get a living out of the phrase. There are just rich and poor, as there always have been and always will be. Point me out a time when men have been equal——"

"I didn't say——"

"Point me out a time when desire for equality has made them happier. No, no. You can't. There always have been rich and poor. I'm no fatalist. Heaven forbid! But our civilization is moulded by great impersonal forces" (his voice grew complacent; it always did when he eliminated the personal), "and there always will be rich and poor. You can't deny it" (and now it was a respectful voice)— "and you can't deny that, in spite of all, the tendency of civilization has on the whole been upward."

"Owing to God, I suppose," flashed Helen.

He stared at her.

"You grab the dollars. God does the rest."

It was no good instructing the girl if she was going to talk about God in that neurotic modern way. Fraternal to the last, he left her for the quieter company of Mrs. Munt. He thought, "She rather reminds me of Dolly."

Helen looked out at the sea.

"Don't ever discuss political economy with Henry," advised her sister. "It'll only end in a cry."

"But he must be one of those men who have reconciled science with religion," said Helen slowly. "I don't like those men. They are scientific themselves, and talk of the survival of the fittest, and cut down the salaries of their clerks, and stunt the independence of all who may menace their comfort, but yet they believe that somehow good—it is always that sloppy 'somehow'—will be the outcome, and that in some mystical way the Mr. Basts of the future will benefit because the Mr. Basts of to-day are in pain."

"He is such a man in theory. But oh, Helen, in theory!"

"But oh, Meg, what a theory!"

"Why should you put things so bitterly, dearie?"

"Because I'm an old maid," said Helen, biting her lip. "I can't think why I go on like this myself." She shook off her sister's hand and went into the house. Margaret, distressed at the day's beginning, followed the Bournemouth steamer with her eyes. She saw that Helen's nerves were exasperated by the unlucky Bast business beyond the bounds of politeness. There might at any minute be a real explosion, which even Henry would notice. Henry must be removed.

"Margaret!" her aunt called. "Magsy! It isn't true, surely, what Mr. Wilcox says, that you want to go away early next week?"

"Not 'want,'" was Margaret's prompt reply; "but there is so much to be settled, and I do want to see the Charles'."

"But going away without taking the Weymouth trip, or even the Lulworth?" said Mrs. Munt, coming nearer. "Without going once more up Nine Barrows Down?"

"I'm afraid so."

Mr. Wilcox rejoined her with, "Good! I did the breaking of the ice."

A wave of tenderness came over her. She put a hand on either shoulder, and looked deeply into the black, bright eyes. What was behind their competent stare? She knew, but was not disquieted.

CHAPTER XXIII

Margaret had no intention of letting things slide, and the evening before she left Swanage she gave her sister a thorough scolding. She censured her, not for disapproving of the engagement, but for throwing over her disapproval a veil of mystery. Helen was equally frank. "Yes," she said, with the air of one looking inwards, "there is a mystery. I can't help it. It's not my fault. It's the way life has been made." Helen in those days was over-interested in the subconscious self. She exaggerated the Punch and Judy aspect of life, and spoke of mankind as puppets, whom an invisible show-man twitches into love and war. Margaret pointed out that if she dwelt on this she, too, would eliminate the personal. Helen was silent for a minute, and then burst into a queer speech, which cleared the air. "Go on and marry him. I think you're splendid; and if anyone can pull it off, you will." Margaret denied that there was anything to "pull off," but she continued: "Yes, there is, and I wasn't up to it with Paul. I can only do what's easy. I can only entice and be enticed. I can't, and won't, attempt difficult rela-tions. If I marry, it will either be a man who's strong enough to boss me or whom I'm strong enough to boss. So I shan't ever marry, for there aren't such men. And Heaven help anyone whom I do marry, for I shall certainly run away from him before you can say 'Jack Robinson.' There! Because I'm uneducated. But you, you're different; you're a heroine."

"Oh, Helen! Am I? Will it be as dreadful for poor Henry as all that?"

"You mean to keep proportion, and that's heroic, it's Greek, and I don't see why it shouldn't succeed with you. Go on and fight with him and help him. Don't ask *me* for help, or even for sympathy. Henceforward I'm going my own way. I mean to be thorough, because thoroughness is easy. I mean to dislike your husband, and to tell him so. I mean to make no concessions to Tibby. If Tibby wants to live with me, he must lump me. I mean to love *you* more than ever. Yes, I do. You and I have built up something real, because it is purely spiritual. There's no veil of mystery over us. Unreality and mystery begin as soon as one touches the body. The popular view is, as usual, exactly the wrong one. Our bothers are over tangible things—money, hus-bands, house-hunting. But Heaven will work of itself."

Margaret was grateful for this expression of affection, and an-swered, "Perhaps." All vistas close in the unseen—no one doubts it—but Helen closed them rather too quickly for her taste. At every turn of speech one was confronted with reality and the absolute. Perhaps Margaret grew too old for metaphysics, perhaps Henry was weaning her from them, but she felt that there was something a little unbalanced in the mind that so readily shreds the visible. The business man who assumes that this life is everything, and the mystic who asserts that it is nothing, fail, on this side and on that, to hit the truth. "Yes, I see, dear; it's about halfway between," Aunt Juley had hazarded in earlier years. No; truth, being alive, was not halfway between anything. It was only to be found by continuous excursions into either realm, and though proportion is the final secret, to espouse it at the outset is to insure sterility.

Helen, agreeing here, disagreeing there, would have talked till midnight, but Margaret, with her packing to do, focussed the conversation on Henry. She might abuse Henry behind his back, but please would she always be civil to him in company? "I definitely dislike him, but I'll do what I can," promised Helen. "Do what you can with my friends in return."

This conversation made Margaret easier. Their inner life was so safe that they could bargain over externals in a way that would have been incredible to Aunt Juley, and impossible for Tibby or Charles. There are moments when the inner life actually "pays," when years of self-scrutiny, conducted for no ulterior motive, are suddenly of practical use. Such moments are still rare in the West; that they come at all promises a fairer future. Margaret, though unable to understand her sister, was assured against estrangement, and returned to London with a more peaceful mind.

The following morning, at eleven o'clock, she presented herself at the offices of the Imperial and West African Rubber Company. She was glad to go there, for Henry had implied his business rather than described it, and the formlessness and vagueness that one associates with Africa itself had hitherto brooded over the main sources of his wealth. Not that a visit to the office cleared things up. There was just the ordinary surface scum of ledgers and polished counters and brass bars that began and stopped for no possible reason, or electric-light globes blossoming in triplets, of little rabbit-hutches faced with glass or wire, of little rabbits. And even when she penetrated to the inner depths, she found only the ordinary table and Turkey carpet, and though the map over the fireplace did depict a helping of West Africa, it was a very ordinary map. Another map hung opposite, on which the whole continent appeared, looking like a whale marked out for a blubber, and by its side was a door, shut, but Henry's voice came through it, dictating a "strong" letter. She might have been at the Porphyrion, or Dempster's Bank, or her own wine-merchant's. Everything seems just alike in these days. But perhaps she was seeing the Imperial side of the company rather than its West African, and Imperialism always had been one of her difficulties.

"One minute!" called Mr. Wilcox on receiving her name. He touched a bell, the effect of which was to produce Charles.

Charles had written his father an adequate letter—more adequate than Evie's, through which a girlish indignation throbbed. And he greeted his future stepmother with propriety.

"I hope that my wife—how do you do?—will give you a decent lunch," was his opening. "I left instructions, but we live in a rough-and-ready way. She expects you back to tea, too, after you have had a look at Howards End. I wonder what you'll think of the place. I wouldn't touch it with tongs myself. Do sit down! It's a measly little place."

"I shall enjoy seeing it," said Margaret, feeling, for the first time, shy.

"You'll see it at its worst, for Bryce decamped abroad last Monday without even arranging for a charwoman to clear up after him. I never saw such a disgraceful mess. It's unbelievable. He wasn't in the house a month."

"I've more than a little bone to pick with Bryce," called Henry from the inner chamber.

"Why did he go so suddenly?"

"Invalid type; couldn't sleep."

"Poor fellow!"

"Poor fiddlesticks!" said Mr. Wilcox, joining them. "He had the impudence to put up notice-boards without as much as saying with your leave or by your leave. Charles flung them down."

"Yes, I flung them down," said Charles modestly.

"I've sent a telegram after him, and a pretty sharp one, too. He, and he in person, is responsible for the upkeep of that house for the next three years."

"The keys are at the farm; we wouldn't have the keys."

"Quite right."

"Dolly would have taken them, but I was in, fortunately."

"What's Mr. Bryce like?" asked Margaret.

But nobody cared. Mr. Bryce was the tenant, who had no right to sublet; to have defined him further was a waste of time. On his misdeeds they descanted profusely, until the girl who had been typing the strong letter came out with it. Mr. Wilcox added his signature. "Now we'll be off," said he.

A motor-drive, a form of felicity detested by Margaret, awaited her. Charles saw them in, civil to the last, and in a moment the offices of the Imperial and West African Rubber Company faded away. But it was not an impressive drive. Perhaps the weather was to blame, being grey and banked high with weary clouds. Perhaps Hertfordshire is scarcely intended for motorists. Did not a gentleman once motor so quickly through Westmoreland that he missed it? and if Westmoreland can be missed, it will fare ill with a county whose delicate structure particularly needs the attentive eye. Hertfordshire is England at its quietest, with little emphasis of river and hill; it is England meditative. If Drayton were with us again to write a new edition of his incomparable poem, he would sing the nymphs of Hertfordshire as indeterminate of feature, with hair obfuscated by the London smoke. Their eyes would be sad, and averted from their fate towards the Northern flats, their leader not Isis or Sabrina, but the slowly flowing Lea. No glory of raiment would be theirs, no urgency of dance; but they would be real nymphs.

The chauffeur could not travel as quickly as he had hoped, for the Great North Road was full of Easter traffic. But he went quite quick enough for Margaret, a poor-spirited creature, who had chickens and children on the brain.

"They're all right," said Mr. Wilcox. "They'll learn—like the swallows and the telegraph-wires."

"Yes, but, while they're learning———"

"The motor's come to stay," he answered. "One must get about. There's a pretty church—oh, you aren't sharp enough. Well, look out, if the road worries you—right outward at the scenery."

She looked at the scenery. It heaved and merged like porridge. Presently it congealed. They had arrived.

Charles's house on the left; on the right the swelling forms of the Six Hills. Their appearance in such a neighbourhood surprised her. They interrupted the stream of residences that was thickening up towards Hilton. Beyond them she saw meadows and a wood, and beneath them she settled that soldiers of the best kind lay buried. She hated war and liked soldiers—it was one of her amiable inconsistencies.

But here was Dolly, dressed up to the nines, standing at the door to greet them, and here were the first drops of the rain. They ran in gaily, and after a long wait in the drawing-room, sat down to the rough-and-ready lunch, every dish in which concealed or exuded cream. Mr. Bryce was the chief topic of conversation. Dolly described his visit with the key, while her father-in-law gave satisfaction by chaffing her and contradicting all she said. It was evidently the custom to laugh at Dolly. He chaffed Margaret, too, and Margaret, roused from a grave meditation, was pleased, and chaffed him back. Dolly seemed surprised, and eyed her curiously. After lunch the two children came down. Margaret disliked babies, but hit it off better with the two-year-old, and sent Dolly into fits of laughter by talking sense to him. "Kiss them now, and come away," said Mr. Wilcox. She came, but refused to kiss them: it was such hard luck on the little things, she said, and though Dolly proffered Chorly-worly and Porgly-woggles in turn, she was obdurate.

By this time it was raining steadily. The car came round with

the hood up, and again she lost all sense of space. In a few minutes they stopped, and Crane opened the door of the car.

"What's happened?" asked Margaret.

"What do you suppose?" said Henry.

A little porch was close up against her face.

"Are we there already?"

"We are."

"Well, I never! In years ago it seemed so far away."

Smiling, but somehow disillusioned, she jumped out, and her
impetus carried her to the front-door. She was about to open it,
when Henry said: "That's no good; it's locked. Who's got the key?"

As he had himself forgotten to call for the key at the farm, no
one replied. He also wanted to know who had left the front gate
open, since a cow had strayed in from the road, and was spoiling
the croquet lawn. Then he said rather crossly: "Margaret, you wait
in the dry. I'll go down for the key. It isn't a hundred yards."

"Mayn't I come too?"

"No; I shall be back before I'm gone."

Then the car turned away, and it was as if a curtain had risen.
For the second time that day she saw the appearance of the earth.

There were the greengage-trees that Helen had once described,
there the tennis lawn, there the hedge that would be glorious with
dog-roses in June, but the vision now was of black and palest
green. Down by the dell-hole more vivid colours were awakening,
and Lent lilies stood sentinel on its margin, or advanced in battal-
ions over the grass. Tulips were a tray of jewels. She could not see
the wych-elm tree, but a branch of the celebrated vine, studded
with velvet knobs, had covered the porch. She was struck by the
fertility of the soil; she had seldom been in a garden where the
flowers looked so well, and even the weeds she was idly plucking
out of the porch were intensely green. Why had poor Mr. Bryce
fled from all this beauty? For she had already decided that the
place was beautiful.

"Naughty cow! Go away!" cried Margaret to the cow, but without indignation.

Harder came the rain, pouring out of a windless sky, and spattering up from the notice-boards of the house-agents, which lay in a row on the lawn where Charles had hurled them. She must have interviewed Charles in another world—where one did have interviews. How Helen would revel in such a notion! Charles dead, all people dead, nothing alive but houses and gardens. The obvious dead, the intangible alive, and—no connection at all between them! Margaret smiled. Would that her own fancies were as clear-cut! Would that she could deal as high-handedly with the world! Smiling and sighing, she laid her hand upon the door. It opened. The house was not locked up at all.

She hesitated. Ought she to wait for Henry? He felt strongly about property, and might prefer to show her over himself. On the other hand, he had told her to keep in the dry, and the porch was beginning to drip. So she went in, and the draught from inside slammed the door behind.

Desolation greeted her. Dirty finger-prints were on the hall-windows, flue and rubbish on its unwashed boards. The civilization of luggage had been here for a month, and then decamped. Dining-room and drawing-room—right and left—were guessed only by their wall-papers. They were just rooms where one could shelter from the rain. Across the ceiling of each ran a great beam. The dining-room and hall revealed theirs openly, but the drawing-room's was match-boarded—because the facts of life must be concealed from ladies? Drawing-room, dining-room, and hall—how petty the names sounded! Here were simply three rooms where children could play and friends shelter from the rain. Yes, and they were beautiful.

Then she opened one of the doors opposite—there were two—and exchanged wall-papers for whitewash. It was the servants' part, though she scarcely realized that: just rooms again, where friends might shelter. The garden at the back was full of flowering cherries and plums. Farther on were hints of the meadow and a black cliff of pines. Yes, the meadow was beautiful.

Penned in by the desolate weather, she recaptured the sense of space which the motor had tried to rob from her. She remembered again that ten square miles are not ten times as wonderful as one square mile, that a thousand square miles are not practically the same as heaven. The phantom of bigness, which London encourages, was laid for ever when she paced from the hall at Howards End to its kitchen and heard the rains run this way and that where the watershed of the roof divided them.

Now Helen came to her mind, scrutinizing half Wessex from the ridge of the Purbeck Downs, and saying: "You will have to lose something." She was not so sure. For instance, she would double her kingdom by opening the door that concealed the stairs.

Now she thought of the map of Africa; of empires; of her father; of the two supreme nations, streams of whose life warmed her blood, but, mingling, had cooled her brain. She paced back into the hall, and as she did so the house reverberated.

"Is that you, Henry?" she called.

There was no answer, but the house reverberated again.

"Henry, have you got in?"

But it was the heart of the house beating, faintly at first, then loudly, martially. It dominated the rain.

It is the starved imagination, not the well-nourished, that is afraid. Margaret flung open the door to the stairs. A noise as of drums seemed to deafen her. A woman, an old woman, was descending, with figure erect, with face impassive, with lips that parted and said dryly:

"Oh! Well, I took you for Ruth Wilcox."

Margaret stammered: "I—— Mrs. Wilcox—I?"

"In fancy, of course—in fancy. You had her way of walking. Good-day." And the old woman passed out into the rain.

CHAPTER XXIV

"It gave her quite a turn," said Mr. Wilcox, when retailing the incident to Dolly at tea-time. "None of you girls have any nerves, really. Of course, a word from me put it all right, but silly old Miss Avery—she frightened you, didn't she, Margaret? There you stood clutching a bunch of weeds. She might have said something, instead of coming down the stairs with that alarming bonnet on. I passed her as I came in. Enough to make the car shy. I believe Miss Avery goes in for being a character; some old maids do." He lit a cigarette. "It is their last resource. Heaven knows what she was doing in the place; but that's Bryce's business, not mine."

"I wasn't as foolish as you suggest," said Margaret. "She only startled me, for the house had been silent so long."

"Did you take her for a spook?" asked Dolly, for whom "spooks" and "going to church" summarized the unseen.

"Not exactly."

"She really did frighten you," said Henry, who was far from discouraging timidity in females. "Poor Margaret! And very naturally. Uneducated classes are so stupid."

"Is Miss Avery uneducated classes?" Margaret asked, and found herself looking at the decoration scheme of Dolly's drawing-room.

"She's just one of the crew at the farm. People like that always assume things. She assumed you'd know who she was. She left all the Howards End keys in the front lobby, and assumed that you'd seen them as you came in, that you'd lock up the house when you'd done, and would bring them on down to her. And there was her niece hunting for them down at the farm. Lack of education makes people very casual. Hilton was full of women like Miss Avery once."

"I shouldn't have disliked it, perhaps."

"Or Miss Avery giving me a wedding present," said Dolly

Which was illogical but interesting. Through Dolly, Margaret was destined to learn a good deal.

"But Charles said I must try not to mind, because she had known his grandmother."

"As usual, you've got the story wrong, my good Dorothea."

"I meant great-grandmother—the one who left Mrs. Wilcox

the house. Weren't both of them and Miss Avery friends when Howards End, too, was a farm?"

Her father-in-law blew out a shaft of smoke. His attitude to his dead wife was curious. He would allude to her, and hear her discussed, but never mentioned her by name. Nor was he interested in the dim, bucolic past. Dolly was—for the following reason.

"Then hadn't Mrs. Wilcox a brother—or was it an uncle? Anyhow, he popped the question, and Miss Avery, she said 'No.' Just imagine, if she'd said 'Yes,' she would have been Charles's aunt. (Oh, I say, that's rather good! 'Charlie's Aunt'! I must chaff him about that this evening.) And the man went out and was killed. Yes, I'm certain I've got it right now. Tom Howard—he was the last of them."

"I believe so," said Mr. Wilcox negligently.

"I say! Howards End—Howards Ended! cried Dolly. "I'm rather on the spot this evening, eh?"

"I wish you'd ask whether Crane's ended."

"Oh, Mr. Wilcox, how *can* you?"

"Because, if he has had enough tea, we ought to go.—Dolly's a good little woman," he continued, "but a little of her goes a long way. I couldn't live near her if you paid me."

Margaret smiled. Though presenting a firm front to outsiders, no Wilcox could live near, or near the possessions of, any other Wilcox. They had the colonial spirit, and were always making for some spot where the white man might carry his burden unobserved. Of course, Howards End was impossible, so long as the younger couple were established in Hilton. His objections to the house were plain as daylight now.

Crane had had enough tea, and was sent to the garage, where their car had been trickling muddy water over Charles's. The downpour had surely penetrated the Six Hills by now, bringing news of our restless civilization. "Curious mounds," said Henry, "but in with you now; another time." He had to be up in London by seven—if possible, by six-thirty. Once more she lost the sense of space; once more trees, houses, people, animals, hills, merged and heaved into one dirtiness, and she was at Wickham Place.

Her evening was pleasant. The sense of flux which had haunted her all the year disappeared for a time. She forgot the luggage and the motor-cars, and the hurrying men who know so much and connect so little. She recaptured the sense of space, which is the basis of all earthly beauty, and, starting from Howards End, she attempted to realize England. She failed— visions do not come when we try, though they may come through trying. But an unexpected love of the island awoke in her, connecting on this side with the joys of the flesh, on that with the inconceivable. Helen and her father had known this love, poor Leonard Bast was groping after it, but it had been hidden from Margaret till this afternoon. It had certainly come through the house and old Miss Avery. Through them: the notion of "through" persisted; her mind trembled towards a conclusion which only the unwise have put into words. Then, veering back into warmth, it dwelt on ruddy bricks, flowering plum-trees, and all the tangible joys of spring.

Henry, after allaying her agitation, had taken her over his property, and had explained to her the use and dimensions of the various rooms. He had sketched the history of the little estate. "It is so unlucky," ran the monologue, "that money wasn't put into it about fifty years ago. Then it had four—five—times the land— thirty acres at least. One could have made something out of it then—a small park, or at all events shrubberies, and rebuilt the house farther away from the road. What's the good of taking it in hand now? Nothing but the meadow left, and even that was heavily mortgaged when I first had to do with things—yes, and the house too. Oh, it was no joke." She saw two women as he spoke, one old, the other young, watching their inheritance melt away. She saw them greet him as a deliverer. "Mismanagement did it— besides, the days for small farms are over. It doesn't pay—except with intensive cultivation. Small holdings, back to the land—ah! philanthropic bunkum. Take it as a rule that nothing pays on a small scale. Most of the land you see (they were standing at an

upper window, the only one which faced west) belongs to the
people at the Park—they made their pile over copper—good
chaps. Avery's Farm, Sishe's—what they call the Common, where
you see that ruined oak—one after the other fell in, and so did
this, as near as is no matter." But Henry had saved it, without fine
feelings or deep insight; but he had saved it, and she loved him
for the deed. "When I had more control I did what I could: sold
off the two and a half animals, and the mangy pony, and the
superannuated tools; pulled down the outhouses; drained;
thinned out I don't know how many guelder-roses and elder-trees;
and inside the house I turned the old kitchen into a hall, and
made a kitchen behind where the dairy was. Garage and so on
came later. But one could still tell it's been an old farm. And yet it
isn't the place that would fetch one of your artistic crew." No, it
wasn't; and if he did not quite understand it, the artistic crew
would still less: it was English, and the wych-elm that she saw
from the window was an English tree. No report had prepared her
for its peculiar glory. It was neither warrior, nor lover, nor god; in
none of these rôles do the English excel. It was a comrade, bending over the house, strength and adventure in its roots, but in its
utmost fingers tenderness, and the girth, that a dozen men could
not have spanned, became in the end evanescent, till pale bud
clusters seemed to float in the air. It was a comrade. House and
tree transcended any similes of sex. Margaret thought of them
now, and was to think of them through many a windy night and
London day, but to compare either to man, to woman, always
dwarfed the vision. Yet they kept within limits of the human.
Their message was not of eternity, but of hope on this side of the
grave. As she stood in the one, gazing at the other, truer relation-
ship had gleamed.

Another touch, and the account of her day is finished. They
entered the garden for a minute, and to Mr. Wilcox's surprise she
was right. Teeth, pigs' teeth, could be seen in the bark of the
wych-elm tree—just the white tips of them showing. "Extraordinary!" he cried. "Who told you?"

"I heard of it one winter in London," was her answer, for she, too, avoided mentioning Mrs. Wilcox by name.

CHAPTER XXV

Evie heard of her father's engagement when she was in for a tennis tournament, and her play went simply to pot. That she should marry and leave him had seemed natural enough; that he, left alone, should do the same was deceitful; and now Charles and Dolly said that it was all her fault. "But I never dreamt of such a thing," she grumbled. "Dad took me to call now and then, and made me ask her to Simpson's. Well, I'm altogether off dad." It was also an insult to their mother's memory; there they all agreed, and Evie had the idea of returning Mrs. Wilcox's lace and jewellery "as a protest." Against what it would protest she was not clear; but being only eighteen, the idea of renunciation appealed to her, the more as she did not care for jewellery or lace. Dolly then suggested that she and Uncle Percy should pretend to break off their engagement, and then perhaps Mr. Wilcox would quarrel with Miss Schlegel, and break off his; or Paul might be cabled for. But at this point Charles told them not to talk nonsense. So Evie settled to marry as soon as possible; it was no good hanging about with these Schlegels eyeing her. The date of her wedding was consequently put forward from September to August, and in the intoxication of presents she recovered much of her good-humour.

Margaret found that she was expected to figure at this function, and to figure largely; it would be such on opportunity, said Henry, for her to get to know his set. Sir James Bidder would be there, and all the Cahills and the Fussells, and his sister-in-law, Mrs. Warrington Wilcox, had fortunately got back from her tour round the world. Henry she loved, but his set promised to be another matter. He had not the knack of surrounding himself with nice people—indeed, for a man of ability and virtue his choice had been singularly unfortunate; he had no guiding

principle beyond a certain preference for mediocrity; he was content to settle one of the greatest things in life haphazard, and so,
while his investments went right, his friends generally went
wrong. She would be told, "Oh, So-and-so's a good sort—a thundering good sort," and find, on meeting him, that he was a brute
or a bore. If Henry had shown real affection, she would have
understood, for affection explains everything. But he seemed
without sentiment. The "thundering good sort" might at any
moment become "a fellow for whom I never did have much use,
and have less now," and be shaken off cheerily into oblivion. Margaret had done the same as a schoolgirl. Now she never forgot
anyone for whom she had once cared; she connected, though the
connection might be bitter, and she hoped that some day Henry
would do the same.

Evie was not to be married from Ducie Street. She had a fancy
for something rural, and, besides, no one would be in London
then, so she left her boxes for a few weeks at Oniton Grange, and
her banns were duly published in the parish church, and for a
couple of days the little town, dreaming between the ruddy hills,
was roused by the clang of our civilization, and drew up by the
roadside to let the motors pass. Oniton had been a discovery of
Mr. Wilcox's—a discovery of which he was not altogether proud.
It was up towards the Welsh border, and so difficult of access that
he had concluded it must be something special. A ruined castle
stood in the grounds. But having got there, what was one to do?
The shooting was bad, the fishing indifferent, and women-folk
reported the scenery as nothing much. The place turned out to be
in the wrong part of Shropshire, damn it, and though he never
damned his own property aloud, he was only waiting to get it off
his hands, and then to let fly. Evie's marriage was its last appearance in public. As soon as a tenant was found, it became a house
for which he never had had much use, and had less now, and, like
Howards End, faded into Limbo.

But on Margaret Oniton was destined to make a lasting impression. She regarded it as her future home, and was anxious to

start straight with the clergy, etc., and, if possible, to see something of the local life. It was a market-town—as tiny a one as England possesses—and had for ages served that lonely valley, and guarded our marches against the Kelt. In spite of the occasion, in spite of the numbing hilarity that greeted her as soon as she got into the reserved saloon at Paddington, her senses were awake and watching, and though Oniton was to prove one of her innumerable false starts, she never forgot it, nor the things that happened there.

The London party only numbered eight—the Fussells, father and son, two Anglo-Indian ladies named Mrs. Plynlimmon and Lady Edser, Mrs. Warrington Wilcox and her daughter, and, lastly, the little girl, very smart and quiet, who figures at so many weddings, and who kept a watchful eye on Margaret, the bride-elect. Dolly was absent—a domestic event detained her at Hilton; Paul had cabled a humorous message; Charles was to meet them with a trio of motors at Shrewsbury. Helen had refused her invitation; Tibby had never answered his. The management was excellent, as was to be expected with anything that Henry undertook; one was conscious of his sensible and generous brain in the background. They were his guests as soon as they reached the train; a special label for their luggage; a courier; a special lunch; they had only to look pleasant and, where possible, pretty. Margaret thought with dismay of her own nuptials—presumably under the management of Tibby. "Mr. Theobald Schlegel and Miss Helen Schlegel request the pleasure of Mrs. Plynlimmon's company on the occasion of the marriage of their sister Margaret." The formula was incredible, but it must soon be printed and sent, and though Wickham Place need not compete with Oniton, it must feed its guests properly, and provide them with sufficient chairs. Her wedding would either be ramshackly or bourgeois—she hoped the latter. Such an affair as the present, staged with a deftness that was almost beautiful, lay beyond her powers and those of her friends.

The low rich purr of a Great Western express is not the worst background for conversation, and the journey passed pleasantly enough. Nothing could have exceeded the kindness of the two men. They raised windows for some ladies, and lowered them for others, they rang the bell for the servant, they identified the colleges as the train slipped past Oxford, they caught books or bag-purses in the act of tumbling on to the floor. Yet there was nothing finicking about their politeness: it had the Public School touch, and, though sedulous, was virile. More battles than Waterloo have been won on our playing-fields, and Margaret bowed to a charm of which she did not wholly approve, and said nothing when the Oxford colleges were identified wrongly. "Male and female created He them"; the journey to Shrewsbury confirmed this questionable statement, and the long glass saloon, that moved so easily and felt so comfortable, became a forcing-house for the idea of sex.

At Shrewbury came fresh air. Margaret was all for sight-seeing, and while the others were finishing their tea at the Raven, she annexed a motor and hurried over the astonishing city. Her chauffeur was not the faithful Crane, but an Italian, who dearly loved making her late. Charles, watch in hand, though with a level brow, was standing in front of the hotel when they returned. It was perfectly all right, he told her; she was by no means the last. And then he dived into the coffee-room, and she heard him say, "For God's sake, hurry the women up; we shall never be off," and Albert Fussell reply, "Not I; I've done my share," and Colonel Fussell opine that the ladies were getting themselves up to kill. Presently Myra (Mrs. Warrington's daughter) appeared, and as she was his cousin, Charles blew her up a little: she had been changing her smart travelling hat for a smart motor hat. Then Mrs. Warrington herself, leading the quiet child; the two Anglo-Indian ladies were always last. Maids, courier, heavy luggage, had already gone on by a branch-line to a station nearer Oniton, but there were five hat-boxes and four dressing-bags to be packed, and five dust-cloaks to be put on, and to be put off at the last moment, because Charles declared them not necessary. The men presided over everything with unfailing good-humour. By half-past five the party was ready, and went out of Shrewsbury by the Welsh Bridge.

Shropshire had not the reticence of Hertfordshire. Though robbed of half its magic by swift movement, it still conveyed the sense of hills. They were nearing the buttresses that force the Severn eastward and make it an English stream, and the sun, sinking over the Sentinels of Wales, was straight in their eyes. Having picked up another guest, they turned southward, avoiding the greater mountains, but conscious of an occasional summit, rounded and mild, whose colouring differed in quality from that of the lower earth, and whose contours altered more slowly. Quiet mysteries were in progress behind those tossing horizons: the West, as ever, was retreating with some secret which may not be worth the discovery, but which no practical man will ever discover.

They spoke of Tariff Reform.

Mrs. Warrington was just back from the Colonies. Like many other critics of Empire, her mouth had been stopped with food, and she could only exclaim at the hospitality with which she had been received, and warn the Mother Country against trifling with young Titans. "They threaten to cut the painter," she cried, "and where shall we be then? Miss Schlegel, you'll undertake to keep Henry sound about Tariff Reform? It is our last hope."

Margaret playfully confessed herself on the other side, and they began to quote from their respective hand-books while the motor carried them deep into the hills. Curious these were rather than impressive, for their outlines lacked beauty, and the pink fields on their summits suggested the handkerchiefs of a giant spread out to dry. An occasional outcrop of rock, an occasional wood, an occasional "forest," treeless and brown, all hinted at wildness to follow, but the main colour was an agricultural green. The air grew cooler; they had surmounted the last gradient, and Oniton lay below them with its church, its radiating houses, its castle, its river-girt peninsula. Close to the castle was a grey mansion, intellectual but kindly, stretching with its grounds across the

peninsula's neck—the sort of mansion that was built all over England in the beginning of the last century, while architecture was
still an expression of the national character. That was the Grange,
remarked Albert, over his shoulder, and then he jammed the
brake on, and the motor slowed down and stopped. "I'm sorry,"
said he, turning round. "Do you mind getting out—by the door
on the right. Steady on."

"What's happened?" asked Mrs. Warrington.

Then the car behind them drew up, and the voice of Charles
was heard saying: "Get out the women at once." There was a con-
course of males, and Margaret and her companions were hustled
out and received into the second car. What had happened? As
it started off again, the door of a cottage opened, and a girl
screamed wildly at them.

"What is it?" the ladies cried.

Charles drove them a hundred yards without speaking. Then
he said: "It's all right. Your car just touched a dog."

"But stop!" cried Margaret, horrified.

"It didn't hurt him."

"Didn't really hurt him?" asked Myra.

"No."

"Do *please* stop!" said Margaret, leaning forward. She was
standing up in the car, the other occupants holding her knees to
steady her. "I want to go back, please."

Charles took no notice.

"We've left Mr. Fussell behind," said another; "and Angelo,
and Crane."

"Yes, but no woman."

"I expect a little of"—Mrs. Warrington scratched her palm—
"will be more to the point than one of us!"

"The insurance company see to that," remarked Charles, "and
Albert will do the talking."

"I want to go back, though, I say!" repeated Margaret, getting angry.

Charles took no notice. The motor, loaded with refugees,

continued to travel very slowly down the hill. "The men are there," chorused the others. "Men will see to it."

"The men *can't* see to it. Oh, this is ridiculous! Charles, I ask you to stop."

"Stopping's no good," drawled Charles.

"Isn't it?" said Margaret, and jumped straight out of the car.

She fell on her knees, cut her gloves, shook her hat over her ear. Cries of alarm followed her. "You've hurt yourself," exclaimed Charles, jumping after her.

"Of course I've hurt myself!" she retorted.

"May I ask what——"

"There's nothing to ask," said Margaret.

"Your hand's bleeding."

"I know."

"I'm in for a frightful row from the pater."

"You should have thought of that sooner, Charles."

Charles had never been in such a position before. It was a woman in revolt who was hobbling away from him, and the sight was too strange to leave any room for anger. He recovered himself when the others caught them up: their sort he understood. He commanded them to go back.

Albert Fussell was seen walking towards them.

"It's all right!" he called. "It wasn't a dog, it was a cat."

"There!" exclaimed Charles triumphantly. "It's only a rotten cat."

"Got room in your car for a little un? I cut as soon as I saw it wasn't a dog; the chauffeurs are tackling the girl." But Margaret walked forward steadily. Why should the chauffeurs tackle the girl? Ladies sheltering behind men, men sheltering behind servants—the whole system's wrong, and she must challenge it.

"Miss Schlegel! 'Pon my word, you've hurt your hand."

"I'm just going to see," said Margaret. "Don't you wait, Mr. Fussell."

The second motor came round the corner. "It is all right, madam," said Crane in his turn. He had taken to call her madam.

"What's all right? The cat?"

"Yes, madam. The girl will receive compensation for it."

"She was a very ruda girla," said Angelo from the third motor thoughtfully.

"Wouldn't you have been rude?"

The Italian spread out his hands, implying that he had not thought of rudeness, but would produce it if it pleased her. The situation became absurd. The gentlemen were again buzzing round Miss Schlegel with offers of assistance, and Lady Edser began to bind up her hand. She yielded, apologizing slightly, and was led back to the car, and soon the landscape resumed its motion, the lonely cottage disappeared, the castle swelled on its cushion of turf, and they had arrived. No doubt she had disgraced herself. But she felt their whole journey from London had been unreal. They had no part with the earth and its emotions. They were dust, and a stink, and cosmopolitan chatter, and the girl whose cat had been killed had lived more deeply than they.

"Oh, Henry," she exclaimed, "I have been so naughty," for she had decided to take up this line. "We ran over a cat. Charles told me not to jump out, but I would, and look!" She held out her bandaged hand. "Your poor Meg went such a flop."

Mr. Wilcox looked bewildered. In evening dress, he was standing to welcome his guests in the hall.

"Thinking it was a dog," added Mrs. Warrington.

"Ah, a dog's a companion!" said Colonel Fussell. "A dog 'll remember you."

"Have you hurt yourself, Margaret?"

"Not to speak about; and it's my left hand."

"Well, hurry up and change."

She obeyed, as did the others. Mr. Wilcox then turned to his son.

"Now, Charles, what's happened?"

Charles was absolutely honest. He described what he believed to have happened. Albert had flattened out a cat, and Miss Schlegel had lost her nerve, as any woman might. She had been got safely into the other car, but when it was in motion had leapt out again, in spite of all that they could say. After walking a little on the road, she had calmed down and had said that she was sorry. His father accepted this explanation, and neither knew that Margaret had artfully prepared the way for it. It fitted in too well with their view of feminine nature. In the smoking-room, after dinner, the Colonel put forward the view that Miss Schlegel had jumped it out of devilry. Well he remembered as a young man, in the harbour of Gibraltar once, how a girl—a handsome girl, too—had jumped overboard for a bet. He could see her now, and all the lads overboard after her. But Charles and Mr. Wilcox agreed it was much more probably nerves in Miss Schlegel's case. Charles was depressed. That woman had a tongue. She would bring worse disgrace on his father before she had done with them. He strolled out on to the castle mound to think the matter over. The evening was exquisite. On three sides of him a little river whispered, full of messages from the west; above his head the ruins made patterns against the sky. He carefully reviewed their dealings with this family, until he fitted Helen, and Margaret, and Aunt Juley into an orderly conspiracy. Paternity had made him suspicious. He had two children to look after, and more coming, and day by day they seemed less likely to grow up rich men. "It is all very well," he reflected, "the pater saying that he will be just to all, but one can't be just indefinitely. Money isn't elastic. What's to happen if Evie has a family? And, come to that, so may the pater. There'll not be enough to go round, for there's none coming in, either through Dolly or Percy. It's damnable!" He looked enviously at the Grange, whose windows poured light and laughter. First and last, this wedding would cost a pretty penny. Two ladies were strolling up and down the garden terrace, and as the syllables "Imperialism" were wafted to his ears, he guessed that one of them was his aunt. She might have helped him, if she too had not had a family to provide for. "Everyone for himself," he repeated—a maxim which had cheered him in the past, but which rang grimly enough among the ruins of Oniton. He lacked his father's ability in business, and so had an ever higher regard for money; unless he could inherit plenty, he feared to leave his children poor.

As he sat thinking, one of the ladies left the terrace and walked into the meadow; he recognized her as Margaret by the white bandage that gleamed on her arm, and put out his cigar, lest the gleam should betray him. She climbed up the mound in zigzags, and at times stooped down, as if she was stroking the turf. It sounds absolutely incredible, but for a moment Charles thought that she was in love with him, and had come out to tempt him. Charles believed in temptresses, who are indeed the strong man's necessary complement, and having no sense of humour, he could not purge himself of the thought by a smile. Margaret, who was engaged to his father, and his sister's wedding-guest, kept on her way without noticing him, and he admitted that he had wronged her on this point. But what was she doing? Why was she stumbling about amongst the rubble and catching her dress in brambles and burrs? As she edged round the keep, she must have got to windward and smelt his cigar-smoke, for she exclaimed, "Hullo! Who's that?"

Charles made no answer.

"Saxon or Kelt?" she continued, laughing in the darkness. "But it doesn't matter. Whichever you are, you will have to listen to me. I love this place. I love Shropshire. I hate London. I am glad that this will be my home. Ah, dear"—she was now moving back towards the house—"what a comfort to have arrived!"

"That woman means mischief," thought Charles, and compressed his lips. In a few minutes he followed her indoors, as the ground was getting damp. Mists were rising from the river, and presently it became invisible, though it whispered more loudly. There had been a heavy downpour in the Welsh hills.

CHAPTER XXVI

Next morning a fine mist covered the peninsula. The weather promised well, and the outline of the castle mound grew clearer each moment that Margaret watched it. Presently she saw the keep, and the sun painted the rubble gold, and charged the white sky with blue. The shadow of the house gathered itself together, and fell over the garden. A cat looked up at her window and mewed. Lastly the river appeared, still holding the mists between its banks and its overhanging alders, and only visible as far as a hill, which cut off its upper reaches.

Margaret was fascinated by Oniton. She had said that she loved it, but it was rather its romantic tension that held her. The rounded Druids of whom she had caught glimpses in her drive, the rivers hurrying down from them to England, the carelessly modelled masses of the lower hills, thrilled her with poetry. The house was insignificant, but the prospect from it would be an eternal joy, and she thought of all the friends she would have to stop in it, and of the conversion of Henry himself to a rural life. Society, too, promised favourably. The rector of the parish had dined with them last night, and she found that he was a friend of her father's, and so knew what to find in her. She liked him. He would introduce her to the town. While, on her other side, Sir James Bidder sat, repeating that she only had to give the word, and he would whip up the county families for twenty miles round. Whether Sir James, who was Garden Seeds, had promised what he could perform, she doubted, but so long as Henry mistook them for the county families when they did call, she was content.

Charles and Albert Fussell now crossed the lawn. They were going for a morning dip, and a servant followed them with their bathing-dresses. She had meant to take a stroll herself before breakfast, but saw that the day was still sacred to men, and amused herself by watching their contretemps. In the first place the key of the bathing-shed could not be found. Charles stood by the riverside with folded hands, tragical, while the servant shouted, and was misunderstood by another servant in the garden. Then came a difficulty about a spring-board, and soon three people were running backwards and forwards over the meadow, with orders and counter orders and recriminations and apologies.

If Margaret wanted to jump from a motor-car, she jumped; if Tibby thought paddling would benefit his ankles, he paddled; if a clerk desired adventure, he took a walk in the dark. But these athletes seemed paralyzed. They could not bathe without their appliances, though the morning sun was calling and the last mists were rising from the dimpling stream. Had they found the life of the body after all? Could not the men whom they despised as milksops beat them, even on their own ground?

She thought of the bathing arrangements as they should be in her day—no worrying of servants, no appliances, beyond good sense. Her reflections were disturbed by the quiet child, who had come out to speak to the cat, but was now watching her watch the men. She called, "Good-morning, dear," a little sharply. Her voice spread consternation. Charles looked round, and though completely attired in indigo blue, vanished into the shed, and was seen no more.

"Miss Wilcox is up——" the child whispered, and then became unintelligible.

"What's that?"

It sounded like, "——cut-yoke—sack-back—"

"I can't hear."

"—On the bed—tissue-paper——"

Gathering that the wedding-dress was on view, and that a visit would be seemly, she went to Evie's room. All was hilarity here. Evie, in a petticoat, was dancing with one of the Anglo-Indian ladies, while the other was adoring yards of white satin. They screamed, they laughed, they sang, and the dog barked.

Margaret screamed a little too, but without conviction. She could not feel that a wedding was so funny. Perhaps something was missing in her equipment.

Evie gasped: "Dolly is a rotter not to be here! Oh, we would rag just then!" Then Margaret went down to breakfast.

Henry was already installed; he ate slowly and spoke little, and was, in Margaret's eyes, the only member of their party who dodged emotion successfully. She could not suppose him indifferent either to the loss of his daughter or to the presence of his future wife. Yet he dwelt intact, only issuing orders occasionally—orders that promoted the comfort of his guests. He inquired after her hand; he set her to pour out the coffee and Mrs. Warrington to pour out the tea. When Evie came down there was a moment's awkwardness, and both ladies rose to vacate their places. "Burton," called Henry, "serve tea and coffee from the sideboard!" It wasn't genuine tact, but it was tact, of a sort—the sort that is as useful as the genuine, and saves even more situations at Board meetings. Henry treated a marriage like a funeral, item by item, never raising his eyes to the whole, and "Death, where is thy sting? Love, where is thy victory?" one would exclaim at the close.

After breakfast she claimed a few words with him. It was always best to approach him formally. She asked for the interview, because he was going on to shoot grouse to-morrow, and she was returning to Helen in town.

"Certainly, dear," said he. "Of course, I have the time. What do you want?"

"Nothing."

"I was afraid something had gone wrong."

"No; I have nothing to say, but you may talk."

Glancing at his watch, he talked of the nasty curve at the lych-gate. She heard him with interest. Her surface could always respond to his without contempt, though all her deeper being might be yearning to help him. She had abandoned any plan of action. Love is the best, and the more she let herself love him, the more chance was there that he would set his soul in order. Such a moment as this, when they sat under fair weather by the walks of their future home, was so sweet to her that its sweetness would surely pierce to him. Each lift of his eyes, each parting of the thatched lip from the clean-shaven, must prelude the tenderness that kills the Monk and the Beast at a single blow. Disappointed a hundred times, she still hoped. She loved him with too clear a vision to fear his cloudiness. Whether he droned trivialities, as to-day, or sprang kisses on her in the twilight, she could pardon him, she could respond.

"If there is this nasty curve," she suggested, "couldn't we walk to the church? Not, of course, you and Evie; but the rest of us might very well go on first, and that would mean fewer carriages."

"One can't have ladies walking through the Market Square. The Fussells wouldn't like it; they were awfully particular at Charles's wedding. My—she—one of our party was anxious to walk, and certainly the church was just round the corner, and I shouldn't have minded; but the Colonel made a great point of it."

"You men shouldn't be so chivalrous," said Margaret thoughtfully.

"Why not?"

She knew why not, but said that she did not know. He then announced that, unless she had anything special to say, he must visit the wine-cellar, and they went off together in search of Burton. Though clumsy and a little inconvenient, Oniton was a genuine country-house. They clattered down flagged passages, looking into room after room, and scaring unknown maids from the performance of obscure duties. The wedding-breakfast must be in readiness when they come back from church, and tea would be served in the garden. The sight of so many agitated and serious people made Margaret smile, but she reflected that they were paid to be serious, and enjoyed being agitated. Here were the lower wheels of the machine that was tossing Evie up into nuptial glory. A little boy blocked their way with pig-pails. His mind could not grasp their greatness, and he said: "By your leave; let me pass, please." Henry asked him where Burton was. But the servants were so new that they did not know one another's names. In the still-room sat the band, who had stipulated for champagne as part of their fee, and who were already drinking beer. Scents of Araby came from the kitchen, mingled with cries. Margaret knew what had happened there, for it happened at Wickham Place. One of the wedding dishes had boiled over, and the cook was throwing cedar-shavings to hide the smell. At last they came upon the butler. Henry gave him the keys, and handed Margaret down the cellar-stairs. Two doors were unlocked. She, who kept all her wine at the bottom of the linen-cupboard, was astonished at the sight. "We shall never get through it!" she cried, and the two men were suddenly drawn into brotherhood, and exchanged smiles. She felt as if she had again jumped out of the car while it was moving.

Certainly Oniton would take some digesting. It would be no small business to remain herself, and yet to assimilate such an establishment. She must remain herself, for his sake as well as her own, since a shadowy wife degrades the husband whom she accompanies; and she must assimilate for reasons of common honesty, since she had no right to marry a man and make him uncomfortable. Her only ally was the power of Home. The loss of Wickham Place had taught her more than its possession. Howards End had repeated the lesson. She was determined to create new sanctities among these hills.

After visiting the wine-cellar, she dressed, and then came the wedding, which seemed a small affair when compared with the preparations for it. Everything went like one o'clock. Mr. Cahill materialized out of space, and was waiting for his bride at the church door. No one dropped the ring or mispronounced the responses, or trod on Evie's train, or cried. In a few minutes the clergymen performed their duty, the register was signed, and they were back in their carriages, negotiating the dangerous curve by the lych-gate. Margaret was convinced that they had not been married at all, and that the Norman church had been intent all the time on other business.

There were more documents to sign at the house, and the breakfast to eat, and then a few more people dropped in for the garden party. There had been a great many refusals, and after all it was not a very big affair—not as big as Margaret's would be. She noted the dishes and the strips of red carpet, that outwardly she might give Henry what was proper. But inwardly she hoped for something better than this blend of Sunday church and fox-hunting. If only someone had been upset! But this wedding had gone off so particularly well—"quite like a Durbar" in the opinion of Lady Edser, and she thoroughly agreed with her.

So the wasted day lumbered forward, the bride and bridegroom drove off, yelling with laughter, and for the second time the sun retreated towards the hills of Wales. Henry, who was more tired than he owned, came up to her in the castle meadow, and, in tones of unusual softness, said that he was pleased. Everything had gone off so well. She felt that he was praising her, too, and blushed; certainly she had done all she could with his intractable friends, and had made a special point of kow-towing to the men. They were breaking camp this evening: only the Warringtons and quiet child would stay the night, and the others were already moving towards the house to finish their packing. "I think it did go off well," she agreed. "Since I had to jump out of the motor, I'm thankful I lighted on my left hand. I am so very glad about it, Henry dear; I only hope that the guests at ours may be half as comfortable. You must all remember that we have no practical person among us, except my aunt, and she is not used to entertainments on a large scale."

"I know," he said gravely. "Under the circumstances, it would be better to put everything into the hands of Harrod's or Whiteley's, or even to go to some hotel."

"You desire a hotel?"

"Yes, because—well, I mustn't interfere with you. No doubt you want to be married from your old home."

"My old home's falling into pieces, Henry. I only want my new. Isn't it a perfect evening——"

"The Alexandrina isn't bad——"

"The Alexandrina," she echoed, more occupied with the threads of smoke that were issuing from their chimneys, and ruling the sunlit slopes with parallels of grey.

"It's off Curzon Street."

"Is it? Let's be married from off Curzon Street."

Then she turned westward, to gaze at the swirling gold. Just where the river rounded the hill the sun caught it. Fairyland must lie above the bend, and its precious liquid was pouring towards

them past Charles's bathing-shed. She gazed so long that her eyes
were dazzled, and when they moved back to the house, she could
not recognize the faces of people who were coming out of it. A
parlour-maid was preceding them.

"Who are those people?" she asked.

"They're callers!" exclaimed Henry. "It's too late for callers."

"Perhaps they're town people who want to see the wedding
presents."

"I'm not at home yet to townees."

"Well, hide among the ruins, and if I can stop them, I will."

He thanked her.

Margaret went forward, smiling socially. She supposed that
these were unpunctual guests, who would have to be content
with vicarious civility, since Evie and Charles were gone, Henry
tired, and the others in their rooms. She assumed the airs of a
hostess; not for long. For one of the group was Helen—Helen in
her oldest clothes, and dominated by that tense, wounding excitement that had made her a terror in their nursery days.

"What is it?" she called. "Oh, what's wrong? Is Tibby ill?"

Helen spoke to her two companions, who fell back. Then she
bore forward furiously.

"They're starving!" she shouted. "I found them starving!"

"Who? Why have you come?"

"The Basts."

"Oh, Helen!" moaned Margaret. "Whatever have you done
now?"

"He has lost his place. He has been turned out of his bank. Yes,
he's done for. We upper classes have ruined him, and I suppose
you'll tell me it's the battle of life. Starving. His wife is ill. Starving.
She fainted in the train."

"Helen, are you mad?"

"Perhaps. Yes. If you like, I'm mad. But I've brought them. I'll
stand injustice no longer. I'll show up the wretchedness that lies
under this luxury, this talk of impersonal forces, this cant about
God doing what we're too slack to do ourselves."

"Have you actually brought two starving people from London to Shropshire, Helen?"

Helen was checked. She had not thought of this, and her hysteria abated. "There was a restaurant car on the train," she said.

"Don't be absurd. They aren't starving, and you know it. Now, begin from the beginning. I won't have such theatrical nonsense. How dare you! Yes, how dare you!" she repeated, as anger filled her, "bursting in to Evie's wedding in this heartless way. My goodness! but you've a perverted notion of philanthropy. Look"—she indicated the house—"servants, people out of the windows. They think it's some vulgar scandal, and I must explain, 'Oh no, it's only my sister screaming, and only two hangers-on of ours, whom she has brought here for no conceivable reason.'"

"Kindly take back that word 'hangers-on,'" said Helen, ominously calm.

"Very well," conceded Margaret, who for all her wrath was determined to avoid a real quarrel. "I, too, am sorry about them, but it beats me why you've brought them here, or why you're here yourself."

"It's our last chance of seeing Mr. Wilcox."

Margaret moved towards the house at this. She was determined not to worry Henry.

"He's going to Scotland. I know he is. I insist on seeing him."

"Yes, to-morrow."

"I knew it was our last chance."

"How do you do, Mr. Bast?" said Margaret, trying to control her voice. "This is an odd business. What view do you take of it?"

"There is Mrs. Bast, too," prompted Helen.

Jacky also shook hands. She, like her husband, was shy, and, furthermore, ill, and, furthermore, so bestially stupid that she could not grasp what was happening. She only knew that the lady had swept down like a whirlwind last night, had paid the rent, redeemed the furniture, provided them with a dinner and a breakfast, and ordered them to meet her at Paddington next morning. Leonard had feebly protested, and when the morning

came, had suggested that they shouldn't go. But she, half mesmer-
ized, had obeyed. The lady had told them to, and they must, and
their bed-sitting-room had accordingly changed into Paddington, and Paddington into a railway carriage, that shook, and grew
hot, and grew cold, and vanished entirely, and reappeared amid
torrents of expensive scent. "You have fainted," said the lady in
an awe-struck voice. "Perhaps the air will do you good." And perhaps it had, for here she was, feeling rather better among a lot
of flowers.

"I'm sure I don't want to intrude," begun Leonard, in answer
to Margaret's question. "But you have been so kind to me in the
past in warning me about the Porphyrion that I wondered—why,
I wondered whether——"

"Whether we could get him back into the Porphyrion again,"
supplied Helen. "Meg, this has been a cheerful business. A bright
evening's work that was on Chelsea Embankment."

Margaret shook her head and returned to Mr. Bast.

"I don't understand. You left the Porphyrion because we suggested it was a bad concern, didn't you?"

"That's right."

"And went into a bank instead?"

"I told you all that," said Helen; "and they reduced their staff
after he had been in a month, and now he's penniless, and I consider that we and our informant are directly to blame."

"I hate all this," Leonard muttered.

"I hope you do, Mr. Bast. But it's no good mincing matters. You
have done yourself no good by coming here. If you intend to con-
front Mr. Wilcox, and to call him to account for a chance remark,
you will make a very great mistake."

"I brought them. I did it all," cried Helen.

"I can only advise you to go at once. My sister has put you in a
false position, and it is kindest to tell you so. It's too late to get to
town, but you'll find a comfortable hotel in Oniton, where Mrs.
Bast can rest, and I hope you'll be my guests there."

"That isn't what I want, Miss Schlegel," said Leonard. "You're very kind, and no doubt it's a false position, but you make me miserable. I seem no good at all."

"It's work he wants," interpreted Helen. "Can't you see?"

Then he said: "Jacky, let's go. We're more bother than we're worth. We're costing these ladies pounds and pounds already to get work for us, and they never will. There's nothing we're good enough to do."

"We would like to find you work," said Margaret rather conventionally. "We want to—I, like my sister. You're only down in your luck. Go to the hotel, have a good night's rest, and some day you shall pay me back the bill, if you prefer it."

But Leonard was near the abyss, and at such moments men see clearly. "You don't know what you're talking about," he said. "I shall never get work now. If rich people fail at one profession, they can try another. Not I. I had my groove, and I've got out of it. I could do one particular branch of insurance in one particular office well enough to command a salary, but that's all. Poetry's nothing, Miss Schlegel. One's thoughts about this and that are nothing. Your money, too, is nothing, if you'll understand me. I mean if a man over twenty once loses his own particular job, it's all over with him. I have seen it happen to others. Their friends gave them money for a little, but in the end they fall over the edge. It's no good. It's the whole world pulling. There always will be rich and poor."

He ceased. "Won't you have something to eat?" said Margaret. "I don't know what to do. It isn't my house, and though Mr. Wilcox would have been glad to see you at any other time—as I say, I don't know what to do, but I undertake to do what I can for you. Helen, offer them something. Do try a sandwich, Mrs. Bast."

They moved to a long table behind which a servant was still standing. Iced cakes, sandwiches innumerable, coffee, claret-cup, champagne, remained almost intact: their overfed guests could do no more. Leonard refused. Jacky thought she could manage a little. Margaret left them whispering together, and had a few more words with Helen.

She said: "Helen, I like Mr. Bast. I agree that he's worth help-ing. I agree that we are directly responsible."

"No indirectly. Via Mr. Wilcox.

"Let me tell you once for all that if you take up that attitude, I'll do nothing. No doubt you're right logically, and are entitled to say a great many scathing things about Henry. Only, I won't have it. So choose.

Helen looked at the sunset.

"If you promise to take them quietly to the George, I will speak to Henry about them—in my own way, mind; there is to be none of this absurd screaming about justice. I have no use for justice. If it was only a question of money, we could do it ourselves. But he wants work, and that we can't give him, but possibly Henry can."

"It's his duty to," grumbled Helen.

"Nor am I concerned with duty. I'm concerned with the charac-ters of various people whom we know, and how, things being as they are, things may be made a little better. Mr. Wilcox hates being asked favours: all business men do. But I am going to ask him, at the risk of a rebuff, because I want to make things a little better."

"Very well. I promise. You take it very calmly."

"Take them off to the George, then, and I'll try. Poor creatures! but they look tired." As they parted, she added: "I haven't nearly done with you, though, Helen. You have been most self-indul-gent. I can't get over it. You have less restraint rather than more as you grow older. Think it over and alter yourself, or we shan't have happy lives."

She rejoined Henry. Fortunately he had been sitting down: these physical matters were important. "Was it townees?" he asked, greeting her with a pleasant smile.

"You'll never believe me," said Margaret, sitting down beside him. "It's all right now, but it was my sister."

"Helen here?" he cried, preparing to rise. "But she refused the invitation. I thought she despised weddings."

"Don't get up. She has not come to the wedding. I've bundled her off to the George."

Inherently hospitable, he protested.

"No; she has two of her protégés with her, and must keep with them."

"Let 'em all come."

"My dear Henry, did you see them?"

"I did catch sight of a brown bunch of a woman, certainly."

"The brown bunch was Helen, but did you catch sight of a seagreen and salmon bunch?"

"What! are they out beanfeasting?"

"No; business. They wanted to see me, and later on I want to talk to you about them."

She was ashamed of her own diplomacy. In dealing with a Wilcox, how tempting it was to lapse from comradeship, and to give him the kind of woman that he desired! Henry took the hint at once, and said: "Why later on? Tell me now. No time like the present."

"Shall I?"

"If it isn't a long story."

"Oh, not five minutes; but there's a sting at the end of it, for I want you to find the man some work in your office."

"What are his qualifications?"

"I don't know. He's a clerk."

"How old?"

"Twenty-five, perhaps."

"What's his name?"

"Bast," said Margaret, and was about to remind him that they had met at Wickham Place, but stopped herself. It had not been a successful meeting.

"Where was he before?"

"Dempster's Bank."

"Why did he leave?" he asked, still remembering nothing.

"They reduced their staff."

"All right; I'll see him."

It was the reward of her tact and devotion through the day. Now she understood why some women prefer influence to rights. Mrs.

Plynlimmon, when condemning suffragettes, had said: "The woman who can't influence her husband to vote the way she wants ought to be ashamed of herself." Margaret had winced, but she was influencing Henry now, and though pleased at her little victory, she knew that she had won it by the methods of the harem.

"I should be glad if you took him," she said, "but I don't know whether he's qualified."

"I'll do what I can. But, Margaret, this mustn't be taken as a precedent."

"No, of course—of course——"

"I can't fit in your protégés every day. Business would suffer."

"I can promise you he's the last. He—he's rather a special case."

"Protégés always are."

She let it stand at that. He rose with a little extra touch of complacency, and held out his hand to help her up. How wide the gulf between Henry as he was and Henry as Helen thought he ought to be! And she herself—hovering as usual between the two, now accepting men as they are, now yearning with her sister for Truth. Love and Truth—their warfare seems eternal. Perhaps the whole visible world rests on it, and if they were one, life itself, like the spirits when Prospero was reconciled to his brother, might vanish into air, into thin air.

"Your protégé has made us late," said he. "The Fussells will just be starting."

On the whole she sided with men as they are. Henry would save the Basts as he had saved Howards End, while Helen and her friends were discussing the ethics of salvation. His was a slap-dash method, but the world has been built slap-dash, and the beauty of mountain and river and sunset may be but the varnish with which the unskilled artificer hides his joins. Oniton, like herself, was imperfect. Its apple-trees were stunted, its castle ruinous. It, too, had suffered in the border warfare between the Anglo-Saxon and the Kelt, between things as they are and as they ought to be. Once more the west was retreating, once again the

orderly stars were dotting the eastern sky. There is certainly no
rest for us on the earth. But there is happiness, and as Margaret
descended the mound on her lover's arm, she felt that she was
having her share.

To her annoyance, Mrs. Bast was still in the garden; the husband and Helen had left her there to finish her meal while they
went to engage rooms. Margaret found this woman repellent. She
had felt, when shaking her hand, an overpowering shame. She
remembered the motive of her call at Wickham Place, and smelt
again odours from the abyss—odours the more disturbing
because they were involuntary. For there was no malice in Jacky.
There she sat, a piece of cake in one hand, an empty champagne
glass in the other, doing no harm to anybody.

"She's overtired," Margaret whispered.

"She's something else," said Henry. "This won't do. I can't have
her in my garden in this state."

"Is she——" Margaret hesitated to add "drunk." Now that she
was going to marry him, he had grown particular. He discounte-
nanced risqué conversations now.

Henry went up to the woman. She raised her face, which
gleamed in the twilight like a puff-ball.

"Madam, you will be more comfortable at the hotel," he
said sharply.

Jacky replied: "If it isn't Hen!"

"Ne crois pas que le mari lui ressemble," apologized Margaret.
"Il est tout à fait différent."

"Henry!" she repeated, quite distinctly.

Mr. Wilcox was much annoyed. "I can't congratulate you on
your protégés," he remarked.

"Hen, don't go. You do love me, dear, don't you?"

"Bless us, what a person!" sighed Margaret, gathering up
her skirts.

Jacky pointed with her cake. "You're a nice boy, you are." She
yawned. "There now, I love you."

"Henry, I am awfully sorry."

"And pray why?" he asked, and looked at her so sternly that she feared he was ill. He seemed more scandalized than the facts demanded.

"To have brought this down on you."

"Pray don't apologize."

The voice continued.

"Why does she call you 'Hen'?" said Margaret innocently. "Has she ever seen you before?"

"Seen Hen before!" said Jacky. "Who hasn't seen Hen? He's serving you like me, my dear. These boys! You wait—— Still we love 'em."

"Are you now satisfied?" Henry asked.

Margaret began to grow frightened. "I don't know what it is all about," she said. "Let's come in."

But he thought she was acting. He thought he was trapped. He saw his whole life crumbling. "Don't you indeed?" he said bitingly. "I do. Allow me to congratulate you on the success of your plan."

"This is Helen's plan, not mine."

"I now understand your interest in the Basts. Very well thought out. I am amused at your caution, Margaret. You are quite right—it was necessary. I am a man, and have lived a man's past. I have the honour to release you from your engagement."

Still she could not understand. She knew of life's seamy side as a theory; she could not grasp it as a fact. More words from Jacky were necessary—words unequivocal, undenied.

"So that——" burst from her, and she went indoors. She stopped herself from saying more.

"So what?" asked Colonel Fussell, who was getting ready to start in the hall.

"We were saying—Henry and I were just having the fiercest argument, my point being——" Seizing his fur coat from a footman, she offered to help him on. He protested, and there was a playful little scene.

"No, let me do that," said Henry, following.

"Thanks so much! You see—he has forgiven me!"

The Colonel said gallantly: "I don't expect there's much to forgive."

He got into the car. The ladies followed him after an interval. Maids, courier, and heavier luggage had been sent on earlier by the branch-line. Still chattering, still thanking their host and patronizing their future hostess, the guests were borne away.

Then Margaret continued: "So that woman has been your mistress?"

"You put it with your usual delicacy," he replied.

"When, please?"

"Why?"

"When, please?"

"Ten years ago."

She left him without a word. For it was not her tragedy: it was Mrs. Wilcox's.

CHAPTER XXVII

Helen began to wonder why she had spent a matter of eight pounds in making some people ill and others angry. Now that the wave of excitement was ebbing, and had left her, Mr. Bast, and Mrs. Bast stranded for the night in a Shropshire hotel, she asked herself what forces had made the wave flow. At all events, no harm was done. Margaret would play the game properly now, and though Helen disapproved of her sister's methods, she knew that the Basts would benefit by them in the long-run.

"Mr. Wilcox is so illogical," she explained to Leonard, who had put his wife to bed, and was sitting with her in the empty coffee-room. "If we told him it was his duty to take you on, he might refuse to do it. The fact is, he isn't properly educated. I don't want to set you against him, but you'll find him a trial."

"I can never thank you sufficiently, Miss Schlegel," was all that Leonard felt equal to.

"I believe in personal responsibility. Don't you? And in

personal everything. I hate—I suppose I oughtn't to say that—but the Wilcoxes are on the wrong tack surely. Or perhaps it isn't their fault. Perhaps the little thing that says 'I' is missing out of the middle of their heads, and then it's a waste of time to blame them. There's a nightmare of a theory that says a special race is being born which will rule the rest of us in the future just because it lacks the little thing that says 'I.' Had you heard that?"

"I get no time for reading."

"Had you thought it, then? That there are two kinds of people—our kind, who live straight from the middle of their heads, and the other kind who can't, because their heads have no middle? They can't say 'I.' They *aren't* in fact, and so they're supermen. Pierpoint Morgan has never said 'I' in his life."

Leonard roused himself. If his benefactress wanted intellectual conversation, she must have it. She was more important than his ruined past. "I never got on to Nietzsche," he said. "But I always understood that those supermen were rather what you may call egoists."

"Oh no, that's wrong," replied Helen. "No superman ever said 'I want,' because 'I want' must lead to the question, 'Who am I?' and so to Pity and to Justice. He only says 'want.' 'Want Europe,' if he's Napoleon; 'want wives,' if he's Bluebeard; 'want Botticelli,' if he's Pierpoint Morgan. Never the 'I'; and if you could pierce through him, you'd find panic and emptiness in the middle."

Leonard was silent for a moment. Then he said: "May I take it, Miss Schlegel, that you and I are both the sort that say 'I'?"

"Of course."

"And your sister too?"

"Of course," repeated Helen, a little sharply. She was annoyed with Margaret, but did not want her discussed. "All presentable people say 'I.' "

"But Mr. Wilcox—he is not perhaps———"

"I don't know that it's any good discussing Mr. Wilcox either."

"Quite so, quite so," he agreed. Helen asked herself why she had snubbed him. Once or twice during the day she had encouraged him to criticize, and then had pulled him up short. Was she afraid of him presuming? If so, it was disgusting of her.

But he was thinking the snub quite natural. Everything she did was natural, and incapable of causing offence. While the Miss Schlegels were together he had felt them scarcely human—a sort of admonitory whirligig. But a Miss Schlegel alone was different. She was in Helen's case unmarried, in Margaret's about to be married, in neither case an echo of her sister. A light had fallen at last into this rich upper world, and he saw that it was full of men and women, some of whom were more friendly to him than others. Helen had become "his" Miss Schlegel, who scolded him and corresponded with him, and had swept down yesterday with grateful vehemence. Margaret, though not unkind, was severe and remote. He would not presume to help her, for instance. He had never liked her, and began to think that his original impression was true, and that her sister did not like her either. Helen was certainly lonely. She, who gave away so much, was receiving too little. Leonard was pleased to think that he could spare her vexation by holding his tongue and concealing what he knew about Mr. Wilcox. Jacky had announced her discovery when he fetched her from the lawn. After the first shock, he did not mind for himself. By now he had no illusions about his wife, and this was only one new stain on the face of a love that had never been pure. To keep perfection perfect, that should be his ideal, if the future gave him time to have ideals. Helen, and Margaret for Helen's sake, must not know.

Helen disconcerted him by turning the conversation to his wife. "Mrs. Bast—does she ever say 'I'?" she asked, half mischievously, and then, "Is she very tired?"

"It's better she stops in her room," said Leonard.

"Shall I sit up with her?"

"No, thank you; she does not need company."

"Mr. Bast, what kind of woman is your wife?"

Leonard blushed up to his eyes.

"You ought to know my ways by now. Does that question offend you?"

"No, oh no, Miss Schlegel, no."

"Because I love honesty. Don't pretend your marriage has been a happy one. You and she can have nothing in common."

He did not deny it, but said shyly: "I suppose that's pretty obvious; but Jacky never meant to do anybody any harm. When things went wrong, or I heard things, I used to think it was her fault, but, looking back, it's more mine. I needn't have married her, but as I have I must stick to her and keep her."

"How long have you been married?"

"Nearly three years."

"What did your people say?"

"They will not have anything to do with us. They had a sort of family council when they heard I was married, and cut us off altogether."

Helen began to pace up and down the room. "My good boy, what a mess!" she said gently. "Who are your people?"

He could answer this. His parents, who were dead, had been in trade; his sisters had married commercial travellers; his brother was a lay-reader.

"And your grandparents?"

Leonard told her a secret that he had held shameful up to now. "They were just nothing at all," he said—"agricultural labourers and that sort."

"So! From which part?"

"Lincolnshire mostly, but my mother's father—he, oddly enough, came from these parts round here."

"From this very Shropshire. Yes, that is odd. My mother's people were Lancashire. But why do your brother and your sisters object to Mrs. Bast?"

"Oh, I don't know."

"Excuse me, you do know. I am not a baby. I can bear anything you tell me, and the more you tell the more I shall be able to help. Have they heard anything against her?"

He was silent.

"I think I have guessed now," said Helen very gravely.

"I don't think so, Miss Schlegel; I hope not."

"We must be honest, even over these things. I have guessed. I am frightfully, dreadfully sorry, but it does not make the least difference to me. I shall feel just the same to both of you. I blame, not your wife for these things, but men."

Leonard left it at that—so long as she did not guess the man. She stood at the window and slowly pulled up the blinds. The hotel looked over a dark square. The mists had begun. When she turned back to him her eyes were shining.

"Don't you worry," he pleaded. "I can't bear that. We shall be all right if I get work. If I could only get work—something regular to do. Then it wouldn't be so bad again. I don't trouble after books as I used. I can imagine that with regular work we should settle down again. It stops one thinking."

"Settle down to what?"

"Oh, just settle down."

"And that's to be life!" said Helen, with a catch in her throat. "How can you, with all the beautiful things to see and do—with music—with walking at night——"

"Walking is well enough when a man's in work," he answered. "Oh, I did talk a lot of nonsense once, but there's nothing like a bailiff in the house to drive it out of you. When I saw him fingering my Ruskins and Stevensons, I seemed to see life straight real, and it isn't a pretty sight. My books are back again, thanks to you, but they'll never be the same to me again, and I shan't ever again think night in the woods is wonderful."

"Why not?" asked Helen, throwing up the window.

"Because I see one must have money."

"Well, you're wrong."

` "I wish I was wrong, but—the clergyman—he has money of his own, or else he's paid; the poet or the musician—just the same; the tramp—he's no different. The tramp goes to the workhouse in the end, and is paid for with other people's money. Miss Schlegel, the real thing's money, and all the rest is a dream."

"You're still wrong. You've forgotten Death."

Leonard could not understand.

"If we lived for ever, what you say would be true. But we have to die, we have to leave life presently. Injustice and greed would be the real thing if we lived for ever. As it is, we must hold to other things, because Death is coming. I love Death——not morbidly, but because He explains. He shows me the emptiness of Money. Death and Money are the eternal foes. Not Death and Life. Never mind what lies behind Death, Mr. Bast, but be sure that the poet and the musician and the tramp will be happier in it than the man who has never learnt to say, 'I am I.' "

"I wonder."

"We are all in a mist—I know, but I can help you this far—men like the Wilcoxes are deeper in the mist than any. Sane, sound Englishmen! building up empires, levelling all the world into what they call common sense. But mention Death to them and they're offended, because Death's really Imperial, and He cries out against them for ever."

"I am as afraid of Death as anyone."

"But not of the idea of Death."

"But what is the difference?"

"Infinite difference," said Helen, more gravely than before.

Leonard looked at her wondering, and had the sense of great things sweeping out of the shrouded night. But he could not receive them, because his heart was still full of little things. As the lost umbrella had spoilt the concert at Queen's Hall, so the lost situation was obscuring the diviner harmonies now. Death, Life and Materialism were fine words, but would Mr. Wilcox take him on as a clerk? Talk as one would, Mr. Wilcox was king of this world, the superman, with his own morality, whose head remained in the clouds.

"I must be stupid," he said apologetically.

While to Helen the paradox became clearer and clearer. 'Death destroys a man: the idea of Death saves him.' Behind the coffins and the skeletons that stay the vulgar mind lies something so immense that all that is great in us responds to it. Men of the world may recoil from the charnel-house that they will one day enter, but Love knows better. Death is his foe, but his peer, and in their age-long struggle the thews of Love have been strengthened, and his vision cleared, until there is no one who can stand against him.

"So never give in," continued the girl, and restated again and again the vague yet convincing plea that the Invisible lodges against the Visible. Her excitement grew as she tried to cut the rope that fastened Leonard to the earth. Woven of bitter experience, it resisted her. Presently the waitress entered and gave her a letter from Margaret. Another note, addressed to Leonard, was inside. They read them, listening to the murmurings of the river.

CHAPTER XXVIII

For many hours Margaret did nothing; then she controlled herself, and wrote some letters. She was too bruised to speak to Henry; she could pity him, and even determine to marry him, but as yet all lay too deep in her heart for speech. On the surface the sense of his degradation was too strong. She could not command voice or look, and the gentle words that she forced out through her pen seemed to proceed from some other person.

"My dearest boy," she began, "this is not to part us. It is everything or nothing, and I mean it to be nothing. It happened long before we ever met, and even if it had happened since, I should be writing the same, I hope. I do understand."

But she crossed out "I do understand"; it struck a false note. Henry could not bear to be understood. She also crossed out, "It is everything or nothing." Henry would resent so strong a grasp of the situation. She must not comment; comment is unfeminine.

"I think that'll about do," she thought.

Then the sense of his degradation choked her. Was he worth all this bother? To have yielded to a woman of that sort was everything, yes, it was, and she could not be his wife. She tried to translate his temptation into her own language, and her brain reeled. Men must be different, even to want to yield to such a temptation. Her belief in comradeship was stifled, and she saw life as from that glass saloon on the Great Western, which sheltered male and female alike from the fresh air. Are the sexes really races, each with its own code of morality, and their mutual love a mere device of Nature to keep things going? Strip human intercourse of the proprieties, and is it reduced to this? Her judgment told her no. She knew that out of Nature's device we have built a magic that will win us immortality. Far more mysterious than the call of sex to sex is the tenderness that we throw into that call; far wider is the gulf between us and the farmyard than between the farmyard and the garbage that nourishes it. We are evolving, in ways that Science cannot measure, to ends that Theology dares not contemplate. "Men did produce one jewel," the gods will say, and, saying, will give us immortality. Margaret knew all this, but for the moment she could not feel it, and transformed the marriage of Evie and Mr. Cahill into a carnival of fools, and her own marriage—too miserable to think of that, she tore up the letter, and then wrote another:

"DEAR MR. BAST,
        "I have spoken to Mr. Wilcox about you, as I promised, and am sorry to say that he has no vacancy for you.
                                        "Yours truly,
                                            "M.J. SCHLEGEL."

She enclosed this in a note to Helen, over which she took less trouble than she might have done; but her head was aching, and she could not stop to pick her words:

"DEAR HELEN,
        "Give him this. The Basts are no good. Henry found the woman drunk on the lawn. I am having a room got ready for you here, and will you please come round at once on getting this? The

Basts are not at all the type we should trouble about. I may go round to them myself in the morning, and do anything that is fair.

"M."

In writing this, Margaret felt that she was being practical. Something might be arranged for the Basts later on, but they must be silenced for the moment. She hoped to avoid a conversation between the woman and Helen. She rang the bell for a servant, but no one answered it; Mr. Wilcox and the Warringtons were gone to bed, and the kitchen was abandoned to Saturnalia. Consequently she went over to the George herself. She did not enter the hotel, for discussion would have been perilous, and, saying that the letter was important, she gave it to the waitress. As she recrossed the square she saw Helen and Mr. Bast looking out of the window of the coffee-room, and feared she was already too late. Her task was not yet over; she ought to tell Henry what she had done.

This came easily, for she saw him in the hall. The night wind had been rattling the pictures against the wall, and the noise had disturbed him.

"Who's there?" he called, quite the householder.

Margaret walked in and past him.

"I have asked Helen to sleep," she said. "She is best here; so don't lock the front-door."

"I thought someone had got in," said Henry.

"At the same time I told the man that we could do nothing for him. I don't know about later, but now the Basts must clearly go."

"Did you say that your sister is sleeping here, after all?"

"Probably."

"Is she to be shown up to your room?"

"I have naturally nothing to say to her; I am going to bed. Will you tell the servants about Helen? Could someone go to carry her bag?"

He tapped a little gong, which had been bought to summon the servants.

"You must make more noise than that if you want them to hear."

Henry opened a door, and down the corridor came shouts of laughter. "Far too much screaming there," he said, and strode towards it. Margaret went upstairs, uncertain whether to be glad that they had met, or sorry. They had behaved as if nothing had happened, and her deepest instincts told her that this was wrong. For his own sake, some explanation was due.

And yet—what could an explanation tell her? A date, a place, a few details, which she could imagine all too clearly. Now that the first shock was over, she saw that there was every reason to premise a Mrs. Bast. Henry's inner life had long laid open to her—his intellectual confusion, his obtuseness to personal influence, his strong but furtive passions. Should she refuse him because his outer life corresponded? Perhaps. Perhaps, if the dishonour had been done to her, but it was done long before her day. She struggled against the feeling. She told herself that Mrs. Wilcox's wrong was her own. But she was not a barren theorist. As she undressed, her anger, her regard for the dead, her desire for a scene, all grew weak. Henry must have it as he liked, for she loved him, and some day she would use her love to make him a better man.

Pity was at the bottom of her actions all through this crisis. Pity, if one may generalize, is at the bottom of woman. When men like us, it is for our better qualities, and however tender their liking, we dare not be unworthy of it, or they will quietly let us go. But unworthiness stimulates woman. It brings out her deeper nature, for good or for evil.

Here was the core of the question. Henry must be forgiven, and made better by love; nothing else mattered. Mrs. Wilcox, that unquiet yet kindly ghost, must be left to her own wrong. To her everything was in proportion now, and she, too, would pity the man who was blundering up and down their lives. Had Mrs. Wilcox known of his trespass? An interesting question, but Margaret fell asleep, tethered by affection, and lulled by the murmurs of the river that descended all the night from Wales. She felt herself at one with her future home, colouring it and coloured by it, and awoke to see, for the second time, Oniton Castle conquering the morning mists.

CHAPTER XXIX

"Henry dear——" was her greeting.

He had finished his breakfast, and was beginning the 'Times.' His sister-in-law was packing. She knelt by him and took the paper from him, feeling that it was unusually heavy and thick. Then, putting her face where it had been, she looked up in his eyes.

"Henry dear, look at me. No, I won't have you shirking. Look at me. There. That's all."

"You're referring to last evening," he said huskily. "I have released you from your engagement. I could find excuses, but I won't. No, I won't. A thousand times no. I'm a bad lot, and must be left at that."

Expelled from his old fortress, Mr. Wilcox was building a new one. He could no longer appear respectable to her, so he defended himself instead in a lurid past. It was not true repentance.

"Leave it where you will, boy. It's not going to trouble us: I know what I'm talking about, and it will make no difference."

"No difference?" he inquired. "No difference, when you find that I am not the fellow you thought?" He was annoyed with Miss Schlegel here. He would have preferred her to be prostrated by the blow, or even to rage. Against the tide of his sin flowed the feeling that she was not altogether womanly. Her eyes gazed too straight; they had read books that are suitable for men only. And though he had dreaded a scene, and though she had determined against one, there was a scene, all the same. It was somehow imperative.

"I am unworthy of you," he began. "Had I been worthy, I should not have released you from your engagement. I know what I am talking about. I can't bear to talk of such things. We had better leave it."

She kissed his hand. He jerked it from her, and, rising to his feet, went on: "You, with your sheltered life, and refined pursuits, and friends, and books, you and your sister, and women like you—I say, how can you guess the temptations that lie round a man?"

"It is difficult for us," said Margaret; "but if we are worth marrying, we do guess."

"Cut off from decent society and family ties, what do you suppose happens to thousands of young fellows overseas? Isolated. No one near. I know by bitter experience, and yet you say it makes 'no difference.'"

"Not to me."

He laughed bitterly. Margaret went to the sideboard and helped herself to one of the breakfast dishes. Being the last down, she turned out the spirit-lamp that kept them warm. She was tender, but grave. She knew that Henry was not so much confessing his soul as pointing out the gulf between the male soul and the female, and she did not desire to hear him on this point.

"Did Helen come?" she asked.

He shook his head.

"But that won't do at all, at all! We don't want her gossiping with Mrs. Bast."

"Good God! no!" he exclaimed, suddenly natural. Then he caught himself up. "Let them gossip. My game's up, though I thank you for your unselfishness—little as my thanks are worth."

"Didn't she send me a message or anything?"

"I heard of none."

"Would you ring the bell, please?"

"What to do?"

"Why, to inquire."

He swaggered up to it tragically, and sounded a peal. Margaret poured herself out some coffee. The butler came, and said that Miss Schlegel had slept at the George, so far as he had heard. Should he go round to the George?

"I'll go, thank you," said Margaret, and dismissed him.

"It is no good," said Henry. "Those things leak out; you cannot stop a story once it has started. I have known cases of other men—I despised them once, I thought that *I'm* different, *I* shall never be tempted. Oh, Margaret——" He came and sat down near her, improvising emotion. She could not bear to listen to him. "We fellows all come to grief once in our time. Will you believe that? There are moments when the strongest man —— 'Let him who standeth, take heed lest he fall.' That's true, isn't it? If you knew all, you would excuse me. I was far from good influences—far even from England. I was very, very lonely, and longed for a woman's voice. That's enough. I have told you too much already for you to forgive me now."

"Yes, that's enough, dear."

"I have"—he lowered his voice—"I have been through hell."

Gravely she considered this claim. Had he? Had he suffered tortures of remorse, or had it been, "There! that's over. Now for respectable life again"? The latter, if she read him rightly. A man who has been through hell does not boast of his virility. He is humble and hides it, if, indeed, it still exists. Only in legend does the sinner come forth penitent, but terrible, to conquer pure woman by his resistless power. Henry was anxious to be terrible, but had not got it in him. He was a good average Englishman, who had slipped. The really culpable point—his faithlessness to Mrs. Wilcox—never seemed to strike him. She longed to mention Mrs. Wilcox.

And bit by bit the story was told her. It was a very simple story. Ten years ago was the time, a garrison town in Cyprus the place. Now and then he asked her whether she could possibly forgive him, and she answered, "I have already forgiven you, Henry." She chose her words carefully, and so saved him from panic. She played the girl, until he could rebuild his fortress and hide his soul from the world. When the butler came to clear away, Henry was in a very different mood—asked the fellow what he was in such a hurry for, complained of the noise last night in the servants' hall. Margaret looked intently at the butler. He, as a handsome young man, was faintly attractive to her as a woman—

an attraction so faint as scarcely to be perceptible, yet the skies would have fallen if she had mentioned it to Henry.

On her return from the George the building operations were complete, and the old Henry fronted her, competent, cynical, and kind. He had made a clean breast, had been forgiven, and the great thing now was to forget his failure, and to send it the way of other unsuccessful investments. Jacky rejoined Howards End and Ducie Street, and the vermilion motor-car, and the Argentine Hard Dollars, and all the things and people for whom he had never had much use, and had less now. Their memory hampered him. He could scarcely attend to Margaret, who brought back disquieting news from the George. Helen and her clients had gone.

"Well, let them go—the man and his wife, I mean, for the more we see of your sister the better."

"But they have gone separately—Helen very early, the Basts just before I arrived. They have left no message. They have answered neither of my notes. I don't like to think what it all means."

"What did you say in the notes?"

"I told you last night."

"Oh—ah—yes! Dear, would you like one turn in the garden?"

Margaret took his arm. The beautiful weather soothed her. But the wheels of Evie's wedding were still at work, tossing the guests outwards as deftly as they had drawn them in, and she could not be with him long. It had been arranged that they should motor to Shrewsbury, whence he would go north, and she back to London with the Warringtons. For a fraction of time she was happy. Then her brain recommenced.

"I am afraid there has been gossiping of some kind at the George. Helen would not have left unless she had heard something. I mismanaged that. It is wretched. I ought to have parted her from that woman at once."

"Margaret!" he exclaimed, loosing her arm impressively.

"Yes—yes, Henry?"

"I am far from a saint—in fact, the reverse—but you have taken me, for better or worse. Bygones must be bygones. You have promised to forgive me. Margaret, a promise is a promise. Never mention that woman again.

"Except for some practical reason—never."

"Practical! You practical!"

"Yes, I'm practical," she murmured, stooping over the mowing machine and playing with the grass which trickled through her fingers like sand.

He had silenced her, but her fears made him uneasy. Not for the first time, he was threatened with blackmail. He was rich and supposed to be moral; the Basts knew that he was not, and might find it profitable to hint as much.

"At all events, you mustn't worry," he said. "This is a man's business." He thought intently. "On no account mention it to anybody."

Margaret flushed at advice so elementary, but he was really paving the way for a lie. If necessary he would deny that he had ever known Mrs. Bast, and prosecute her for libel. Perhaps he never had known her. Here was Margaret, who behaved as if he had not. There the house. Round them were half a dozen gardeners, clearing up after his daughter's wedding. All was so solid and spruce, that the past flew up out of sight like a spring-blind, leaving only the last five minutes unrolled.

Glancing at these, he saw that the car would be round during the next five, and plunged into action. Gongs were tapped, orders issued, Margaret was sent to dress, and the housemaid to sweep up the long trickle of grass that she had left across the hall. As is Man to the Universe, so was the mind of Mr. Wilcox to the minds of some men—a concentrated light upon a tiny spot, a little Ten Minutes moving self-contained through its appointed years. No Pagan he, who lives for the Now, and may be wiser than all philosophers. He lived for the five minutes that have past, and the five to come; he had the business mind.

How did he stand now, as his motor slipped out of Oniton and breasted the great round hills? Margaret had heard a certain rumour, but was all right. She had forgiven him, God bless her, and he felt the manlier for it. Charles and Evie had not heard it, and never must hear. No more must Paul. Over his children he felt great tenderness, which he did not try to track to a cause: Mrs. Wilcox was too far back in his life. He did not connect her with the sudden aching love that he felt for Evie. Poor little Evie! he trusted that Cahill would make her a decent husband.

And Margaret? How did she stand?

She had several minor worries. Clearly her sister had heard something. She dreaded meeting her in town. And she was anxious about Leonard, for whom they certainly were responsible. Nor ought Mrs. Bast to starve. But the main situation had not altered. She still loved Henry. His actions, not his disposition, had disappointed her, and she could bear that. And she loved her future home. Standing up in the car, just where she had leapt from it two days before, she gazed back with deep emotion upon Oniton. Besides the Grange and the Castle keep, she could now pick out the church and the black-and-white gables of the George. There was the bridge, and the river nibbling its green peninsula. She could even see the bathing-shed, but while she was looking for Charles's new spring-board, the forehead of the hill rose up and hid the whole scene.

She never saw it again. Day and night the river flows down into England, day after day the sun retreats into the Welsh mountains, and the tower chimes, "See the Conquering Hero." But the Wilcoxes have no part in the place, nor in any place. It is not their names that recur in the parish register. It is not their ghosts that sigh among the alders at evening. They have swept into the valley and swept out of it, leaving a little dust and a little money behind.

CHAPTER XXX

Tibby was now approaching his last year at Oxford. He had moved out of college, and was contemplating the Universe, or such portions of it as concerned him, from his comfortable lodgings in Long Wall. He was not concerned with much. When a young man is untroubled by passions and sincerely indifferent to public opinion, his outlook is necessarily limited. Tibby neither wished to strengthen the position of the rich nor to improve that of the poor, and so was well content to watch the elms nodding behind the mildly embattled parapets of Magdalen. There are worse lives. Though selfish, he was never cruel; though affected in manner, he never posed. Like Margaret, he disdained the heroic equipment, and it was only after many visits that men discovered Schlegel to possess a character and a brain. He had done well in Mods, much to the surprise of those who attended lectures and took proper exercise, and was now glancing disdainfully at Chinese in case he should some day consent to qualify as a Student Interpreter. To him thus employed Helen entered. A telegram had preceded her.

He noticed, in a distant way, that his sister had altered. As a rule he found her too pronounced, and had never come across this look of appeal, pathetic yet dignified—the look of a sailor who has lost everything at sea.

"I have come from Oniton," she began. "There has been a great deal of trouble there."

"Who's for lunch?" said Tibby, picking up the claret, which was warming in the hearth. Helen sat down submissively at the table. "Why such an early start?" he asked.

"Sunrise or something—hen I could get away."

"So I surmise. Why?"

"I don't know what's to be done, Tibby. I am very much upset at a piece of news that concerns Meg, and do not want to face her, and I am not going back to Wickham Place. I stopped here to tell you this."

The landlady came in with the cutlets. Tibby put a marker in the leaves of his Chinese Grammar and helped them. Oxford— the Oxford of the vacation—dreamed and rustled outside, and indoors the little fire was coated with grey where the sunshine touched it. Helen continued her odd story.

"Give Meg my love and say that I want to be alone. I mean to go to Munich or else Bonn."

"Such a message is easily given," said her brother.

"As regards Wickham Place and my share of the furniture, you and she are to do exactly as you like. My own feeling is that everything may just as well be sold. What does one want with dusty economic books, which have made the world no better, or with mother's hideous cheffoniers? I have also another commission for you. I want you to deliver a letter." She got up. "I haven't written it yet. Why shouldn't I post it, though?" She sat down again. "My head is rather wretched. I hope that none of your friends are likely to come in."

Tibby locked the door. His friends often found it in this condition. Then he asked whether anything had gone wrong at Evie's wedding.

"Not there," said Helen, and burst into tears.

He had known her hysterical—it was one of her aspects with which he had no concern—and yet these tears touched him as something unusual. They were nearer the things that did concern him, such as music. He laid down his knife and looked at her curiously. Then, as she continued to sob, he went on with his lunch.

The time came for the second course, and she was still crying. Apple Charlotte was to follow, which spoils by waiting. "Do you mind Mrs. Marlett coming in?" he asked, "or shall I take it from her at the door?"

"Could I bathe my eyes, Tibby?"

He took her to his bedroom, and introduced the pudding in her absence. Having helped himself, he put it down to warm in the hearth. His hand stretched towards the Grammar, and soon he was turning over the pages, raising his eyebrows scornfully, perhaps at human nature, perhaps at Chinese. To him thus employed Helen returned. She had pulled herself together, but the grave appeal had not vanished from her eyes.

"Now for the explanation," she said. "Why didn't I begin with it? I have found out something about Mr. Wilcox. He has behaved very wrongly indeed, and ruined two people's lives. It all came on me very suddenly last night; I am very much upset, and I do not know what to do. Mrs. Bast——"

"Oh, those people!"

Helen seemed silenced.

"Shall I lock the door again?"

"No thanks, Tibbikins. You're being very good to me. I want to tell you the story before I go abroad. You must do exactly what you like—treat it as part of the furniture. Meg cannot have heard it yet, I think. But I cannot face her and tell her that the man she is going to marry has misconducted himself. I don't even know whether she ought to be told. Knowing as she does that I dislike him, she will suspect me, and think that I want to ruin her match. I simply don't know what to make of such a thing. I trust your judgment. What would you do?"

"I gather he has had a mistress," said Tibby.

Helen flushed with shame and anger. "And ruined two people's lives. And goes about saying that personal actions count for nothing, and there always will be rich and poor. He met her when he was trying to get rich out in Cyprus—I don't wish to make him worse than he is, and no doubt she was ready enough to meet him. But there it is. They met. He goes his way and she goes hers. What do you suppose is the end of such women?"

He conceded that it was a bad business.

"They end in two ways: Either they sink till the lunatic asylums and the workhouses are full of them, and cause Mr. Wilcox to write letters to the papers complaining of our national degeneracy, or else they entrap a boy into marriage before it is too late. She—I can't blame her."

"But this isn't all," she continued after a long pause, during which the landlady served them with coffee. "I come now to the business that took us to Oniton. We went all three. Acting on Mr. Wilcox's advice, the man throws up a secure situation and takes an insecure one, from which he is dismissed. There are certain excuses, but in the main Mr. Wilcox is to blame, as Meg herself admitted. It is only common justice that he should employ the man himself. But he meets the woman, and, like the cur that he is, he refuses, and tries to get rid of them. He makes Meg write. Two notes came from her late that evening—one for me, one for Leonard, dismissing him with barely a reason. I couldn't understand. Then it comes out that Mrs. Bast had spoken to Mr. Wilcox on the lawn while we left her to get rooms, and was still speaking about him when Leonard came back to her. This Leonard knew all along. He thought it natural he should be ruined twice. Natural! Could you have contained yourself?"

"It is certainly a very bad business," said Tibby.

His reply seemed to calm his sister. "I was afraid that I saw it out of proportion. But you are right outside it, and you must know. In a day or two—or perhaps a week—take whatever steps you think fit. I leave it in your hands."

She concluded her charge.

"The facts as they touch Meg are all before you," she added; and Tibby sighed and felt it rather hard that, because of his open mind, he should be empanelled to serve as a juror. He had never been interested in human beings, for which one must blame him, but he had had rather too much of them at Wickham Place. Just as some people cease to attend when books are mentioned, so Tibby's attention wandered when "personal relations" came under discussion. Ought Margaret to know what Helen knew the Basts to know? Similar questions had vexed him from infancy, and at Oxford he had learned to say that the importance of human beings has been vastly over-rated by specialists. The epigram, with its faint whiff of the eighties, meant nothing. But he might have let it off now if his sister had not been ceaselessly beautiful.

"You see, Helen—have a cigarette—I don't see what I'm to do."

"Then there's nothing to be done. I dare say you are right. Let them marry. There remains the question of compensation."

"Do you want me to adjudicate that too? Had you not better consult an expert?"

"This part is in confidence," said Helen. "It has nothing to do with Meg, and do not mention it to her. The compensation—I do not see who is to pay it if I don't, and I have already decided on the minimum sum. As soon as possible I am placing it to your account, and when I am in Germany you will pay it over for me. I shall never forget your kindness, Tibbikins, if you do this."

"What is the sum?"

"Five thousand."

"Good God alive!" said Tibby, and went crimson.

"Now, what is the good of driblets? To go through life having done one thing—to have raised one person from the abyss: not these puny gifts of shillings and blankets—making the grey more grey. No doubt people will think me extraordinary."

"I don't care a damn what people think!" cried he, heated to unusual manliness of diction. "But it's half what you have."

"Not nearly half." She spread out her hands over her soiled skirt. "I have far too much, and we settled at Chelsea last spring that three hundred a year is necessary to set a man on his feet. What I give will bring in a hundred and fifty between two. It isn't enough."

He could not recover. He was not angry or even shocked, and he saw that Helen would still have plenty to live on. But it amazed him to think what haycocks people can make of their lives. His delicate intonations would not work, and he could only blurt out that the five thousand pounds would mean a great deal of bother for him personally.

"I didn't expect you to understand me."

"I? I understand nobody."

"But you'll do it?"

"Apparently."

"I leave you two commissions, then. The first concerns Mr. Wilcox, and you are to use your discretion. The second concerns the money, and is to be mentioned to no one, and carried out literally. You will send a hundred pounds on account tomorrow."

He walked with her to the station, passing through those streets whose serried beauty never bewildered him and never fatigued. The lovely creature raised domes and spires into the cloudless blue, and only the ganglion of vulgarity round Carfax showed how evanescent was the phantom, how faint its claim to represent England. Helen, rehearsing her commission, noticed nothing: the Basts were in her brain, and she retold the crisis in a meditative way, which might have made other men curious. She was seeing whether it would hold. He asked her once why she had taken the Basts right into the heart of Evie's wedding. She stopped like a frightened animal and said, "Does that seem to you so odd?" Her eyes, the hand laid on the mouth, quite haunted him, until they were absorbed into the figure of St. Mary the Virgin, before whom he paused for a moment on the walk home.

It is convenient to follow him in the discharge of his duties. Margaret summoned him the next day. She was terrified at Helen's flight, and he had to say that she had called in at Oxford. Then she said:" Did she seem worried at any rumour about Henry?" He answered, "Yes." "I knew it was that!" she exclaimed. "I'll write to her." Tibby was relieved.

He then sent the cheque to the address that Helen gave him, and stated that later on he was instructed to forward five thousand pounds. An answer came back, very civil and quiet in tone—such an answer as Tibby himself would have given. The cheque was returned, the legacy refused, the writer being in no need of money. Tibby forwarded this to Helen, adding in the fulness of his heart that Leonard Bast seemed somewhat a monumental person after all. Helen's reply was frantic. He was to take no notice. He was to go down at once and say that she commanded acceptance. He went. A scurf of books and china ornaments awaited him. The Basts had just been evicted for not paying their rent, and had wandered no one knew whither. Helen had begun bungling with her money by this time, and had even sold out her shares in the Nottingham and Derby Railway. For some weeks she did nothing. Then she reinvested, and, owing to the good advice of her stock-brokers, became rather richer than she had been before.

CHAPTER XXXI

Houses have their own ways of dying, falling as variously as the generations of men, some with a tragic roar, some quietly, but to an after-life in the city of ghosts, while from others—and thus was the death of Wickham Place—the spirit slips before the body perishes. It had decayed in the spring, disintegrating the girls more than they knew, and causing either to accost unfamiliar regions. By September it was a corpse, void of emotion, and scarcely hallowed by the memories of thirty years of happiness. Through its round-topped doorway passed furniture, and pictures, and books, until the last room was gutted and the last van had rumbled away. It stood for a week or two longer, open-eyed, as if astonished at its own emptiness. Then it fell. Navvies came, and spilt it back into the grey. With their muscles and their beery good temper, they were not the worst of undertakers for a house which had always been human, and had not mistaken culture for an end.

The furniture, with a few exceptions, went down into Hertfordshire, Mr. Wilcox having most kindly offered Howards End as a warehouse. Mr. Bryce had died abroad—an unsatisfactory affair—and as there seemed little guarantee that the rent would be paid regularly, he cancelled the agreement, and resumed possession himself. Until he relet the house, the Schlegels were welcome to stack their furniture in the garage and lower rooms. Margaret demurred, but Tibby accepted the offer gladly; it saved him from coming to any decision about the future. The plate and the more valuable pictures found a safer home in London, but the bulk of the things went country-ways, and were entrusted to the guardianship of Miss Avery.

Shortly before the move, our hero and heroine were married. They have weathered the storm, and may reasonably expect peace. To have no illusions and yet to love—what stronger surety can a woman find? She had seen her husband's past as well as his heart. She knew her own heart with a thoroughness that commonplace people believe impossible. The heart of Mrs. Wilcox was alone hidden, and perhaps it is superstitious to speculate on the feelings of the dead. They were married quietly—really quietly, for as the day approached she refused to go through another Oniton. Her brother gave her away, her aunt, who was out of health, presided over a few colourless refreshments. The Wilcoxes were represented by Charles, who witnessed the marriage settlement, and by Mr. Cahill. Paul did send a cablegram. In a few minutes, and without the aid of music, the clergyman made them man and wife, and soon the glass shade had fallen that cuts off married couples from the world. She, a monogamist, regretted the cessation of some of life's innocent odours; he, whose instincts were polygamous, felt morally braced by the change, and less liable to the temptations that had assailed him in the past.

They spent their honeymoon near Innsbruck. Henry knew of a reliable hotel there, and Margaret hoped for a meeting with her sister. In this she was disappointed. As they came south, Helen retreated over the Brenner, and wrote an unsatisfactory postcard from the shores of the Lake of Garda, saying that her plans were uncertain and had better be ignored. Evidently she disliked meeting Henry. Two months are surely enough to accustom an outsider to a situation which a wife has accepted in two days, and Margaret had again to regret her sister's lack of self-control. In a long letter she pointed out the need of charity in sexual matters: so little is known about them; it is hard enough for those who are personally touched to judge; then how futile must be the verdict of Society. "I don't say there is no standard, for that would destroy morality; only that there can be no standard until our impulses are classified and better understood." Helen thanked her for her kind letter—rather a curious reply. She moved south again, and spoke of wintering in Naples.

Mr. Wilcox was not sorry that the meeting failed. Helen left him time to grow skin over his wound. There were still moments when it pained him. Had he only known that Margaret was awaiting him—Margaret, so lively and intelligent, and yet so submissive—he would have kept himself worthier of her. Incapable of grouping the past, he confused the episode of Jacky with another episode that had taken place in the days of his bachelorhood. The two made one crop of wild oats, for which he was heartily sorry, and he could not see that those oats are of a darker stock which are rooted in another's dishonour. Unchastity and infidelity were as confused to him as to the Middle Ages, his only moral teacher. Ruth (poor old Ruth!) did not enter into his calculations at all, for poor old Ruth had never found him out.

His affection for his present wife grew steadily. Her cleverness gave him no trouble, and, indeed, he liked to see her reading poetry or something about social questions; it distinguished her from the wives of other men. He had only to call, and she clapped the book up and was ready to do what he wished. Then they would argue so jollily, and once or twice she had him in quite a tight corner, but as soon as he grew really serious, she gave in. Man is for war, woman for the recreation of the warrior, but he does not dislike it if she makes a show of fight. She cannot win in a real battle, having no muscles, only nerves. Nerves make her jump out of a moving motor-car, or refuse to be married fashionably. The warrior may well allow her to triumph on such occasions; they move not the imperishable plinth of things that touch his peace.

Margaret had a bad attack of these nerves during the honeymoon. He told her—casually, as was his habit—that Oniton Grange was let. She showed her annoyance, and asked rather crossly why she had not been consulted.

"I didn't want to bother you," he replied. "Besides, I have only heard for certain this morning."

"Where are we to live?" said Margaret, trying to laugh. "I loved the place extraordinarily. Don't you believe in having a permanent home, Henry?"

He assured her that she misunderstood him. It is home life that distinguishes us from the foreigner. But he did not believe in a damp home.

"This is news. I never heard till this minute that Oniton was damp."

"My dear girl!"—he flung out his hand—"have you eyes? have you a skin? How could it be anything but damp in such a situation? In the first place, the Grange is on clay, and built where the castle moat must have been; then there's that detestable little river, steaming all night like a kettle. Feel the cellar walls; look up under the eaves. Ask Sir James or anyone. Those Shropshire valleys are notorious. The only possible place for a house in Shropshire is on a hill; but, for my part, I think the country is too far from London, and the scenery nothing special."

Margaret could not resist saying, "Why did you go there, then?"

"I—because——" He drew his head back and grew rather angry. "Why have we come to the Tyrol, if it comes to that? One might go on asking such questions indefinitely."

One might; but he was only gaining time for a plausible answer. Out it came, and he believed it as soon as it was spoken.

"The truth is, I took Oniton on account of Evie. Don't let this go any further."

"Certainly not."

"I shouldn't like her to know that she nearly let me in for a very bad bargain. No sooner did I sign the agreement than she got engaged. Poor little girl! She was so keen on it all, and wouldn't even wait to make proper inquiries about the shooting. Afraid it would get snapped up—just like all of your sex. Well, no harm's done. She has had her country wedding, and I've got rid of my house to some fellows who are starting a preparatory school."

"Where shall we live, then, Henry? I should enjoy living somewhere."

"I have not yet decided. What about Norfolk?"

Margaret was silent. Marriage had not saved her from the sense of flux. London was but a foretaste of this nomadic civilization which is altering human nature so profoundly, and throws upon personal relations a stress greater than they have ever borne before. Under cosmopolitanism, if it comes, we shall receive no help from the earth. Trees and meadows and mountains will only be a spectacle, and the binding force that they once exercised on character must be entrusted to Love alone. May Love be equal to the task!

"It is now what?" continued Henry. "Nearly October. let us camp for the winter at Ducie Street, and look out for something in the spring."

"If possible, something permanent. I can't be as young as I was, for these alterations don't suit me."

"But, my dear, which would you rather have—alterations or rheumatism?"

"I see your point," said Margaret, getting up. "If Oniton is really damp, it is impossible, and must be inhabited by little boys. Only, in the spring, let us look before we leap. I will take warning by Evie, and not hurry you. Remember that you have a free hand this time. These endless moves must be bad for the furniture, and are certainly expensive."

"What a practical little woman it is! What's it been reading? Theo—theo—how much?"

"Theosophy."

So Ducie Street was her first fate—a pleasant enough fate. The house, being only a little larger than Wickham Place, trained her for the immense establishment that was promised in the spring. They were frequently away, but at home life ran fairly regularly. In the morning Henry went to the business, and his sandwich—a relic this of some prehistoric craving—was always cut by her own hand. He did not rely upon the sandwich for lunch, but liked to have it by him in case he grew hungry at eleven. When he had gone, there was the house to look after, and the servants to humanize, and several kettles of Helen's to keep on the boil. Her conscience pricked her a little about the Basts; she was not sorry to have lost sight of them. No doubt Leonard was worth helping, but being Henry's wife, she preferred to help someone else. As for theatres and discussion societies, they attracted her less and less. She began to "miss" new movements, and to spend her spare time re-reading or thinking, rather to the concern of her Chelsea friends. They attributed the change to her marriage, and perhaps some deep instinct did warn her not to travel further from her husband than was inevitable. Yet the main cause lay deeper still; she had outgrown stimulants, and was passing from words to things. It was doubtless a pity not to keep up with Wedekind or John, but some closing of the gates is inevitable after thirty, if the mind itself is to become a creative power.

CHAPTER XXXII

She was looking at plans one day in the following spring—they had finally decided to go down into Sussex and build—when Mrs. Charles Wilcox was announced.

"Have you heard the news?" Dolly cried, as soon as she entered the room. "Charles is so ang—I mean he is sure you know about it, or, rather, that you don't know."

"Why, Dolly!" said Margaret, placidly kissing her. "Here's a surprise! How are the boys and the baby?"

Boys and the baby were well, and in describing a great row that there had been at the Hilton Tennis Club, Dolly forgot her news. The wrong people had tried to get in. The rector, as representing the older inhabitants, had said—Charles had said—the tax-collector had said—Charles had regretted not saying—and she closed the description with, "But lucky you, with four courts of your own at Midhurst."

"It will be very jolly," replied Margaret.

"Are those the plans? Does it matter me seeing them?"

"Of course not."

"Charles has never seen the plans."

"They have only just arrived. Here is the ground floor—no, that's rather difficult. Try the elevation. We are to have a good many gables and a picturesque sky-line."

"What makes it smell so funny?" said Dolly, after a moment's inspection. She was incapable of understanding plans or maps.

"I suppose the paper."

"And *which* way up is it?"

"Just the ordinary way up. That's the sky-line, and the part that smells strongest is the sky."

"Well, ask me another. Margaret—oh—what was I going to say? How's Helen?"

"Quite well."

"Is she never coming back to England? Everyone thinks it's awfully odd she doesn't."

"So it is," said Margaret, trying to conceal her vexation. She was getting rather sore on this point. "Helen is odd, awfully. She has now been away eight months."

"But hasn't she any address?"

"A poste restante somewhere in Bavaria is her address. Do write her a line. I will look it up for you."

"No, don't bother. That's eight months she has been away, surely?"

"Exactly. She left just after Evie's wedding. It would be eight months."

"Just when baby was born, then?"

"Just so."

Dolly sighed, and stared enviously round the drawing-room. She was beginning to lose her brightness and good looks. The Charles' were not well off, for Mr. Wilcox, having brought up his children with expensive tastes, believed in letting them shift for themselves. After all, he had not treated them generously. Yet another baby was expected, she told Margaret, and they would have to give up the motor. Margaret sympathized, but in a formal fashion, and Dolly little imagined that the step-mother was urging Mr. Wilcox to make them a more liberal allowance. She sighed again, and at last the particular grievance was remembered. "Oh yes," she cried, "that is it: Miss Avery has been unpacking your packing-cases."

"Why has she done that? How unnecessary!"

"Ask another. I suppose you ordered her to."

"I gave no such orders. Perhaps she was airing the things. She did undertake to light an occasional fire."

"It was far more than an air," said Dolly solemnly. " The floor sounds covered with books. Charles sent me to know what is to be done, for he feels certain you don't know."

"Books!" cried Margaret, moved by the holy word. "Dolly, are you serious? Has she been touching our books?"

"Hasn't she, though! What used to be the hall's full of them. Charles thought for certain you knew of it."

"I am very much obliged to you, Dolly. What can have come over Miss Avery? I must go down about it at once. Some of the books are my brother's, and are quite valuable. She had no right to open any of the cases."

"I say she's dotty. She was the one that never got married, you know. Oh, I say, perhaps she thinks your books are wedding-presents to herself. Old maids are taken that way sometimes. Miss Avery hates us all like poison ever since her frightful dust-up with Evie."

"I hadn't heard of that," said Margaret. A visit from Dolly had its compensations.

"Didn't you know she gave Evie a present last August, and Evie returned it, and then—oh, goloshes! You never read such a letter as Miss Avery wrote."

"But it was wrong of Evie to return it. It wasn't like her to do such a heartless thing."

"But the present was so expensive."

"Why does that make any difference, Dolly?"

"Still, when it costs over five pounds—I didn't see it, but it was a lovely enamel pendant from a Bond Street shop. You can't very well accept that kind of thing from a farm woman. Now, can you?"

"You accepted a present from Miss Avery when you were married."

"Oh, mine was old earthenware stuff—not worth a halfpenny. Evie's was quite different. You'd have to ask anyone to the wedding who gave you a pendant like that. Uncle Percy and Albert and father and Charles all said it was quite impossible, and when four men agree, what is a girl to do? Evie didn't want to upset the old thing, so thought a sort of joking letter best, and returned the pendant straight to the shop to save Miss Avery trouble."

"But Miss Avery said——"

Dolly's eyes grew round. "It was a perfectly awful letter. Charles said it was the letter of a madman. In the end she had the pendant back again from the shop and threw it into the duck-pond."

"Did she give any reasons?"

"We think she meant to be invited to Oniton, and so climb into society."

"She's rather old for that," said Margaret pensively. "May not she have given the present to Evie in remembrance of her mother?"

"That's a notion. Give everyone their due, eh? Well, I suppose I ought to be toddling. Come along Mr. Muff—you want a new coat, but I don't know who'll give it you, I'm sure;" and addressing her apparel with mournful humour, Dolly moved from the room.

Margaret followed her to ask whether Henry knew about Miss Avery's rudeness.

"Oh yes."

"I wonder, then, why he let me ask her to look after the house."

"But she's only a farm woman," said Dolly, and her explanation proved correct. Henry only censured the lower classes when it suited him. He bore with Miss Avery as with Crane—because he could get good value out of them. "I have patience with a man who knows his job," he would say, really having patience with the job, and not the man. Paradoxical as it may sound, he had something of the artist about him; he would pass over an insult of his daughter sooner than lose a good charwoman for his wife.

Margaret judged it better to settle the little trouble herself. Parties were evidently ruffled. With Henry's permission, she wrote a pleasant note to Miss Avery, asking her to leave the cases untouched. Then, at the first convenient opportunity, she went down herself, intending to repack her belongings and store them properly in the local warehouse: the plan had been amateurish and a failure. Tibby promised to accompany her, but at the last moment begged to be excused. So, for the second time in her life, she entered the house alone.

CHAPTER XXXIII

The day of her visit was exquisite, and the last of unclouded happiness that she was to have for many months. Her anxiety about Helen's extraordinary absence was still dormant, and as for a possible brush with Miss Avery—that only gave zest to the expedition. She had also eluded Dolly's invitation to luncheon. Walking straight up from the station, she crossed the village green and entered the long chestnut avenue that connects it with the church. The church itself stood in the village once. But it there attracted so many worshippers that the devil, in a pet, snatched it from its foundations, and poised it on an inconvenient knoll, three-quarters of a mile away. If this story is true, the chestnut avenue must have been planted by the angels. No more tempting approach could be imagined for the lukewarm Christian, and if he still finds the walk too long, the devil is defeated all the same, Science having built Holy Trinity, a Chapel of Ease, near the Charles', and roofed it with tin.

Up the avenue Margaret strolled slowly, stopping to watch the sky that gleamed through the upper branches of the chestnuts, or to finger the little horseshoes on the lower branches. Why has not England a great mythology? Our folklore has never advanced beyond daintiness, and the greater melodies about our country-side have all issued through the pipes of Greece. Deep and true as the native imagination can be, it seems to have failed here. It has stopped with the witches and the fairies. It cannot vivify one fraction of a summer field, or give names to half a dozen stars. England still waits for the supreme moment of her literature—for the great poet who shall voice her, or, better still, for the thousand little poets whose voices shall pass into our common talk.

At the church the scenery changed. The chestnut avenue opened into a road, smooth but narrow, which led into the untouched country. She followed it for over a mile. Its little hesitations pleased her. Having no urgent destiny, it strolled downhill or up as it wished, taking no trouble about the gradients, nor about the view, which nevertheless expanded. The great estates that throttle the south of Hertfordshire were less obtrusive here, and the appearance of the land was neither aristocratic nor suburban. To define it was difficult, but Margaret knew what it was not: it was not snobbish. Though its contours were slight, there was a touch of freedom in their sweep to which Surrey will never attain, and the distant brow of the Chilterns towered like a mountain. "Left to itself," was Margaret's opinion, "this county would vote Liberal." The comradeship, not passionate, that is our highest gift as a nation, was promised by it, as by the low brick farm where she called for the key.

But the inside of the farm was disappointing. A most finished young person received her. "Yes, Mrs. Wilcox; no, Mrs. Wilcox; oh yes, Mrs. Wilcox, auntie received your letter quite duly. Auntie has gone up to your little place at the present moment. Shall I send the servant to direct you?" Followed by: "Of course, auntie does not generally look after your place; she only does it to oblige a neighbour as something exceptional. It gives her something to do. She spends quite a lot of her time there. My husband says to me sometimes, 'Where's auntie?' I say, 'Need you ask? She's at Howards End.' Yes, Mrs. Wilcox. Mrs. Wilcox, could I prevail upon you to accept a piece of cake? Not if I cut it for you?"

Margaret refused the cake, but unfortunately this acquired her gentility in the eyes of Miss Avery's niece.

"I cannot let you go on alone. Now don't. You really mustn't. I will direct you myself if it comes to that. I must get my hat. Now"—roguishly—"Mrs. Wilcox, don't you move while I'm gone."

Stunned, Margaret did not move from the best parlour, over

which the touch of art nouveau had fallen. But the other rooms looked in keeping, though they conveyed the peculiar sadness of a rural interior. Here had lived an elder race, to which we look back with disquietude. The country which we visit at weekends was really a home to it, and the graver sides of life, the deaths, the partings, the yearnings for love, have their deepest expression in the heart of the fields. All was not sadness. The sun was shining without. The thrush sang his two syllables on the budding guelder-rose. Some children were playing uproariously in heaps of golden straw. It was the presence of sadness at all that surprised Margaret, and ended by giving her a feeling of completeness. In these English farms, if anywhere, one might see life steadily and see it whole, group in one vision its transitoriness and its eternal youth, connect—connect without bitterness until all men are brothers. But her thoughts were interrupted by the return of Miss Avery's niece, and were so tranquillizing that she suffered the interruption gladly.

It was quicker to go out by the back door, and, after due explanations, they went out by it. The niece was now mortified by innumerable chickens, who rushed up to her feet for food, and by a shameless and maternal sow. She did not know what animals were coming to. But her gentility withered at the touch of the sweet air. The wind was rising, scattering the straw and ruffling the tails of the ducks as they floated in families over Evie's pendant. One of those delicious gales of spring, in which leaves still in bud seem to rustle, swept over the land and then fell silent. "Georgie," sang the thrush. "Cuckoo," came furtively from the cliff of pine-trees. "Georgie, pretty Georgie," and the other birds joined in with nonsense. The hedge was a half-painted picture which would be finished in a few days. Celandines grew on its banks, lords and ladies and primroses in the defended hollows; the wild rose-bushes, still bearing their withered hips, showed also the promise of blossom. Spring had come, clad in no classical garb, yet fairer than all springs; fairer even than she who walks through the myrtles of Tuscany with the graces before her and the zephyr behind.

The two women walked up the lane full of outward civility. But Margaret was thinking how difficult it was to be earnest about furniture on such a day, and the niece was thinking about hats. Thus engaged, they reached Howards End. Petulant cries of "Auntie!" severed the air. There was no reply, and the front door was locked.

"Are you sure that Miss Avery is up here?" asked Margaret.

"Oh yes, Mrs. Wilcox, quite sure. She is here daily."

Margaret tried to look in through the dining-room window, but the curtain inside was drawn tightly. So with the drawing-room and the hall. The appearance of these curtains was familiar, yet she did not remember them being there on her other visit: her impression was that Mr. Bryce had taken everything away. They tried the back. Here again they received no answer, and could see nothing; the kitchen-window was fitted with a blind, while the pantry and scullery had pieces of wood propped up against them, which looked ominously like the lids of packing-cases. Margaret thought of her books, and she lifted up her voice also. At the first cry she succeeded.

"Well, well!" replied someone inside the house. "If it isn't Mrs. Wilcox come at last!"

"Have you got the key, auntie?"

"Madge, go away," said Miss Avery, still invisible.

"Auntie, it's Mrs. Wilcox——"

Margaret supported her. "Your niece and I have come together——"

"Madge, go away. This is no moment for your hat."

The poor woman went red. "Auntie gets more eccentric lately," she said nervously.

"Miss Avery!" called Margaret. "I have come about the furniture. Could you kindly let me in?"

"Yes, Mrs. Wilcox," said the voice, "of course." But after that came silence. They called again without response. They walked round the house disconsolately.

"I hope Miss Avery is not ill," hazarded Margaret.

"Well, if you'll excuse me," said Madge, "perhaps I ought to be leaving you now. The servants need seeing to at the farm. Auntie is so odd at times." Gathering up her elegancies, she retired defeated, and, as if her departure had loosed a spring, the front door opened at once.

Miss Avery said, "Well, come right in, Mrs. Wilcox!" quite pleasantly and calmly.

"Thank you so much," began Margaret, but broke off at the sight of an umbrella-stand. It was her own.

"Come right into the hall first," said Miss Avery. She drew the curtain, and Margaret uttered a cry of despair. For an appalling thing had happened. The hall was fitted up with the contents of the library from Wickham Place. The carpet had been laid, the big work-table drawn up near the window; the bookcases filled the wall opposite the fireplace, and her father's sword—this is what bewildered her particularly—had been drawn from its scabbard and hung naked amongst the sober volumes. Miss Avery must have worked for days.

"I'm afraid this isn't what we meant," she began. "Mr. Wilcox and I never intended the cases to be touched. For instance, these books are my brother's. We are storing them for him and for my sister, who is abroad. When you kindly undertook to look after things, we never expected you to do so much."

"The house has been empty long enough," said the old woman.

Margaret refused to argue. "I dare say we didn't explain," she said civilly. "It has been a mistake, and very likely our mistake."

"Mrs. Wilcox, it has been mistake upon mistake for fifty years. The house is Mrs. Wilcox's, and she would not desire it to stand empty any longer."

To help the poor decaying brain, Margaret said:

"Yes, Mrs. Wilcox's house, the mother of Mr. Charles."

"Mistake upon mistake," said Miss Avery. "Mistake upon mistake."

"Well, I don't know," said Margaret, sitting down in one of her own chairs. "I really don't know what's to be done." She could not help laughing.

The other said: "Yes, it should be a merry house enough."

"I don't know—I dare say. Well, thank you very much, Miss Avery. Yes, that's all right. Delightful."

"There is still the parlour." She went through the door opposite and drew a curtain. Light flooded the drawing-room and the drawing-room furniture from Wickham Place. "And the dining-room." More curtains were drawn, more windows were flung open to the spring. "Then through here——" Miss Avery continued passing and repassing through the hall. Her voice was lost, but Margaret heard her pulling up the kitchen blind. "I've not finished here yet," she announced, returning. "There's still a deal to do. The farm lads will carry your great wardrobes upstairs, for there is no need to go into expense at Hilton."

"It is all a mistake," repeated Margaret, feeling that she must put her foot down. "A misunderstanding. Mr. Wilcox and I are not going to live at Howards End."

"Oh, indeed. On account of his hay fever?"

"We have settled to build a new home for ourselves in Sussex, and part of this furniture—my part—will go down there presently." She looked at Miss Avery intently, trying to understand the kink in her brain. Here was no maundering old woman. Her wrinkles were shrewd and humorous. She looked capable of scathing wit and also of high but unostentatious nobility.

"You think that you won't come back to live here, Mrs. Wilcox, but you will."

"That remains to be seen," said Margaret, smiling. "We have no intention of doing so for the present. We happen to need a much larger house. Circumstances oblige us to give big parties. Of course, some day—one never knows, does one?"

Miss Avery retorted: "Some day! Tcha! tcha! Don't talk about some day. You are living here now."

"Am I?"

"You are living here, and have been for the last ten minutes, if you ask me."

It was a senseless remark, but with a queer feeling of disloyalty

Margaret rose from her chair. She felt that Henry had been obscurely censured. They went into the dining-room, where the sunlight poured in upon her mother's cheffonier, and upstairs, where many an old god peeped from a new niche. The furniture fitted extraordinarily well. In the central room—over the hall, the room that Helen had slept in four years ago—Miss Avery had placed Tibby's old bassinette.

"The nursery," she said.

Margaret turned away without speaking.

At last everything was seen. The kitchen and lobby were still stacked with furniture and straw, but, as far as she could make out, nothing had been broken or scratched. A pathetic display of ingenuity! Then they took a friendly stroll in the garden. It had gone wild since her last visit. The gravel sweep was weedy, and grass had sprung up at the very jaws of the garage. And Evie's rockery was only bumps. Perhaps Evie was responsible for Miss Avery's oddness. But Margaret suspected that the cause lay deeper, and that the girl's silly letter had but loosed the irritation of years.

"It's a beautiful meadow," she remarked. It was one of those open-air drawing-rooms that have been formed, hundreds of years ago, out of the smaller fields. So the boundary hedge zigzagged down the hill at right angles, and at the bottom there was a little green annex—a sort of powder-closet for the cows.

"Yes, the maidy's well enough," said Miss Avery, "for those, that is, who don't suffer from sneezing." And she cackled maliciously. "I've seen Charlie Wilcox go out to my lads in hay time—oh, they ought to do this—they mustn't do that—he'd learn them to be lads. And just then the tickling took him. He has it from his father, with other things. There's not one Wilcox that can stand up against a field in June—I laughed fit to burst while he was courting Ruth."

"My brother gets hay fever too," said Margaret.

"This house lies too much on the land for them. Naturally, they were glad enough to slip in at first. But Wilcoxes are better than nothing, as I see you've found."

Margaret laughed.

"They keep a place going, don't they? Yes, it is just that."

"They keep England going, it is my opinion."

But Miss Avery upset her by replying: "Ay, they breed like rabbits. Well, well, it's a funny world. But He who made it knows
what He wants in it, I suppose. If Mrs. Charlie is expecting her
fourth, it isn't for us to repine."

"They breed and they also work," said Margaret, conscious of
some invitation to disloyalty, which was echoed by the very
breeze and by the songs of the birds. "It certainly is a funny
world, but so long as men like my husband and his sons govern
it, I think it'll never be a bad one—never really bad."

"No, better'n nothing," said Miss Avery, and turned to the
wych-elm.

On their way back to the farm she spoke of her old friend
much more clearly than before. In the house Margaret had wondered whether she quite distinguished the first wife from the
second. Now she said: "I never saw much of Ruth after her grandmother died, but we stayed civil. It was a very civil family. Old
Mrs. Howard never spoke against anybody, nor let anyone be
turned away without food. Then it was never 'Trespassers will be
prosecuted' in their land, but would people please not come in?
Mrs. Howard was never created to run a farm."

"Had they no men to help them?" Margaret asked.

Miss Avery replied: "Things went on until there were no men."

"Until Mr. Wilcox came along," corrected Margaret, anxious
that her husband should receive his dues.

"I suppose so; but Ruth should have married a—no disrespect
to you to say this, for I take it you were intended to get Wilcox
any way, whether she got him first or no."

"Whom should she have married?"

"A soldier!" exclaimed the old woman. "Some real soldier."

Margaret was silent. It was a criticism of Henry's character far
more trenchant than any of her own. She felt dissatisfied.

"But that's all over," she went on. "A better time is coming now, though you've kept me long enough waiting. In a couple of weeks I'll see your lights shining through the hedge of an evening. Have you ordered in coals?"

"We are not coming," said Margaret firmly. She respected Miss Avery too much to humour her. "No. Not coming. Never coming. It has all been a mistake. The furniture must be repacked at once, and I am very sorry, but I am making other arrangements, and must ask you to give me the keys."

"Certainly, Mrs. Wilcox," said Miss Avery, and resigned her duties with a smile.

Relieved at this conclusion, and having sent her compliments to Madge, Margaret walked back to the station. She had intended to go to the furniture warehouse and give directions for removal, but the muddle had turned out more extensive than she expected, so she decided to consult Henry. It was as well that she did this. He was strongly against employing the local man whom he had previously recommended, and advised her to store in London after all.

But before this could be done an unexpected trouble fell upon her.

CHAPTER XXXIV

It was not unexpected entirely. Aunt Juley's health had been bad all the winter. She had had a long series of colds and coughs, and had been too busy to get rid of them. She had scarcely promised her niece "to really take my tiresome chest in hand," when she caught a chill and developed acute pneumonia. Margaret and Tibby went down to Swanage. Helen was telegraphed for, and that spring party that after all gathered in that hospitable house had all the pathos of fair memories. On a perfect day, when the sky seemed blue porcelain, and the waves of the discreet little bay beat gentlest of tattoes upon the sand, Margaret hurried up through the rhododendrons, confronted again by the senselessness of Death. One death may explain itself, but it throws no light upon another: the groping inquiry must begin anew. Preachers or scientists may generalize, but we know that no generality is possible about those whom we love; not one heaven awaits them, not even one oblivion. Aunt Juley, incapable of tragedy, slipped out of life with odd little laughs and apologies for having stopped in it so long. She was very weak; she could not rise to the occasion, or realize the great mystery which all agree must await her; it only seemed to her that she was quite done up—more done up than ever before; that she saw and heard and felt less every moment; and that, unless something changed, she would soon feel nothing. Her spare strength she devoted to plans: could not Margaret take some steamer expeditions? were mackerel cooked as Tibby liked them? She worried herself about Helen's absence, and also that she should be the cause of Helen's return. The nurses seemed to think such interests quite natural, and perhaps hers was an average approach to the Great Gate. But Margaret saw Death stripped of any false romance; whatever the idea of Death may contain, the process can be trivial and hideous.

"Important—Margaret dear, take the Lulworth when Helen comes."

"Helen won't be able to stop, Aunt Juley. She has telegraphed that she can only get away just to see you. She must go back to Germany as soon as you are well."

"How very odd of Helen! Mr. Wilcox——"

"Yes, dear?"

"Can he spare you?"

Henry wished her to come, and had been very kind. Yet again Margaret said so.

Mrs. Munt did not die. Quite outside her will, a more dignified power took hold of her and checked her on the downward slope. She returned, without emotion, as fidgety as ever. On the fourth day she was out of danger.

"Margaret—important," it went on: "I should like you to have some companion to take walks with. Do try Miss Conder."

"I have been a little walk with Miss Conder."

"But she is not really interesting. If only you had Helen."

"I have Tibby, Aunt Juley."

"No, but he has to do his Chinese. Some real companion is what you need. Really, Helen is odd."

"Helen is odd, very," agreed Margaret.

"Not content with going abroad, why does she want to go back there at once?"

"No doubt she will change her mind when she sees us. She has not the least balance."

That was the stock criticism about Helen, but Margaret's voice trembled as she made it. By now she was deeply pained at her sister's behaviour. It may be unbalanced to fly out of England, but to stop away eight months argues that the heart is awry as well as the head. A sick-bed could recall Helen, but she was deaf to more human calls; after a glimpse at her aunt, she would retire into her nebulous life behind some poste restante. She scarcely existed; her letters had become dull and infrequent; she had no wants and no curiosity. And it was all put down to poor Henry's account! Henry, long pardoned by his wife, was still too infamous to be greeted by his sister-in-law. It was morbid, and, to her alarm, Margaret fancied that she could trace the growth of morbidity back in Helen's life for nearly four years. The flight from Oniton; the unbalanced patronage of the Basts; the explosion of grief up on the Downs—all connected with Paul, an insignificant boy whose lips had kissed hers for a fraction of time. Margaret and Mrs. Wilcox had feared that they might kiss again. Foolishly: the real danger was reaction. Reaction against the Wilcoxes had eaten into her life until she was scarcely sane. At twenty-five she had an idée fixe. What hope was there for her as an old woman?

The more Margaret thought about it the more alarmed she became. For many months she had put the subject away, but it was too big to be slighted now. There was almost a taint of madness. Were all Helen's actions to be governed by a tiny mishap, such as may happen to any young man or woman? Can human nature be constructed on lines so insignificant? The blundering

little encounter at Howards End was vital. It propagated itself
where graver intercourse lay barren; it was stronger than sisterly
intimacy, stronger than reason or books. In one of her moods
Helen had confessed that she still "enjoyed" it in a certain sense.
Paul had faded, but the magic of his caress endured. And where
there is enjoyment of the past there may also be reaction—propa-
gation at both ends.

Well, it is odd and sad that our minds should be such seed-
beds, and we without power to choose the seed. But man is an
odd, sad creature as yet, intent on pilfering the earth, and heed-
less of the growths within himself. He cannot be bored about
psychology. He leaves it to the specialist, which is as if he should
leave his dinner to be eaten by a steam-engine. He cannot be
bothered to digest his own soul. Margaret and Helen have been
more patient, and it is suggested that Margaret has succeeded—so
far as success is yet possible. She does understand herself, she has
some rudimentary control over her own growth. Whether Helen
has succeeded one cannot say.

The day that Mrs. Munt rallied Helen's letter arrived. She had
posted it at Munich, and would be in London herself on the
morrow. It was a disquieting letter, though the opening was affectionate and sane.

"DEAREST MEG,

"Give Helen's love to Aunt Juley. Tell her that I love, and
have loved, her ever since I can remember. I shall be in London
Thursday.

"My address will be care of the bankers. I have not yet settled on a hotel, so write or wire to me there and give me detailed
news. If Aunt Juley is much better, or if, for a terrible reason, it
would be no good my coming down to Swanage, you must not
think it odd if I do not come. I have all sorts of plans in my head.
I am living abroad at present, and want to get back as quickly as
possible. Will you please tell me where our furniture is. I should
like to take out one or two books; the rest are for you.

"Forgive me, dearest Meg. This must read like rather a tire-some letter, but all letters are from your loving

"HELEN."

It was a tiresome letter, for it tempted Margaret to tell a lie. If she wrote that Aunt Juley was still in danger her sister would come. Unhealthiness is contagious. We cannot be in contact with those who are in a morbid state without ourselves deteriorating. To "act for the best" might do Helen good, but would do herself harm and, at the risk of disaster, she kept her colours flying a little longer. She replied that their aunt was much better, and awaited developments.

Tibby approved of her reply. Mellowing rapidly, he was a pleas-anter companion than before. Oxford had done much for him. He had lost his peevishness, and could hide his indifference to people and his interest in food. But he had not grown more human. The years between eighteen and twenty-two, so magical for most, were leading him gently from boyhood to middle age. He had never known young-manliness, that quality which warms the heart till death, and gives Mr. Wilcox an imperishable charm. He was frigid, through no fault of his own, and without cruelty. He thought Helen wrong and Margaret right, but the family trouble was for him what a scene behind footlights is for most people. He had only one suggestion to make, and that was characteristic.

"Why don't you tell Mr. Wilcox?"

"About Helen?"

"Perhaps he has come across that sort of thing."

"He would do all he could, but——"

"Oh, you know best. But he is practical."

It was the student's belief in experts. Margaret demurred for one or two reasons. Presently Helen's answer came. She sent a telegram requesting the address of the furniture, as she would now return at once. Margaret replied, "Certainly not; meet me at the bankers at four." She and Tibby went up to London. Helen was not at the bankers, and they were refused her address. Helen had passed into chaos.

Margaret put her arm round her brother. He was all that she had left, and never had he seemed more unsubstantial.

"Tibby love, what next?"

He replied: "It is extraordinary."

"Dear, your judgment's often clearer than mine. Have you any notion what's at the back?"

"None, unless it's something mental."

"Oh—that!" said Margaret. "Quite impossible." But the suggestion had been uttered, and in a few minutes she took it up herself. Nothing else explained. And London agreed with Tibby. The mask fell off the city, and she saw it for what it really is—a caricature of infinity. The familiar barriers, the streets along which she moved, the houses between which she had made her little journeys for so many years, became negligible suddenly. Helen seemed one with grimy trees and the traffic and the slowly-flowing slabs of mud. She had accomplished a hideous act of renunciation and returned to the One. Margaret's own faith held firm. She knew the human soul will be merged, if it be merged at all, with the stars and the sea. Yet she felt that her sister had been going amiss for many years. It was symbolic the catastrophe would come now, on a London afternoon, while rain fell slowly.

Henry was the only hope. Henry was definite. He might know of some paths in the chaos that were hidden from them, and she determined to take Tibby's advice and lay the whole matter in his hands. They must call at his office. He could not well make it worse. She went for a few moments into St. Paul's, whose dome stands out of the welter so bravely, as if preaching the gospel of form. But within, St. Paul's is as its surroundings—echoes and whispers, inaudible songs, invisible mosaics, wet footmarks crossing and recrossing the floor. Si monumentum requiris, circumspice: it points us back to London. There was no hope of Helen here.

Henry was unsatisfactory at first. That she had expected. He was overjoyed to see her back from Swanage, and slow to admit the growth of a new trouble. When they told him of their search, he only chaffed Tibby and the Schlegels generally, and declared that it was "just like Helen" to lead her relatives a dance.

"That is what we all say," replied Margaret. "But why should it be just like Helen? Why should she be allowed to be so queer, and to grow queerer?"

"Don't ask me. I'm a plain man of business. I live and let live. My advice to you both is, don't worry. Margaret, you've got black marks again under your eyes. You know that's strictly forbidden. First your aunt—then your sister. No, we aren't going to have it. Are we, Theobald?" He rang the bell. "I'll give you some tea, and then you go straight to Ducie Street. I can't have my girl looking as old as her husband."

"All the same, you have not quite seen our point," said Tibby.

Mr. Wilcox, who was in good spirits, retorted, "I don't suppose I ever shall." He leant back, laughing at the gifted but ridiculous family, while the fire flickered over the map of Africa. Margaret motioned to her brother to go on. Rather diffident, he obeyed her.

"Margaret's point is this," he said. "Our sister may be mad."

Charles, who was working in the inner room, looked round.

"Come in, Charles," said Margaret kindly. "Could you help us at all? We are again in trouble."

"I'm afraid I cannot. What are the facts? We are all mad more or less, you know, in these days."

"The facts are as follows," replied Tibby, who had at times a pedantic lucidity. "The facts are that she has been in England for three days and will not see us. She has forbidden the bankers to give us her address. She refuses to answer questions. Margaret finds her letters colourless. There are other facts, but these are the most striking."

"She has never behaved like this before, then?" asked Henry.

"Of course not!" said his wife, with a frown.

"Well, my dear, how am I to know?"

A senseless spasm of annoyance came over her. "You know quite well that Helen never sins against affection," she said. "You must have noticed that much in her, surely."

"Oh yes; she and I have always hit it off together."

"No, Henry—can't you see?—I don't mean that."

She recovered herself, but not before Charles had observed her. Stupid and attentive, he was watching the scene.

"I was meaning that when she was eccentric in the past, one could trace it back to the heart in the long-run. She behaved oddly because she cared for someone, or wanted to help them. There's no possible excuse for her now. She is grieving us deeply, and that is why I am sure that she is not well. 'Mad' is too terrible a word, but she is not well. I shall never believe it. I shouldn't discuss my sister with you if I thought she was well—trouble you about her, I mean."

Henry began to grow serious. Ill-health was to him something perfectly definite. Generally well himself, he could not realize that we sink to it by slow gradations. The sick had no rights; they were outside the pale; one could lie to them remorselessly. When his first wife was seized, he had promised to take her down into Hertfordshire, but meanwhile arranged with a nursing-home instead. Helen, too, was ill. And the plan that he sketched out for her capture, clever and well-meaning as it was, drew its ethics from the wolf-pack.

"You want to get hold of her?" he said. "That's the problem, isn't it? She has got to see a doctor."

"For all I know she has seen one already."

"Yes, yes; don't interrupt." He rose to his feet and thought intently. The genial, tentative host disappeared, and they saw instead the man who had carved money out of Greece and Africa, and bought forests from the natives for a few bottles of gin. "I've got it," he said at last. "It's perfectly easy. Leave it to me. We'll send her down to Howards End."

"How will you do that?"

"After her books. Tell her that she must unpack them herself. Then you can meet her there."

"But, Henry, that's just what she won't let me do. It's part of her—whatever it is—never to see me."

"Of course you won't tell her you're going. When she is there, looking at the cases, you'll just stroll in. If nothing is wrong with her, so much the better. But there'll be the motor round the corner, and we can run her up to a specialist in no time."

Margaret shook her head. "It's quite impossible."

"Why?"

"It doesn't seem impossible to me," said Tibby; "it is surely a very tippy plan."

"It is impossible, because——" She looked at her husband sadly. "It's not the particular language that Helen and I talk, if you see my meaning. It would do splendidly for other people, whom I don't blame."

"But Helen doesn't talk," said Tibby. "That's our whole difficulty. She won't talk your particular language, and on that account you think she's ill."

"No, Henry; it's sweet of you, but I couldn't."

"I see," he said; "you have scruples."

"I suppose so."

"And sooner than go against them you would have your sister suffer. You could have got her down to Swanage by a word, but you had scruples. And scruples are all very well. I am as scrupulous as any man alive, I hope; but when it is a case like this, when there is a question of madness——"

"I deny it's madness."

"You said just now——"

"It's madness when I say it, but not when you say it."

Henry shrugged his shoulders. "Margaret! Margaret!" he groaned. "No education can teach a woman logic. Now, my dear, my time is valuable. Do you want me to help you or not?"

"Not in that way."

"Answer my question. Plain question, plain answer. Do——"

Charles surprised them by interrupting. "Pater, we may as well keep Howards End out of it," he said.

"Why, Charles?"

Charles could give no reason; but Margaret felt as if, over tremendous distance, a salutation had passed between them.

"The whole house is at sixes and sevens," he said crossly. "We don't want any more mess."

"Who's 'we'?" asked his father. "My boy, pray, who's 'we'?"

"I am sure I beg your pardon," said Charles. "I appear always to be intruding."

By now Margaret wished she had never mentioned her trouble to her husband. Retreat was impossible. He was determined to push the matter to a satisfactory conclusion, and Helen faded as he talked. Her fair, flying hair and eager eyes counted for nothing, for she was ill, without rights, and any of her friends might hunt her. Sick at heart, Margaret joined in the chase. She wrote her sister a lying letter, at her husband's dictation; she said the furniture was all at Howards End, but could be seen on Monday next at 3 p.m., when a charwoman would be in attendance. It was a cold letter, and the more plausible for that. Helen would think she was offended. And on Monday next she and Henry were to lunch with Dolly, and then ambush themselves in the garden.

After they had gone, Mr. Wilcox said to his son: "I can't have this sort of behaviour, my boy. Margaret's too sweet-natured to mind, but I mind for her."

Charles made no answer.

"Is anything wrong with you, Charles, this afternoon?"

"No, pater; but you may be taking on a bigger business than you reckon."

"How?"

"Don't ask me."

CHAPTER XXXV

One speaks of the moods of spring, but the days that are her true children have only one mood: they are all full of the rising and dropping of winds, and the whistling of birds. New flowers may come out, the green embroidery of the hedges increase, but the same heaven broods overhead, soft, thick, and blue, the same figures, seen and unseen, are wandering by coppice and meadow. The morning that Margaret had spent with Miss Avery, and the afternoon she set out to entrap Helen, were the scales of a single balance. Time might never have moved, rain never have fallen, and man alone, with his schemes and ailments, was troubling Nature until he saw her through a veil of tears.

She protested no more. Whether Henry was right or wrong, he was most kind, and she knew of no other standard by which to judge him. She must trust him absolutely. As soon as he had taken up a business, his obtuseness vanished. He profited by the slightest indications, and the capture of Helen promised to be staged as deftly as the marriage of Evie.

They went down in the morning as arranged, and he discovered that their victim was actually in Hilton. On his arrival he called at all the livery-stables in the village, and had a few minutes' serious conversation with the proprietors. What he said, Margaret did not know—perhaps not the truth; but news arrived after lunch that a lady had come by the London train, and had taken a fly to Howards End.

"She was bound to drive," said Henry. "There will be her books."

"I cannot make it out," said Margaret for the hundredth time.

"Finish your coffee, dear. We must be off."

"Yes, Margaret, you know you must take plenty," said Dolly.

Margaret tried, but suddenly lifted her hand to her eyes. Dolly stole glances at her father-in-law which he did not answer. In the silence the motor came round to the door.

"You're not fit for it," he said anxiously. "Let me go alone. I know exactly what to do."

"Oh yes, I am fit," said Margaret, uncovering her face. "Only most frightfully worried. I cannot feel that Helen is really alive. Her letters and telegrams seem to have come from someone else. Her voice isn't in them. I don't believe your driver really saw her at the station. I wish I'd never mentioned it. I know that Charles is vexed. Yes, he is——" She seized Dolly's hand and kissed it. "There, Dolly will forgive me. There. Now we'll be off."

Henry had been looking at her closely. He did not like this breakdown.

"Don't you want to tidy yourself?" he asked.

"Have I time?"

"Yes, plenty."

She went to the lavatory by the front door, and as soon as the bolt slipped, Mr. Wilcox said quietly:

"Dolly, I'm going without her."

Dolly's eyes lit up with vulgar excitement. She followed him on tip-toe out to the car.

"Tell her I thought it best."

"Yes, Mr. Wilcox, I see."

"Say anything you like. All right."

The car started well, and with ordinary luck would have got away. But Porgly-woggles, who was playing in the garden, chose this moment to sit down in the middle of the path. Crane, in trying to pass him, ran one wheel over a bed of wallflowers. Dolly screamed. Margaret, hearing the noise, rushed out hatless, and was in time to jump on the footboard. She said not a single word: he was only treating her as she had treated Helen, and her rage at his dishonesty only helped to indicate what Helen would feel against them. She thought, "I deserve it: I am punished for lowering my colours." And she accepted his apologies with a calmness that astonished him.

"I still consider you are not fit for it," he kept saying.

"Perhaps I was not at lunch. But the whole thing is spread clearly before me now."

"I was meaning to act for the best."

"Just lend me your scarf, will you. This wind takes one's hair so."

"Certainly, dear girl. Are you all right now?"

"Look! My hands have stopped trembling."

"And have quite forgiven me? Then listen. Her cab should already have arrived at Howards End. (We're a little late, but no matter.) Our first move will be to send it down to wait at the farm, as, if possible, one doesn't want a scene before servants. A certain gentleman"—he pointed at Crane's back—"won't drive in, but will wait a little short of the front gate, behind the laurels. Have you still the keys of the house?"

"Yes."

"Well, they aren't wanted. Do you remember how the house stands?"

"Yes."

"If we don't find her in the porch, we can stroll round into the garden. Our object——"

Here they stopped to pick up the doctor.

"I was just saying to my wife, Mansbridge, that our main object is not to frighten Miss Schlegel. The house, as you know, is my property, so it should seem quite natural for us to be there. The trouble is evidently nervous—wouldn't you say so, Margaret?"

The doctor, a very young man, began to ask questions about Helen. Was she normal? Was there anything congenital or heredi- tary? Had anything occurred that was likely to alienate her from her family?

"Nothing," answered Margaret, wondering what would have happened if she had added: "Though she did resent my hus- band's immorality."

"She always was highly strung," pursued Henry, leaning back in the car as it shot past the church. "A tendency to spiritualism and those things, though nothing serious. Musical, literary, artis- tic, but I should say normal—a very charming girl."

Margaret's anger and terror increased every moment. How dare these men label her sister! What horrors lay ahead! What imperti- nences that shelter under the name of science! The pack was turning on Helen, to deny her human rights, and it seemed to Margaret that all Schlegels were threatened with her. "Were they normal?" What a question to ask! And it is always those who know nothing about human nature, who are bored by psychology and shocked by physiology, who ask it. However piteous her sister's state, she knew that she must be on her side. They would be mad together if the world chose to consider them so.

It was now five minutes past three. The car slowed down by the farm, in the yard of which Miss Avery was standing. Henry asked her whether a cab had gone past. She nodded, and the next moment they caught sight of it, at the end of the lane. The car ran silently like a beast of prey. So unsuspicious was Helen that she was sitting in the porch, with her back to the road. She had come. Only her head and shoulders were visible. She sat framed in the vine, and one of her hands played with the buds. The wind ruffled her hair, the sun glorified it; she was as she had always been.

Margaret was seated next to the door. Before her husband could prevent her, she slipped out. She ran to the garden gate, which was shut, passed through it, and deliberately pushed it in his face. The noise alarmed Helen. Margaret saw her rise with an unfamiliar movement, and, rushing into the porch, learnt the simple explanation of all their fears—her sister was with child.

"Is the truant all right?" called Henry.

She had time to whisper: "Oh, my darling——" The keys of the house were in her hand. She unlocked Howards End and thrust Helen into it. "Yes, all right," she said, and stood with her back to the door.

CHAPTER XXXVI

"Margaret, you look upset!" said Henry.

Mansbridge had followed. Crane was at the gate, and the flyman had stood up on the box. Margaret shook her head at them; she could not speak any more. She remained clutching the keys, as if all their future depended on them. Henry was asking more questions. She shook her head again. His words had no sense. She heard him wonder why she had let Helen in. "You might have given me a knock with the gate," was another of his remarks. Presently she heard herself speaking. She, or someone for her, said "Go away." Henry came nearer. He repeated, "Margaret, you look upset again. My dear, give me the keys. What are you doing with Helen?"

"Oh, dearest, do go away, and I will manage it all."

"Manage what?"

He stretched out his hand for the keys. She might have obeyed if it had not been for the doctor.

"Stop that at least," she said piteously; the doctor had turned back, and was questioning the driver of Helen's cab. A new feeling came over her; she was fighting for women against men. She did not care about rights, but if men came into Howards End, it should be over her body.

"Come, this is an odd beginning," said her husband.

The doctor came forward now, and whispered two words to Mr. Wilcox—the scandal was out. Sincerely horrified, Henry stood gazing at the earth.

"I cannot help it," said Margaret. "Do wait. It's not my fault. Please all four of you to go away now."

Now the flyman was whispering to Crane.

"We are relying on you to help us, Mrs. Wilcox," said the young doctor. "Could you go in and persuade your sister to come out?"

"On what grounds?" said Margaret, suddenly looking him straight in the eyes.

Thinking it professional to prevaricate, he murmured something about a nervous breakdown.

"I beg your pardon, but it is nothing of the sort. You are not qualified to attend my sister, Mr. Mansbridge. If we require your services, we will let you know."

"I can diagnose the case more bluntly if you wish," he retorted.

"You could, but you have not. You are, therefore, not qualified to attend my sister."

"Come, come, Margaret!" said Henry, never raising his eyes. "This is a terrible business, an appalling business. It's doctor's orders. Open the door."

"Forgive me, but I will not."

"I don't agree."

Margaret was silent.

"This business is as broad as it's long," contributed the doctor.

"We had better all work together. You need us, Mrs. Wilcox, and we need you."

"Quite so," said Henry.

"I do not need you in the least," said Margaret.

The two men looked at each other anxiously.

"No more does my sister, who is still many weeks from her confinement."

"Margaret, Margaret!"

"Well, Henry, send your doctor away. What possible use is he now?"

Mr. Wilcox ran his eye over the house. He had a vague feeling that he must stand firm and support the doctor. He himself might need support, for there was trouble ahead.

"It all turns on affection now," said Margaret. "Affection. Don't you see?" Resuming her usual methods, she wrote the word on the house with her finger. "Surely you see. I like Helen very much, you not so much. Mr. Mansbridge doesn't know her. That's all. And affection, when reciprocated, gives rights. Put that down in your note-book, Mr. Mansbridge. It's a useful formula."

Henry told her to be calm.

"You don't know what you want yourselves," said Margaret, folding her arms. "For one sensible remark I will let you in. But you cannot make it. You would trouble my sister for no reason. I will not permit it. I'll stand here all the day sooner."

"Mansbridge," said Henry in a low voice, "perhaps not now."

The pack was breaking up. At a sign from his master, Crane also went back into the car.

"Now, Henry, you," she said gently. None of her bitterness had been directed at him. "Go away now, dear. I shall want your advice later, no doubt. Forgive me if I have been cross. But, seriously, you must go."

He was too stupid to leave her. Now it was Mr. Mansbridge who called in a low voice to him.

"I shall soon find you down at Dolly's," she called, as the gate at last clanged between them. The fly moved out of the way, the motor backed, turned a little, backed again, and turned in the narrow road. A string of farm carts came up in the middle; but she waited through all, for there was no hurry. When all was over and the car had started, she opened the door. "Oh, my darling!" she said. "My darling, forgive me." Helen was standing in the hall.

CHAPTER XXXVII

Margaret bolted the door on the inside. Then she would have kissed her sister, but Helen, in a dignified voice, that came strangely from her, said:

"Convenient! You did not tell me that the books were unpacked. I have found nearly everything that I want."

"I told you nothing that was true."

"It has been a great surprise, certainly. Has Aunt Juley been ill?"

"Helen, you wouldn't think I'd invent that?"

"I suppose not," said Helen, turning away, and crying a very little. "But one loses faith in everything after this."

"We thought it was illness, but even then—— I haven't behaved worthily."

Helen selected another book.

"I ought not to have consulted anyone. What would our father have thought of me?"

She did not think of questioning her sister, nor of rebuking her. Both might be necessary in the future, but she had first to purge a greater crime than any that Helen could have committed—that want of confidence that is the work of the devil.

"Yes, I am annoyed," replied Helen. "My wishes should have been respected. I would have gone through this meeting if it was necessary, but after Aunt Juley recovered, it was not necessary. Planning my life, as I now have to do——"

"Come away from those books," called Margaret. "Helen, do talk to me."

"I was just saying that I have stopped living haphazard. One

can't go through a great deal of—— " she missed out the noun—
"without planning one's actions in advance. I am going to have a
child in June, and in the first place conversations, discussions,
excitement, are not good for me. I will go through them if necessary, but only then. In the second place I have no right to trouble
people. I cannot fit in with England as I know it. I have done
something that the English never pardon. It would not be right
for them to pardon it. So I must live where I am not known."

"But why didn't you tell me, dearest?"

"Yes," replied Helen judicially. "I might have, but decided
to wait."

"I believe you would never have told me."

"Oh yes, I should. We have taken a flat in Munich."

Margaret glanced out of window.

"By 'we' I mean myself and Monica. But for her, I am and have
been and always wish to be alone."

"I have not heard of Monica."

"You wouldn't have. She's an Italian—by birth at least. She
makes her living by journalism. I met her originally on Garda.
Monica is much the best person to see me through."

"You are very fond of her, then."

"She has been extraordinarily sensible with me."

Margaret guessed at Monica's type—'Italiano Inglesiato' they
had named it: the crude feminist of the South, whom one respects
but avoids. And Helen had turned to it in her need!

"You must not think that we shall never meet," said Helen, with
a measured kindness. "I shall always have a room for you when you
can be spared, and the longer you can be with me the better. But
you haven't understood yet, Meg, and of course it is difficult for
you. This is a shock to you. It isn't to me, who have been thinking
over our futures for many months, and they won't be changed by
a slight contretemps, such as this. I cannot live in England."

"Helen, you've not forgiven me for my treachery. You *couldn't*
talk like this to me if you had."

"Oh, Meg dear, why do we talk at all?" She dropped a book

and sighed wearily. Then, recovering herself, she said: "Tell me, how is it that all the books are down here?"

"Series of mistakes."

"And a great deal of the furniture has been unpacked."

"All."

"Who lives here, then?"

"No one."

"I suppose you are letting it, though."

"The house is dead," said Margaret, with a frown. "Why worry on about it?"

"But I am interested. You talk as if I had lost all my interest in life. I am still Helen, I hope. Now this hasn't the feel of a dead house. The hall seems more alive even than in the old days, when it held the Wilcoxes' own things."

"Interested, are you? Very well, I must tell you, I suppose. My husband lent it on condition we—but by a mistake all our things were unpacked, and Miss Avery, instead of——" She stopped. "Look here, I can't go on like this. I warn you I won't. Helen, why should you be so miserably unkind to me, simply because you hate Henry?"

"I don't hate him now," said Helen. "I have stopped being a schoolgirl, and, Meg, once again, I'm not being unkind. But as for fitting in with your English life—no, put it out of your head at once. Imagine a visit from me at Ducie Street! It's unthinkable."

Margaret could not contradict her. It was appalling to see her quietly moving forward with her plans, not bitter or excitable, neither asserting innocence nor confessing guilt, merely desiring freedom and the company of those who would not blame her. She had been through—how much? Margaret did not know. But it was enough to part her from old habits as well as old friends.

"Tell me about yourself," said Helen, who had chosen her books, and was lingering over the furniture.

"There's nothing to tell."

"But your marriage has been happy, Meg?"

"Yes, but I don't feel inclined to talk."

"You feel as I do."

"Not that, but I can't."

"No more can I. It is a nuisance, but no good trying."

Something had come between them. Perhaps it was Society, which henceforward would exclude Helen. Perhaps it was a third life, already potent as a spirit. They could find no meeting-place. Both suffered acutely, and were not comforted by the knowledge that affection survived.

"Look here, Meg, is the coast clear?"

"You mean that you want to go away from me?"

"I suppose so—dear old lady! it isn't any use. I knew we should have nothing to say. Give my love to Aunt Juley and Tibby, and take more yourself than I can say. Promise to come and see me in Munich later."

"Certainly, dearest."

"For that is all we can do."

It seemed so. Most ghastly of all was Helen's common sense: Monica had been extraordinarily good for her.

"I am glad to have seen you and the things." She looked at the bookcase lovingly, as if she was saying farewell to the past.

Margaret unbolted the door. She remarked: "The car has gone, and here's your cab."

She led the way to it, glancing at the leaves and the sky. The spring had never seemed more beautiful. The driver, who was leaning on the gate, called out, "Please, lady, a message," and handed her Henry's visiting-card through the bars.

"How did this come?" she asked.

Crane had returned with it almost at once.

She read the card with annoyance. It was covered with instructions in domestic French. When she and her sister had talked she was to come back for the night to Dolly's. "Il faut dormir sur ce sujet." While Helen was to be found "une comfortable chambre à l'hotel." The final sentence displeased her greatly until she remembered that the Charles' had only one spare room, and so could not invite a third guest.

"Henry would have done what he could," she interpreted.

Helen had not followed her into the garden. The door once open, she lost her inclination to fly. She remained in the hall, going from bookcase to table. She grew more like the old Helen, irresponsible and charming.

"This *is* Mr. Wilcox's house?" she inquired.

"Surely you remember Howards End?"

"Remember? I who remember everything! But it looks to be ours now."

"Miss Avery was extraordinary," said Margaret, her own spirits lightening a little. Again she was invaded by a slight feeling of disloyalty. But it brought her relief, and she yielded to it. "She loved Mrs. Wilcox, and would rather furnish her house with our things than think of it empty. In consequence here are all the library books."

"Not all the books. She hasn't unpacked the Art Books, in which she may show her sense. And we never used to have the sword here."

"The sword looks well, though."

"Magnificent."

"Yes, doesn't it?"

"Where's the piano, Meg?"

"I warehoused that in London. Why?"

"Nothing."

"Curious, too, that the carpet fits."

"The carpet's a mistake," announced Helen. "I know that we had it in London, but this floor ought to be bare. It is far too beautiful."

"You still have a mania for under-furnishing. Would you care to come into the dining-room before you start? There's no carpet there."

They went in, and each minute their talk became more natural.

"Oh, *what* a place for mother's cheffonier!" cried Helen.

"Look at the chairs, though."

"Oh, look at them! Wickham Place faced north, didn't it?"

"North-west."

"Anyhow, it is thirty years since any of those chairs have felt the sun. Feel. Their dear little backs are quite warm."

"But why has Miss Avery made them set to partners? I shall just——"

"Over here, Meg. Put it so that anyone sitting will see the lawn."

Margaret moved a chair. Helen sat down in it.

"Ye-es. The window's too high."

"Try a drawing-room chair."

"No, I don't like the drawing-room so much. The beam has been match-boarded. It would have been so beautiful otherwise."

"Helen, what a memory you have for some things! You're perfectly right. It's a room that men have spoilt through trying to make it nice for women. Men don't know what we want——"

"And never will."

"I don't agree. In two thousand years they'll know."

"But the chairs show up wonderfully. Look where Tibby spilt the soup."

"Coffee. It was coffee surely."

Helen shook her head. "Impossible. Tibby was far too young to be given coffee at that time."

"Was father alive?"

"Yes."

"Then you're right and it must have been soup. I was thinking of much later—that unsuccessful visit of Aunt Juley's, when she didn't realize that Tibby had grown up. It was coffee then, for he threw it down on purpose. There was some rhyme, 'Tea, coffee—coffee, tea,' that she said to him every morning at breakfast. Wait a minute—how did it go?"

"I know—no, I don't. What a detestable boy Tibby was!"

"But the rhyme was simply awful. No decent person could have put up with it."

"Ah, that greengage tree," cried Helen, as if the garden was also part of their childhood. "Why do I connect it with dumb-bells? And there come the chickens. The grass wants cutting. I love yellowhammers——"

Margaret interrupted her. "I have got it," she announced.

> "'Tea, tea, coffee, tea,
> Or chocolaritee.'

"That every morning for three weeks. No wonder Tibby was wild."

"Tibby is moderately a dear now," said Helen.

"There! I knew you'd say that in the end. Of course he's a dear. A bell rang.

"Listen! what's that?"

Helen said, "Perhaps the Wilcoxes are beginning the siege."

"What nonsense—listen!"

And the triviality faded from their faces, though it left something behind—the knowledge that they never could be parted because their love was rooted in common things. Explanations and appeals had failed; they had tried for a common meeting-ground, and had only made each other unhappy. And all the time their salvation was lying round them—the past sanctifying the present; the present, with wild heart-throb, declaring that there would after all be a future, with laughter and the voices of children. Helen, still smiling, came up to her sister. She said, "It is always Meg." They looked into each other's eyes. The inner life had paid.

Solemnly the clapper tolled. No one was in the front. Margaret went to the kitchen, and struggled between packing-cases to the window. Their visitor was only a little boy with a tin can. And triviality returned.

"Little boy, what do you want?"

"Please, I am the milk."

"Did Miss Avery send you?" said Margaret, rather sharply.

"Yes, please."

"Then take it back and say we require no milk." While she called to Helen, "No, it's not the siege, but possibly an attempt to provision us against one."

"But I like milk," cried Helen. "Why send it away?"

"Do you? Oh, very well. But we've nothing to put it in, and he wants the can."

"Please, I'm to call in the morning for the can," said the boy.

"The house will be locked up then."

"In the morning would I bring eggs, too?"

"Are you the boy whom I saw playing in the stacks last week?" The child hung his head.

"Well, run away and do it again."

"Nice little boy," whispered Helen. "I say, what's your name? Mine's Helen."

"Tom."

That was Helen all over. The Wilcoxes, too, would ask a child its name, but they never told their names in return.

"Tom, this one here is Margaret. And at home we've another called Tibby."

"Mine are lop-eareds," replied Tom, supposing Tibby to be a rabbit.

"You're a very good and rather a clever little boy. Mind you come again.—Isn't he charming?"

"Undoubtedly," said Margaret. "He is probably the son of Madge, and Madge is dreadful. But this place has wonderful powers."

"What do you mean?"

"I don't know."

"Because I probably agree with you."

"It kills what is dreadful and makes what is beautiful live."

"I do agree," said Helen, as she sipped the milk. "But you said that the house was dead not half an hour ago."

"Meaning that I was dead. I felt it."

"Yes, the house has a surer life than we, even if it was empty, and, as it is, I can't get over that for thirty years the sun has never shone full on our furniture. After all, Wickham Place was a grave. Meg, I've a startling idea."

"What is it?"

"Drink some milk to steady you."

Margaret obeyed.

"No, I won't tell you yet," said Helen, "because you may laugh or be angry. Let's go upstairs first and give the rooms an airing."

They opened window after window, till the inside, too, was rustling to the spring. Curtains blew, picture-frames tapped cheerfully. Helen uttered cries of excitement as she found this bed obviously in its right place, that in its wrong one. She was angry with Miss Avery for not having moved the wardrobes up. "Then one would see really." She admired the view. She was the Helen who had written the memorable letters four years ago. As they leant out, looking westward, she said: "About my idea. Couldn't you and I camp out in this house for the night?"

"I don't think we could well do that," said Margaret.

"Here are beds, tables, towels——"

"I know; but the house isn't supposed to be slept in, and Henry's suggestion was——"

"I require no suggestions. I shall not alter anything in my plans. But it would give me so much pleasure to have one night here with you. It will be something to look back on. Oh, Meg lovey, do let's!"

"But, Helen, my pet," said Margaret, "we can't without getting Henry's leave. Of course, he would give it, but you said yourself that you couldn't visit at Ducie Street now, and this is equally intimate."

"Ducie Street is his house. This is ours. Our furniture, our sort of people coming to the door. Do let us camp out, just one night, and Tom shall feed us on eggs and milk. Why not? It's a moon."

Margaret hesitated. "I feel Charles wouldn't like it," she said at last. "Even our furniture annoyed him, and I was going to clear it out when Aunt Juley's illness prevented me. I sympathize with Charles. He feels it's his mother's house. He loves it in rather an untaking way. Henry I could answer for—not Charles."

"I know he won't like it," said Helen. "But I am going to pass out of their lives. What difference will it make in the long run if they say, 'And she even spent the night at Howards End'?"

"How do you know you'll pass out of their lives? We have thought that twice before."

"Because my plans——"

"—which you change in a moment."

"Then because my life is great and theirs are little," said Helen, taking fire. "I know of things they can't know of, and so do you. We *know* that there's poetry. We *know* that there's death. They can only take them on hearsay. We know this is our house, because it feels ours. Oh, they may take the title-deeds and the doorkeys, but for this one night we are at home."

"It would be lovely to have you once more alone," said Margaret. "It may be a chance in a thousand."

"Yes, and we could talk." She dropped her voice. "It won't be a very glorious story. But under that wych-elm—honestly, I see little happiness ahead. Cannot I have this one night with you?"

"I needn't say how much it would mean to me."

"Then let us."

"It is no good hesitating. Shall I drive down to Hilton now and get leave?"

"Oh, we don't want leave."

But Margaret was a loyal wife. In spite of imagination and poetry—perhaps on account of them—she could sympathize with the technical attitude that Henry would adopt. If possible, she would be technical, too. A night's lodging—and they demanded no more—need not involve the discussion of general principles.

"Charles may so no," grumbled Helen.

"We shan't consult him."

"Go if you like; I should have stopped without leave."

It was the touch of selfishness, which was not enough to mar Helen's character, and even added to its beauty. She would have stopped without leave, and escaped to Germany the next morning. Margaret kissed her.

"Expect me back before dark. I am looking forward to it so much. It is like you to have thought of such a beautiful thing."

"Not a thing, only an ending," said Helen rather sadly; and the sense of tragedy closed in on Margaret again as soon as she left the house.

She was afraid of Miss Avery. It is disquieting to fulfil a

prophecy, however superficially. She was glad to see no watching figure as she drove past the farm, but only little Tom, turning somersaults in the straw.

CHAPTER XXXVIII

The tragedy began quietly enough, and, like many another talk, by the man's deft assertion of his superiority. Henry heard her arguing with the driver, stepped out and settled the fellow, who was inclined to be rude, and then led the way to some chairs on the lawn. Dolly, who had not been "told," ran out with offers of tea. He refused them, and ordered them to wheel baby's perambulator away, as they desired to be alone.

"But the diddums can't listen; he isn't nine months old," she pleaded.

"That's not what I was saying," retorted her father-in-law.

Baby was wheeled out of earshot, and did not hear about the crisis till later years. It was now the turn of Margaret.

"Is it what we feared?" he asked.

"It is."

"Dear girl," he began, "there is a troublesome business ahead of us, and nothing but the most absolute honesty and plain speech will see us through." Margaret bent her head. "I am obliged to question you on subjects we'd both prefer to leave untouched. As you know, I am not one of your Bernard Shaws who consider nothing sacred. To speak as I must will pain me, but there are occasions—— We are husband and wife, not children. I am a man of the world, and you are a most exceptional woman."

All Margaret's senses forsook her. She blushed, and looked past him at the Six Hills, covered with spring herbage. Noting her colour, he grew still more kind.

"I see that you feel as I felt when—— My poor little wife! Oh, be brave! Just one or two questions, and I have done with you. Was your sister wearing a wedding-ring?"

Margaret stammered a "No."

There was an appalling silence.

"Henry, I really came to ask a favour about Howards End."

"One point at a time. I am now obliged to ask for the name of her seducer."

She rose to her feet and held the chair between them. Her colour had ebbed, and she was grey. It did not displease him that she should receive his question thus.

"Take your time," he counselled her. "Remember that this is far worse for me than for you."

She swayed; he feared she was going to faint. Then speech came, and she said slowly: "Seducer? No; I do not know her seducer's name."

"Would she not tell you?"

"I never even asked her who seduced her," said Margaret, dwelling on the hateful word thoughtfully.

"That is singular." Then he changed his mind. "Natural perhaps, dear girl, that you shouldn't ask. But until his name is known, nothing can be done. Sit down. How terrible it is to see you so upset! I knew you weren't fit for it. I wish I hadn't taken you."

Margaret answered, "I like to stand, if you don't mind, for it gives me a pleasant view of the Six Hills."

"As you like."

"Have you anything else to ask me, Henry?"

"Next you must tell me whether you have gathered anything. I have often noticed your insight, dear. I only wish my own was as good. You may have guessed something, even though your sister said nothing. The slightest hint would help us."

"Who is 'we'?"

"I thought it best to ring up Charles."

"That was unnecessary," said Margaret, growing warmer. "This news will give Charles disproportionate pain."

"He has at once gone to call on your brother."

"That too was unnecessary."

"Let me explain, dear, how the matter stands. You don't think that I and my son are other than gentlemen? It is in Helen's interests that we are acting. It is still not too late to save her name."

Then Margaret hit out for the first time. "Are we to make her seducer marry her?" she asked.

"If possible. Yes."

"But, Henry, suppose he turned out to be married already? One has heard of such cases."

"In that case he must pay heavily for his misconduct, and be thrashed within an inch of his life."

So her first blow missed. She was thankful of it. What had tempted her to imperil both of their lives? Henry's obtuseness had saved her as well as himself. Exhausted with anger, she sat down again, blinking at him as he told her as much as he thought fit. At last she said: "May I ask you my question now?"

"Certainly, my dear."

"To-morrow Helen goes to Munich——"

"Well, possibly she is right."

"Henry, let a lady finish. To-morrow she goes; to-night, with your permission, she would like to sleep at Howards End."

It was the crisis of his life. Again she would have recalled the words as soon as they were uttered. She had not led up to them with sufficient care. She longed to warn him that they were far more important than he supposed. She saw him weighing them, as if they were a business proposition.

"Why Howards End?" he said at last. "Would she not be more comfortable, as I suggested, at the hotel?"

Margaret hastened to give him reasons. "It is an odd request, but you know what Helen is and what women in her state are." He frowned, and moved irritably. "She has the idea that one night in your house would give her pleasure and do her good. I think she's right. Being one of those imaginative girls, the presence of all our books and furniture soothes her. This is a fact. It is the end of her girlhood. Her last words to me were, 'A beautiful ending.' "

"She values the old furniture for sentimental reasons, in fact."

"Exactly. You have quite understood. It is her last hope of being with it."

"I don't agree there, my dear! Helen will have her share of the goods wherever she goes—possibly more than her share, for you are so fond of her that you'd give her anything of yours that she fancies, wouldn't you? and I'd raise no objection. I could understand it if it was her old home, because a home, or a house"—he changed the word, designedly; he had thought of a telling point—"because a house in which one has once lived becomes in a sort of way sacred, I don't know why. Associations and so on. Now Helen has no associations with Howards End, though I and Charles and Evie have. I do not see why she wants to stay the night there. She will only catch cold."

"Leave it that you don't see," cried Margaret. "Call it fancy. But realize that fancy is a scientific fact. Helen is fanciful, and wants to."

Then he surprised her—a rare occurrence. He shot an unexpected bolt. "If she wants to sleep one night, she may want to sleep two. We shall never get her out of the house, perhaps."

"Well?" said Margaret, with the precipice in sight. "And suppose we don't get her out of the house? Would it matter? She would do no one any harm."

Again the irritated gesture.

"No, Henry," she panted, receding. "I didn't mean that. We will only trouble Howards End for this one night. I take her to London to-morrow——"

"Do you intend to sleep in a damp house, too?"

"She cannot be left alone."

"That's quite impossible! Madness. You must be here to meet Charles."

"I have already told you that your message to Charles was unnecessary, and I have no desire to meet him."

"Margaret—my Margaret——"

"What has this business to do with Charles? If it concerns me little, it concerns you less, and Charles not at all."

"As the future owner of Howards End," said Mr. Wilcox, arching his fingers, "I should say that it did concern Charles."

"In what way? Will Helen's condition depreciate the property?"

"My dear, you are forgetting yourself."

"I think you yourself recommended plain speaking."

They looked at each other in amazement. The precipice was at their feet now.

"Helen commands my sympathy," said Henry. "As your husband, I shall do all for her that I can, and I have no doubt that she will prove more sinned against than sinning. But I cannot treat her as if nothing has happened. I should be false to my position in society if I did."

She controlled herself for the last time. "No, let us go back to Helen's request," she said. "It is unreasonable, but the request of an unhappy girl. To-morrow she will go to Germany, and trouble society no longer. To-night she asks to sleep in your empty house—a house which you do not care about, and which you have not occupied for over a year. May she? Will you give my sister leave? Will you forgive her—as you hope to be forgiven, and as you have actually been forgiven? Forgive her for one night only. That will be enough."

"As I have actually been forgiven——?"

"Never mind for the moment what I mean by that," said Margaret. "Answer my question."

Perhaps some hint of her meaning did dawn on him. If so, he blotted it out. Straight from his fortress he answered: "I seem rather unaccommodating, but I have some experience of life, and know how one thing leads to another. I am afraid that your sister had better sleep at the hotel. I have my children and the memory of my dear wife to consider. I am sorry, but see that she leaves my house at once."

"You have mentioned Mrs. Wilcox."

"I beg your pardon?"

"A rare occurrence. In reply, may I mention Mrs. Bast?"

"You have not been yourself all day," said Henry, and rose from his seat with face unmoved. Margaret rushed at him and seized both his hands. She was transfigured.

"Not any more of this!" she cried. "You shall see the connection if it kills you, Henry! You have had a mistress—I forgave you. My sister has a lover—you drive her from the house. Do you see the connection? Stupid, hypocritical, cruel—oh, contemptible!—a man who insults his wife when she's alive and cants with her memory when she's dead. A man who ruins a woman for his pleasure, and casts her off to ruin other men. And gives bad financial advice, and then says he is not responsible. These men are you. You can't recognize them, because you cannot connect. I've had enough of your unweeded kindness. I've spoilt you long enough. All your life you have been spoiled. Mrs. Wilcox spoiled you. No one has ever told what you are—muddled, criminally muddled. Men like you use repentance as a blind, so don't repent. Only say to yourself, 'What Helen has done, I've done.' "

"The two cases are different," Henry stammered. His real retort was not quite ready. His brain was still in a whirl, and he wanted a little longer.

"In what way different? You have betrayed Mrs. Wilcox, Helen only herself. You remain in society, Helen can't. You have had only pleasure, she may die. You have the insolence to talk to me of differences, Henry?"

Oh, the uselessness of it! Henry's retort came.

"I perceive you are attempting blackmail. It is scarcely a pretty weapon for a wife to use against her husband. My rule through life has been never to pay the least attention to threats, and I can only repeat what I said before: I do not give you and your sister leave to sleep at Howards End."

Margaret loosed his hands. He went into the house, wiping first one and then the other on his handkerchief. For a little she stood looking at the Six Hills, tombs of warriors, breasts of the spring. Then she passed out into what was now the evening.

CHAPTER XXXIX

Charles and Tibby met at Ducie Street, where the latter was staying. Their interview was short and absurd. They had nothing in common but the English language, and tried by its help to express what neither of them understood. Charles saw in Helen the family foe. He had singled her out as the most dangerous of the Schlegels, and, angry as he was, looked forward to telling his wife how right he had been. His mind was made up at once: the girl must be got out of the way before she disgraced them farther. If occasion offered she might be married to a villain or, possibly, to a fool. But this was a concession to morality, it formed no part of his main scheme. Honest and hearty was Charles's dislike, and the past spread itself out very clearly before him; hatred is a skilful compositor. As if they were heads in a note-book, he ran through all the incidents of the Schlegels' campaign: the attempt to compromise his brother, his mother's legacy, his father's marriage, the introduction of the furniture, the unpacking of the same. He had not yet heard of the request to sleep at Howards End; that was to be their master-stroke and the opportunity for his. But he already felt that Howards End was the objective, and, though he disliked the house, was determined to defend it.

Tibby, on the other hand, had no opinions. He stood above the conventions: his sister had a right to do what she thought right. It is not difficult to stand above the conventions when we leave no hostages among them; men can always be more unconventional than women, and a bachelor of independent means need encounter no difficulties at all. Unlike Charles, Tibby had money enough; his ancestors had earned it for him, and if he shocked the people in one set of lodgings he had only to move into another. His was the Leisure without sympathy—an attitude as fatal as the strenuous: a little cold culture may be raised on it, but no art. His sisters had seen the family danger, and had never forgotten to discount the gold islets that raised them from the sea. Tibby gave all the praise to himself, and so despised the struggling and the submerged.

Hence the absurdity of the interview; the gulf between them was economic as well as spiritual. But several facts passed: Charles pressed for them with an impertinence that the undergraduate could not withstand. On what date had Helen gone abroad? To whom? (Charles was anxious to fasten the scandal on Germany.) Then, changing his tactics, he said roughly: "I suppose you realize that you are your sister's protector?"

"In what sense?"

"If a man played about with my sister, I'd send a bullet through him, but perhaps you don't mind."

"I mind very much," protested Tibby.

"Who d'ye suspect, then? Speak out, man. One always suspects someone."

"No one. I don't think so." Involuntarily he blushed. He had remembered the scene in his Oxford rooms.

"You are hiding something," said Charles. As interviews go, he got the best of this one. "When you saw her last, did she mention anyone's name? Yes or no!" he thundered, so that Tibby started.

"In my rooms she mentioned some friends, called the Basts ——"

"Who are the Basts?"

"People—friends of hers at Evie's wedding."

"I don't remember. But, by great Scott! I do. My aunt told me about some tag-rag. Was she full of them when you saw her? Is there a man? Did she speak of the man? Or—look here—have you had any dealings with him?"

Tibby was silent. Without intending it, he had betrayed his sister's confidence; he was not enough interested in human life to see where things will lead to. He had a strong regard for honesty, and his word, once given, had always been kept up to now. He was deeply vexed, not only for the harm he had done Helen, but for the flaw he had discovered in his own equipment.

"I see—you are in his confidence. They met at your rooms. Oh, what a family, what a family! God help the poor pater——"

And Tibby found himself alone.

CHAPTER XL

Leonard—he would figure at length in a newspaper report, but that evening he did not count for much. The foot of the tree was in shadow, since the moon was still hidden behind the house. But above, to right, to left, down the long meadow the moonlight was streaming. Leonard seemed not a man, but a cause.

Perhaps it was Helen's way of falling in love—a curious way to Margaret, whose agony and whose contempt of Henry were yet imprinted with his image. Helen forgot people. They were husks that had enclosed her emotion. She could pity, or sacrifice herself, or have instincts, but had she ever loved in the noblest way, where man and woman, having lost themselves in sex, desire to lose sex itself in comradeship?

Margaret wondered, but said no word of blame. This was Helen's evening. Troubles enough lay ahead of her—the loss of friends and of social advantages, the agony, the supreme agony, of motherhood, which is even yet not a matter of common knowledge. For the present let the moon shine brightly and the breezes of the spring blow gently, dying away from the gale of the day, and let the earth, who brings increase, bring peace. Not even to herself dare she blame Helen. She could not assess her trespass by any moral code; it was everything or nothing. Morality can tell us that murder is worse than stealing, and group most sins in an order all must approve, but it cannot group Helen. The surer its pronouncements on this point, the surer may we be that morality is not speaking. Christ was evasive when they questioned Him. It is those that cannot connect who hasten to cast the first stone.

This was Helen's evening—won at what cost, and not to be marred by the sorrows of others. Of her own tragedy Margaret never uttered a word.

"One isolates," said Helen slowly. "I isolated Mr. Wilcox from the other forces that were pulling Leonard downhill. Consequently, I was full of pity, and almost of revenge. For weeks I had blamed Mr. Wilcox only, and so, when your letters came——"

"I need never have written them," sighed Margaret. "They never shielded Henry. How hopeless it is to tidy away the past, even for others!"

"I did not know that it was your own idea to dismiss the Basts."

"Looking back, that was wrong of me."

"Looking back, darling, I know that it was right. It is right to save the man whom one loves. I am less enthusiastic about justice now. But we both thought you wrote at his dictation. It seemed the last touch of his callousness. Being very much wrought up by this time—and Mrs. Bast was upstairs. I had not seen her, and had talked for a long time to Leonard—I had snubbed him for no reason, and that should have warned me I was in danger. So when the notes came I wanted us to go to you for an explanation. He said that he guessed the explanation—he knew of it, and you mustn't know. I pressed him to tell me. He said no one must know; it was something to do with his wife. Right up to the end we were Mr. Bast and Miss Schlegel. I was going to tell him that he must be frank with me when I saw his eyes, and guessed that Mr. Wilcox had ruined him in two ways, not one. I drew him to me. I made him tell me. I felt very lonely myself. He is not to blame. He would have gone on worshipping me. I want never to see him again, though it sounds appalling. I wanted to give him money and feel finished. Oh, Meg, the little that is known about these things!"

She laid her face against the tree.

"The little, too, that is known about growth! Both times it was loneliness, and the night, and panic afterwards. Did Leonard grow out of Paul?"

Margaret did not speak for a moment. So tired was she that her attention had actually wandered to the teeth—the teeth that had been thrust into the tree's bark to medicate it. From where she sat she could see them gleam. She had been trying to count them. "Leonard is a better growth than madness," she said. "I was afraid that you would react against Paul until you went over the verge."

"I did react until I found poor Leonard. I am steady now. I

shan't ever *like* your Henry, dearest Meg, or even speak kindly about him, but all that blinding hate is over. I shall never rave against Wilcoxes any more. I understand how you married him, and you will now be very happy."

Margaret did not reply.

"Yes," repeated Helen, her voice growing more tender, "I do at last understand."

"Except Mrs. Wilcox, dearest, no one understands our little movements."

"Because in death—I agree."

"Not quite. I feel that you and I and Henry are only fragments of that woman's mind. She knows everything. She is everything. She is the house, and the tree that leans over it. People have their own deaths as well as their own lives, and even if there is nothing beyond death, we shall differ in our nothingness. I cannot believe that knowledge such as hers will perish with knowledge such as mine. She knew about realities. She knew when people were in love, though she was not in the room. I don't doubt that she knew when Henry deceived her."

"Good-night, Mrs. Wilcox," called a voice.

"Oh, good-night, Miss Avery."

"Why should Miss Avery work for us?" Helen murmured.

"Why, indeed?"

Miss Avery crossed the lawn and merged into the hedge that divided it from the farm. An old gap, which Mr. Wilcox had filled up, had reappeared, and her track through the dew followed the path that he had turfed over, when he improved the garden and made it possible for games.

"This is not quite our house yet," said Helen. "When Miss Avery called, I felt we are only a couple of tourists."

"We shall be that everywhere, and for ever."

"But affectionate tourists——"

"But tourists who pretend each hotel is their home."

"I can't pretend very long," said Helen. "Sitting under this tree one forgets, but I know that to-morrow I shall see the moon rise out of Germany. Not all your goodness can alter the facts of the case. Unless you will come with me."

Margaret thought for a moment. In the past year she had grown so fond of England that to leave it was a real grief. Yet what detained her? No doubt Henry would pardon her outburst, and go on blustering and muddling into a ripe old age. But what was the good? She had just as soon vanish from his mind.

"Are you serious in asking me, Helen? Should I get on with your Monica?"

"You would not, but I am serious in asking you."

"Still, no more plans now. And no more reminiscences."

They were silent for a little. It was Helen's evening.

The present flowed by them like a stream. The tree rustled. It had made music before they were born, and would continue after their deaths, but its song was of the moment. The moment had passed. The tree rustled again. Their senses were sharpened, and they seemed to apprehend life. Life passed. The tree rustled again.

"Sleep now," said Margaret.

The peace of the country was entering into her. It has no commerce with memory, and little with hope. Least of all is it concerned with the hopes of the next five minutes. It is the peace of the present, which passes understanding. Its murmur came "now," and "now" once more as they trod the gravel, and "now," as the moonlight fell upon their father's sword. They passed upstairs, kissed, and amidst the endless iterations fell asleep. The house had enshadowed the tree at first, but as the moon rose higher the two disentangled, and were clear for a few moments at midnight. Margaret awoke and looked into the garden. How incomprehensible that Leonard Bast should have won her this night of peace! Was he also part of Mrs. Wilcox's mind?

CHAPTER XLI

Far different was Leonard's development. The months after Oniton, whatever minor troubles they might bring him, were all overshadowed by Remorse. When Helen looked back she could philosophize, or she could look into the future and plan for her child. But the father saw nothing beyond his own sin. Weeks afterwards, in the midst of other occupations, he would suddenly cry out, "Brute—you brute, I couldn't have——" and be rent into two people who held dialogues. Or brown rain would descend, blotting out faces and the sky. Even Jacky noticed the change in him. Most terrible were his sufferings when he awoke from sleep. Sometimes he was happy at first, but grew conscious of a burden hanging to him and weighing down his thoughts when they would move. Or little irons scorched his body. Or a sword stabbed him. He would sit at the edge of his bed, holding his heart and moaning, "Oh what *shall* I do, whatever *shall* I do?" Nothing brought ease. He could put distance between him and the trespass, but it grew in his soul.

Remorse is not among the eternal verities. The Greeks were right to dethrone her. Her action is too capricious, as though the Erinyes selected for punishment only certain men and certain sins. And of all means to regeneration Remorse is surely the most wasteful. It cuts away healthy tissues with the poisoned. It is a knife that probes far deeper than the evil. Leonard was driven straight through its torments and emerged pure, but enfeebled—a better man, who would never lose control of himself again, but also a smaller man, who had less to control. Nor did purity mean peace. The use of the knife can become a habit as hard to shake off as passion itself, and Leonard continued to start with a cry out of dreams.

He built up a situation that was far enough from the truth. It never occurred to him that Helen was to blame. He forgot the intensity of their talk, the charm that had been lent him by sincerity, the magic of Oniton under darkness and of the whispering river. Helen loved the absolute. Leonard had been ruined absolutely, and had appeared to her as a man apart, isolated from the world. A real man, who cared for adventure and beauty, who desired to live decently and pay his way, who could have travelled more gloriously through life than the Juggernaut car that was crushing him. Memories of Evie's wedding had warped her, the starched servants, the yards of uneaten food, the rustle of overdressed women, motor-cars oozing grease on the gravel rubbish on a pretentious band. She had tasted the lees of this on her arrival: in the darkness, after failure, they intoxicated her. She and the victim seemed alone in a world of unreality, and she loved him absolutely, perhaps for half an hour.

In the morning she was gone. The note that she left, tender and hysterical in tone, and intended to be most kind, hurt her lover terribly. It was as if some work of art had been broken by him, some picture in the National Gallery slashed out of its frame. When he recalled her talents and her social position, he felt that the first passer-by had a right to shoot him down. He was afraid of the waitress and the porters at the railway-station. He was afraid at first of his wife, though later he was to regard her with a strange new tenderness, and to think, "There is nothing to choose between us, after all."

The expedition to Shropshire crippled the Basts permanently. Helen in her flight forgot to settle the hotel bell, and took their return tickets away with her; they had to pawn Jacky's bangles to get home, and the smash came a few days afterwards. It is true that Helen offered him five thousand pounds, but such a sum meant nothing to him. He could not see that the girl was desperately righting herself, and trying to save something out of the disaster, if it was only five thousand pounds. But he had to live somehow. He turned to his family, and degraded himself to a professional beggar. There was nothing else for him to do.

"A letter from Leonard," thought Blanche, his sister; "and after all this time." She hid it, so that her husband should not see, and when he had gone to his work read it with some emotion, and sent the prodigal a little money out of her dress allowance.

"A letter from Leonard!" said the other sister, Laura, a few days later. She showed it to her husband. He wrote a cruel, insolent reply, but sent more money than Blanche, so Leonard soon wrote to him again.

And during the winter the system was developed. Leonard realized that they need never starve, because it would be too painful for his relatives. Society is based on the family, and the clever wastrel can exploit this indefinitely. Without a generous thought on either side, pounds and pounds passed. The donors disliked Leonard, and he grew to hate them intensely. When Laura censured his immoral marriage, he thought bitterly, "She minds that! What would she say if she knew the truth?" When Blanche's husband offered him work, he found some pretext for avoiding it. He had wanted work keenly at Oniton, but too much anxiety had shattered him, he was joining the unemployable. When his brother, the lay-reader, did not reply to a letter, he wrote again, saying that he and Jacky would come down to his village on foot. He did not intend this as blackmail. Still, the brother sent a postal order, and it became part of the system. And so passed his winter and his spring.

In the horror there are two bright spots. He never confused the past. He remained alive, and blessed are those who live, if it is only to a sense of sinfulness. The anodyne of muddledom, by which most men blur and blend their mistakes, never passed Leonard's lips—

> "And if I drink oblivion of a day,
> So shorten I the stature of my soul."

It is a hard saying, and a hard man wrote it, but it lies at the root of all character.

And the other bright spot was his tenderness for Jacky. He pitied her with nobility now—not the contemptuous pity of a man who sticks to a woman through thick and thin. He tried to be less irritable. He wondered what her hungry eyes desired—

nothing that she could express, or that he or any man could give her. Would she ever receive the justice that is mercy—the justice for by-products that the world is too busy to bestow? She was fond of flowers, generous with money, and not revengeful. If she had borne him a child he might have cared for her. Unmarried, Leonard would never have begged; he would have flickered out and died. But the whole of life is mixed. He had to provide for Jacky, and went down dirty paths that she might have a few feathers and the dishes of food that suited her.

One day he caught sight of Margaret and her brother. He was in St. Paul's. He had entered the cathedral partly to avoid the rain and partly to see a picture that had educated him in former years. But the light was bad, the picture ill placed, and Time and Judgment were inside him now. Death alone still charmed him, with her lap of poppies, on which all men shall sleep. He took one glance, and turned aimlessly away towards a chair. Then down the nave he saw Miss Schlegel and her brother. They stood in the fairway of passengers, and their faces were extremely grave. He was perfectly certain that they were in trouble about their sister.

Once outside—and he fled immediately—he wished that he had spoken to them. What was his life? What were a few angry words, or even imprisonment? He had done wrong—that was the true terror. Whatever they might know, he would tell them everything he knew. He re-entered St. Paul's. But they had moved in his absence, and had gone to lay their difficulties before Mr. Wilcox and Charles.

The sight of Margaret turned remorse into new channels. He desired to confess, and though the desire is proof of a weakened nature, which is about to lose the essence of human intercourse, it did not take an ignoble form. He did not suppose that confession would bring him happiness. It was rather that he yearned to get clear of the tangle. So does the suicide yearn. The impulses are akin, and the crime of suicide lies rather in its disregard for the feelings of those whom we leave behind. Confession need harm no one—it can satisfy that test—and though it was un-English, and ignored by our Anglican cathedral, Leonard had a right to decide upon it.

Moreover, he trusted Margaret. He wanted her hardness now. That cold, intellectual nature of hers would be just, if unkind. He would do whatever she told him, even if he had to see Helen. That was the supreme punishment she would exact. And perhaps she would tell him how Helen was. That was the supreme reward.

He knew nothing about Margaret, not even whether she was married to Mr. Wilcox, and tracking her out took several days. That evening he toiled through the wet to Wickham Place, where the new flats were now appearing. Was he also the cause of their move? Were they expelled from society on his account? Thence to a public library, but could find no satisfactory Schlegel in the directory. On the morrow he searched again. He hung about outside Mr. Wilcox's office at lunch time, and, as the clerks came out said: "Excuse me, sir, but is your boss married?" Most of them stared, some said, "What's that to you?" but one, who had not yet acquired reticence, told him what he wished. Leonard could not learn the private address. That necessitated more trouble with directories and tubes. Ducie Street was not discovered till the Monday, the day that Margaret and her husband went down on their hunting expedition to Howards End.

He called at about four o'clock. The weather had changed, and the sun shone gaily on the ornamental steps—black and white marble in triangles. Leonard lowered his eyes to them after ringing the bell. He felt in curious health: doors seemed to be opening and shutting inside his body, and he had been obliged to sleep sitting up in bed, with his back propped against the wall. When the parlourmaid came he could not see her face; the brown rain had descended suddenly.

"Does Mrs. Wilcox live here?" he asked.

"She's out," was the answer.

"When will she be back?"

"I'll ask," said the parlourmaid.

Margaret had given instructions that no one who mentioned her name should ever be rebuffed. Putting the door on the chain —for Leonard's appearance demanded this—she went through to the smoking-room, which was occupied by Tibby. Tibby was asleep. He had had a good lunch. Charles Wilcox had not yet rung him up for the distracting interview. He said drowsily: "I don't know. Hilton. Howards End. Who is it?"

"I'll ask, sir."

"No, don't bother."

"They have taken the car to Howards End," said the parlour-maid to Leonard.

He thanked her, and asked whereabouts that place was.

"You appear to want to know a good deal," she remarked. But Margaret had forbidden her to be mysterious. She told him against her better judgment that Howards End was in Hertfordshire.

"Is it a village, please?"

"Village! It's Mr. Wilcox's private house—at least, it's one of them. Mrs. Wilcox keeps her furniture there. Hilton is the village."

"Yes. And when will they be back?"

"Mr. Schlegel doesn't know. We can't know everything, can we?" She shut him out, and went to attend to the telephone, which was ringing furiously.

He loitered away another night of agony. Confession grew more difficult. As soon as possible he went to bed. He watched a patch of moonlight cross the floor of their lodging, and, as sometimes happens when the mind is overtaxed, he fell asleep for the rest of the room, but kept awake for the patch of moonlight. Horrible! Then began one of those disintegrating dialogues. Part of him said: "Why horrible? It's ordinary light from the moon." "But it moves." "So does the moon." "But it is a clenched fist." "Why not?" "But it is going to touch me." "Let it." And, seeming to gather motion, the patch ran up his blanket. Presently a blue snake appeared; then another, parallel to it. "Is there life in the moon?" "Of course." "But I thought it was uninhabited." "Not by

Time, Death, Judgment, and the smaller snakes." "Smaller snakes!" said Leonard indignantly and aloud. "What a notion!" By a rending effort of the will he woke the rest of the room up. Jacky, the bed, their food, their clothes on the chair, gradually entered his consciousness, and the horror vanished outwards, like a ring that is spreading through water.

"I say, Jacky, I'm going out for a bit."

She was breathing regularly. The patch of light fell clear of the striped blanket, and began to cover the shawl that lay over her feet. Why had he been afraid? He went to the window, and saw that the moon was descending through a clear sky. He saw her volcanoes, and the bright expanses that a gracious error has named seas. They paled, for the sun, who had lit them up, was coming to light the earth. Sea of Serenity, Sea of Tranquillity, Ocean of the Lunar Storms, merged into one lucent drop, itself to slip into the sempiternal dawn. And he had been afraid of the moon!

He dressed among the contending lights, and went through his money. It was running low again, but enough for a return ticket to Hilton. As it clinked Jacky opened her eyes.

"Hullo, Len! What ho, Len!"

"What ho, Jacky! see you again later."

She turned over and slept.

The house was unlocked, their landlord being a salesman at Covent Garden. Leonard passed out and made his way down to the station. The train, though it did not start for an hour, was already drawn up at the end of the platform, and he lay down in it and slept. With the first jolt he was in daylight; they had left the gateways of King's Cross, and were under blue sky. Tunnels followed, and after each the sky grew bluer, and from the embankment at Finsbury Park he had his first sight of the sun. It rolled along behind the eastern smokes—a wheel, whose fellow was the descending moon—and as yet it seemed the servant of the blue sky, not its lord. He dozed again. Over Tewin Water it was day. To the left fell the shadow of the embankment and its arches; to the right Leonard saw up into the Tewin Woods and towards the church, with its wild legend of immortality. Six forest trees—that is a fact—grow out of one of the graves in Tewin churchyard. The grave's occupant—that is the legend—is an atheist, who declared that if God existed, six forest trees would grow out of her grave. These things in Hertfordshire; and farther afield lay the house of a hermit—Mrs. Wilcox had known him—who barred himself up, and wrote prophecies, and gave all he had to the poor. While, powdered in between, were the villas of business men, who saw life more steadily, though with the steadiness of the half-closed eye. Over all the sun was streaming, to all the birds were singing, to all the primroses were yellow, and the speedwell blue, and the country, however they interpreted her, was uttering her cry of "now." She did not free Leonard yet, and the knife plunged deeper into his heart as the train drew up at Hilton. But remorse had become beautiful.

Hilton was asleep, or at the earliest, breakfasting. Leonard noticed the contrast when he stepped out of it into the country. Here men had been up since dawn. Their hours were ruled, not by a London office, but by the movements of the crops and the sun. That they were men of the finest type only the sentimentalist can declare. But they kept to the life of daylight. They are England's hope. Clumsily they carry forward the torch of the sun, until such time as the nation sees fit to take it up. Half clodhopper, half board-school prig, they can still throw back to a nobler stock, and breed yeomen.

At the chalk pit a motor passed hm. In it was another type, whom Nature favours—the Imperial. Healthy, ever in motion, it hopes to inherit the earth. It breeds as quickly as the yeoman, and as soundly; strong is the temptation to acclaim it as a super-yeoman, who carries his country's virtue overseas. But the Imperialist is not what he thinks or seems. He is a destroyer. He prepares the way for cosmopolitanism, and though his ambitions may be fulfilled, the earth that he inherits will be grey.

To Leonard, intent on his private sin, there came the conviction of innate goodness elsewhere. It was not the optimism which he had been taught at school. Again and again must the drums tap, and the goblins stalk over the universe before joy can be purged of the superficial. It was rather paradoxical, and arose from his sorrow. Death destroys a man, but the idea of death saves him—that is the best account of it that has yet been given. Squalor and tragedy can beckon to all that is great in us, and strengthen the wings of love. They can beckon; it is not certain that they will, for they are not love's servants. But they can beckon, and the knowledge of this incredible truth comforted him.

As he approached the house all thought stopped. Contradictory notions stood side by side in his mind. He was terrified but happy, ashamed, but had done no sin. He knew the confession: "Mrs. Wilcox, I have done wrong," but sunrise had robbed its meaning, and he felt rather on a supreme adventure.

He entered a garden, steadied himself against a motor-car that he found in it, found a door open and entered a house. Yes, it would be very easy. From a room to the left he heard voices, Margaret's amongst them. His own name was called aloud, and a man whom he had never seen said, "Oh, is he there? I am not surprised. I now thrash him within an inch of his life."

"Mrs. Wilcox," said Leonard, "I have done wrong."

The man took him by the collar and cried, "Bring me a stick." Women were screaming. A stick, very bright, descended. It hurt him, not where it descended, but in the heart. Books fell over him in a shower. Nothing had sense.

"Get some water," commanded Charles, who had all through kept very calm. "He's shamming. Of course I only used the blade. Here, carry him out into the air."

Thinking that he understood these things, Margaret obeyed him. They laid Leonard, who was dead, on the gravel; Helen poured water over him.

"That's enough," said Charles.

"Yes, murder's enough," said Miss Avery, coming out of the house with the sword.

CHAPTER XLII

When Charles left Ducie Street he had caught the first train home, but had no inkling of the newest development until late at night. Then his father, who had dined alone, sent for him, and in very grave tones inquired for Margaret.

"I don't know where she is, pater," said Charles. "Dolly kept back dinner nearly an hour for her."

"Tell me when she comes in."

Another hour passed. The servants went to bed, and Charles visited his father again, to receive further instructions. Mrs. Wilcox had still not returned.

"I'll sit up for her as late as you like, but she can hardly be coming. Isn't she stopping with her sister at the hotel?"

"Perhaps," said Mr. Wilcox thoughtfully—"perhaps."

"Can I do anything for you, sir?"

"Not to-night, my boy."

Mr. Wilcox liked being called sir. He raised his eyes and gave his son more open a look of tenderness than he usually ventured. He saw Charles as little boy and strong man in one. Though his wife had proved unstable his children were left to him.

After midnight he tapped on Charles's door. "I can't sleep," he said. "I had better have a talk with you and get it over."

He complained of the heat. Charles took him out into the garden, and they paced up and down in their dressing-gowns. Charles became very quiet as the story unrolled; he had known all along that Margaret was as bad as her sister.

"She will feel differently in the morning," said Mr. Wilcox, who had of course said nothing about Mrs. Bast. "But I cannot let this kind of thing continue without comment. I am morally certain that she is with her sister at Howards End. The house is mine—and, Charles, it will be yours—and when I say that no one is to live there, I mean that no one is to live there." I won't have it. He looked angrily at the moon. "To my mind this question is connected with something far greater, the rights of property itself."

"Undoubtedly," said Charles.

Mr. Wilcox lined his arm in his son's, but somehow liked him less as he told him more. "I don't want you to conclude that my wife and I had anything of the nature of a quarrel. She was only overwrought, as who would not be? I shall do what I can for Helen, but on the understanding that they clear out of the house at once. Do you see? That is a sine qua non."

"Then at eight to-morrow I may go up in the car?"

"Eight or earlier. Say that you are acting as my representative, and, of course, use no violence, Charles."

On the morrow, as Charles returned, leaving Leonard dead upon the gravel, it did not seem to him that he had used violence. Death was due to heart disease. His stepmother herself had said so, and even Miss Avery had acknowledged that he only used the flat of the sword. On his way through the village he informed the police, who thanked him, and said there must be an inquest. He found his father in the garden shading his eyes from the sun.

"It has been pretty horrible," said Charles gravely. "They were there, and they had the man up there with them too."

"What—what man?"

"I told you last night. His name was Bast."

"My God! is it possible?" said Mr. Wilcox. "In your mother's house! Charles, in your mother's house!"

"I know, pater. That was what I felt. As a matter of fact, there is no need to trouble about the man. He was in the last stages of heart disease, and just before I could show him what I thought of him he went off. The police are seeing about it at this moment."

Mr. Wilcox listened attentively.

"I got up there—oh, it couldn't have been more than half-past seven. The Avery woman was lighting a fire for them. They were still upstairs. I waited in the drawing-room. We were all moderately civil and collected, though I had my suspicions. I gave them your message, and Mrs. Wilcox said, 'Oh yes, I see; yes,' in that way of hers."

"Nothing else?"

"I promised to tell you, 'with her love,' that she was going to Germany with her sister this evening. That was all we had time for."

Mr. Wilcox seemed relieved.

"Because by then I suppose the man got tired of hiding, for suddenly Mrs. Wilcox screamed out his name. I recognized it, and I went for him in the hall. Was I right, pater? I thought things were going a little too far."

"Right, my dear boy? I don't know. But you would have been no son of mine if you hadn't. Then did he just—just—crumple up as you said?" He shrunk from the simple word.

"He caught hold of the bookcase, which came down over him. So I merely put the sword down and carried him into the garden. We all thought he was shamming. However, he's dead right enough. Awful business!"

"Sword?" cried his father, with anxiety in his voice. "What sword? Whose sword?"

"A sword of theirs."

"What were you doing with it?"

"Well, didn't you see, pater, I had to snatch up the first thing handy. I hadn't a riding-whip or stick. I caught him once or twice over the shoulders with the flat of their old German sword."

"Then what?"

"He pulled over the bookcase, as I said, and fell," said Charles, with a sigh. It was no fun doing errands for his father, who was never quite satisfied.

"But the real cause was heart disease? Of that you're sure?"

"That or a fit. However, we shall hear more than enough at the inquest on such unsavoury topics."

They went into breakfast. Charles had a racking headache, consequent on motoring before food. He was also anxious about the future, reflecting that the police must detain Helen and Margaret for the inquest and ferret the whole thing out. He saw himself obliged to leave Hilton. One could not afford to live near the scene of a scandal—it was not fair on one's wife. His comfort was that the pater's eyes were opened at last. There would be a horrible smash up, and probably a separation from Margaret; then they would all start again, more as they had been in his mother's time.

"I think I'll go round to the police-station," said his father when breakfast was over.

"What for?" cried Dolly, who had still not been "told."

"Very well, sir. Which car will you have?"

"I think I'll walk."

"It's a good half-mile," said Charles, stepping into the garden. "The sun's very hot for April. Shan't I take you up, and then, perhaps, a little spin round by Tewin?"

"You go on as if I didn't know my own mind," said Mr. Wilcox fretfully. Charles hardened his mouth. "You young fellows' one idea is to get into a motor. I tell you, I want to walk: I'm very fond of walking."

"Oh, all right; I'm about the house if you want me for anything. I thought of not going up to the office to-day, if that is your wish."

"It is, indeed, my boy," said Mr. Wilcox, and laid a hand on his sleeve.

Charles did not like it; he was uneasy about his father, who did not seem himself this morning. There was a petulant touch about him—more like a woman. Could it be that he was growing old? The Wilcoxes were not lacking in affection; they had it royally, but they did not know how to use it. It was the talent in the napkin, and, for a warm-hearted man, Charles had conveyed very little joy. As he watched his father shuffling up the road, he had a vague regret—a wish that something had been different somewhere—a wish (though he did not express it thus) that he had been taught to say "I" in his youth. He meant to make up for Margaret's defection, but knew that his father had been very happy with her until yesterday. How had she done it? By some dishonest trick, no doubt—but how?

Mr. Wilcox reappeared at eleven, looking very tired. There was to be an inquest on Leonard's body to-morrow, and the police required his son to attend.

"I expected that," said Charles. "I shall naturally be the most important witness there."

CHAPTER XLIII

Out of the turmoil and horror that had begun with Aunt Juley's illness and was not even to end with Leonard's death, it seemed impossible to Margaret that healthy life should re-emerge. Events succeeded in a logical, yet senseless, train. People lost their humanity, and took values as arbitrary as those in a pack of playing-cards. It was natural that Henry should do this and cause Helen to do that, and then think her wrong for doing it; natural that she herself should think him wrong; natural that Leonard should want to know how Helen was, and come, and Charles be angry with him for coming—natural, but unreal. In this jangle of causes and effects what had become of their true selves? Here Leonard lay dead in the garden, from natural causes; yet life was a deep, deep river, death a blue sky, life was a house, death a wisp of hay, a flower, a tower, life and death were anything and everything, except this ordered insanity, where the king takes the queen, and the ace the king. Ah, no; there was beauty and adventure behind, such as the man at her feet had yearned for; there was hope this side of the grave; there were truer relationships beyond the limits that fetter us now. As a prisoner looks up and sees stars beckoning, so she, from the turmoil and horror of those days, caught glimpses of the diviner wheels.

And Helen, dumb with fright, but trying to keep calm for the child's sake, and Miss Avery, calm, but murmuring tenderly, "No one ever told the lad he'll have a child"—they also reminded her that horror is not the end. To what ultimate harmony we tend she did not know, but there seemed great chance that a child would be born into the world, to take the great chances of beauty and adventure that the world offers. She moved through the sunlit garden, gathering narcissi, crimson-eyed and white. There was nothing else to be done; the time for telegrams and anger was over, and it seemed wisest that the hands of Leonard should be folded on his breast and be filled with flowers. Here was the father; leave it at that. Let Squalor be turned into Tragedy, whose eyes are the stars, and whose hands hold the sunset and the dawn.

And even the influx of officials, even the return of the doctor, vulgar and acute, could not shake her belief in the eternity of beauty. Science explained people, but could not understand them. After long centuries among the bones and muscles it might be advancing to knowledge of the nerves, but this would never give understanding. One could open the heart to Mr. Mansbridge and his sort without discovering its secrets to them, for they wanted everything down in black and white, and black and white was exactly what they were left with.

They questioned her closely about Charles. She never suspected why. Death had come, and the doctor agreed that it was due to heart disease. They asked to see her father's sword. She explained that Charles's anger was natural, but mistaken. Miserable questions about Leonard followed, all of which she answered unfalteringly. Then back to Charles again. "No doubt Mr. Wilcox may have induced death," she said; "but if it wasn't one thing it would have been another, as you yourselves know." At last they thanked her, and took the sword and the body down to Hilton. She began to pick up the books from the floor.

Helen had gone to the farm. It was the best place for her, since she had to wait for the inquest. Though, as if things were not hard enough, Madge and her husband had raised trouble; they did not see why they should receive the offscourings of Howards End. And, of course, they were right. The whole world was going to be right, and amply avenge any brave talk against the conventions. "Nothing matters," the Schlegels had said in the past, "except one's self-respect and that of one's friends." When the time came, other things mattered terribly. However, Madge had yielded, and

Helen was assured of peace for one day and night, and to-morrow she would return to Germany.

As for herself, she determined to go too. No message came from Henry; perhaps he expected her to apologize. Now that she had time to think over her own tragedy, she was unrepentant. She neither forgave him for his behaviour nor wished to forgive him. Her speech to him seemed perfect. She would not have altered a word. It had to be uttered once in a life, to adjust the lopsidedness of the world. It was spoken not only to her husband, but to thousands of men like him—a protest against the inner darkness in high places that comes with a commercial age. Though he would build up his life without hers, she could not apologize. He had refused to connect, on the clearest issue that can be laid before a man, and their love must take the consequences.

No, there was nothing more to be done. They had tried not to go over the precipice, but perhaps the fall was inevitable. And it comforted her to think that the future was certainly inevitable: cause and effect would go jangling forward to some goal doubtless, but to none that she could imagine. At such moments the soul retires within, to float upon the bosom of a deeper stream, and has communion with the dead, and sees the world's glory not diminished, but different in kind to what she has supposed. She alters her focus until trivial things are blurred. Margaret had been tending this way all the winter. Leonard's death brought her to the goal. Alas! that Henry should fade away as reality emerged, and only her love for him should remain clear, stamped with his image like the cameos we rescue out of dreams.

With unfaltering eye she traced his future. He would soon present a healthy mind to the world again, and what did he or the world care if he was rotten at the core? He would grow into a rich, jolly old man, at times a little sentimental about women, but emptying his glass with anyone. Tenacious of power, he would keep Charles and the rest dependent, and retire from business reluctantly and at an advanced age. He would settle down—though she could not realize this. In her eyes Henry was always moving and causing others to move, until the ends of the earth met. But in time he must get too tired to move, and settle down. What next? The inevitable word. The release of the soul to its appropriate Heaven.

Would they meet in it? Margaret believed in immortality for herself. An eternal future had always seemed natural to her. And Henry believed in it for himself. Yet, would they meet again? Are there not rather endless levels beyond the grave, as the theory that he had censured teaches? And his level, whether higher or lower, could it possibly be the same as hers?

Thus gravely meditating, she was summoned by him. He sent up Crane in the motor. Other servants passed like water, but the chauffeur remained, though impertinent and disloyal. Margaret disliked Crane, and he knew it.

"Is it the keys that Mr. Wilcox wants?" she asked.

"He didn't say, madam."

"You haven't any note for me?"

"He didn't say, madam."

After a moment's thought she locked up Howards End. It was pitiable to see in it the stirrings of warmth that would be quenched for ever. She raked out the fire that was blazing in the kitchen, and spread the coals in the gravelled yard. She closed the windows and drew the curtains. Henry would probably sell the place now.

She was determined not to spare him, for nothing new had happened as far as they were concerned. Her mood might never have altered from yesterday evening. He was standing a little outside Charles's gate, and motioned the car to stop. When his wife got out he said hoarsely: "I prefer to discuss things with you outside."

"It will be more appropriate in the road, I am afraid," said Margaret. "Did you get my message?"

"What about?"

"I am going to Germany with my sister. I must tell you now that I shall make it my permanent home. Our talk last night was more important than you have realized. I am unable to forgive you and am leaving you."

"I am extremely tired," said Henry, in injured tones. "I have been walking about all the morning, and wish to sit down."

"Certainly, if you will consent to sit on the grass."

The Great North Road should have been bordered all its length with glebe. Henry's kind had filched most of it. She moved to the scrap opposite, wherein were the Six Hills. They sat down on the farther side, so that they could not be seen by Charles or Dolly.

"Here are your keys," said Margaret. She tossed them towards him. They fell on the sunlit slope of grass, and he did not pick them up.

"I have something to tell you," he said gently.

She knew this superficial gentleness, this confession of hastiness, that was only intended to enhance her admiration of the male.

"I don't want to hear it," she replied. "My sister is going to be ill. My life is going to be with her now. We must manage to build up something, she and I and her child."

"Where are you going?"

"Munich. We start after the inquest, if she is not too ill."

"After the inquest?"

"Yes."

"Have you realized what the verdict at the inquest will be?"

"Yes, heart disease."

"No, my dear; manslaughter."

Margaret drove her fingers through the grass. The hill beneath her moved as if it was alive.

"Manslaughter," repeated Mr. Wilcox. "Charles may go to prison. I dare not tell him. I don't know what to do—what to do. I'm broken—I'm ended."

No sudden warmth arose in her. She did not see that to break him was her only hope. She did not enfold the sufferer in her arms. But all through that day and the next a new life began to move. The verdict was brought in. Charles was committed for trial. It was against all reason that he should be punished, but the law, being made in his image, sentenced him to three years' imprisonment. Then Henry's fortress gave way. He could bear no one but his wife, he shambled up to Margaret afterwards and asked her to do what she could with him. She did what seemed easiest—she took him down to recruit at Howards End.

CHAPTER XLIV

Tom's father was cutting the big meadow. He passed again and again amid whirring blades and sweet odours of grass, encompassing with narrowing circles the sacred centre of the field. Tom was negotiating with Helen.

"I haven't any idea," she replied. "Do you suppose baby may, Meg?"

Margaret put down her work and regarded them absently.

"What was that?" she asked.

"Tom wants to know whether baby is old enough to play with hay?"

"I haven't the least notion," answered Margaret, and took up her work again.

"Now, Tom, baby is not to stand; he is not to lie on his face; he is not to lie so that his head wags; he is not to be teased or tickled; and he is not to be cut into two or more pieces by the cutter. Will you be as careful as all that?"

Tom held out his arms.

"That child is a wonderful nursemaid," remarked Margaret.

"He is fond of baby. That's why he does it!" was Helen's answer. "They're going to be lifelong friends."

"Starting at the ages of six and one?"

"Of course. It will be a great thing for Tom."

"It may be a greater thing for baby."

Fourteen months had passed, but Margaret still stopped at Howards End. No better plan had occurred to her. The meadow was being recut, the great red poppies were reopening in the garden. July would follow with the little red poppies among the wheat, August with the cutting of the wheat. These little events would become part of her year after year. Every summer she would fear lest the well should give out, every winter lest the pipes should freeze; every westerly gale might blow the wych-elm down and bring the end of all things, and so she could not read or talk during a westerly gale. The air was tranquil now. She and her sister were sitting on the remains of Evie's rockery, where the lawn merged into the field.

"What a time they all are!" said Helen. "What can they be doing inside?" Margaret, who was growing less talkative, made no answer. The noise of the cutter came intermittently, like the breaking of waves. Close by them a man was preparing to scythe out one of the dell-holes.

"I wish Henry was out to enjoy this," said Helen. "This lovely weather and to be shut up in the house! It's very hard."

"It has to be," said Margaret. "The hay-fever is his chief objection against living here, but he thinks it worth while."

"Meg, is or isn't he ill? I can't make out."

"Not ill. Eternally tired. He has worked very hard all his life, and noticed nothing. Those are the people who collapse when they do notice a thing."

"I suppose he worries dreadfully about his part of the tangle."

"Dreadfully. That is why I wish Dolly had not come, too, to-day. Still, he wanted them all to come. It has to be."

"Why does he want them?"

Margaret did not answer.

"Meg, may I tell you something? I like Henry."

"You'd be odd if you didn't," said Margaret.

"I usen't to."

"Usen't!" She lowered her eyes a moment to the black abyss of the past. They had crossed it, always excepting Leonard and Charles. They were building up a new life, obscure, yet gilded with tranquillity. Leonard was dead; Charles had two years more in prison. One usen't always to see clearly before that time. It was different now.

"I like Henry because he does worry."

"And he likes you because you don't."

Helen sighed. She seemed humiliated, and buried her face in her hands. After a time she said: "About love," a transition less abrupt than it appeared.

Margaret never stopped working.

"I mean a woman's love for a man. I supposed I should hang my life on to that once, and was driven up and down and about as if something was worrying through me. But everything is peaceful now; I seem cured. That Herr Förstmeister, whom Frieda keeps writing about, must be a noble character, but he doesn't see that I shall never marry him or anyone. It isn't shame or mistrust of myself. I simply couldn't. I'm ended. I used to be so dreamy about a man's love as a girl, and think that for good or evil love must be the great thing. But it hasn't been; it has been itself a dream. Do you agree?"

"I do not agree. I do not."

"I ought to remember Leonard as my lover," said Helen, stepping down into the field. "I tempted him, and killed him, and it is surely the least I can do. I would like to throw out all my heart to Leonard on such an afternoon as this. But I cannot. It is no good pretending. I am forgetting him." Her eyes filled with tears. "How nothing seems to match—how, my darling, my precious——" She broke off. "Tommy!"

"Yes, please?"

"Baby's not to try and stand.—There's something wanting in me. I see you loving Henry, and understanding him better daily, and I know that death wouldn't part you in the least. But I—— Is it some awful appalling, criminal defect?"

Margaret silenced her. She said: "It is only that people are far more different than is pretended. All over the world men and women are worrying because they cannot develop as they are supposed to develop. Here and there they have the matter out, and it comforts them. Don't fret yourself, Helen. Develop what you have; love your child. I do not love children. I am thankful to have none. I can play with their beauty and charm, but that is all—nothing real, not one scrap of what there ought to be. And others—others go farther still, and move outside humanity altogether. A place, as well as a person, may catch the glow. Don't you see that all this leads to comfort in the end? It is part of the battle against sameness. Differences—eternal differences, planted by God in a single family, so that there may always be colour; sorrow perhaps, but colour in the daily grey. Then I can't have you worrying about Leonard. Don't drag in the personal when it will not come. Forget him."

"Yes, yes, but what has Leonard got out of life?"

"Perhaps an adventure."

"Is that enough?"

"Not for us. But for him."

Helen took up a bunch of grass. She looked at the sorrel, and the red and white and yellow clover, and the quaker grass, and the daisies, and the bents that composed it. She raised it to her face.

"Is it sweetening yet?" asked Margaret.

"No, only withered."

"It will sweeten to-morrow."

Helen smiled. "Oh, Meg, you are a person," she said. "Think of the racket and torture this time last year. But now I couldn't stop unhappy if I tried. What a change—and all through you!"

"Oh, we merely settled down. You and Henry learnt to understand one another and to forgive, all through the autumn and the winter."

"Yes, but who settled us down?"

Margaret did not reply. The scything had begun, and she took off her pince-nez to watch it.

"You!" cried Helen. "You did it all, sweetest, though you're too stupid to see. Living here was your plan—I wanted you; he wanted you; and everyone said it was impossible, but you knew. Just think of our lives without you, Meg—I and baby with Monica, revolting by theory, he handed about from Dolly to Evie. But you picked up the pieces, and made us a home. Can't it strike you—even for a moment—that your life has been heroic? Can't you remember the two months after Charles's arrest, when you began to act, and did all?"

"You were both ill at the time," said Margaret. "I did the obvious things. I had two invalids to nurse. Here was a house, ready furnished and empty. It was obvious. I didn't know myself it would turn into a permanent home. No doubt I have done a little towards straightening the tangle, but things that I can't phrase have helped me."

"I hope it will be permanent," said Helen, drifting away to other thoughts.

"I think so. There are moments when I feel Howards End peculiarly our own."

"All the same, London's creeping."

She pointed over the meadow—over eight or nine meadows, but at the end of them was a red rust.

"You see that in Surrey and even Hampshire now," she continued. "I can see it from the Purbeck Downs. And London is only part of something else, I'm afraid. Life's going to be melted down, all over the world."

Margaret knew that her sister spoke truly. Howards End, Oniton, the Purbeck Downs, the Oderberge, were all survivals, and the melting-pot was being prepared for them. Logically, they had no right to be alive. One's hope was in the weakness of logic. Were they possibly the earth beating time?

"Because a thing is going strong now, it need not go strong for ever," she said. "This craze for motion has only set in during the last hundred years. It may be followed by a civilization that won't be a movement, because it will rest on the earth. All the signs are against it now, but I can't help hoping, and very early in the morning in the garden I feel that our house is the future as well as the past."

They turned and looked at it. Their own memories coloured it now, for Helen's child had been born in the central room of the nine. Then Margaret said, "Oh, take care—!" for something moved behind the window of the hall, and the door opened.

"The conclave's breaking at last. I'll go."

It was Paul.

Helen retreated with the children far into the field. Friendly voices greeted her. Margaret rose, to encounter a man with a heavy black moustache.

"My father has asked for you," he said with hostility.

She took her work and followed him.

"We have been talking business," he continued, "but I dare say you knew all about it beforehand."

"Yes, I did."

Clumsy of movement—for he had spent all his life in the saddle—Paul drove his foot against the paint of the front door. Mrs. Wilcox gave a little cry of annoyance. She did not like anything scratched; she stopped in the hall to take Dolly's boa and gloves out of a vase.

Her husband was lying in a great leather chair in the dining-room, and by his side, holding his hand rather ostentatiously, was Evie. Dolly, dressed in purple, sat near the window. The room was a little dark and airless; they were obliged to keep it like this until the carting of the hay. Margaret joined the family without speaking; the five of them had met already at tea, and she knew quite well what was going to be said. Averse to wasting her time, she went on sewing. The clock struck six.

"Is this going to suit everyone?" said Henry in a weary voice. He used the old phrases, but their effect was unexpected and shadowy. "Because I don't want you all coming here later on and complaining that I have been unfair."

"It's apparently got to suit us," said Paul.

"I beg your pardon, my boy. You have only to speak, and I will leave the house to you instead."

Paul frowned ill-temperedly, and began scratching at his arm. "As I've given up the outdoor life that suited me, and I have come home to look after the business, it's no good my settling down here," he said at last. "It's not really the country, and it's not the town."

"Very well. Does my arrangement suit you, Evie?"

"Of course, father."

"And you, Dolly?"

Dolly raised her faded little face, which sorrow could wither but not steady. "Perfectly splendidly," she said. "I thought Charles wanted it for the boys, but last time I saw him he said no, because we cannot possibly live in this part of England again. Charles says we ought to change our name, but I cannot think what to, for Wilcox just suits Charles and me, and I can't think of any other name."

There was a general silence. Dolly looked nervously round, fearing that she had been inappropriate. Paul continued to scratch his arm.

"Then I leave Howards End to my wife absolutely," said Henry. "And let everyone understand that; and after I am dead let there be no jealousy and no surprise."

Margaret did not answer. There was something uncanny in her triumph. She, who had never expected to conquer anyone, had charged straight through these Wilcoxes and broken up their lives.

"In consequence, I leave my wife no money," said Henry. "That is her own wish. All that she would have had will be divided among you. I am also giving you a great deal in my lifetime, so that you may be independent of me. That is her wish, too. She also is giving away a great deal of money. She intends to diminish her income by half during the next ten years; she intends when she dies to leave the house to her—to her nephew, down in the field. Is all that clear? Does everyone understand?"

Paul rose to his feet. He was accustomed to natives, and a very little shook him out of the Englishman. Feeling manly and cynical, he said: "Down in the field? Oh, come! I think we might have had the whole establishment, piccaninnies included."

Mrs. Cahill whispered: "Don't, Paul. You promised you'd take care." Feeling a woman of the world, she rose and prepared to take her leave.

Her father kissed her. "Good-bye, old girl," he said; "don't you worry about me."

"Good-bye, dad."

Then it was Dolly's turn. Anxious to contribute, she laughed nervously, and said: "Good-bye, Mr. Wilcox. It does seem curious that Mrs. Wilcox should have left Margaret Howards End, and yet she get it, after all."

From Evie came a sharply-drawn breath. "Good-bye," she said to Margaret, and kissed her.

And again and again fell the word, like the ebb of a dying sea.

"Good-bye."

"Good-bye, Dolly."

"So long, father."

"Good-bye, my boy; always take care of yourself."

"Good-bye, Mrs. Wilcox."

"Good-bye."

Margaret saw their visitors to the gate. Then she returned to her husband and laid her head in his hands. He was pitiably tired. But Dolly's remark had interested her. At last she said: "Could you tell me, Henry, what was that about Mrs. Wilcox having left me Howards End?"

Tranquilly he replied: "Yes, she did. But that is a very old story. When she was ill and you were so kind to her she wanted to make you some return, and, not being herself at the time, scribbled 'Howards End' on a piece of paper. I went into it thoroughly, and, as it was clearly fanciful, I set it aside, little knowing what my Margaret would be to me in the future."

Margaret was silent. Something shook her life in its inmost recesses, and she shivered.

"I didn't do wrong, did I?" he asked, bending down.

"You didn't, darling. Nothing has been done wrong."

From the garden came laughter. "Here they are at last!" exclaimed Henry, disengaging himself with a smile. Helen rushed into the gloom, holding Tom by one hand and carrying her baby on the other. There were shouts of infectious joy.

"The field's cut!" Helen cried excitedly—"the big meadow! We've seen to the very end, and it'll be such a crop of hay as never!"

Weybridge, 1908–1910.

· · ·

The Story of a Panic

I

Eustace's career—if career it can be called—certainly dates from that afternoon in the chestnut woods above Ravello. I confess at once that I am a plain, simple man, with no pretensions to literary style. Still, I do flatter myself that I can tell a story without exaggerating, and I have therefore decided to give an unbiassed account of the extraordinary events of eight years ago.

Ravello is a delightful place with a delightful little hotel in which we met some charming people. There were the two Miss Robinsons, who had been there for six weeks with Eustace, their nephew, then a boy of about fourteen. Mr. Sandbach had also been there some time. He had held a curacy in the north of England, which he had been compelled to resign on account of ill-health, and while he was recruiting at Ravello he had taken in hand Eustace's education—which was then sadly deficient—and was endeavouring to fit him for one of our great public schools. Then there was Mr. Leyland, a would-be artist, and, finally, there was the nice landlady, Signora Scafetti, and the nice English-speaking waiter, Emmanuele—though at the time of which I am speaking Emmanuele was away, visiting a sick father.

To this little circle, I, my wife, and my two daughters made, I venture to think, a not unwelcome addition. But though I liked most of the company well enough, there were two of them to whom I did not take at all. They were the artist, Leyland, and the Miss Robinsons' nephew, Eustace.

Leyland was simply conceited and odious, and, as those qualities will be amply illustrated in my narrative, I need not enlarge upon them here. But Eustace was something besides: he was indescribably repellent.

I am fond of boys as a rule, and was quite disposed to be friendly. I and my daughters offered to take him out—'No, walking was such a fag.' Then I asked him to come and bathe—'No, he could not swim.'

"Every English boy should be able to swim," I said, "I will teach you myself."

"There, Eustace dear," said Miss Robinson; "here is a chance for you."

But he said he was afraid of the water!—a boy afraid!—and of course I said no more.

I would not have minded so much if he had been a really studious boy, but he neither played hard nor worked hard. His favourite occupations were lounging on the terrace in an easy chair and loafing along the high road, with his feet shuffling up the dust and his shoulders stooping forward. Naturally enough, his features were pale, his chest contracted, and his muscles undeveloped. His aunts thought him delicate; what he really needed was discipline.

That memorable day we all arranged to go for a picnic up in the chestnut woods—all, that is, except Janet, who stopped behind to finish her water-colour of the Cathedral—not a very successful attempt, I am afraid.

I wander off into these irrelevant details, because in my mind I cannot separate them from an account of the day; and it is the same with the conversation during the picnic: all is imprinted on my brain together. After a couple of hours' ascent, we left the donkeys that had carried the Miss Robinsons and my wife, and all proceeded on foot to the head of the valley—Vallone Fontana Caroso is its proper name, I find.

I have visited a good deal of fine scenery before and since, but have found little that has pleased me more. The valley ended in a vast hollow, shaped like a cup, into which radiated ravines from the precipitous hills around. Both the valley and the ravines and the ribs of hill that divided the ravines were covered with leafy chestnut, so that the general appearance was that of a many-fingered green hand, palm upwards, which was clutching convulsively to keep us in its grasp. Far down the valley we could see Ravello and the sea, but that was the only sign of another world.

"Oh, what a perfectly lovely place," said my daughter Rose. "What a picture it would make!"

"Yes," said Mr. Sandbach. "Many a famous European gallery would be proud to have a landscape a tithe as beautiful as this upon its walls."

"On the contrary," said Leyland, "it would make a very poor picture. Indeed, it is not paintable at all."

"And why is that?" said Rose, with far more deference than he deserved.

"Look, in the first place," he replied, "how intolerably straight against the sky is the line of the hill. It would need breaking up and diversifying. And where we are standing the whole thing is out of perspective. Besides, all the colouring is monotonous and crude."

"I do not know anything about pictures," I put in, "and I do not pretend to know: but I know what is beautiful when I see it, and I am thoroughly content with this."

"Indeed, who could help being contented!" said the elder Miss Robinson; and Mr. Sandbach said the same.

"Ah!" said Leyland, "you all confuse the artistic view of Nature with the photographic."

Poor Rose had brought her camera with her, so I thought this positively rude. I did not wish any unpleasantness; so I merely turned away and assisted my wife and Miss Mary Robinson to put out the lunch—not a very nice lunch.

"Eustace, dear," said his aunt, "come and help us here."

He was in a particularly bad temper that morning. He had, as usual, not wanted to come, and his aunts had nearly allowed him to stop at the hotel to vex Janet. But I, with their permission, spoke to him rather sharply on the subject of exercise; and the result was that he had come, but was even more taciturn and moody than usual.

Obedience was not his strong point. He invariably questioned every command, and only executed it grumbling. I should always insist on prompt and cheerful obedience, if I had a son.

"I'm—coming—Aunt—Mary," he at last replied, and dawdled to cut a piece of wood to make a whistle, taking care not to arrive till we had finished.

"Well, well, sir!" said I, "you stroll in at the end and profit by our labours." He sighed, for he could not endure being chaffed. Miss Mary, very unwisely, insisted on giving him the wing of the chicken, in spite of all my attempts to prevent her. I remember that I had a moment's vexation when I thought that, instead of enjoying the sun, and the air, and the woods, we were all engaged in wrangling over the diet of a spoilt boy.

But, after lunch, he was a little less in evidence. He withdrew to a tree trunk, and began to loosen the bark from his whistle. I was thankful to see him employed, for once in a way. We reclined, and took a *dolce far niente*.

Those sweet chestnuts of the South are puny striplings compared with our robust Northerners. But they clothed the contours of the hills and valleys in a most pleasing way, their veil being only broken by two clearings, in one of which we were sitting.

And because these few trees were cut down, Leyland burst into a petty indictment of the proprietor.

"All the poetry is going from Nature," he cried, "her lakes and marshes are drained, her seas banked up, her forests cut down. Everywhere we see the vulgarity of desolation spreading."

I have had some experience of estates, and answered that cutting was very necessary for the health of the larger trees. Besides, it was unreasonable to expect the proprietor to derive no income from his lands.

"If you take the commercial side of landscape, you may feel pleasure in the owner's activity. But to me the mere thought that a tree is convertible into cash is disgusting."

"I see no reason," I observed politely, "to despise the gifts of Nature because they are of value."

It did not stop him. "It is no matter," he went on, "we are all hopelessly steeped in vulgarity. I do not except myself. It is through us, and to our shame, that the Nereids have left the waters and the Oreads the mountains, that the woods no longer give shelter to Pan."

"Pan!" cried Mr. Sandbach, his mellow voice filling the valley as if it had been a great green church, "Pan is dead. That is why the woods do not shelter him." And he began to tell the striking story of the mariners who were sailing near the coast at the time of the birth of Christ, and three times heard a loud voice saying: "The great God Pan is dead."

"Yes. The great God Pan is dead," said Leyland. And he abandoned himself to that mock misery in which artistic people are so fond of indulging. His cigar went out, and he had to ask me for a match.

"How very interesting," said Rose. "I do wish I knew some ancient history."

"It is not worth your notice," said Mr. Sandbach. "Eh, Eustace?"

Eustace was finishing his whistle. He looked up, with the irritable frown in which his aunts allowed him to indulge, and made no reply.

The conversation turned to various topics and then died out. It was a cloudless afternoon in May, and the pale green of the young chestnut leaves made a pretty contrast with the dark blue of the sky. We were all sitting at the edge of the small clearing for the sake of the view, and the shade of the chestnut saplings behind us was manifestly insufficient. All sounds died away—at least that is my account: Miss Robinson says that the clamour of the birds was the first sign of uneasiness that she discerned. All sounds died away, except that, far in the distance, I could hear two boughs of a great chestnut grinding together as the tree swayed. The grinds grew shorter and shorter, and finally that sound stopped also. As I looked over the green valley, everything was absolutely motionless and still; and that feeling of suspense which one so often experiences when Nature is in repose, began to steal over me.

Suddenly, we were all electrified by the excruciating noise of
Eustace's whistle. I never heard any instrument give forth so ear-
splitting and discordant a sound.

"Eustace, dear," said Miss Mary Robinson, "you might have
thought of your poor Aunt Julia's head."

Leyland who had apparently been asleep, sat up.

"It is astonishing how blind a boy is to anything that is elevating or beautiful," he observed. "I should not have thought he
could have found the wherewithal out here to spoil our pleasure
like this."

Then the terrible silence fell upon us again. I was now standing up and watching a catspaw of wind that was running down
one of the ridges opposite, turning the light green to dark as it
travelled. A fanciful feeling of foreboding came over me; so I
turned away, to find to my amazement, that all the others were
also on their feet, watching it too.

It is not possible to describe coherently what happened next:
but I, for one, am not ashamed to confess that, though the fair
blue sky was above me, and the green spring woods beneath me,
and the kindest of friends around me, yet I became terribly
frightened, more frightened than I ever wish to become again,
frightened in a way I never have known either before or after. And
in the eyes of the others, too, I saw blank, expressionless fear,
while their mouths strove in vain to speak and their hands to ges-
ticulate. Yet, all around us were prosperity, beauty, and peace, and
all was motionless, save the catspaw of wind, now travelling up
the ridge on which we stood.

Who moved first has never been settled. It is enough to say
that in one second we were tearing away along the hill-side. Leyland was in front, then Mr. Sandbach, then my wife. But I only
saw for a brief moment; for I ran across the little clearing and
through the woods and over the undergrowth and the rocks and
down the dry torrent beds into the valley below. The sky might
have been black as I ran, and the trees short grass, and the hillside
a level road; for I saw nothing and heard nothing and felt nothing,

since all the channels of sense and reason were blocked. It was not the spiritual fear that one has known at other times, but brutal overmastering physical fear, stopping up the ears, and dropping clouds before the eyes, and filling the mouth with foul tastes. And it was no ordinary humiliation that survived; for I had been afraid, not as a man, but as a beast.

II

I cannot describe our finish any better than our start; for our fear passed away as it had come, without cause. Suddenly I was able to see, and hear, and cough, and clear my mouth. Looking back, I saw that the others were stopping too; and, in a short time, we were all together, though it was long before we could speak, and longer before we dared to.

No one was seriously injured. My poor wife had sprained her ankle, Leyland had torn one of his nails on a tree trunk, and I myself had scraped and damaged my ear. I never noticed it till I had stopped.

We were all silent, searching one another's faces. Suddenly Miss Mary Robinson gave a terrible shriek. "Oh, merciful heavens! where is Eustace?" And then she would have fallen, if Mr. Sandbach had not caught her.

"We must go back, we must go back at once," said my Rose, who was quite the most collected of the party. "But I hope—I feel he is safe."

Such was the cowardice of Leyland, that he objected. But, finding himself in a minority, and being afraid of being left alone, he gave in. Rose and I supported my poor wife, Mr. Sandbach and Miss Robinson helped Miss Mary, and we returned slowly and silently, taking forty minutes to ascend the path that we had descended in ten.

Our conversation was naturally disjointed, as no one wished to offer an opinion on what had happened. Rose was the most talkative: she startled us all by saying that she had very nearly stopped where she was.

"Do you mean to say that you weren't—that you didn't feel compelled to go?" said Mr. Sandbach.

"Oh, of course, I did feel frightened"—she was the first to use the word—"but I somehow felt that if I could stop on it would be quite different, that I shouldn't be frightened at all, so to speak." Rose never did express herself clearly: still, it is greatly to her credit that she, the youngest of us, should have held on so long at that terrible time.

"I should have stopped, I do believe," she continued, "if I had not seen mamma go."

Rose's experience comforted us a little about Eustace. But a feeling of terrible foreboding was on us all, as we painfully climbed the chestnut-covered slopes and neared the little clearing. When we reached it our tongues broke loose. There, at the further side, were the remains of our lunch, and close to them, lying motionless on his back, was Eustace.

With some presence of mind I at once cried out: "Hey, you young monkey! jump up!" But he made no reply, nor did he answer when his poor aunts spoke to him. And, to my unspeakable horror, I saw one of those green lizards dart out from under his shirt-cuff as we approached.

We stood watching him as he lay there so silently, and my ears began to tingle in expectation of the outbursts of lamentations and tears.

Miss Mary fell on her knees beside him and touched his hand, which was convulsively entwined in the long grass.

As she did so, he opened his eyes and smiled.

I have often seen that peculiar smile since, both on the possessor's face and on the photographs of him that are beginning to get into the illustrated papers. But, till then, Eustace had always worn a peevish, discontented frown; and we were all unused to this disquieting smile, which always seemed to be without adequate reason.

His aunts showered kisses on him, which he did not reciprocate, and then there was an awkward pause. Eustace seemed so natural and undisturbed; yet, if he had not had astonishing experiences himself, he ought to have been all the more astonished at our extraordinary behaviour. My wife, with ready tact, endeavoured to behave as if nothing had happened.

"Well, Mr. Eustace," she said, sitting down as she spoke, to ease her foot, "how have you been amusing yourself since we have been away?"

"Thank you, Mrs. Tyler, I have been very happy."

"And where have you been?"

"Here."

"And lying down all the time, you idle boy?"

"No, not all the time."

"What were you doing before?"

"Oh; standing or sitting."

"Stood and sat doing nothing! Don't you know the poem 'Satan finds some mischief still for——' "

"Oh, my dear madam, hush! hush!" Mr. Sandbach's voice broke in; and my wife, naturally mortified by the interruption, said no more and moved away. I was surprised to see Rose immediately take her place, and, with more freedom than she generally displayed, run her fingers through the boy's tousled hair.

"Eustace! Eustace!" she said, hurriedly, "tell me everything—every single thing."

Slowly he sat up—till then he had lain on his back.

"Oh, Rose——," he whispered, and, my curiosity being aroused, I moved nearer to hear what he was going to say. As I did so, I caught sight of some goats' footmarks in the moist earth beneath the trees.

"Apparently you have had a visit from some goats," I observed. "I had no idea they fed up here."

Eustace laboriously got on to his feet and came to see; and when he saw the footmarks he lay down and rolled on them, as a dog rolls in dirt.

After that there was a grave silence, broken at length by the solemn speech of Mr. Sandbach.

"My dear friends," he said, "it is best to confess the truth bravely. I know that what I am going to say now is what you are all now feeling. The Evil One has been very near us in bodily form. Time may yet discover some injury that he has wrought among us. But, at present, for myself at all events, I wish to offer up thanks for a merciful deliverance."

With that he knelt down, and, as the others knelt, I knelt too, though I do not believe in the Devil being allowed to assail us in visible form, as I told Mr. Sandbach afterwards. Eustace came too, and knelt quietly enough between his aunts after they had beckoned to him. But when it was over he at once got up, and began hunting for something.

"Why! Someone has cut my whistle in two," he said. (I had seen Leyland with an open knife in his hand—a superstitious act which I could hardly approve.)

"Well, it doesn't matter," he continued.

"And why doesn't it matter?" said Mr. Sandbach, who has ever since tried to entrap Eustace into an account of that mysterious hour.

"Because I don't want it any more."

"Why?"

At that he smiled; and, as no one seemed to have anything more to say, I set off as fast as I could through the wood, and hauled up a donkey to carry my poor wife home. Nothing occurred in my absence, except that Rose had again asked Eustace to tell her what had happened; and he, this time, had turned away his head, and had not answered her a single word.

As soon as I returned, we all set off. Eustace walked with difficulty, almost with pain, so that, when we reached the other donkeys, his aunts wished him to mount one of them and ride all the way home. I make it a rule never to interfere between relatives, but I put my foot down at this. As it turned out, I was perfectly right, for the healthy exercise, I suppose, began to thaw

Eustace's sluggish blood and loosen his stiffened muscles. He stepped out manfully, for the first time in his life, holding his head up and taking deep draughts of air into his chest. I observed with satisfaction to Miss Mary Robinson, that Eustace was at last taking some pride in his personal appearance.

Mr. Sandbach sighed, and said that Eustace must be carefully watched, for we none of us understood him yet. Miss Mary Robinson being very much—over much, I think—guided by him, sighed too.

"Come, come, Miss Robinson," I said, "there's nothing wrong with Eustace. Our experiences are mysterious, not his. He was astonished at our sudden departure, that's why he was so strange when we returned. He's right enough—improved, if anything."

"And is the worship of athletics, the cult of insensate activity, to be counted as an improvement?" put in Leyland, fixing a large, sorrowful eye on Eustace, who had stopped to scramble on to a rock to pick some cyclamen. "The passionate desire to rend from Nature the few beauties that have been still left her—that is to be counted as an improvement too?"

It is mere waste of time to reply to such remarks, especially when they come from an unsuccessful artist, suffering from a damaged finger. I changed the conversation by asking what we should say at the hotel. After some discussion, it was agreed that we should say nothing, either there or in our letters home. Importunate truth-telling, which brings only bewilderment and discomfort to the hearers, is, in my opinion, a mistake; and, after a long discussion, I managed to make Mr. Sandbach acquiesce in my view.

Eustace did not share in our conversation. He was racing about, like a real boy, in the wood to the right. A strange feeling of shame prevented us from openly mentioning our fright to him. Indeed, it seemed almost reasonable to conclude that it had made but little impression on him. So it disconcerted us when he bounded back with an armful of flowering acanthus, calling out:

"Do you suppose Gennaro'll be there when we get back?"

Gennaro was the stop-gap waiter, a clumsy, impertinent fisher-lad, who had been had up from Minori in the absence of the nice English-speaking Emmanuele. It was to him that we owed our scrappy lunch; and I could not conceive why Eustace desired to see him, unless it was to make mock with him of our behaviour.

"Yes, of course he will be there," said Miss Robinson. "Why do you ask, dear?"

"Oh, I thought I'd like to see him."

"And why?" snapped Mr. Sandbach.

"Because, because I do, I do; because, because I do." He danced away into the darkening wood to the rhythm of his words.

"This is very extraordinary," said Mr. Sandbach. "Did he like Gennaro before?"

"Gennaro has only been here two days," said Rose, "and I know that they haven't spoken to each other a dozen times."

Each time Eustace returned from the wood his spirits were higher. Once he came whooping down on us as a wild Indian, and another time he made believe to be a dog. The last time he came back with a poor dazed hare, too frightened to move, sitting on his arm. He was getting too uproarious, I thought; and we were all glad to leave the wood, and start upon the steep staircase path that leads down into Ravello. It was late and turning dark; and we made all the speed we could, Eustace scurrying in front of us like a goat.

Just where the staircase path debouches on the white high road, the next extraordinary incident of this extraordinary day occurred. Three old women were standing by the wayside. They, like ourselves, had come down from the woods, and they were resting their heavy bundles of fuel on the low parapet of the road. Eustace stopped in front of them, and, after a moment's delibera-tion, stepped forward and—kissed the left-hand one on the cheek!

"My good fellow!" exclaimed Mr. Sandbach, "are you quite crazy?"

Eustace said nothing, but offered the old woman some of his flowers, and then hurried on. I looked back; and the old woman's companions seemed as much astonished at the proceeding as we were. But she herself had put the flowers in her bosom, and was murmuring blessings.

This salutation of the old lady was the first example of Eustace's strange behaviour, and we were both surprised and alarmed. It was useless talking to him, for he either made silly replies, or else bounded away without replying at all.

He made no reference on the way home to Gennaro, and I hoped that that was forgotten. But, when we came to the Piazza, in front of the Cathedral, he screamed out: "Gennaro! Gennaro!" at the top of his voice, and began running up the little alley that led to the hotel. Sure enough, there was Gennaro at the end of it, with his arms and legs sticking out of the nice little English-speaking waiter's dress suit, and a dirty fisherman's cap on his head—for, as the poor landlady truly said, however much she superintended his toilette, he always managed to introduce something incongruous into it before he had done.

Eustace sprang to meet him, and leapt right up into his arms, and put his own arms round his neck. And this in the presence, not only of us, but also of the landlady, the chambermaid, the facchino, and of two American ladies who were coming for a few days' visit to the little hotel.

I always make a point of behaving pleasantly to Italians, however little they may deserve it; but this habit of promiscuous intimacy was perfectly intolerable, and could only lead to familiarity and mortification for all. Taking Miss Robinson aside, I asked her permission to speak seriously to Eustace on the subject of intercourse with social inferiors. She granted it; but I determined to wait till the absurd boy had calmed down a little from the excitement of the day. Meanwhile, Gennaro, instead of attending to the wants of the two new ladies, carried Eustace into the house, as if it was the most natural thing in the world.

"Ho capito," I heard him say as he passed me. 'Ho capito' is the Italian for 'I have understood'; but, as Eustace had not spoken to him, I could not see the force of the remark. It served to increase our bewilderment, and, by the time we sat down at the dinner-table, our imaginations and our tongues were alike exhausted.

I omit from this account the various comments that were made, as few of them seem worthy of being recorded. But, for three or four hours, seven of us were pouring forth our bewilderment in a stream of appropriate and inappropriate exclamations. Some traced a connection between our behaviour in the afternoon and the behaviour of Eustace now. Others saw no connection at all. Mr. Sandbach still held to the possibility of infernal influences, and also said that he ought to have a doctor. Leyland only saw the development of "that unspeakable Philistine, the boy." Rose maintained, to my surprise, that everything was excusable; while I began to see that the young gentleman wanted a sound thrashing. The poor Miss Robinsons swayed helplessly about between these diverse opinions; inclining now to careful supervision, now to acquiescence, now to corporal chastisement, now to Eno's Fruit Salt.

Dinner passed off fairly well, though Eustace was terribly fidgety, Gennaro as usual dropping the knives and spoons, and hawking and clearing his throat. He only knew a few words of English, and we were all reduced to Italian for making known our wants. Eustace, who had picked up a little somehow, asked for some oranges. To my annoyance, Gennaro, in his answer made use of the second person singular—a form only used when addressing those who are both intimates and equals. Eustace had brought it on himself; but an impertinence of this kind was an affront to us all, and I was determined to speak, and to speak at once.

When I heard him clearing the table I went in, and, summoning up my Italian, or rather Neapolitan—the Southern dialects are execrable—I said, "Gennaro! I heard you address Signor Eustace with 'Tu.'"

"It is true."

"You are not right. You must use 'Lei' or 'Voi'—more polite forms. And remember that, though Signor Eustace is sometimes silly and foolish—this afternoon for example—yet you must always behave respectfully to him; for he is a young English gentleman, and you are a poor Italian fisher-boy."

I know that speech sounds terribly snobbish, but in Italian one can say things that one would never dream of saying in English. Besides, it is no good speaking delicately to persons of that class. Unless you put things plainly, they take a vicious pleasure in misunderstanding you.

An honest English fisherman would have landed me one in the eye in a minute for such a remark, but the wretched down-trodden Italians have no pride. Gennaro only sighed, and said: "It is true."

"Quite so," I said, and turned to go. To my indignation I heard him add: "But sometimes it is not important."

"What do you mean?" I shouted.

He came close up to me with horrid gesticulating fingers.

"Signor Tytler, I wish to say this. If Eustazio asks me to call him 'Voi,' I will call him 'Voi.' Otherwise, no."

With that he seized up a tray of dinner things, and fled from the room with them; and I heard two more wine-glasses go on the courtyard floor.

I was now fairly angry, and strode out to interview Eustace. But he had gone to bed, and, the landlady, to whom I also wished to speak, was engaged. After more vague wonderings, obscurely expressed owing to the presence of Janet and the two American ladies, we all went to bed, too, after a harassing and most extraordinary day.

III

But the day was nothing to the night.

I suppose I had slept for about four hours, when I woke suddenly thinking I heard a noise in the garden. And, immediately, before my eyes were open, cold terrible fear seized me—not fear of something that was happening, like the fear in the wood, but fear of something that might happen.

Our room was on the first floor, looking out on to the garden—or terrace, it was rather: a wedge-shaped block of ground covered with roses and vines, and intersected with little asphalt paths. It was bounded on the small side by the house; round the two long sides ran a wall, only three feet above the terrace level, but with a good twenty feet drop over it into the olive yards, for the ground fell very precipitously away.

Trembling all over I stole to the window. There, pattering up and down the asphalt paths, was something white. I was too much alarmed to see clearly; and in the uncertain light of the stars the thing took all manner of curious shapes. Now it was a great dog, now an enormous white bat, now a mass of quickly travelling cloud. It would bounce like a ball, or take short flights like a bird, or glide slowly like a wraith. It gave no sound—save the pattering sound of what, after all, must be human feet. And at last the obvious explanation forced itself upon my disordered mind; and I realized that Eustace had got out of bed, and that we were in for something more.

I hastily dressed myself, and went down into the dining-room which opened upon the terrace. The door was already unfastened. My terror had almost entirely passed away, but for quite five minutes I struggled with a curious cowardly feeling, which bade me not interfere with the poor strange boy, but leave him to his ghostly patterings, and merely watch him from the window, to see he took no harm.

But better impulses prevailed and, opening the door, I called out:

"Eustace! what on earth are you doing? Come in at once."

He stopped his antics, and said: "I hate my bedroom. I could not stop in it, it is too small."

"Come! come! I'm tired of affectation. You've never complained of it before."

"Besides I can't see anything—no flowers, no leaves, no sky: only a stone wall." The outlook of Eustace's room certainly was limited: but, as I told him, he had never complained of it before.

"Eustace, you talk like a child. Come in! Prompt obedience, if you please."

He did not move.

"Very well: I shall carry you in by force." I added, and made a few steps towards him. But I was soon convinced of the futility of pursuing a boy through a tangle of asphalt paths, and went in instead, to call Mr. Sandbach and Leyland to my aid.

When I returned with them he was worse than ever. He would not even answer us when we spoke, but began singing and chattering to himself in a most alarming way.

"It's a case for the doctor now," said Mr. Sandbach, gravely tapping his forehead.

He had stopped his running and was singing, first low, then loud—singing five-finger exercises, scales, hymn tunes, scraps of Wagner—anything that came into his head. His voice—a very untuneful voice—grew stronger and stronger, and he ended with a tremendous shout which boomed like a gun among the mountains, and awoke everyone who was still sleeping in the hotel. My poor wife and the two girls appeared at their respective windows, and the American ladies were heard violently ringing their bell.

"Eustace," we all cried, "stop! stop, dear boy and come into the house."

He shook his head, and started off again—talking this time. Never have I listened to such an extraordinary speech. At any other time it would have been ludicrous, for here was a boy, with no sense of beauty and a puerile command of words, attempting to tackle themes which the greatest poets have found almost beyond their power. Eustace Robinson, aged fourteen, was standing in his nightshirt saluting, praising, and blessing, the great forces and manifestations of Nature.

He spoke first of night and the stars and planets above his head, of the swarms of fire-flies below him, of the invisible sea below the fire-flies, of the great rocks covered with anemones and shells that were slumbering in the invisible sea. He spoke of the rivers and water-falls, of the ripening bunches of grapes, of the smoking cone of Vesuvius and the hidden fire-channels that made the smoke, of the myriads of lizards who were lying curled up in the crannies of the sultry earth, of the showers of white rose-leaves that were tangled in his hair. And then he spoke of the rain and the wind by which all things are changed, of the air through which all things live, and of the woods in which all things can be hidden.

Of course, it was all absurdly high faluting: yet I could have kicked Leyland for audibly observing that it was 'a diabolical cari-cature of all that was most holy and beautiful in life.'

"And then,"—Eustace was going on in the pitiable conversa-tional doggerel which was his only mode of expression—"and then there are men, but I can't make them out so well." He knelt down by the parapet, and rested his head on his arms.

"Now's the time," whispered Leyland. I hate stealth, but we darted forward and endeavoured to catch hold of him from be-hind. He was away in a twinkling, but turned round at once to look at us. As far as I could see in the starlight, he was crying. Leyland rushed at him again, and we tried to corner him among the asphalt paths, but without the slightest approach to success.

We returned, breathless and discomfited, leaving him to his madness in the further corner of the terrace. But my Rose had an inspiration.

"Papa," she called from the window, "if you get Gennaro, he might be able to catch him for you."

I had no wish to ask a favour of Gennaro, but, as the landlady had by now appeared on the scene, I begged her to summon him from the charcoal-bin in which he slept, and make him try what he could do.

She soon returned, and was shortly followed by Gennaro, attired in a dress coat, without either waistcoat, shirt, or vest, and a ragged pair of what had been trousers, cut short above the knees for purposes of wading. The landlady, who had quite picked up English ways, rebuked him for the incongruous and even inde-cent appearance which he presented.

"I have a coat and I have trousers. What more do you desire?"

"Never mind, Signora Scafetti," I put in. "As there are no ladies here, it is not of the slightest consequence." Then, turning to Gennaro, I said: "The aunts of Signor Eustace wish you to fetch him into the house."

He did not answer.

"Do you hear me? He is not well. I order you to fetch him into the house."

"Fetch! fetch!" said Signora Scafetti, and shook him roughly by the arm.

"Eustazio is well where he is."

"Fetch! fetch!" Signora Scafetti screamed, and let loose a flood of Italian, most of which, I am glad to say, I could not follow. I glanced up nervously at the girls' window, but they hardly know as much as I do, and I am thankful to say that none of us caught one word of Gennaro's answer.

The two yelled and shouted at each other for quite ten minutes, at the end of which Gennaro rushed back to his charcoal-bin and Signora Scafetti burst into tears, as well she might, for she greatly valued her English guests.

"He says," she sobbed, "that Signor Eustace is well where he is, and that he will not fetch him. I can do no more."

But I could, for, in my stupid British way, I have got some insight into the Italian character. I followed Mr. Gennaro to his place of repose, and found him wriggling down on to a dirty sack.

"I wish you to fetch Signor Eustace to me," I began.

He hurled at me an unintelligible reply.

"If you fetch him, I will give you this." And out of my pocket I took a new ten lira note.

This time he did not answer.

"This note is equal to ten lire in silver," I continued, for I knew that the poor-class Italian is unable to conceive of a single large sum.

"I know it."

"That is, two hundred soldi."

"I do not desire them. Eustazio is my friend."

I put the note into my pocket.

"Besides, you would not give it me."

"I am an Englishman. The English always do what they promise."

"That is true." It is astonishing how the most dishonest of nations trust us. Indeed they often trust us more than we trust one another. Gennaro knelt up on his sack. It was too dark to see his face, but I could feel his warm garlicky breath coming out in gasps, and I knew that the eternal avarice of the South had laid hold upon him.

"I could not fetch Eustazio to the house. He might die there."

"You need not do that," I replied patiently. "You need only bring him to me; and I will stand outside in the garden." And to this, as if it were something quite different, the pitiable youth consented.

"But give me first the ten lire."

"No"—for I knew the kind of person with whom I had to deal. Once faithless, always faithless.

We returned to the terrace, and Gennaro, without a single word, pattered off towards the pattering that could be heard at the remoter end. Mr. Sandbach, Leyland, and myself moved away a little from the house, and stood in the shadow of the white climbing roses, practically invisible.

We heard "Eustazio" called, followed by absurd cries of pleasure from the poor boy. The pattering ceased, and we heard them talking. Their voices got nearer, and presently I could discern them through the creepers, the grotesque figure of the young man, and the slim little white-robed boy. Gennaro had his arm round Eustace's neck, and Eustace was talking away in his fluent, slip-shod Italian.

"I understand almost everything," I heard him say. "The trees, hills, stars, water, I can see all. But isn't it odd! I can't make out men a bit. Do you know what I mean?"

"Ho capito," said Gennaro gravely, and took his arm off Eustace's shoulder. But I made the new note crackle in my pocket;

and he heard it. He stuck his hand out with a jerk; and the unsuspecting Eustace gripped it in his own.

"It is odd!" Eustace went on—they were quite close now—"It almost seems as if—as if——"

I darted out and caught hold of his arm, and Leyland got hold of the other arm, and Mr. Sandbach hung on to his feet. He gave shrill heart-piercing screams; and the white roses, which were falling early that year, descended in showers on him as we dragged him into the house.

As soon as we entered the house he stopped shrieking; but floods of tears silently burst forth, and spread over his upturned face.

"Not to my room," he pleaded. "It is so small."

His infinitely dolorous look filled me with strange pity, but what could I do? Besides, his window was the only one that had bars to it.

"Never mind, dear boy," said kind Mr. Sandbach. "I will bear you company till the morning."

At this his convulsive struggles began again. "Oh, please not that. Anything but that. I will promise to lie still and not to cry more than I can help, if I am left alone."

So we laid him on the bed, and drew the sheets over him, and left him sobbing bitterly, and saying: "I nearly saw everything, and now I can see nothing at all."

We informed the Miss Robinsons of all that had happened, and returned to the dining-room, where we found Signora Scafetti and Gennaro whispering together. Mr. Sandbach got pen and paper, and began writing to the English doctor at Naples. I at once drew out the note, and flung it down on the table to Gennaro.

"Here is your pay," I said sternly, for I was thinking of the Thirty Pieces of Silver.

"Thank you very much, sir," said Gennaro, and grabbed it.

He was going off, when Leyland, whose interest and indifference were always equally misplaced, asked him what Eustace had meant by saying 'he could not make out men a bit.'

"I cannot say. Signor Eustazio" (I was glad to observe a little deference at last) "has a subtle brain. He understands many things."

"But I heard you say you understood," Leyland persisted.

"I understand, but I cannot explain. I am a poor Italian fisherlad. Yet, listen: I will try." I saw to my alarm that his manner was changing, and tried to stop him. But he sat down on the edge of the table and started off, with some absolutely incoherent remarks.

"It is sad," he observed at last. "What has happened is very sad. But what can I do? I am poor. It is not I."

I turned away in contempt. Leyland went on asking questions. He wanted to know who it was that Eustace had in his mind when he spoke.

"That is easy to say," Gennaro gravely answered. "It is you, it is I. It is all in this house, and many outside it. If he wishes for mirth, we discomfort him. If he asks to be alone, we disturb him. He longed for a friend, and found none for fifteen years. Then he found me, and the first night I—I who have been in the woods and understood things too—betray him to you, and send him in to die. But what could I do?"

"Gently, gently," said I.

"Oh, assuredly he will die. He will lie in the small room all night, and in the morning he will be dead. That I know for certain."

"There, that will do," said Mr. Sandbach. "I shall be sitting with him."

"Filomena Giusti sat all night with Caterina, but Caterina was dead in the morning. They would not let her out, though I begged, and prayed, and cursed, and beat the door, and climbed the wall. They were ignorant fools, and thought I wished to carry her away. And in the morning she was dead."

"What is all this?" I asked Signora Scafetti.

"All kinds of stories will get about," she replied, "and he, least of anyone, has reason to repeat them."

"And I am alive now," he went on, "because I had neither parents nor relatives nor friends, so that, when the first night came, I could run through the woods, and climb the rocks, and plunge into the water, until I had accomplished my desire!"

We heard a cry from Eustace's room—a faint but steady sound, like the sound of wind in a distant wood, heard by one standing in tranquillity.

"That" said Gennaro, "was the last noise of Caterina. I was hanging on to her window then, and it blew out past me."

And, lifting up his hand, in which my ten lira note was safely packed, he solemnly cursed Mr. Sandbach, and Leyland, and myself, and Fate, because Eustace was dying in the upstairs room. Such is the working of the Southern mind; and I verily believe that he would not have moved even then, had not Leyland, that unspeakable idiot, upset the lamp with his elbow. It was a patent self-extinguishing lamp, bought by Signora Scafetti at my special request, to replace the dangerous thing that she was using. The result was, that it went out; and the mere physical change from light to darkness had more power over the ignorant animal nature of Gennaro than the most obvious dictates of logic and reason.

I felt, rather than saw, that he had left the room, and shouted out to Mr. Sandbach: "Have you got the key of Eustace's room in your pocket?" But Mr. Sandbach and Leyland were both on the floor, having mistaken each other for Gennaro, and some more precious time was wasted in finding a match. Mr. Sandbach had only just time to say that he had left the key in the door, in case the Miss Robinsons wished to pay Eustace a visit, when we heard a noise on the stairs, and there was Gennaro, carrying Eustace down.

We rushed out and blocked up the passage, and they lost heart and retreated to the upper landing.

"Now they are caught," cried Signora Scafetti. "There is no other way out."

We were cautiously ascending the staircase, when there was a terrific scream from my wife's room, followed by a heavy thud on the asphalt path. They had leapt out of her window.

I reached the terrace just in time to see Eustace jumping over the parapet of the garden wall. This time I knew for certain he would be killed. But he alighted in an olive tree, looking like a great white moth, and from the tree he slid on to the earth. And as soon as his bare feet touched the clods of earth he uttered a strange loud cry, such as I should not have thought the human voice could have produced, and disappeared among the trees below.

"He has understood and he is saved," cried Gennaro, who was still sitting on the asphalt path. "Now, instead of dying he will live!"

"And you, instead of keeping the ten lire, will give them up," I retorted, for at this theatrical remark I could contain myself no longer.

"The ten lire are mine," he hissed back, in a scarcely audible voice. He clasped his hand over his breast to protect his ill-gotten gains, and, as he did so, he swayed forward and fell upon his face on the path. He had not broken any limbs, and a leap like that would never have killed an Englishman, for the drop was not great. But those miserable Italians have no stamina. Something had gone wrong inside him, and he was dead.

The morning was still far off, but the morning breeze had begun, and more rose leaves fell on us as we carried him in. Signora Scafetti burst into screams at the sight of the dead body, and, far down the valley towards the sea, there still resounded the shouts and the laughter of the escaping boy.

· · ·

The Other Side
of the Hedge

My pedometer told me that I was twenty-five; and, though it is a shocking thing to stop walking, I was so tired that I sat down on a milestone to rest. People outstripped me, jeering as they did so, but I was too apathetic to feel resentful, and even when Miss Eliza Dimbleby, the great educationist, swept past, exhorting me to persevere, I only smiled and raised my hat.

At first I thought I was going to be like my brother, whom I had had to leave by the roadside a year or two round the corner. He had wasted his breath on singing, and his strength on helping others. But I had travelled more wisely, and now it was only the monotony of the highway that oppressed me—dust under foot and brown crackling hedges on either side, ever since I could remember.

And I had already dropped several things—indeed, the road behind was strewn with the things we all had dropped; and the white dust was settling down on them, so that already they looked no better than stones. My muscles were so weary that I could not even bear the weight of those things I still carried. I slid off the milestone into the road, and lay there prostrate, with my face to the great parched hedge, praying that I might give up.

A little puff of air revived me. It seemed to come from the hedge; and, when I opened my eyes, there was a glint of light through the tangle of boughs and dead leaves. The hedge could not be as thick as usual. In my weak, morbid state, I longed to force my way in, and see what was on the other side. No one was in sight, or I should not have dared to try. For we of the road do not admit in conversation that there is another side at all.

I yielded to the temptation, saying to myself that I would come back in a minute. The thorns scratched my face, and I had to use my arms as a shield, depending on my feet alone to push me forward. Halfway through I would have gone back, for in the passage all the things I was carrying were scraped off me, and my clothes were torn. But I was so wedged that return was impossible, and I had to wriggle blindly forward, expecting every moment that my strength would fail me, and that I should perish in the undergrowth.

Suddenly cold water closed round my head, and I seemed sinking down for ever. I had fallen out of the hedge into a deep pool. I rose to the surface at last, crying for help, and I heard someone on the opposite bank laugh and say: "Another!" And then I was twitched out and laid panting on the dry ground.

Even when the water was out of my eyes, I was still dazed, for I had never been in so large a space, nor seen such grass and sunshine. The blue sky was no longer a strip, and beneath it the earth had risen grandly into hills—clean, bare buttresses, with beech trees in their folds, and meadows and clear pools at their feet. But the hills were not high, and there was in the landscape a sense of human occupation—so that one might have called it a park, or garden, if the words did not imply a certain triviality and constraint.

As soon as I got my breath, I turned to my rescuer and said: "Where does this place lead to?"

"Nowhere, thank the Lord!" said he, and laughed. He was a man of fifty or sixty—just the kind of age we mistrust on the road—but there was no anxiety in his manner, and his voice was that of a boy of eighteen.

"But it must lead somewhere!" I cried, too much surprised at his answer to thank him for saving my life.

"He wants to know where it leads!" he shouted to some men on the hill side, and they laughed back, and waved their caps.

I noticed then that the pool into which I had fallen was really a moat which bent round to the left and to the right, and that the hedge followed it continually. The hedge was green on this side—its roots showed through the clear water, and fish swam about in them—and it was wreathed over with dog-roses and Traveller's Joy. But it was a barrier, and in a moment I lost all pleasure in the grass, the sky, the trees, the happy men and women, and realized that the place was but a prison, for all its beauty and extent.

We moved away from the boundary, and then followed a path almost parallel to it, across the meadows. I found it difficult walking, for I was always trying to out-distance my companion, and there was no advantage in doing this if the place led nowhere. I had never kept step with anyone since I left my brother.

I amused him by stopping suddenly and saying disconsolately, "This is perfectly terrible. One cannot advance: one cannot progress. Now we of the road——"

"Yes. I know."

"I was going to say, we advance continually."

"I know."

"We are always learning, expanding, developing. Why, even in my short life I have seen a great deal of advance—the Transvaal War, the Fiscal Question, Christian Science, Radium. Here for example——"

I took out my pedometer, but it still marked twenty-five, not a degree more.

"Oh, it's stopped! I meant to show you. It should have registered all the time I was walking with you. But it makes me only twenty-five."

"Many things don't work in here," he said. "One day a man brought in a Lee-Metford, and that wouldn't work."

"The laws of science are universal in their application. It must be the water in the moat that has injured the machinery. In normal conditions everything works. Science and the spirit of emulation—those are the forces that have made us what we are."

I had to break off and acknowledge the pleasant greetings of people whom we passed. Some of them were singing, some talking, some engaged in gardening, hay-making, or other rudimentary industries. They all seemed happy; and I might have been happy too, if I could have forgotten that the place led nowhere.

I was startled by a young man who came sprinting across our path, took a little fence in fine style, and went tearing over a ploughed field till he plunged into a lake, across which he began to swim. Here was true energy, and I exclaimed: "A cross-country race! Where are the others?"

"There are no others," my companion replied; and, later on, when we passed some long grass from which came the voice of a girl singing exquisitely to herself, he said again: "There are no others." I was bewildered at the waste in production, and murmured to myself, "What does it all mean?"

He said: "It means nothing but itself"—and he repeated the words slowly, as if I were a child.

"I understand," I said quietly, "but I do not agree. Every achievement is worthless unless it is a link in the chain of development. And I must not trespass on your kindness any longer. I must get back somehow to the road, and have my pedometer mended."

"First you must see the gates," he replied, "for we have gates, though we never use them."

I yielded politely, and before long we reached the moat again, at a point where it was spanned by a bridge. Over the bridge was a big gate, as white as ivory, which was fitted into a gap in the boundary hedge. The gate opened outwards, and I exclaimed in amazement, for from it ran a road—just such a road as I had left—dusty under foot, with brown crackling hedges on either side as far as the eye could reach.

"That's my road!" I cried.

He shut the gate and said: "But not your part of the road. It is through this gate that humanity went out countless ages ago, when it was first seized with the desire to walk."

I denied this, observing that the part of the road I myself had left was not more than two miles off. But with the obstinacy of his years he repeated: "It is the same road. This is the beginning, and though it seems to run straight away from us, it doubles so often, that it is never far from our boundary and sometimes touches it."

He stooped down by the moat, and traced on its moist margin an absurd figure like a maze. As we walked back through the meadows, I tried to convince him of his mistake.

"The road sometimes doubles, to be sure, but that is part of our discipline. Who can doubt that its general tendency is onward? To what goal we know not—it may be to some mountain where we shall touch the sky, it may be over precipices into the sea. But that it goes forward—who can doubt that? It is the thought of that that makes us strive to excel, each in his own way, and gives us an impetus which is lacking with you. Now that man who passed us—it's true that he ran well, and jumped well, and swam well; but we have men who can run better, and men who can jump better, and who can swim better. Specialization has produced results which would surprise you. Similarly, that girl——"

Here I interrupted myself to exclaim: "Good gracious me! I could have sworn it was Miss Eliza Dimbleby over there, with her feet in the fountain!"

He believed that it was.

"Impossible! I left her on the road, and she is due to lecture this evening at Tunbridge Wells. Why, her train leaves Cannon Street in—of course my watch has stopped like everything else. She is the last person to be here."

"People always are astonished at meeting each other. All kinds come through the hedge, and come at all times—when they are drawing ahead in the race, when they are lagging behind, when they are left for dead. I often stand near the boundary listening to the sounds of the road—you know what they are—and wonder if anyone will turn aside. It is my great happiness to help someone out of the moat, as I helped you. For our country fills up slowly, though it was meant for all mankind."

"Mankind have other aims," I said gently, for I thought him well-meaning; "and I must join them." I bade him good evening, for the sun was declining, and I wished to be on the road by nightfall. To my alarm, he caught hold of me, crying: "You are not to go yet!" I tried to shake him off, for we had no interests in common, and his civility was becoming irksome to me. But for all my struggles the tiresome old man would not let go; and, as wrestling is not my speciality, I was obliged to follow him.

It was true that I could have never found alone the place where I came in, and I hoped that, when I had seen the other sights about which he was worrying, he would take me back to it. But I was determined not to sleep in the country, for I mistrusted it, and the people too, for all their friendliness. Hungry though I was, I would not join them in their evening meals of milk and fruit, and, when they gave me flowers, I flung them away as soon as I could do so unobserved. Already they were lying down for the night like cattle—some out on the bare hillside, others in groups under the beeches. In the light of an orange sunset I hurried on with my unwelcome guide, dead tired, faint for want of food, but murmuring indomitably: "Give me life, with its struggles and victories, with its failures and hatreds, with its deep moral meaning and its unknown goal!"

At last we came to a place where the encircling moat was spanned by another bridge, and where another gate interrupted the line of the boundary hedge. It was different from the first gate; for it was half transparent like horn, and opened inwards. But through it, in the waning light, I saw again just such a road as I had left—monotonous, dusty, with brown crackling hedges on either side, as far as the eye could reach.

I was strangely disquieted at the sight, which seemed to deprive me of all self-control. A man was passing us, returning for the night to the hills, with a scythe over his shoulder and a can of some liquid in his hand. I forgot the destiny of our race. I forgot the road that lay before my eyes, and I sprang at him, wrenched the can out of his hand, and began to drink.

It was nothing stronger than beer, but in my exhausted state it overcame me in a moment. As in a dream, I saw the old man shut the gate, and heard him say; "This is where your road ends, and through this gate humanity—all that is left of it—will come in to us."

Though my senses were sinking into oblivion, they seemed to expand ere they reached it. They perceived the magic song of nightingales, and the odour of invisible hay, and stars piercing the fading sky. The man whose beer I had stolen lowered me down gently to sleep off its effects, and, as he did so, I saw that he was my brother.

· · ·

THE CELESTIAL OMNIBUS

I

The boy who resided at Agathox Lodge, 28, Buckingham Park Road, Surbiton, had often been puzzled by the old sign-post that stood almost opposite. He asked his mother about it, and she replied that it was a joke, and not a very nice one, which had been made many years back by some naughty young men, and that the police ought to remove it. For there were two strange things about this sign-post: firstly, it pointed up a blank alley, and, secondly, it had painted on it, in faded characters, the words, "To Heaven."

"What kind of young men were they?" he asked.

"I think your father told me that one of them wrote verses, and was expelled from the University and came to grief in other ways. Still, it was a long time ago. You must ask your father about it. He will say the same as I do, that it was put up as a joke."

"So it doesn't mean anything at all?"

She sent him up-stairs to put on his best things, for the Bonses were coming to tea, and he was to hand the cake-stand.

It struck him, as he wrenched on his tightening trousers, that he might do worse than ask Mr. Bons about the sign-post. His father, though very kind, always laughed at him—shrieked with laughter whenever he or any other child asked a question or spoke. But Mr. Bons was serious as well as kind. He had a beautiful house and lent one books, he was a churchwarden, and a candidate for the County Council; he had donated to the Free Library enormously, he presided over the Literary Society, and had Members of Parliament to stop with him—in short, he was probably the wisest person alive.

Yet even Mr. Bons could only say that the sign-post was a joke—the joke of a person named Shelley.

"Of course!" cried the mother; "I told you so, dear. That was the name."

"Had you never heard of Shelley?" asked Mr. Bons.

"No," said the boy, and hung his head.

"But is there no Shelley in the house?"

"Why, yes!" exclaimed the lady, in much agitation. "Dear Mr. Bons, we aren't such Philistines as that. Two at the least. One a wedding present, and the other, smaller print, in one of the spare rooms."

"I believe we have seven Shelleys," said Mr. Bons, with a slow smile. Then he brushed the cake crumbs off his stomach, and, together with his daughter, rose to go.

The boy, obeying a wink from his mother, saw them all the way to the garden gate, and when they had gone he did not at once return to the house, but gazed for a little up and down Buckingham Park Road.

His parents lived at the right end of it. After No. 39 the quality of the houses dropped very suddenly, and 64 had not even a separate servants' entrance. But at the present moment the whole road looked rather pretty, for the sun had just set in splendour, and the inequalities of rent were drowned in a saffron afterglow. Small birds twittered, and the breadwinners' train shrieked musically down through the cutting—that wonderful cutting which has drawn to itself the whole beauty out of Surbiton, and clad itself, like any Alpine valley, with the glory of the fir and the silver birch and the primrose. It was this cutting that had first stirred desires within the boy—desires for something just a little different, he knew not what, desires that would return whenever things were sunlit, as they were this evening, running up and down inside him, up and down, up and down, till he would feel quite unusual all over, and as likely as not would want to cry. This evening he was even sillier, for he slipped across the road towards the sign-post and began to run up the blank alley.

The alley runs between high walls—the walls of the gardens of "Ivanhoe" and "Belle Vista" respectively. It smells a little all the way, and is scarcely twenty yards long, including the turn at the end. So not unnaturally the boy soon came to a standstill. "I'd like to kick that Shelley," he exclaimed, and glanced idly at a piece of paper which was pasted on the wall. Rather an odd piece of paper, and he read it carefully before he turned back. This is what he read:

S. AND C. R. C. C.
Alteration in Service
Owing to lack of patronage the Company are regretfully compelled to suspend the hourly service, and to retain only the
Sunrise and Sunset Omnibuses,
which will run as usual. It is to be hoped that the public will patronize an arrangement which is intended for their convenience. As an extra inducement, the Company will, for the first time, now issue
Return Tickets!
(available one day only), which may be obtained of the driver. Passengers are again reminded that *no tickets are issued at the other end*, and that no complaints in this connection will receive consideration from the Company. Nor will the Company be responsible for any negligence or stupidity on the part of Passengers, nor for Hailstorms, Lightning, Loss of Tickets, nor for any Act of God.

For the Direction.

Now he had never seen this notice before, nor could he imagine where the omnibus went to. S. of course was for Surbiton, and R.C.C. meant Road Car Company. But what was the meaning of the other C.? Coombe and Malden, perhaps, or possibly "City." Yet it could not hope to compete with the South-Western. The whole thing, the boy reflected, was run on hopelessly unbusinesslike lines. Why no tickets from the other end? And what an hour to start! Then he realized that unless the notice was a hoax, an omnibus must have been starting just as he was wishing the Bonses good-bye. He peered at the ground through the gathering dusk, and there he saw what might or might not be the marks of wheels. Yet nothing had come out of the alley. And he had never seen an omnibus at any time in the Buckingham Park Road. No: it must be a hoax, like the sign-posts, like the fairy tales, like the dreams upon which he would wake suddenly in the night. And with a sigh he stepped from the alley—right into the arms of his father.

Oh, how his father laughed! "Poor, poor Popsey!" he cried. "Diddums! Diddums! Diddums think he'd walky-palky up to Evvink!" And his mother, also convulsed with laughter, appeared on the steps of Agathox Lodge. "Don't, Bob!" she gasped. "Don't be so naughty! Oh, you'll kill me! Oh, leave the boy alone!"

But all that evening the joke was kept up. The father implored to be taken too. Was it a very tiring walk? Need one wipe one's shoes on the door-mat? And the boy went to bed feeling faint and sore, and thankful for only one thing—that he had not said a word about the omnibus. It was a hoax, yet through his dreams it grew more and more real, and the streets of Surbiton, through which he saw it driving, seemed instead to become hoaxes and shadows. And very early in the morning he woke with a cry, for he had had a glimpse of its destination.

He struck a match, and its light fell not only on his watch but also on his calendar, so that he knew it to be half-an-hour to sunrise. It was pitch dark, for the fog had come down from London in the night, and all Surbiton was wrapped in its embraces. Yet he sprang out and dressed himself, for he was determined to settle once for all which was real: the omnibus or the streets. "I shall be a fool one way or the other," he thought, "until I know." Soon he was shivering in the road under the gas lamp that guarded the entrance to the alley.

To enter the alley itself required some courage. Not only was it horribly dark, but he now realized that it was an impossible terminus for an omnibus. If it had not been for a policeman, whom he heard approaching through the fog, he would never have made the attempt. The next moment he had made the attempt and failed. Nothing. Nothing but a blank alley and a very silly boy gaping at its dirty floor. It *was* a hoax. "I'll tell papa and mamma," he decided. "I deserve it. I deserve that they should know. I am too silly to be alive." And he went back to the gate of Agathox Lodge.

There he remembered that his watch was fast. The sun was not risen; it would not rise for two minutes. "Give the bus every chance," he thought cynically, and returned into the alley.

But the omnibus was there.

II

It had two horses, whose sides were still smoking from their journey, and its two great lamps shone through the fog against the alley's walls, changing their cobwebs and moss into tissues of fairyland. The driver was huddled up in a cape. He faced the blank wall, and how he had managed to drive in so neatly and so silently was one of the many things that the boy never discovered. Nor could he imagine how ever he would drive out.

"Please," his voice quavered through the foul brown air, "Please, is that an omnibus?"

"Omnibus est," said the driver, without turning round. There was a moment's silence. The policeman passed, coughing, by the entrance of the alley. The boy crouched in the shadow, for he did not want to be found out. He was pretty sure, too, that it was a Pirate; nothing else, he reasoned, would go from such odd places and at such odd hours.

"About when do you start?" He tried to sound nonchalant.

"At sunrise."

"How far do you go?"

"The whole way."

"And can I have a return ticket which will bring me all the way back?"

"You can."

"Do you know, I half think I'll come." The driver made no answer. The sun must have risen, for he unhitched the brake. And scarcely had the boy jumped in before the omnibus was off.

How? Did it turn? There was no room. Did it go forward? There was a blank wall. Yet it was moving—moving at a stately pace through the fog, which had turned from brown to yellow. The thought of warm bed and warmer breakfast made the boy feel faint. He wished he had not come. His parents would not have approved. He would have gone back to them if the weather had not made it impossible. The solitude was terrible; he was the only passenger. And the omnibus, though well-built, was cold and somewhat musty. He drew his coat round him, and in so doing chanced to feel his pocket. It was empty. He had forgotten his purse.

"Stop!" he shouted. "Stop!" And then, being of a polite disposition, he glanced up at the painted notice-board so that he might call the driver by name. "Mr. Browne! stop; O, do please stop!"

Mr. Browne did not stop, but he opened a little window and looked in at the boy. His face was a surprise, so kind it was and modest.

"Mr. Browne, I've left my purse behind. I've not got a penny. I can't pay for the ticket. Will you take my watch, please? I am in the most awful hole."

"Tickets on this line," said the driver, "whether single or return, can be purchased by coinage from no terrene mint. And a chronometer, though it had solaced the vigils of Charlemagne, or measured the slumbers of Laura, can acquire by no mutation the double-cake that charms the fangless Cerberus of Heaven!" So saying, he handed in the necessary ticket, and, while the boy said "Thank you," continued: "Titular pretensions, I know it well, are vanity. Yet they merit no censure when uttered on a laughing lip, and in an homonymous world are in some sort useful, since they do serve to distinguish one Jack from his fellow. Remember me, therefore, as Sir Thomas Browne."

"Are you a Sir? Oh, sorry!" He had heard of these gentlemen drivers. "It is good of you about the ticket. But if you go on at this rate, however does your bus pay?"

"It does not pay. It was not intended to pay. Many are the faults of my equipage; it is compounded too curiously of foreign woods; its cushions tickle erudition rather than promote repose; and my horses are nourished not on the evergreen pastures of the moment, but on the dried bents and clovers of Latinity. But that it pays!—that error at all events was never intended and never attained."

"Sorry again," said the boy rather hopelessly. Sir Thomas looked sad, fearing that, even for a moment, he had been the cause of sadness. He invited the boy to come up and sit beside him on the box, and together they journeyed on through the fog, which was now changing from yellow to white. There were no houses by the road; so it must be either Putney Heath or Wimbledon Common.

"Have you been a driver always?"

"I was a physician once."

"But why did you stop? Weren't you good?"

"As a healer of bodies I had scant success, and several score of my patients preceded me. But as a healer of the spirit I have succeeded beyond my hopes and my deserts. For though my draughts were not better nor subtler than those of other men, yet, by reason of the cunning goblets wherein I offered them, the queasy soul was ofttimes tempted to sip and be refreshed."

"The queasy soul," he murmured; "if the sun sets with trees in front of it, and you suddenly come strange all over, is that a queasy soul?"

"Have you felt that?"

"Why yes."

After a pause he told the boy a little, a very little, about the journey's end. But they did not chatter much, for the boy, when he liked a person, would as soon sit silent in his company as speak, and this, he discovered, was also the mind of Sir Thomas

Browne and of many others with whom he was to be acquainted.
He heard, however, about the young man Shelley, who was now
quite a famous person, with a carriage of his own, and about
some of the other drivers who are in the service of the Company.
Meanwhile the light grew stronger, though the fog did not dis-
perse. It was now more like mist than fog, and at times would
travel quickly across them, as if it was part of a cloud. They had
been ascending, too, in a most puzzling way; for over two hours
the horses had been pulling against the collar, and even if it were
Richmond Hill they ought to have been at the top long ago. Perhaps it was Epsom, or even the North Downs; yet the air seemed
keener than that which blows on either. And as to the name of
their destination, Sir Thomas Browne was silent.

Crash!

"Thunder, by Jove!" said the boy, "and not so far off either. Listen to the echoes! It's more like mountains."

He thought, not very vividly, of his father and mother. He saw
them sitting down to sausages and listening to the storm. He saw
his own empty place. Then there would be questions, alarms, theories, jokes, consolations. They would expect him back at lunch.
To lunch he would not come, nor to tea, but he would be in for
dinner, and so his day's truancy would be over. If he had had his
purse he would have bought them presents—not that he should
have known what to get them.

Crash!

The peal and the lightning came together. The cloud quivered
as if it were alive, and torn streamers of mist rushed past. "Are
you afraid?" asked Sir Thomas Browne.

"What is there to be afraid of? Is it much farther?"

The horses of the omnibus stopped just as a ball of fire
burst up and exploded with a ringing noise that was deafening
but clear, like the noise of a blacksmith's forge. All the cloud was
shattered.

"Oh, listen, Sir Thomas Browne! No, I mean look; we shall get
a view at last. No, I mean listen; that sounds like a rainbow!"

The noise had died into the faintest murmur, beneath which another murmur grew, spreading stealthily, steadily, in a curve that widened but did not vary. And in widening curves a rainbow was spreading from the horses' feet into the dissolving mists.

"But how beautiful! What colours! Where will it stop? It is more like the rainbows you can tread on. More like dreams."

The colour and the sound grew together. The rainbow spanned an enormous gulf. Clouds rushed under it and were pierced by it, and still it grew, reaching forward, conquering the darkness, until it touched something that seemed more solid than a cloud.

The boy stood up. "What is that out there?" he called. "What does it rest on, out at that other end?"

In the morning sunshine a precipice shone forth beyond the gulf. A precipice—or was it a castle? The horses moved. They set their feet upon the rainbow.

"Oh, look!" the boy shouted. "Oh, listen! Those caves—or are they gateways? Oh, look between those cliffs at those ledges. I see people! I see trees!"

"Look also below," whispered Sir Thomas. "Neglect not the diviner Acheron."

The boy looked below, past the flames of the rainbow that licked against their wheels. The gulf also had cleared, and in its depths there flowed an everlasting river. One sunbeam entered and struck a green pool, and as they passed over he saw three maidens rise to the surface of the pool, singing, and playing with something that glistened like a ring.

"You down in the water——" he called.

They answered, "You up on the bridge——" There was a burst of music. "You up on the bridge, good luck to you. Truth in the depth, truth on the height."

"You down in the water, what are you doing?"

Sir Thomas Browne replied: "They sport in the mancipiary possession of their gold"; and the omnibus arrived.

III

The boy was in disgrace. He sat locked up in the nursery of Agathox Lodge, learning poetry for a punishment. His father had said, "My boy! I can pardon anything but untruthfulness," and had caned him, saying at each stroke, "There is *no* omnibus, *no* driver, *no* bridge, *no* mountain; you are a *truant*, a *guttersnipe*, a *liar*." His father could be very stern at times. His mother had begged him to say he was sorry. But he could not say that. It was the greatest day of his life, in spite of the caning and the poetry at the end of it.

He had returned punctually at sunset—driven not by Sir Thomas Browne, but by a maiden lady who was full of quiet fun. They had talked of omnibuses and also of barouche landaus. How far away her gentle voice seemed now! Yet it was scarcely three hours since he had left her up the alley.

His mother called through the door. "Dear, you are to come down and to bring your poetry with you."

He came down, and found that Mr. Bons was in the smoking-room with his father. It had been a dinner party.

"Here is the great traveller!" said his father grimly. "Here is the young gentleman who drives in an omnibus over rainbows, while young ladies sing to him." Pleased with his wit, he laughed.

"After all," said Mr. Bons, smiling, "there is something a little like it in Wagner. It is odd how, in quite illiterate minds, you will find glimmers of Artistic Truth. The case interests me. Let me plead for the culprit. We have all romanced in our time, haven't we?"

"Hear how kind Mr. Bons is," said his mother, while his father said, "Very well. Let him say his Poem, and that will do. He is going away to my sister on Tuesday, and *she* will cure him of this alley-slopering." (Laughter.) "Say your Poem."

The boy began. " 'Standing aloof in giant ignorance.' "

His father laughed again—roared. "One for you, my son! 'Standing aloof in giant ignorance!' I never knew these poets

talked sense. Just describes you. Here, Bons, you go in for poetry.
Put him through it, will you, while I fetch up the whisky?"

"Yes, give me the Keats," said Mr. Bons. "Let him say his Keats
to me."

So for a few moments the wise man and the ignorant boy were
left alone in the smoking-room.

"'Standing aloof in giant ignorance, of thee I dream and of
the Cyclades, as one who sits ashore and longs perchance to
visit——'"

"Quite right. To visit what?"

"'To visit dolphin coral in deep seas,'" said the boy, and burst
into tears.

"Come, come! why do you cry?"

"Because—because all these words that only rhymed before,
now that I've come back they're me."

Mr. Bons laid the Keats down. The case was more interesting
that he had expected. "*You?*" he exclaimed. "This sonnet, *you?*"

"Yes—and look further on: 'Aye, on the shores of darkness
there is light, and precipices show untrodden green.' It *is* so, sir.
All these things are true."

"I never doubted it," said Mr. Bons, with closed eyes.

"You—then you believe me? You believe in the omnibus and
the driver and the storm and that return ticket I got for nothing
and——"

"Tut, tut! No more of your yarns, my boy. I meant that I never
doubted the essential truth of Poetry. Some day, when you have
read more, you will understand what I mean."

"But Mr. Bons, it *is* so. There *is* light upon the shores of darkness. I have seen it coming. Light and a wind."

"Nonsense," said Mr. Bons.

"If I had stopped! They tempted me. They told me to give up
my ticket—for you cannot come back if you lose your ticket.
They called from the river for it, and indeed I was tempted, for I
have never been so happy as among those precipices. But I
thought of my mother and father, and that I must fetch them. Yet

they will not come, though the road starts opposite our house. It has all happened as the people up there warned me, and Mr. Bons has disbelieved me like every one else. I have been caned. I shall never see that mountain again."

"What's that about me?" said Mr. Bons, sitting up in his chair very suddenly.

"I told them about you, and how clever you were, and how many books you had, and they said, 'Mr. Bons will certainly disbelieve you.' "

"Stuff and nonsense, my young friend. You grow impertinent. I—well—I will settle the matter. Not a word to your father. I will cure you. To-morrow evening I will myself call here to take you for a walk, and at sunset we will go up this alley opposite and hunt for your omnibus, you silly little boy."

His face grew serious, for the boy was not disconcerted, but leapt about the room singing, "Joy! joy! I told them you would believe me. We will drive together over the rainbow. I told them that you would come." After all, could there be anything in the story? Wagner? Keats? Shelley? Sir Thomas Browne? Certainly the case was interesting.

And on the morrow evening, though it was pouring with rain, Mr. Bons did not omit to call at Agathox Lodge.

The boy was ready, bubbling with excitement, and skipping about in a way that rather vexed the President of the Literary Society. They took a turn down Buckingham Park Road, and then—having seen that no one was watching them —slipped up the alley. Naturally enough (for the sun was setting) they ran straight against the omnibus.

"Good heavens!" exclaimed Mr. Bons. "Good gracious heavens!"

It was not the omnibus in which the boy had driven first, nor yet that in which he had returned. There were three horses—black, gray, and white, the gray being the finest. The driver, who turned round at the mention of goodness and of heaven, was a sallow man with terrifying jaws and sunken eyes. Mr. Bons, on seeing him, gave a cry as if of recognition, and began to tremble violently.

The boy jumped in.

"Is it possible?" cried Mr. Bons. "Is the impossible possible?"

"Sir; come in, sir. It is such a fine omnibus. Oh, here is his name—Dan some one."

Mr. Bons sprang in too. A blast of wind immediately slammed the omnibus door, and the shock jerked down all the omnibus blinds, which were very weak on their springs.

"Dan . . . Show me. Good gracious heavens! we're moving."

"Hooray!" said the boy.

Mr. Bons became flustered. He had not intended to be kidnapped. He could not find the door-handle, nor push up the blinds. The omnibus was quite dark, and by the time he had struck a match, night had come on outside also. They were moving rapidly.

"A strange, a memorable adventure," he said, surveying the interior of the omnibus, which was large, roomy, and constructed with extreme regularity, every part exactly answering to every other part. Over the door (the handle of which was outside) was written, "Lasciate ogni baldanza voi che entrate"—at least, that was what was written, but Mr. Bons said that it was Lashy arty something, and that baldanza was a mistake for speranza. His voice sounded as if he was in church. Meanwhile, the boy called to the cadaverous driver for two return tickets. They were handed in without a word. Mr. Bons covered his face with his hand and again trembled. "Do you know who that is!" he whispered, when the little window had shut upon them. "It is the impossible."

"Well, I don't like him as much as Sir Thomas Browne, though I shouldn't be surprised if he had even more in him."

"More in him?" He stamped irritably. "By accident you have made the greatest discovery of the century, and all you can say is that there is more in this man. Do you remember those vellum books in my library, stamped with red lilies? This—sit still, I bring you stupendous news!—this is the man who wrote them."

The boy sat quite still. "I wonder if we shall see Mrs. Gamp?" he asked, after a civil pause.

"Mrs.——?"

"Mrs. Gamp and Mrs. Harris. I like Mrs. Harris. I came upon them quite suddenly. Mrs. Gamp's bandboxes have moved over the rainbow so badly. All the bottoms have fallen out, and two of the pippins off her bedstead tumbled into the stream."

"Out there sits the man who wrote my vellum books!" thundered Mr. Bons, "and you talk to me of Dickens and of Mrs. Gamp?"

"I know Mrs. Gamp so well," he apologized. "I could not help being glad to see her. I recognized her voice. She was telling Mrs. Harris about Mrs. Prig."

"Did you spend the whole day in her elevating company?"

"Oh, no. I raced. I met a man who took me out beyond to a race-course. You run, and there are dolphins out at sea."

"Indeed. Do you remember the man's name?"

"Achilles. No; he was later. Tom Jones."

Mr. Bons sighed heavily. "Well, my lad, you have made a miserable mess of it. Think of a cultured person with your opportunities! A cultured person would have known all these characters and known what to have said to each. He would not have wasted his time with a Mrs. Gamp or a Tom Jones. The creations of Homer, of Shakespeare, and of Him who drives us now, would alone have contented him. He would not have raced. He would have asked intelligent questions."

"But, Mr. Bons," said the boy humbly, "you will be a cultured person. I told them so."

"True, true, and I beg you not to disgrace me when we arrive. No gossiping. No running. Keep close to my side, and never speak to these Immortals unless they speak to you. Yes, and give me the return tickets. You will be losing them."

The boy surrendered the tickets, but felt a little sore. After all, he had found the way to this place. It was hard first to be disbelieved and then to be lectured. Meanwhile, the rain had stopped, and moonlight crept into the omnibus through the cracks in the blinds.

"But how is there to be a rainbow?" cried the boy.

"You distract me," snapped Mr. Bons. "I wish to meditate on beauty. I wish to goodness I was with a reverent and sympathetic person."

The lad bit his lip. He made a hundred good resolutions. He would imitate Mr. Bons all the visit. He would not laugh, or run, or sing, or do any of the vulgar things that must have disgusted his new friends last time. He would be very careful to pronounce their names properly, and to remember who knew whom. Achilles did not know Tom Jones—at least, so Mr. Bons said. The Duchess of Malfi was older than Mrs. Gamp—at least, so Mr. Bons said. He would be self-conscious, reticent, and prim. He would never say he liked any one. Yet, when the blind flew up at a chance touch of his head, all these good resolutions went to the winds, for the omnibus had reached the summit of a moonlit hill, and there was the chasm, and there, across it, stood the old precipices, dreaming, with their feet in the everlasting river. He exclaimed, "The mountain! Listen to the new tune in the water! Look at the camp fires in the ravines," and Mr. Bons, after a hasty glance, retorted, "Water? Camp fires? Ridiculous rubbish. Hold your tongue. There is nothing at all."

Yet, under his eyes, a rainbow formed, compounded not of sunlight and storm, but of moonlight and the spray of the river. The three horses put their feet upon it. He thought it the finest rainbow he had seen, but did not dare to say so, since Mr. Bons said that nothing was there. He leant out—the window had opened—and sang the tune that rose from the sleeping waters.

"The prelude to Rhinegold?" said Mr. Bons suddenly. "Who taught you these *leit motifs*?" He, too, looked out of the window. Then he behaved very oddly. He gave a choking cry, and fell back on to the omnibus floor. He writhed and kicked. His face was green.

"Does the bridge make you dizzy?" the boy asked.

"Dizzy!" gasped Mr. Bons. "I want to go back. Tell the driver."

But the driver shook his head.

"We are nearly there," said the boy. "They are asleep. Shall I call? They will be so pleased to see you, for I have prepared them."

Mr. Bons moaned. They moved over the lunar rainbow, which ever and ever broke away behind their wheels. How still the night was! Who would be sentry at the Gate?

"I am coming," he shouted, again forgetting the hundred resolutions. "I am returning—I, the boy."

"The boy is returning," cried a voice to other voices, who repeated, "The boy is returning."

"I am bringing Mr. Bons with me."

Silence.

"I should have said Mr. Bons is bringing me with him."

Profound silence.

"Who stands sentry?"

"Achilles."

And on the rocky causeway, close to the springing of the rainbow bridge, he saw a young man who carried a wonderful shield.

"Mr. Bons, it is Achilles, armed."

"I want to go back," said Mr. Bons.

The last fragment of the rainbow melted, the wheels sang upon the living rock, the door of the omnibus burst open. Out leapt the boy—he could not resist—and sprang to meet the warrior, who, stooping suddenly, caught him on his shield.

"Achilles!" he cried, "let me get down, for I am ignorant and vulgar, and I must wait for that Mr. Bons of whom I told you yesterday."

But Achilles raised him aloft. He crouched on the wonderful shield, on heroes and burning cities, on vineyards graven in gold, on every dear passion, every joy, on the entire image of the Mountain that he had discovered, encircled, like it, with an everlasting stream. "No, no," he protested, "I am not worthy. It is Mr. Bons who must be up here."

But Mr. Bons was whimpering, and Achilles trumpeted and cried, "Stand upright upon my shield!"

"Sir, I did not mean to stand! something made me stand. Sir, why do you delay? Here is only the great Achilles, whom you knew."

Mr. Bons screamed, "I see no one. I see nothing. I want to go back." Then he cried to the driver, "Save me! Let me stop in your chariot. I have honoured you. I have quoted you. I have bound you in vellum. Take me back to my world."

The driver replied, "I am the means and not the end. I am the food and not the life. Stand by yourself, as that boy has stood. I cannot save you. For poetry is a spirit; and they that would worship it must worship in spirit and in truth."

Mr. Bons—he could not resist—crawled out of the beautiful omnibus. His face appeared, gaping horribly. His hands followed, one gripping the step, the other beating the air. Now his shoulders emerged, his chest, his stomach. With a shriek of "I see London," he fell—fell against the hard, moonlit rock, fell into it as if it were water, fell through it, vanished, and was seen by the boy no more.

"Where have you fallen to, Mr. Bons? Here is a procession arriving to honour you with music and torches. Here come the men and women whose names you know. The mountain is awake, the river is awake, over the race-course the sea is awaking those dolphins, and it is all for you. They want you——"

There was the touch of fresh leaves on his forehead. Some one had crowned him.

ΤΕΛΟΣ

. . .

From the *Kingston Gazette, Surbiton Times,*
and *Raynes Park Observer.*

The body of Mr. Septimus Bons has been found in a shockingly mutilated condition in the vicinity of the Bermondsey gas-works. The deceased's pockets contained a sovereign-purse, a silver cigar-case, a bijou pronouncing dictionary, and a couple of omnibus tickets. The unfortunate gentleman had apparently been hurled from a considerable height. Foul play is suspected, and a thorough investigation is pending by the authorities.

· · ·

OTHER KINGDOM

"'*Quem*, whom; *fugis*, are you avoiding; *ah demens*, you silly ass; *habitarunt di quoque*, gods too have lived in; *silvas*, the woods.' Go ahead!"

I always brighten the classics—it is part of my system—and therefore I translated *demens* by "silly ass." But Miss Beaumont need not have made a note of the translation, and Ford, who knows better, need not have echoed after me. "Whom are you avoiding, you silly ass, gods too have lived in the woods."

"Ye—es," I replied, with scholarly hesitation. "Ye—es. *Silvas*—woods, wooded spaces, the country generally. Yes. *Demens*, of course, is *de—mens*. 'Ah, witless fellow! Gods, I say, even gods have dwelt in the woods ere now.'"

"But I thought gods always lived in the sky," said Mrs. Worters, interrupting our lesson for I think the third-and-twentieth time.

"Not always," answered Miss Beaumont. As she spoke she inserted "witless fellow" as an alternative to "silly ass."

"I always thought they lived in the sky."

"Oh, no, Mrs. Worters," the girl repeated. "Not always." And finding her place in the note-book she read as follows: "Gods. Where. Chief deities—Mount Olympus. Pan—most places, as name implies. Oreads—mountains. Sirens, Tritons, Nereids—water (salt). Naiads—water (fresh). Satyrs, Fauns, etc.—woods. Dryads—trees."

"Well, dear, you have learnt a lot. And will you now tell me what good it has done you?"

"It has helped me—" faltered Miss Beaumont. She was very earnest over her classics. She wished she could have said what good they had done her.

Ford came to her rescue. "Of course it's helped you. The classics are full of tips. They teach you how to dodge things."

I begged my young friend not to dodge his Virgil lesson.

"But they do!" he cried. "Suppose that long-haired brute Apollo wants to give you a music lesson. Well, out you pop into the laurels. Or Universal Nature comes along. You aren't feeling particularly keen on Universal Nature, so you turn into a reed."

"Is Jack mad?" asked Mrs. Worters.

But Miss Beaumont had caught the allusions—which were quite ingenious I must admit. "And Croesus?" she inquired. "What was it one turned into to get away from Croesus?"

I hastened to tidy up her mythology. "Midas, Miss Beaumont, not Croesus. And he turns you—you don't turn yourself: he turns you into gold."

"There's no dodging Midas," said Ford.

"Surely—" said Miss Beaumont. She had been learning Latin not quite a fortnight, but she would have corrected the Regius Professor.

He began to tease her. "Oh, there's no dodging Midas! He just comes, he touches you, and you pay him several thousand per cent at once. You're gold—a young golden lady—if he touches you."

"I won't be touched!" she cried, relapsing into her habitual frivolity.

"Oh, but he'll touch you."

"He sha'n't!"

"He will."

"He sha'n't!"

"He will."

Miss Beaumont took up her Virgil and smacked Ford over the head with it.

"Evelyn! Evelyn!" said Mrs. Worters. "Now you are forgetting yourself. And you also forget my question. What good has Latin done you?"

"Mr. Ford—what good has Latin done you?"

"Mr. Inskip—what good has Latin done us?"

So I was let in for the classical controversy. The arguments for the study of Latin are perfectly sound, but they are difficult to remember, and the afternoon sun was hot, and I needed my tea. But I had to justify my existence as a coach, so I took off my eye-glasses and breathed on them and said, "My dear Ford, what a question!"

"It's all right for Jack," said Mrs. Worters. "Jack has to pass his entrance examination. But what's the good of it for Evelyn? None at all."

"No, Mrs. Worters," I persisted, pointing my eye-glasses at her. "I cannot agree. Miss Beaumont is—in a sense—new to our civilization. She is entering it, and Latin is one of the subjects in her entrance examination also. No one can grasp modern life without some knowledge of its origins."

"But why should she grasp modern life?" said the tiresome woman.

"Well, there you are!" I retorted, and shut up my eye-glasses with a snap.

"Mr. Inskip, I am not there. Kindly tell me what's the good of it all. Oh, I've been through it myself: Jupiter, Venus, Juno, I know the lot of them. And many of the stories not at all proper."

"Classical education," I said drily, "is not entirely confined to classical mythology. Though even the mythology has its value. Dreams if you like, but there is value in dreams."

"I too have dreams," said Mrs. Worters, "but I am not so foolish as to mention them afterwards."

Mercifully we were interrupted. A rich virile voice close behind us said, "Cherish your dreams!" We had been joined by our host, Harcourt Worters—Mrs. Worters' son, Miss Beaumont's *fiancé*, Ford's guardian, my employer: I must speak of him as Mr. Worters.

"Let us cherish our dreams!" he repeated. "All day I've been fighting, haggling, bargaining. And to come out on to this lawn and see you all learning Latin, so happy, so passionless, so Arcadian——"

He did not finish the sentence, but sank into the chair next to Miss Beaumont, and possessed himself of her hand. As he did so she sang: "Áh yoù sílly àss góds lìve in woóds!"

"What have we here?" said Mr. Worters with a slight frown.

With the other hand she pointed to me.

"Virgil—" I stammered. "Colloquial translation——"

"Oh, I see; a colloquial translation of poetry." Then his smile returned. "Perhaps if gods live in woods, that is why woods are so dear. I have just bought Other Kingdom Copse!"

Loud exclamations of joy. Indeed, the beeches in that copse are as fine as any in Hertfordshire. Moreover, it, and the meadow by which it is approached, have always made an ugly notch in the rounded contours of the Worters estate. So we were all very glad that Mr. Worters had purchased Other Kingdom. Only Ford kept silent, stroking his head where the Virgil had hit it, and smiling a little to himself as he did so.

"Judging from the price I paid, I should say there was a god in every tree. But price, this time was no object." He glanced at Miss Beaumont. "You admire beeches, Evelyn, do you not?"

"I forget always which they are. Like this?"

She flung her arms up above her head, close together, so that she looked like a slender column. Then her body swayed and her delicate green dress quivered over it with the suggestion of countless leaves.

"My dear child!" exclaimed her lover.

"No: that is a silver birch," said Ford.

"Oh, of course. Like this, then." And she twitched up her skirts so that for a moment they spread out in great horizontal layers, like the layers of a beech.

We glanced at the house, but none of the servants were looking. So we laughed, and said she ought to go on the variety stage.

"Ah, this is the kind I like!" she cried, and practised the beech-tree again.

"I thought so," said Mr. Worters. "I thought so. Other Kingdom Copse is yours."

"Mine——?" She had never had such a present in her life. She could not realize it.

"The purchase will be drawn up in your name. You will sign the deed. Receive the wood, with my love. It is a second engagement ring."

"But is it—is it mine? Can I—do what I like there?"

"You can," said Mr. Worters, smiling.

She rushed at him and kissed him. She kissed Mrs. Worters. She would have kissed myself and Ford if we had not extruded elbows. The joy of possession had turned her head.

"It's mine! I can walk there, work there, live there. A wood of my own! Mine for ever."

"Yours, at all events, for ninety-nine years."

"Ninety-nine years?" I regret to say there was a tinge of disappointment in her voice.

"My dear child! Do you expect to live longer?"

"I suppose I can't," she replied, and flushed a little. "I don't know."

"Ninety-nine seems long enough to most people. I have got this house, and the very lawn you are standing on, on a lease of ninety-nine years. Yet I call them my own, and I think I am justified. Am I not?"

"Oh, yes."

"Ninety-nine years is practically for ever. Isn't it?"

"Oh, yes. It must be."

Ford possesses a most inflammatory notebook. Outside it is labelled "Private," inside it is headed "Practically a book." I saw him make an entry in it now, "Eternity: practically ninety-nine years."

Mr. Worters, as if speaking to himself, now observed: "My goodness! My goodness! How land has risen! Perfectly astounding."

I saw that he was in need of a Boswell, so I said: "Has it, indeed?"

"My dear Inskip. Guess what I could have got that wood for ten years ago! But I refused. Guess why."

We could not guess why.

"Because the transaction would not have been straight." A most becoming blush spread over his face as he uttered the noble word. "Not straight. Straight legally. But not morally straight. We were to force the hands of the man who owned it. I refused. The others—decent fellows in their way—told me I was squeamish. I said, 'Yes. Perhaps I am. My name is plain Harcourt Worters—not a well known name if you go outside the City and my own country, but a name which, where it is known, carries, I flatter myself, some weight. And I will not sign my name to this. That is all. Call me squeamish if you like. But I will not sign. It is just a fad of mine. Let us call it a fad.'" He blushed again. Ford believes that his guardian blushes all over—that if you could strip him and make him talk nobly he would look like a boiled lobster. There is a picture of him in this condition in the notebook.

"So the man who owned it then didn't own it now?" said Miss Beaumont, who had followed the narrative with some interest.

"Oh, no!" said Mr. Worters.

"Why no!" said Mrs. Worters absently, as she hunted in the grass for her knitting-needle. "Of course not. It belongs to the widow."

"Tea!" cried her son, springing vivaciously to his feet. "I see tea and I want it. Come, mother. Come along, Evelyn. I can tell you it's no joke, a hard day in the battle of life. For life is practically a battle. To all intents and purposes a battle. Except for a few lucky fellows who can read books, and so avoid the realities. But I——"

His voice died away as he escorted the two ladies over the smooth lawn and up the stone steps to the terrace, on which the footman was placing tables and little chairs and a silver kettle-stand. More ladies came out of the house. We could just hear their shouts of excitement as they also were told of the purchase of Other Kingdom.

I like Ford. The boy has the makings of a scholar and—though for some reason he objects to the word—of a gentleman. It amused me now to see his lip curl with the vague cynicism of youth. He cannot understand the footman and the solid silver kettle-stand. They make him cross. For he has dreams—not exactly spiritual dreams: Mr. Worters is the man for those—but dreams of the tangible and the actual: robust dreams, which take him, not to heaven, but to another earth. There are no footmen in this other earth, and the kettle-stands, I suppose, will not be made of silver, and I know that everything is to be itself, and not practically something else. But what this means, and, if it means anything, what the good of it is, I am not prepared to say. For though I have just said "there is value in dreams," I only said it to silence old Mrs. Worters.

"Go ahead, man! We can't have tea till we've got through something."

He turned his chair away from the terrace, so that he could sit looking at the meadows and at the stream that runs through the meadows, and at the beech-trees of Other Kingdom that rise beyond the stream. Then, most gravely and admirably, he began to construe the Eclogues of Virgil.

II

Other Kingdom Copse is just like any other beech copse, and I am therefore spared the fatigue of describing it. And the stream in front of it, like many other streams, is not crossed by a bridge in the right place, and you must either walk round a mile or else you must paddle. Miss Beaumont suggested that we should paddle.

Mr. Worters accepted the suggestion tumultuously. It only became evident gradually that he was not going to adopt it.

"What fun! What fun! We will paddle to your kingdom. If only—if only it wasn't for the tea-things."

"But you can carry the tea-things on your back."

"Why, yes! so I can. Or the servants could."

"Harcourt—no servants. This is my picnic, and my wood. I'm going to settle everything. I didn't tell you: I've got all the food. I've been in the village with Mr. Ford."

"In the village——?"

"Yes. We got biscuits and oranges and half a pound of tea. That's all you'll have. He carried them up. And he'll carry them over the stream. I want you just to lend me some tea-things—not the best ones. I'll take care of them. That's all."

"Dear creature. . . ."

"Evelyn," said Mrs. Worters, "how much did you and Jack pay for that tea?"

"For the half-pound, tenpence."

Mrs. Worters received the announcement in gloomy silence.

"Mother!" cried Mr. Worters. "Why, I forgot! How could we go padding with mother!"

"Oh, but, Mrs. Worters, we could carry you over."

"Thank you, dearest child. I am sure you could."

"Alas! alas! Evelyn. Mother is laughing at us. She would sooner die than be carried. And alas! there are my sisters, and Mrs. Osgood: she has a cold, tiresome woman. No: we shall have to go round by the bridge."

"But some of us——" began Ford. His guardian cut him short with a quick look.

So we went round—a procession of eight. Miss Beaumont led us. She was full of fun—at least so I thought at the time, but when I reviewed her speeches afterwards I could not find in them anything amusing. It was all this kind of thing: "Single file! Pretend you're in church and don't talk. Mr. Ford, turn out your toes. Harcourt—at the bridge throw to the Naiad a pinch of tea. She has a headache. She has had a headache for nineteen hundred years." All that she said was quite stupid. I cannot think why I liked it at the time.

As we approached the copse she said, "Mr. Inskip, sing, and we'll sing after you: Áh yoù sílly àss góds lìve in woóds." I cleared my throat and gave out the abominable phrase, and we all chanted it as if it were a litany. There was something attractive about Miss Beaumont. I was not surprised that Harcourt had picked her out of "Ireland" and had brought her home, without money, without connections, almost without antecedents, to be his bride. It was daring of him, but he knew himself to be a daring fellow. She brought him nothing; but that he could afford, he had so vast a surplus of spiritual and commercial goods. "In time," I heard him tell his mother, "in time Evelyn will repay me a thousandfold." Meanwhile there was something attractive about her. If it were my place to like people, I could have liked her very much.

"Stop singing!" she cried. We had entered the wood. "Welcome, all of you." We bowed. Ford, who had not been laughing, bowed down to the ground. "And now be seated. Mrs. Worters—will you sit there—against that tree with a green trunk? It will show up your beautiful dress."

"Very well, dear, I will," said Mrs. Worters.

"Anna—there. Mr. Inskip next to her. Then Ruth and Mrs. Osgood. Oh, Harcourt—do sit a little forward, so that you'll hide the house. I don't want to see the house at all."

"I won't!" laughed her lover, "I want my back against a tree, too."

"Miss Beaumont," asked Ford, "where shall I sit?" He was standing at attention, like a soldier.

"Oh, look at all these Worters!" she cried, "and one little Ford in the middle of them!" For she was at that state of civilization which appreciates a pun.

"Shall I stand, Miss Beaumont? Shall I hide the house from you if I stand?"

"Sit down, Jack, you baby!" cried his guardian, breaking in with needless asperity. "Sit down!"

"He may just as well stand if he will," said she. "Just pull back your soft hat, Mr. Ford. Like a halo. Now you hide even the smoke from the chimneys. And it makes you look beautiful."

"Evelyn! Evelyn! You are too hard on the boy. You'll tire him. He's one of those bookworms. He's not strong. Let him sit down."

"Aren't you strong?" she asked.

"I am strong!" he cried. It is quite true. Ford has no right to be strong, but he is. He never did his dumb-bells or played in his school fifteen. But the muscles came. He thinks they came while he was reading Pindar.

"Then you may just as well stand, if you will."

"Evelyn! Evelyn! childish, selfish maiden! If poor Jack gets tired I will take his place. Why don't you want to see the house? Eh?"

Mrs. Worters and the Miss Worters moved uneasily. They saw that their Harcourt was not quite pleased. Theirs not to question why. It was for Evelyn to remove his displeasure, and they glanced at her.

"Well, why don't you want to see your future home? I must say—though I practically planned the house myself—that it looks very well from here. I like the gables. Miss! Answer me!"

I felt for Miss Beaumont. A home-made gable is an awful thing, and Harcourt's mansion looked like a cottage with the dropsy. But what would she say?

She said nothing.

"Well?"

It was as if he had never spoken. She was as merry, as smiling, as pretty as ever, and she said nothing. She had not realized that a question requires an answer.

For us the situation was intolerable. I had to save it by making a tactful reference to the view, which, I said, reminded me a little of the country near Veii. It did not—indeed it could not, for I have never been near Veii. But it is part of my system to make classical allusions. And at all events I saved the situation.

Miss Beaumont was serious and rational at once. She asked me the date of Veii. I made a suitable answer.

"I do like the classics," she informed us. "They are so natural. Just writing down things."

"Ye—es," said I. "But the classics have their poetry as well as their prose. They're more than a record of facts."

"Just writing down things," said Miss Beaumont, and smiled as if the silly definition pleased her.

Harcourt had recovered himself. "A very just criticism," said he. "It is what I always feel about the ancient world. It takes us but a very little way. It only writes things down."

"What do you mean?" asked Evelyn.

"I mean this—though it is presumptuous to speak in the presence of Mr. Inskip. This is what I mean. The classics are not everything. We owe them an enormous debt; I am the last to undervalue it; I, too, went through them at school. They are full of elegance and beauty. But they are not everything. They were written before men began to really feel." He coloured crimson. "Hence, the chilliness of classical art—its lack of—of a something. Whereas later things—Dante—a Madonna of Raphael—some bars of Mendelssohn——" His voice tailed reverently away. We sat with our eyes on the ground, not liking to look at Miss Beaumont. It is a fairly open secret that she also lacks a something. She has not yet developed her soul.

The silence was broken by the still small voice of Mrs. Worters saying that she was faint with hunger.

The young hostess sprang up. She would let none of us help her: it was her party. She undid the basket and emptied out the biscuits and oranges from their bags, and boiled the kettle and poured out the tea, which was horrible. But we laughed and talked with the frivolity that suits the open air, and even Mrs. Worters expectorated her flies with a smile. Over us all there stood the silent, chivalrous figure of Ford, drinking tea carefully lest it should disturb his outline. His guardian, who is a wag, chaffed him and tickled his ankles and calves.

"Well, this is nice!" said Miss Beaumont. "I am happy."

"Your wood, Evelyn!" said the ladies.

"Her wood for ever!" cried Mr. Worters. "It is an unsatisfactory arrangement, a ninety-nine years' lease. There is no feeling of permanency. I reopened negotiations. I have bought her the wood for ever—all right, dear, all right: don't make a fuss."

"But I must!" she cried. "For everything's perfect! Every one so kind—and I didn't know most of you a year ago. Oh, it is so wonderful—and now a wood—a wood of my own—a wood for ever.

All of you coming to tea with me here! Dear Harcourt—dear people—and just where the house would come and spoil things, there is Mr. Ford!"

"Ha! Ha!" laughed Mr. Worters, and slipped his hand up round the boy's ankle. What happened I do not know, but Ford collapsed on to the ground with a sharp cry. To an outsider it might have sounded like a cry of anger or pain. We, who knew better, laughed uproariously.

"Down he goes! Down he goes!" And they struggled playfully, kicking up the mould and the dry leaves.

"Don't hurt my wood!" cried Miss Beaumont.

Ford gave another sharp cry. Mr. Worters withdrew his hand. "Victory!" he exclaimed. "Evelyn! behold the family seat!" But Miss Beaumont, in her butterfly fashion, had left us, and was strolling away into her wood.

We packed up the tea-things and then split into groups. Ford went with the ladies. Mr. Worters did me the honour to stop by me.

"Well!" he said, in accordance with his usual formula, "and how go the classics?"

"Fairly well."

"Does Miss Beaumont show any ability?"

"I should say that she does. At all events she has enthusiasm."

"You do not think it is the enthusiasm of a child? I will be frank with you, Mr. Inskip. In many ways Miss Beaumont's practically a child. She has everything to learn: she acknowledges as much herself. Her new life is so different—so strange. Our habits—our thoughts—she has to be initiated into them all."

I saw what he was driving at, but I am not a fool, and I replied: "And how can she be initiated better than through the classics?"

"Exactly, exactly," said Mr. Worters. In the distance we heard her voice. She was counting the beech-trees. "The only question is—this Latin and Greek—what will she do with it? Can she make anything of it? Can she—well, it's not as if she will ever have to teach it to others."

"That is true." And my features might have been observed to become undecided.

"Whether, since she knows so little—I grant you she has enthusiasm. But ought one not to divert her enthusiasm—say to English literature? She scarcely knows her Tennyson at all. Last night in the conservatory I read her that wonderful scene between Arthur and Guinevere. Greek and Latin are all very well, but I sometimes feel we ought to begin at the beginning."

"You feel," said I, "that for Miss Beaumont the classics are something of a luxury."

"A luxury. That is the exact word, Mr. Inskip. A luxury. A whim. It is all very well for Jack Ford. And here we come to another point. Surely she keeps Jack back? Her knowledge must be elementary."

"Well, her knowledge is elementary: and I must say that it's difficult to teach them together. Jack has read a good deal, one way and another, whereas Miss Beaumont, though diligent and enthusiastic——"

"So I have been feeling. The arrangement is scarcely fair on Jack?"

"Well, I must admit——"

"Quite so. I ought never to have suggested it. It must come to an end. Of course, Mr. Inskip, it shall make no difference to you, this withdrawal of a pupil."

"The lessons shall cease at once, Mr. Worters."

Here she came up to us. "Harcourt, there are seventy-eight trees. I have had such a count."

He smiled down at her. Let me remember to say that he is tall and handsome, with a strong chin and liquid brown eyes, and a high forehead and hair not at all gray. Few things are more striking than a photograph of Mr. Harcourt Worters.

"Seventy-eight trees?"

"Seventy-eight."

"Are you pleased?"

"Oh, Harcourt——!"

I began to pack up the tea-things. They both saw and heard me. It was their own fault if they did not go further.

"I'm looking forward to the bridge," said he. "A rustic bridge at the bottom, and then, perhaps, an asphalt path from the house over the meadow, so that in all weathers we can walk here dry-shod. The boys come into the wood—look at all these initials—and I thought of putting a simple fence, to prevent any one but ourselves——"

"Harcourt!"

"A simple fence," he continued, "just like what I have put round my garden and the fields. Then at the other side of the copse, away from the house, I would put a gate, and have keys—two keys, I think—one for me and one for you—not more; and I would bring the asphalt path——"

"But Harcourt——"

"But Evelyn!"

"I—I—I——"

"You—you—you——?"

"I—I don't want an asphalt path."

"No? Perhaps you are right. Cinders perhaps. Yes. Or even gravel."

"But Harcourt—I don't want a path at all. I—I—can't afford a path."

He gave a roar of triumphant laughter. "Dearest! As if you were going to be bothered? The path's part of my present."

"The wood is your present," said Miss Beaumont. "Do you know—I don't care for the path. I'd rather always come as we came today. And I don't want a bridge. No—nor a fence either. I don't mind the boys and their initials. They and the girls have always come up to Other Kingdom and cut their names together in the bark. It's called the Fourth Time of Asking. I don't want it to stop."

"Ugh!" He pointed to a large heart transfixed by an arrow. "Ugh! Ugh!" I suspect that he was gaining time.

"They cut their names and go away, and when the first child is born they come again and deepen the cuts. So for each child. That's how you know: the initials that go right through to the wood are the fathers and mothers of large families, and the scratches in the bark that soon close up are boys and girls who were never married at all."

"You wonderful person! I've lived here all my life and never heard a word of this. Fancy folk-lore in Hertfordshire! I must tell the Archdeacon: he will be delighted——"

"And Harcourt, I don't want this to stop."

"My dear girl, the villagers will find other trees! There's nothing particular in Other Kingdom."

"But——"

"Other Kingdom shall be for us. You and I alone. Our initials only." His voice sank to a whisper.

"I don't want it fenced in." Her face was turned to me; I saw that it was puzzled and frightened. "I hate fences. And bridges. And all paths. It is my wood. Please: you gave me the wood."

"Why, yes!" he replied, soothing her. But I could see that he was angry. "Of course. But aha! Evelyn, the meadow's mine; I have a right to fence there—between my domain and yours!"

"Oh, fence me out if you like! Fence me out as much as you like! But never in. Oh, Harcourt, never in. I must be on the outside, I must be where any one can reach me. Year by year— while the initials deepen—the only thing worth feeling—and at last they close up—but one has felt them."

"Our initials!" he murmured, seizing upon the one word which he had understood and which was useful to him. "Let us carve our initials now. You and I—a heart if you like it, and an arrow and everything. H. W.—E. B."

"H. W.," she repeated, "and E. B."

He took out his penknife and drew her away in search of an unsullied tree. "E. B., Eternal Blessing. Mine! Mine! My haven from the world! My temple of purity. Oh, the spiritual exaltation—you cannot understand it, but you will! Oh, the seclusion of Paradise. Year after year alone together, all in all to each other —year after year, soul to soul, E. B., Everlasting Bliss!"

He stretched out his hand to cut the initials. As he did so she seemed to awake from a dream. "Harcourt!" she cried, "Harcourt! What's that? What's that red stuff on your finger and thumb?"

III

Oh, my goodness! Oh, all ye goddesses and gods! Here's a mess. Mr. Worters has been reading Ford's inflammatory note-book.

"It is my own fault," said Ford. "I should have labelled it 'Practically Private.' How could he know he was not meant to look inside?"

I spoke out severely, as an *employé* should. "My dear boy, none of that. The label came unstuck. That was why Mr. Worters opened the book. He never suspected it was private. See—the label's off."

"Scratched off," Ford retorted grimly, and glanced at his ankle.

I affected not to understand. "The point is this. Mr. Worters is thinking the matter over for four-and-twenty hours. If you take my advice you will apologize before that time elapses."

"And if I don't?"

"You know your own affairs of course. But don't forget that you are young and practically ignorant of life, and that you have scarcely any money of your own. As far as I can see, your career practically depends on the favour of Mr. Worters. You have laughed at him. He does not like being laughed at. It seems to me that your course is obvious."

"Apology?"

"Complete."

"And if I don't?"

"Departure."

He sat down on the stone steps and rested his head on his knees. On the lawn below us was Miss Beaumont, draggling about with some croquet balls. Her lover was out in the meadow, superintending the course of the asphalt path. For the path is to be made, and so is the bridge, and the fence is to be built round

Other Kingdom after all. In time Miss Beaumont saw how unreasonable were her objections. Of her own accord, one evening in the drawing-room, she gave her Harcourt permission to do what he liked. "That wood looks nearer," said Ford.

"The inside fences have gone: that brings it nearer. But my dear boy—you must settle what you're going to do."

"How much has he read?"

"Naturally he only opened the book. From what you showed me of it, one glance would be enough."

"Did he open at the poems?"

"Poems?"

"Did he speak of the poems?"

"No. Were they about him?"

"They were not about him."

"Then it wouldn't matter if he saw them."

"It is sometimes a compliment to be mentioned," said Ford, looking up at me. The remark had a stinging fragrance about it— such a fragrance as clings to the mouth after admirable wine. It did not taste like the remark of a boy. I was sorry that my pupil was likely to wreck his career; and I told him again that he had better apologize.

"I won't speak of Mr. Worters' claim for an apology. That's an aspect on which I prefer not to touch. The point is, if you don't apologize, you go—where?"

"To an aunt at Peckham."

I pointed to the pleasant, comfortable landscape, full of cows and carriage-horses out at grass, and civil retainers. In the midst of it stood Mr. Worters, radiating energy and wealth, like a terrestrial sun. "My dear Ford—don't be heroic! Apologize."

Unfortunately I raised my voice a little, and Miss Beaumont heard me, down on the lawn.

"Apologize?" she cried. "What about?" And as she was not interested in the game, she came up the steps towards us, trailing her croquet mallet behind her. Her walk was rather listless. She was toning down at last.

"Come indoors!" I whispered. "We must get out of this."

"Not a bit of it!" said Ford.

"What is it?" she asked, standing beside him on the step.

He swallowed something as he looked up at her. Suddenly I understood. I knew the nature and the subject of his poems. I was not so sure now that he had better apologize. The sooner he was kicked out of the place the better.

In spite of my remonstrances, he told her about the book, and her first remark was: "Oh, do let me see it!" She had no "proper feeling" of any kind. Then she said: "But why do you both look so sad?"

"We are awaiting Mr. Worters' decision," said I.

"Mr. Inskip! What nonsense! Do you suppose Harcourt'll be angry?"

"Of course he is angry, and rightly so."

"But why?"

"Ford has laughed at him."

"But what's that!" And for the first time there was anger in her voice. "Do you mean to say he'll punish some one who laughs at him? Why, for what else—for whatever reason are we all here? Not to laugh at each other! I laugh at people all day. At Mr. Ford. At you. And so does Harcourt. Oh, you've misjudged him! He won't—he couldn't be angry with people who laughed."

"Mine is not nice laughter," said Ford. "He could not well forgive me."

"You're a silly boy." She sneered at him. "You don't know Harcourt. So generous in every way. Why, he'd be as furious as I should be if you apologized. Mr. Inskip, isn't that so?"

"He has every right to an apology, I think."

"Right? What's a right? You use too many new words. 'Rights' —'apologies'—'society'—'position' —I don't follow it. What are we all here for, anyhow?"

Her discourse was full of trembling lights and shadows—frivolous one moment, the next moment asking why Humanity is here. I did not take the Moral Science Tripos, so I could not tell her.

"One thing I know—and that is that Harcourt isn't as stupid as you two. He soars above conventions. He doesn't care about 'rights' and 'apologies.' He knows that all laughter is nice, and that the other nice things are money and the soul and so on."

The soul and so on! I wonder that Harcourt out in the meadows did not have an apoplectic fit.

"Why, what a poor business your life would be," she continued, "if you all kept taking offence and apologizing! Forty million people in England and all of them touchy! How one would laugh if it was true! Just imagine!" And she did laugh. "Look at Harcourt though. He knows better. He isn't petty like that. Mr. Ford! He isn't petty like that. Why, what's wrong with your eyes?"

He rested his head on his knees again, and we could see his eyes no longer. In dispassionate tones she informed me that she thought he was crying. Then she tapped him on the hair with her mallet and said: "Cry-baby! Cry-cry-baby! Crying about nothing!" and ran laughing down the steps. "All right!" she shouted from the lawn. "Tell the cry-baby to stop. I'm going to speak to Harcourt!"

We watched her go in silence. Ford had scarcely been crying. His eyes had only become large and angry. He used such swear-words as he knew, and then got up abruptly, and went into the house. I think he could not bear to see her disillusioned. I had no such tenderness, and it was with considerable interest that I watched Miss Beaumont approach her lord.

She walked confidently across the meadow, bowing to the workmen as they raised their hats. Her languor had passed, and with it her suggestion of "tone." She was the same crude, unsophisticated person that Harcourt had picked out of Ireland—beautiful and ludicrous in the extreme, and—if you go in for pathos—extremely pathetic.

I saw them meet, and soon she was hanging on his arm. The motion of his hand explained to her the construction of bridges. Twice she interrupted him: he had to explain everything again. Then she got in her word, and what followed was a good deal better than a play. Their two little figures parted and met and parted again, she gesticulating, he most pompous and calm. She pleaded, she argued and—if satire can carry half a mile—she tried to be satirical. To enforce one of her childish points she made two steps back. Splash! She was floundering in the little stream.

That was the *dénouement* of the comedy. Harcourt rescued her, while the workmen crowded round in an agitated chorus. She was wet quite as far as her knees, and muddy over her ankles. In this state she was conducted towards me, and in time I began to hear words; "Influenza—a slight immersion—clothes are of no consequence beside health—pray, dearest, don't worry—yes, it must have been a shock—bed! bed! I insist on bed! Promise? Good girl. Up the steps to bed then."

They parted on the lawn, and she came obediently up the steps. Her face was full of terror and bewilderment.

"So you've had a wetting, Miss Beaumont!"

"Wetting? Oh, yes. But, Mr. Inskip—I don't understand: I've failed."

I expressed surprise.

"Mr. Ford is to go—at once. I've failed."

"I'm sorry."

"I've failed with Harcourt. He's offended. He won't laugh. He won't let me do what I want. Latin and Greek began it: I wanted to know about gods and heroes and he wouldn't let me: then I wanted no fence round Other Kingdom and no bridge and no path—and look! Now I ask that Mr. Ford, who has done nothing, sha'n't be punished for it—and he is to go away for ever."

"Impertinence is not 'nothing,' Miss Beaumont." For I must keep in with Harcourt.

"Impertinence is nothing!" she cried. "It doesn't exist. It's a sham, like 'claims' and 'position' and 'rights.' It's part of the great dream."

"What 'great dream'?" I asked, trying not to smile.

"Tell Mr. Ford—here comes Harcourt; I must go to bed. Give my love to Mr. Ford, and tell him 'to guess.' I shall never see him again, and I won't stand it. Tell him to guess. I am sorry I called

him a cry-baby. He was not crying like a baby. He was crying like
a grown-up person, and now I have grown up too."

I judged it right to repeat this conversation to my employer.

IV

The bridge is built, the fence finished, and Other Kingdom lies
tethered by a ribbon of asphalt to our front door. The seventy-
eight trees therein certainly seem nearer, and during the windy
nights that followed Ford's departure we could hear their
branches sighing, and would find in the morning that beech-
leaves had been blown right up against the house. Miss Beaumont
made no attempt to go out, much to the relief of the ladies, for
Harcourt had given the word that she was not to go out unat-
tended, and the boisterous weather deranged their petticoats. She
remained indoors, neither reading nor laughing, and dressing no
longer in green, but in brown.

Not noticing her presence, Mr. Worters looked in one day and
said with a sigh of relief: "That's all right. The circle's completed."

"Is it indeed!" she replied.

"You there, you quiet little mouse? I only meant that our lords,
the British workmen, have at last condescended to complete their
labours, and have rounded us off from the world. I—in the end I
was a naughty, domineering tyrant, and disobeyed you. I didn't
have the gate out at the further side of the copse. Will you forgive me?"

"Anything, Harcourt, that pleases you, is certain to please me."

The ladies smiled at each other, and Mr. Worters said: "That's
right, and as soon as the wind goes down we'll all progress
together to your wood, and take possession of it formally, for it
didn't really count that last time."

"No, it didn't really count that last time," Miss Beaumont echoed.

"Evelyn says this wind never will go down," remarked Mrs.
Worters. "I don't know how she knows."

"It will never go down, as long as I am in the house."

"Really?" he said gaily. "Then come out now, and send it down with me."

They took a few turns up and down the terrace. The wind lulled for a moment, but blew fiercer than ever during lunch. As we ate, it roared and whistled down the chimney at us, and the trees of Other Kingdom frothed like the sea. Leaves and twigs flew from them, and a bough, a good-sized bough, was blown on to the smooth asphalt path, and actually switchbacked over the bridge, up the meadow, and across our very lawn. (I venture to say "our," as I am now staying on as Harcourt's secretary.) Only the stone steps prevented it from reaching the terrace and perhaps breaking the dining-room window. Miss Beaumont sprang up and, napkin in hand, ran out and touched it.

"Oh, Evelyn——" the ladies cried.

"Let her go," said Mr. Worters tolerantly. "It certainly is a remarkable incident, remarkable. We must remember to tell the Archdeacon about it."

"Harcourt," she cried, with the first hint of returning colour in her cheeks, "mightn't we go up to the copse after lunch, you and I?"

Mr. Worters considered.

"Of course, not if you don't think best."

"Inskip, what's your opinion?"

I saw what his own was, and cried, "Oh, let's go!" though I detest the wind as much as any one.

"Very well. Mother, Anna, Ruth, Mrs. Osgood—we'll all go."

And go we did, a lugubrious procession; but the gods were good to us for once, for as soon as we were started, the tempest dropped, and there ensued an extraordinary calm. After all, Miss Beaumont was something of a weather prophet. Her spirits improved every minute. She tripped in front of us along the asphalt path, and ever and anon turned round to say to her lover some gracious or alluring thing. I admired her for it. I admire people who know on which side their bread's buttered.

"Evelyn, come here!"

"Come here yourself."

"Give me a kiss."

"Come and take it then."

He ran after her, and she ran away, while all our party laughed melodiously.

"Oh, I am so happy!" she cried. "I think I've everything I want in all the world. Oh dear, those last few days indoors! But oh, I am so happy now!" She had changed her brown dress for the old flowing green one, and she began to do her skirt dance in the open meadow, lit by sudden gleams of the sunshine. It was really a beautiful sight, and Mr. Worters did not correct her, glad perhaps that she should recover her spirits, even if she lost her tone. Her feet scarcely moved, but her body so swayed and her dress spread so gloriously around her, that we were transported with joy. She danced to the song of a bird that sang passionately in Other Kingdom, and the river held back its waves to watch her (one might have supposed), and the winds lay spell-bound in their cavern, and the great clouds spell-bound in the sky. She danced away from our society and our life, back, back through the centuries till houses and fences fell and the earth lay wild to the sun. Her garment was as foliage upon her, the strength of her limbs as boughs, her throat the smooth upper branch that salutes the morning or glistens to the rain. Leaves move, leaves hide it as hers was hidden by the motion of her hair. Leaves move again and it is ours, as her throat was ours again when, parting the tangle, she faced us crying, "Oh!" crying, "Oh Harcourt! I never was so happy. I have all that there is in the world."

But he, entrammelled in love's ecstasy, forgetting certain Madonnas of Raphael, forgetting, I fancy, his soul, sprang to inarm her with, "Evelyn! Eternal Bliss! Mine to eternity! Mine!" and she sprang away. Music was added and she sang, "Oh Ford! oh Ford, among all these Worters, I am coming through you to my Kingdom. Oh Ford, my lover while I was a woman, I will never forget you, never, as long as I have branches to shade you from the sun," and, singing, crossed the stream.

Why he followed her so passionately, I do not know. It was play, she was in his own domain which a fence surrounds, and she could not possibly escape him. But he dashed round by the bridge as if all their love was at stake, and pursued her with fierceness up the hill. She ran well, but the end was a foregone conclusion, and we only speculated whether he would catch her outside or inside the copse. He gained on her inch by inch; now they were in the shadow of the trees; he had practically grasped her, he had missed; she had disappeared into the trees themselves, he following.

"Harcourt is in high spirits," said Mrs. Osgood, Anna, and Ruth.

"Evelyn!" we heard him shouting within.

We proceeded up the asphalt path.

"Evelyn! Evelyn!"

"He's not caught her yet, evidently."

"Where are you, Evelyn?"

"Miss Beaumont must have hidden herself rather cleverly."

"Look here," cried Harcourt, emerging, "have you seen Evelyn?"

"Oh, no, she's certainly inside."

"So I thought."

"Evelyn must be dodging round one of the trunks. You go this way, I that. We'll soon find her."

We searched, gaily at first, and always with a feeling that Miss Beaumont was close by, that the delicate limbs were just behind this bole, the hair and the drapery quivering among those leaves. She was beside us, above us; here was her footstep on the purple-brown earth—her bosom, her neck—she was everywhere and nowhere. Gaiety turned to irritation, irritation to anger and fear. Miss Beaumont was apparently lost. "Evelyn! Evelyn!" we continued to cry. "Oh, really, it is beyond a joke."

Then the wind arose, the more violent for its lull, and we were driven into the house by a terrific storm. We said, "At all events she will come back now." But she did not come, and the rain hissed and rose up from the dry meadows like incense smoke, and smote the quivering leaves to applause. Then it lightened. Ladies screamed, and we saw Other Kingdom as one who claps the hands, and heard it as one who roars with laughter in the thunder. Not even the Archdeacon can remember such a storm. All Harcourt's seedlings were ruined, and the tiles flew off his gables right and left. He came to me presently with a white, drawn face, saying: "Inskip, can I trust you?"

"You can, indeed."

"I have long suspected it; she has eloped with Ford."

"But how——" I gasped.

"The carriage is ready—we'll talk as we drive." Then, against the rain he shouted: "No gate in the fence, I know, but what about a ladder? While I blunder, she's over the fence, and he——"

"But you were so close. There was not the time."

"There is time for anything," he said venomously, "where a treacherous woman is concerned. I found her no better than a savage, I trained her, I educated her. But I'll break them both. I can do that; I'll break them soul and body."

No one can break Ford now. The task is impossible. But I trembled for Miss Beaumont.

We missed the train. Young couples had gone by it, several young couples, and we heard of more young couples in London, as if all the world were mocking Harcourt's solitude. In desperation we sought the squalid suburb that is now Ford's home. We swept past the dirty maid and the terrified aunt, swept upstairs, to catch him if we could red-handed. He was seated at the table, reading the *Œdipus Coloneus* of Sophocles.

"That won't take in me!" shouted Harcourt. "You've got Miss Beaumont with you, and I know it."

"No such luck," said Ford.

He stammered with rage. "Inskip—you hear that? 'No such luck'! Quote the evidence against him. I can't speak."

So I quoted her song. "'Oh Ford! Oh Ford, among all these Worters, I am coming through you to my Kingdom! Oh Ford, my lover while I was a woman, I will never forget you, never, as long as I have branches to shade you from the sun.' Soon after that, we lost her."

"And—and on another occasion she sent a message of similar effect. Inskip, bear witness. He was to 'guess' something."

"I have guessed it," said Ford.

"So you practically——"

"Oh, no, Mr. Worters, you mistake me. I have not practically guessed. I have guessed. I could tell you if I chose, but it would be no good, for she has not practically escaped you. She has escaped you absolutely, for ever and ever, as long as there are branches to shade men from the sun."

. . .

THE CURATE'S FRIEND

It is uncertain how the Faun came to be in Wiltshire. Perhaps he came over with the Roman legionaries to live with his friends in camp, talking to them of Lucretilis, or Garganus or of the slopes of Etna; they in the joy of their recall forgot to take him on board, and he wept in exile; but at last he found that our hills also understood his sorrows, and rejoiced when he was happy. Or, perhaps he came to be there because he had been there always. There is nothing particularly classical about a faun: it is only that the Greeks and Italians have ever had the sharpest eyes. You will find him in the "Tempest" and the "Benedicite;" and any country which has beech clumps and sloping grass and very clear streams may reasonably produce him.

How I came to see him is a more difficult question. For to see him there is required a certain quality, for which truthfulness is too cold a name and animal spirits too coarse a one, and he alone knows how this quality came to be in me. No man has the right to call himself a fool, but I may say that I then presented the perfect semblance of one. I was facetious without humour and serious without conviction. Every Sunday I would speak to my rural parishioners about the other world in the tone of one who has been behind the scenes, or I would explain to them the errors of the Pelagians, or I would warn them against hurrying from one dissipation to another. Every Tuesday I gave what I called "straight talks to my lads"—talks which led straight past anything awkward. And every Thursday I addressed the Mother's Union on the duties of wives or widows, and gave them practical hints on the management of a family of ten.

I took myself in, and for a time I certainly took in Emily. I have never known a girl attend so carefully to my sermons, or laugh so heartily at my jokes. It is no wonder that I became engaged. She has made an excellent wife, freely correcting her husband's absurdities, but allowing no one else to breathe a word against them; able to talk about the sub-conscious self in the drawing-room, and yet have an ear for the children crying in the nursery, or the plates breaking in the scullery. An excellent wife—better than I ever imagined. But she has not married me.

Had we stopped indoors that afternoon nothing would have happened. It was all owing to Emily's mother, who insisted on our tea-ing out. Opposite the village, across the stream, was a small chalk down, crowned by a beech copse, and a few Roman earth-works. (I lectured very vividly on those earthworks: they have since proved to be Saxon). Hither did I drag up a tea-basket and a heavy rug for Emily's mother, while Emily and a little friend went on in front. The little friend—who has played all through a much less important part than he supposes—was a pleasant youth, full of intelligence and poetry, especially of what he called the poetry of earth. He longed to wrest earth's secret from her, and I have seen him press his face passionately into the grass, even when he has believed himself to be alone. Emily was at that time full of vague aspirations, and, though I should have preferred them all to centre in me, yet it seemed unreasonable to deny her such other opportunities for self-culture as the neighbourhood provided.

It was then my habit, on reaching the top of any eminence, to exclaim facetiously "And who will stand on either hand and keep the bridge with me?" at the same moment violently agitating my arms or casting my wide-awake at an imaginary foe. Emily and the friend received my sally as usual, nor could I detect any in-sincerity in their mirth. Yet I was convinced that some one was present who did not think I had been funny, and any public speaker will understand my growing uneasiness.

I was somewhat cheered by Emily's mother, who puffed up exclaiming, "Kind Harry, to carry the things! What should we do without you, even now! Oh, what a view! Can you see the dear

Cathedral? No. Too hazy. Now *I'm* going to sit *right* on the rug."
She smiled mysteriously. "The downs in September, you know."

We gave some perfunctory admiration to the landscape, which
is indeed only beautiful to those who admire land, and to them
perhaps the most beautiful in England. For here is the body of the
great chalk spider who straddles over our island—whose legs are
the south downs and the north downs and the Chilterns, and the
tips of whose toes poke out at Cromer and Dover. He is a clean
creature, who grows as few trees as he can, and those few in tidy
clumps, and he loves to be tickled by quickly flowing streams. He
is pimpled all over with earth-works, for from the beginning of
time men have fought for the privilege of standing on him, and
the oldest of our temples is built upon his back.

But in those days I liked my country snug and pretty, full of
gentlemen's residences and shady bowers and people who touch
their hats. The great sombre expanses on which one may walk for
miles and hardly shift a landmark or meet a genteel person were
still intolerable to me. I turned away as soon as propriety allowed
and said "And may I now prepare the cup that cheers?"

Emily's mother replied: "Kind man, to help me. I always do say
that tea out is worth the extra effort. I wish we led simpler lives."
We agreed with her. I spread out the food. "Won't the kettle
stand? Oh, but *make* it stand." I did so. There was a little cry, faint
but distinct, as of something in pain.

"How silent it all is up here!" said Emily.

I dropped a lighted match on the grass, and again I heard the
little cry.

"What is that?" I asked.

"I only said it was so silent," said Emily.

"Silent, indeed," echoed the little friend.

Silent! the place was full of noises. If the match had fallen in a
drawing-room it could not have been worse, and the loudest
noise came from beside Emily herself. I had exactly the sensation
of going to a great party, of waiting to be announced in the echo-
ing hall, where I could hear the voices of the guests, but could not

yet see their faces. It is a nervous moment for a self-conscious man, especially if all the voices should be strange to him, and he has never met his host.

"My dear Harry!" said the elder lady, "never mind about that match. That'll smoulder away and harm no one. Tea-ee-ee! I always say—and you will find Emily the same—that as the magic hour of five approaches, no matter how good a lunch, one begins to feel a sort of——"

Now the Faun is of the kind who capers upon the Neo-Attic reliefs, and if you do not notice his ears or see his tail, you take him for a man and are horrified.

"Bathing!" I cried wildly. "Such a thing for our village lads, but I quite agree—more supervision—I blame myself. Go away, bad boy, go away!"

"What will he think of next!" said Emily, while the creature beside her stood up and beckoned to me. I advanced struggling and gesticulating with tiny steps and horrified cries, exorcising the apparition with my hat. Not otherwise had I advanced the day before, when Emily's nieces showed me their guinea pigs. And by no less hearty laughter was I greeted now. Until the strange fingers closed upon me, I still thought that here was one of my parishioners and did not cease to exclaim, "Let me go, naughty boy, let go!" And Emily's mother, believing herself to have detected the joke, replied, "Well I must confess they are naughty boys and reach one even on the rug: the downs in September, as I said before."

Here I caught sight of the tail, uttered a wild shriek and fled into the beech copse behind.

"Harry would have been a born actor," said Emily's mother as I left them.

I realized that a great crisis in my life was approaching, and that if I failed in it I might permanently lose my self-esteem. Already in the wood I was troubled by a multitude of voices—the voices of the hill beneath me, of the trees over my head, of the very insects in the bark of the tree. I could even hear the stream licking little pieces out of the meadows, and the meadows dreamily protesting. Above the din—which is no louder than the flight of a bee—rose the Faun's voice saying, "Dear priest, be placid, be placid: why are you frightened?"

"I am not frightened," said I—and indeed I was not. "But I am grieved: you have disgraced me in the presence of ladies."

"No one else has seen me," he said, smiling idly. "The women have tight boots and the man has long hair. Those kinds never see. For years I have only spoken to children, and they lose sight of me as soon as they grow up. But you will not be able to lose sight of me, and until you die you will be my friend. Now I begin to make you happy: lie upon your back or run races, or climb trees, or shall I get you blackberries, or harebells, or wives—"

In a terrible voice I said to him, "Get thee behind me!" He got behind me. "Once for all," I continued, "let me tell you that it is vain to tempt one whose happiness consists in giving happiness to others."

"I cannot understand you," he said ruefully. "What is to tempt?"

"Poor woodland creature!" said I, turning round. "How could you understand? It was idle of me to chide you. It is not in your little nature to comprehend a life of self-denial. Ah! if only I could reach you!"

"You have reached him," said the hill.

"If only I could touch you!"

"You have touched him," said the hill.

"But I will never leave you," burst out the Faun. "I will sweep out your shrine for you, I will accompany you to the meetings of matrons. I will enrich you at the bazaars."

I shook my head. "For these things I care not at all. And indeed I was minded to reject your offer of service altogether. There I was wrong. You shall help me—you shall help me to make others happy."

"Dear priest, what a curious life! People whom I have never seen—people who cannot see me—why should I make them happy?"

"My poor lad—perhaps in time you will learn why. Now begone: commence. On this very hill sits a young lady for whom I have a high regard. Commence with her. Aha! your face falls. I thought as much. You *cannot* do anything. Here is the conclusion of the whole matter!"

"I can make her happy," he replied, "if you order me; and when I have done so, perhaps you will trust me more."

Emily's mother had started home, but Emily and the little friend still sat beside the tea-things—she in her white piqué dress and biscuit straw, he in his rough but well-cut summer suit. The great pagan figure of the Faun towered insolently above them.

The friend was saying, "And have you never felt the appalling loneliness of a crowd?"

"All that," replied Emily, "have I felt, and very much more——"

Then the Faun laid his hands upon them. They, who had only intended a little cultured flirtation, resisted him as long as they could, but were gradually urged into each other's arms, and embraced with passion.

"Miscreant!" I shouted, bursting from the wood. "You have betrayed me."

"I know it: I care not," cried the little friend. "Stand aside. You are in the presence of that which you do not understand. In the great solitude we have found ourselves at last."

"Remove your accursed hands!" I shrieked to the Faun.

He obeyed and the little friend continued more calmly: "It is idle to chide. What should you know, poor clerical creature, of the mystery of love of the eternal man and the eternal woman, of the self-effectuation of a soul?"

"That is true," said Emily angrily. "Harry, you would never have made me happy. I shall treat you as a friend, but how could I give myself to a man who makes such silly jokes? When you played the buffoon at tea, your hour was sealed. I must be treated seriously: I must see infinities broadening around me as I rise. You may not approve of it, but so I am. In the great solitude I have found myself at last."

"Wretched girl!" I cried. "Great solitude! O pair of helpless puppets——"

The little friend began to lead Emily away, but I heard her whisper to him: "Dear, we can't possibly leave the basket for Harry after this: and mother's rug; do you mind having that in the other hand?"

So they departed and I flung myself upon the ground with every appearance of despair.

"Does he cry?" said the Faun.

"He does not cry," answered the hill. "His eyes are as dry as pebbles."

My tormentor made me look at him. "I see happiness at the bottom of your heart," said he.

"I trust I have my secret springs," I answered stiffly. And then I prepared a scathing denunciation, but of all the words I might have said, I only said one and it began with "D."

He gave a joyful cry, "Oh, now you really belong to us. To the end of your life you will swear when you are cross and laugh when you are happy. Now laugh!"

There was a great silence. All nature stood waiting, while a curate tried to conceal his thoughts not only from nature but from himself. I thought of my injured pride, of my baffled unselfishness, of Emily, whom I was losing through no fault of her own, of the little friend, who just then slipped beneath the heavy tea basket, and that decided me, and I laughed.

That evening, for the first time, I heard the chalk downs singing to each other across the valleys, as they often do when the air is quiet and they have had a comfortable day. From my study window I could see the sunlit figure of the Faun, sitting before the beech copse as a man sits before his house. And as night came on I knew for certain that not only was he asleep, but that the hills and woods were asleep also. The stream, of course, never slept, any more than it ever freezes. Indeed, the hour of darkness is really the hour of water, which has been somewhat stifled all day by the great pulsings of the land. That is why you can feel it and hear it from a greater distance in the night, and why a bath after sundown is most wonderful.

The joy of that first evening is still clear in my memory, in spite of all the happy years that have followed. I remember it when I ascend my pulpit—I have a living now—and look down upon the best people sitting beneath me pew after pew, generous and contented, upon the worse people, crowded in the aisles, upon the whiskered tenors of the choir, and the high-browed curates and the church-wardens fingering their bags, and the supercilious vergers who turn late comers from the door. I remember it also when I sit in my comfortable bachelor rectory, amidst the carpet slippers that good young ladies have worked for me, and the oak brackets that have been carved for me by good young men; amidst my phalanx of presentation teapots and my illuminated testimonials and all the other offerings of people who believe that I have given them a helping hand, and who really have helped me out of the mire themselves. And though I try to communicate that joy to others—as I try to communicate anything else that seems good—and though I sometimes succeed, yet I can tell no one exactly how it came to me. For if I breathed one word of that, my present life, so agreeable and profitable, would come to an end, my congregation would depart, and so should I, and instead of being an asset to my parish, I might find myself an expense to the nation. Therefore in the place of the lyrical and rhetorical treatment, so suitable to the subject, so congenial to my profession, I have been forced to use the unworthy medium of a narrative, and to delude you by declaring that this is a short story, suitable for reading in the train.

· · ·

The Road from Colonus

I

For no very intelligible reason, Mr. Lucas had hurried ahead of his party. He was perhaps reaching the age at which independence becomes valuable, because it is so soon to be lost. Tired of attention and consideration, he liked breaking away from the younger members, to ride by himself, and to dismount unassisted. Perhaps he also relished that more subtle pleasure of being kept waiting for lunch, and of telling the others on their arrival that it was of no consequence.

So, with childish impatience, he battered the animal's sides with his heels, and made the muleteer bang it with a thick stick and prick it with. a sharp one, and jolted down the hill sides through clumps of flowering shrubs and stretches of anemones and asphodel, till he heard the sound of running water, and came in sight of the group of plane trees where they were to have their meal.

Even in England those trees would have been remarkable, so huge were they, so interlaced, so magnificently clothed in quivering green. And here in Greece they were unique, the one cool spot in that hard brilliant landscape, already scorched by the heat of an April sun. In their midst was hidden a tiny Khan or country inn, a frail mud building with a broad wooden balcony in which sat an old woman spinning, while a small brown pig, eating orange peel, stood beside her. On the wet earth below squatted two children, playing some primaeval game with their fingers; and their mother, none too clean either, was messing with some rice inside. As Mrs. Forman would have said, it was all very

Greek, and the fastidious Mr. Lucas felt thankful that they were
bringing their own food with them, and should eat it in the
open air.

Still, he was glad to be there—the muleteer had helped him
off—and glad that Mrs. Forman was not there to forestall his
opinions—glad even that he should not see Ethel for quite half an
hour. Ethel was his youngest daughter, still unmarried. She was
unselfish and affectionate, and it was generally understood that
she was to devote her life to her father, and be the comfort of his
old age. Mrs. Forman always referred to her as Antigone, and Mr.
Lucas tried to settle down to the role of Oedipus, which seemed
the only one that public opinion allowed him.

He had this in common with Oedipus, that he was growing
old. Even to himself it had become obvious. He had lost interest
in other people's affairs, and seldom attended when they spoke to
him. He was fond of talking himself but often forgot what he was
going to say, and even when he succeeded, it seldom seemed
worth the effort. His phrases and gestures had become stiff and
set, his anecdotes, once so successful, fell flat, his silence was as
meaningless as his speech. Yet he had led a healthy, active life, had
worked steadily, made money, educated his children. There was
nothing and no one to blame: he was simply growing old.

At the present moment, here he was in Greece, and one of the
dreams of his life was realized. Forty years ago he had caught the
fever of Hellenism, and all his life he had felt that could he but
visit that land, he would not have lived in vain. But Athens had
been dusty, Delphi wet, Thermopylae flat, and he had listened
with amazement and cynicism to the rapturous exclamations of
his companions. Greece was like England: it was a man who was
growing old, and it made no difference whether that man looked
at the Thames or the Eurotas. It was his last hope of contradicting
that logic of experience, and it was failing.

Yet Greece had done something for him, though he did not
know it. It had made him discontented, and there are stirrings
of life in discontent. He knew that he was not the victim of

continual ill-luck. Something great was wrong, and he was pitted against no mediocre or accidental enemy. For the last month a strange desire had possessed him to die fighting.

"Greece is the land for young people," he said to himself as he stood under the plane trees, "but I will enter into it, I will possess it. Leaves shall be green again, water shall be sweet, the sky shall be blue. They were so forty years ago, and I will win them back. I do mind being old, and I will pretend no longer."

He took two steps forward, and immediately cold waters were gurgling over his ankle.

"Where does the water come from?" he asked himself. "I do not even know that." He remembered that all the hill sides were dry; yet here the road was suddenly covered with flowing streams.

He stopped still in amazement, saying: "Water out of a tree— out of a hollow tree? I never saw nor thought of that before."

For the enormous plane that leant towards the Khan was hollow—it had been burnt out for charcoal—and from its living trunk there gushed an impetuous spring, coating the bark with fern and moss, and flowing over the mule track to create fertile meadows beyond. The simple country folk had paid to beauty and mystery such tribute as they could, for in the rind of the tree a shrine was cut, holding a lamp and a little picture of the Virgin, inheritor of the Naiad's and Dryad's joint abode.

"I never saw anything so marvellous before," said Mr. Lucas. "I could even step inside the trunk and see where the water comes from."

For a moment he hesitated to violate the shrine. Then he remembered with a smile his own thought—"the place shall be mine; I will enter it and possess it"—and leapt almost agressively on to a stone within.

The water pressed up steadily and noiselessly from the hollow roots and hidden crevices of the plane, forming a wonderful amber pool ere it spilt over the lip of bark on to the earth outside. Mr. Lucas tasted it and it was sweet, and when he looked up the black funnel of the trunk he saw sky which was blue, and some leaves which were green; and he remembered, without smiling, another of his thoughts.

Others had been before him—indeed he had a curious sense of companionship. Little votive offerings to the presiding Power were fastened on to the bark—tiny arms and legs and eyes in tin, grotesque models of the brain or the heart—all tokens of some recovery of strength or wisdom or love. There was no such thing as the solitude of nature, for the sorrows and joys of humanity had pressed even into the bosom of a tree. He spread out his arms and steadied himself against the soft charred wood, and then slowly leant back, till his body was resting on the trunk behind. His eyes closed, and he had the strange feeling of one who is moving, yet at peace—the feeling of the swimmer, who, after long struggling with chopping seas, finds that after all the tide will sweep him to his goal.

So he lay motionless, conscious only of the stream below his feet, and that all things were a stream, in which he was moving.

He was aroused at last by a shock—the shock of an arrival perhaps, for when he opened his eyes, something unimagined, indefinable, had passed over all things, and made them intelligible and good.

There was meaning in the stoop of the old woman over her work, and in the quick motions of the little pig, and in her diminishing globe of wool. A young man came singing over the streams on a mule, and there was beauty in his pose and sincerity in his greeting. The sun made no accidental patterns upon the spreading roots of the trees, and there was intention in the nodding clumps of asphodel, and in the music of the water. To Mr. Lucas, who, in a brief space of time, had discovered not only Greece, but England and all the world and life, there seemed nothing ludicrous in the desire to hang within the tree another votive offering—a little model of an entire man.

"Why, here's papa, playing at being Merlin."

All unnoticed they had arrived—Ethel, Mrs. Forman, Mr. Graham, and the English-speaking dragoman. Mr. Lucas peered out at them suspiciously. They had suddenly become unfamiliar, and all that they did seemed strained and coarse.

"Allow me to give you a hand," said Mr. Graham, a young man who was always polite to his elders.

Mr. Lucas felt annoyed. "Thank you, I can manage perfectly well by myself," he replied. His foot slipped as he stepped out of the tree, and went into the spring.

"Oh papa, my papa!" said Ethel, "what are you doing? Thank goodness I have got a change for you on the mule."

She tended him carefully, giving him clean socks and dry boots, and then sat him down on the rug beside the lunch basket, while she went with the others to explore the grove.

They came back in ecstasies, in which Mr. Lucas tried to join. But he found them intolerable. Their enthusiasm was superficial, commonplace, and spasmodic. They had no perception of the coherent beauty that was flowering around them. He tried at least to explain his feelings, and what he said was:

"I am altogether pleased with the appearance of this place. It impresses me very favourably. The trees are fine, remarkably fine for Greece, and there is something very poetic in the spring of clear running water. The people too seem kindly and civil. It is decidedly an attractive place."

Mrs. Forman upbraided him for his tepid praise.

"Oh, it is a place in a thousand!" she cried "I could live and die here! I really would stop if I had not to be back at Athens! It reminds me of the Colonus of Sophocles."

"Well, I must stop," said Ethel. "I positively must."

"Yes, do! You and your father! Antigone and Oedipus. Of course you must stop at Colonus!"

Mr. Lucas was almost breathless with excitement. When he stood within the tree, he had believed that his happiness would be independent of locality. But these few minutes' conversation had undeceived him. He no longer trusted himself to journey through the world, for old thoughts, old wearinesses might be waiting to rejoin him as soon as he left the shade of the planes, and the music of the virgin water. To sleep in the Khan with the gracious, kind-eyed country people, to watch the bats flit about within the globe of shade, and see the moon turn the golden patterns into silver—one such night would place him beyond relapse, and confirm him for ever in the kingdom he had regained. But all his lips could say was: "I should be willing to put in a night here."

"You mean a week, papa! It would be sacrilege to put in less."

"A week then, a week," said his lips, irritated at being corrected, while his heart was leaping with joy. All through lunch he spoke to them no more, but watched the place he should know so well, and the people who would so soon be his companions and friends. The inmates of the Khan only consisted of an old woman, a middle-aged woman, a young man and two children, and to none of them had he spoken, yet he loved them as he loved everything that moved or breathed or existed beneath the benedictory shade of the planes.

"*En route!*" said the shrill voice of Mrs. Forman. "Ethel! Mr. Graham! The best of things must end."

"To-night," thought Mr. Lucas, "they will light the little lamp by the shrine. And when we all sit together on the balcony, perhaps they will tell me which offerings they put up."

"I beg your pardon, Mr. Lucas," said Graham, "but they want to fold up the rug you are sitting on."

Mr. Lucas got up, saying to himself: "Ethel shall go to bed first, and then I will try to tell them about my offering too—for it is a thing I must do. I think they will understand if I am left with them alone."

Ethel touched him on the cheek. "Papa! I've called you three times. All the mules are here."

"Mules? What mules?"

"Our mules. We're all waiting. Oh, Mr. Graham, do help my father on."

"I don't know what you're talking about, Ethel."

"My dearest papa, we must start. You know we have to get to Olympia to-night."

Mr. Lucas in pompous, confident tones replied: "I always did wish, Ethel, that you had a better head for plans. You know perfectly well that we are putting in a week here. It is your own suggestion."

Ethel was startled into impoliteness. "What a perfectly ridiculous idea. You must have known I was joking. Of course I meant I wished we could."

"Ah! if we could only do what we wished!" sighed Mrs. Forman, already seated on her mule.

"Surely," Ethel continued in calmer tones, "you didn't think I meant it."

"Most certainly I did. I have made all my plans on the supposition that we are stopping here, and it will be extremely inconvenient, indeed, impossible for me to start."

He delivered this remark with an air of great conviction, and Mrs. Forman and Mr. Graham had to turn away to hide their smiles.

"I am sorry I spoke so carelessly; it was wrong of me. But, you know, we can't break up our party, and even one night here would make us miss the boat at Patras."

Mrs. Forman, in an aside, called Mr. Graham's attention to the excellent way in which Ethel managed her father.

"I don't mind about the Patras boat. You said that we should stop here, and we are stopping."

It seemed as if the inhabitants of the Khan had divined in some mysterious way that the altercation touched them. The old woman stopped her spinning, while the young man and the two children stood behind Mr. Lucas, as if supporting him.

Neither arguments nor entreaties moved him. He said little, but he was absolutely determined, because for the first time he saw his daily life aright. What need had he to return to England? Who would miss him? His friends were dead or cold. Ethel loved him in a way, but, as was right, she had other interests. His other children he seldom saw. He had only one other relative, his sister Julia, whom he both feared and hated. It was no effort to struggle.

He would be a fool as well as a coward if he stirred from the place which brought him happiness and peace.

At last Ethel, to humour him, and not disinclined to air her modern Greek, went into the Khan with the astonished dragoman to look at the rooms. The woman inside received them with loud welcomes, and the young man, when no one was looking, began to lead Mr. Lucas' mule to the stable.

"Drop it, you brigand!" shouted Graham, who always declared that foreigners could understand English if they chose. He was right, for the man obeyed, and they all stood waiting for Ethel's return.

She emerged at last, with close-gathered skirts, followed by the dragoman bearing the little pig, which he had bought at a bargain.

"My dear papa, I will do all I can for you, but stop in that Khan—no."

"Are there—fleas?" asked Mrs. Forman.

Ethel intimated that "fleas" was not the word.

"Well, I am afraid that settles it," said Mrs. Forman, "I know how particular Mr. Lucas is."

"It does not settle it," said Mr. Lucas. "Ethel, you go on. I do not want you. I don't know why I ever consulted you. I shall stop here alone."

"That is absolute nonsense," said Ethel, losing her temper. "How can you be left alone at your age? How would you get your meals or your bath? All your letters are waiting for you at Patras. You'll miss the boat. That means missing the London operas, and upsetting all your engagements for the month. And as if you could travel by yourself!"

"They might knife you," was Mr. Graham's contribution.

The Greeks said nothing; but whenever Mr. Lucas looked their way, they beckoned him towards the Khan. The children would even have drawn him by the coat, and the old woman on the balcony stopped her almost completed spinning, and fixed him with mysterious appealing eyes. As he fought, the issue assumed gigantic proportions, and he believed that he was not merely stopping because he had regained youth or seen beauty or found happiness, but because in that place and with those people a supreme event was awaiting him which would transfigure the face of the world. The moment was so tremendous that he abandoned words and arguments as useless, and rested on the strength of his mighty unrevealed allies: silent men, murmuring water, and whispering trees. For the whole place called with one voice, articulate to him, and his garrulous opponents became every minute more meaningless and absurd. Soon they would be tired and go chattering away into the sun, leaving him to the cool grove and the moonlight and the destiny he foresaw.

Mrs. Forman and the dragoman had indeed already started, amid the piercing screams of the little pig, and the struggle might have gone on indefinitely if Ethel had not called in Mr. Graham.

"Can you help me?" she whispered. "He is absolutely unmanageable."

"I'm no good at arguing—but if I could help you in any other way——" and he looked down complacently at his well-made figure.

Ethel hesitated. Then she said: "Help me in any way you can. After all, it is for his good that we do it."

"Then have his mule led up behind him."

So when Mr. Lucas thought he had gained the day, he suddenly felt himself lifted off the ground, and sat sideways on the saddle, and at the same time the mule started off at a trot. He said nothing, for he had nothing to say, and even his face showed little emotion as he felt the shade pass and heard the sound of the water cease. Mr. Graham was running at his side, hat in hand, apologizing.

"I know I had no business to do it, and I do beg your pardon awfully. But I do hope that some day you too will feel that I was —damn!"

A stone had caught him in the middle of the back. It was thrown by the little boy, who was pursuing them along the mule track. He was followed by his sister, also throwing stones.

Ethel screamed to the dragoman, who was some way ahead with Mrs. Forman, but before he could rejoin them, another adversary appeared. It was the young Greek, who had cut them off in front, and now dashed down at Mr. Lucas' bridle. Fortunately Graham was an expert boxer, and it did not take him a moment to beat down the youth's feeble defence, and to send him sprawling with a bleeding mouth into the asphodel. By this time the dragoman had arrived, the children, alarmed at the fate of their brother, had desisted, and the rescue party, if such it is to be considered, retired in disorder to the trees.

"Little devils!" said Graham, laughing with triumph. "That's the modern Greek all over. Your father meant money if he stopped, and they consider we were taking it out of their pocket."

"Oh, they are terrible—simple savages! I don't know how I shall ever thank you. You've saved my father."

"I only hope you didn't think me brutal."

"No," replied Ethel with a little sigh. "I admire strength."

Meanwhile the cavalcade reformed, and Mr. Lucas, who, as Mrs. Forman said, bore his disappointment wonderfully well, was put comfortably on to his mule. They hurried up the opposite hillside, fearful of another attack, and it was not until they had left the eventful place far behind that Ethel found an opportunity to speak to her father and ask his pardon for the way she had treated him.

"You seemed so different, dear father, and you quite frightened me. Now I feel that you are your old self again."

He did not answer, and she concluded that he was not unnaturally offended at her behaviour.

By one of those curious tricks of mountain scenery, the place they had left an hour before suddenly reappeared far below them. The Khan was hidden under the green dome, but in the open there still stood three figures, and through the pure air rose up a faint cry of defiance or farewell.

Mr. Lucas stopped irresolutely, and let the reins fall from his hand.

"Come, father dear," said Ethel gently.

He obeyed, and in another moment a spur of the hill hid the dangerous scene for ever.

II

It was breakfast time, but the gas was alight, owing to the fog. Mr. Lucas was in the middle of an account of a bad night he had spent. Ethel, who was to be married in a few weeks, had her arms on the table, listening.

"First the door bell rang, then you came back from the theatre. Then the dog started, and after the dog the cat. And at three in the morning a young hooligan passed by singing. Oh yes: then there was the water gurgling in the pipe above my head."

"I think that was only the bath water running away," said Ethel, looking rather worn.

"Well, there's nothing I dislike more than running water. It's perfectly impossible to sleep in the house. I shall give it up. I shall give notice next quarter. I shall tell the landlord plainly, 'The reason I am giving up the house is this: it is perfectly impossible to sleep in it.' If he says—says—well, what has he got to say?"

"Some more toast, father?"

"Thank you, my dear." He took it, and there was an interval of peace.

But he soon recommenced. "I'm not going to submit to the practising next door as tamely as they think. I wrote and told them so—didn't I?"

"Yes," said Ethel, who had taken care that the letter should not reach. "I have seen the governess, and she has promised to arrange it differently. And Aunt Julia hates noise. It will sure to be all right."

Her aunt, being the only unattached member of the family, was coming to keep house for her father when she left him. The reference was not a happy one, and Mr. Lucas commenced a series of half articulate sighs, which was only stopped by the arrival of the post.

"Oh, what a parcel!" cried Ethel. "For me! What can it be! Greek stamps. This is most exciting!"

It proved to be some asphodel bulbs, sent by Mrs. Forman from Athens for planting in the conservatory.

"Doesn't it bring it all back! You remember the asphodels, father. And all wrapped up in Greek newspapers. I wonder if I can read them still. I used to be able to, you know."

She rattled on, hoping to conceal the laughter of the children next door—a favourite source of querulousness at breakfast time.

"Listen to me! 'A rural disaster.' Oh, I've hit on something sad. But never mind. 'Last Tuesday at Plataniste, in the province of Messenia, a shocking tragedy occurred. A large tree'—aren't I getting on well?—'blew down in the night and'—wait a minute—oh, dear! 'crushed to death the five occupants of the little Khan there, who had apparently been sitting in the balcony. The bodies of Maria Rhomaides, the aged proprietress, and of her daughter, aged forty-six, were easily recognizable, whereas that of her grandson'—oh, the rest is really too horrid: I wish I had never tried it, and what's more I feel to have heard the name Plataniste before. We didn't stop there, did we, in the spring?"

"We had lunch," said Mr. Lucas, with a faint expression of trouble on his vacant face. "Perhaps it was where the dragoman bought the pig."

"Of course," said Ethel in a nervous voice. "Where the dragoman bought the little pig. How terrible!"

"Very terrible!" said her father, whose attention was wandering to the noisy children next door. Ethel suddenly started to her feet with genuine interest.

"Good gracious!" she exclaimed. "This is an old paper. It happened not lately but in April—the night of Tuesday the eighteenth—and we—we must have been there in the afternoon."

"So we were," said Mr. Lucas. She put her hand to her heart, scarcely able to speak.

"Father, dear father, I must say it: you wanted to stop there. All those people, those poor half savage people, tried to keep you, and they're dead. The whole place, it says, is in ruins, and even the stream has changed its course. Father, dear, if it had not been for me, and if Arthur had not helped me, you must have been killed."

Mr. Lucas waved his hand irritably. "It is not a bit of good speaking to the governess, I shall write to the landlord and say, 'The reason I am giving up the house is this: the dog barks, the children next door are intolerable, and I cannot stand the noise of running water.'"

Ethel did not check his babbling. She was aghast at the narrowness of the escape, and for a long time kept silence. At last she said: "Such a marvellous deliverance does make one believe in Providence."

Mr. Lucas, who was still composing his letter to the landlord, did not reply.

. . .

REVIEW

The Season's Great Novel "Howards End"

BY

ARCHIBALD MARSHALL

LONDON DAILY MAIL
NOVEMBER 17, 1910

Mr. E. M. Forster is not a new novelist in the sense of coming before the public with a first book. "Howards End," which has become a general subject of talk in literary circles, is his fourth novel, but with it he may be said to have arrived, as the phrase goes. He showed much of his power in his last book, "A Room with a View," but "Howards End" is a riper work altogether, and raises its author to a place among contemporary novelists which few even of those whose earlier work shows promise succeed in attaining to.

"Howards End" is the name of a house, a little, old, rather inconvenient country house, not so very far from London. It belongs to the Wilcoxes, capable, business-like people, all clear and sane and effective on the outside, all muddled and wrong about the deeper things that really matter—matter at least to people like the Schlegels, who are contrasted with them throughout the story. The house also plays its part throughout. Mrs. Wilcox, to whom it actually belongs, and who loves it, dies suddenly, and leaves a pencilled note to say that she should like it to go to Margaret Schlegel, the elder of the two orphan sisters, knowing that she will cherish it as a possession, and feeling perhaps that her own bustling family will never value it beyond its appropriateness or otherwise as the sort of house they want to live in. But Mr. Wilcox tears up the paper, and Margaret hears nothing of the bequest until at the very end of the story, when she is married to Mr. Wilcox as his second wife and many other things have happened between them.

THE CONTRAST
OF CHARACTER

The Schlegels, always on the look-out for originality, come across a pathetic, ineffective little clerk with leanings toward adventure both of the mind and body. He is married to a woman of no intelligence at all, who has entrapped him in his youth, and there is a breathless scene when Helen Schlegel rushes the pair of them down to Shropshire, where Mr. Wilcox is marrying off his daughter, and the startling fact bursts upon Margaret, whose own marriage is about to take place, that Mr. Wilcox during the lifetime of his first wife has had relations with the unspeakable and irresponsible 'Jacky.'

Helen also discovers the fact, and her piercing sympathy with the troubles of the poor little clerk brings about her sudden undoing. The way in which the truth, when it comes out, forms the pivot of the final struggle between Margaret's essential rightness of mind and her husband's crude and illogical want of principal is realised in a masterly way.

In the end there is happiness between the warring factions. Love and reason have triumphed. Unfortunately it is just here that Mr. Forster, having elaborated his theme at great length throughout the book, hastily takes leave of us with a very slight gathering up of the threads, and we are left wondering exactly how the happiness we are assured has descended once more upon Howards End can have come about. We are not quite satisfied with his sketched-in explanation, and Mr. Wilcox's conversion somehow recalls that of Mr. Dombey.

THE OLD CANONS
OF FICTION

But the faults of this book are as nothing compared to its merits. The way in which the characters—even those minor ones who have not been mentioned above—are made to live before us is of the essence of all great fiction. "Howards End" is essentially a novel of character, but where it differs from a good deal of clever modern work done more or less upon the same lines is that Mr. Forster has gone back to the old canons of fiction and exhibited his characters in action. That is to say, he has made it his business to tell us a story about them. Things are always happening in "Howards End," and although there is a great deal of talk, and very good talk, both from the characters themselves and also from the author, it is not all talk. That is why "Howards End" will be widely read. There will be many who read it for the story alone, and they will be right to do so, for the best novels have always contained the best stories.

When Margaret Schlegel was looking out for a new house in London Mr. Wilcox suggested that his unoccupied house in Ducie-street might suit her. When she was engaged to him they looked over the house with the idea of living in it, and he told her that Ducie-street had huge drawbacks. "There's a mews behind."

Margaret could not help laughing. It was the first she had heard of the mews behind Ducie-street. When she was a possible tenant it had suppressed itself, not consciously, but automatically. The breezy Wilcox manner, though genuine, lacked the clearness of vision that is imperative for truth. When Henry lived in Ducie-street he remembered the mews; when he tried to let he forgot it; and if anyone remarked that the mews must be either there or not, he would have felt annoyed, and afterwards have found some opportunity of stigmatising the speaker as academic. So does my grocer stigmatise me when I complain of the quality of his sultanas, and he answers in one breath that they are the best sultanas, and how can I expect the best sultanas at that price? It is a flaw inherent in the business mind, and Margaret may do well to be tender to it, considering all that the business mind has done for England.

This little passage is typical of Mr. Forster's method. He takes infinite trouble to devise little episodes and illustrations to show up his characters, instead of telling us what they are like. It is, of course, the method of the old, good novelists, but the clever moderns are apt to forget it. Invention means trouble, and it is much easier to write pages of analysis; only they are not so easy to read.

MR. FORSTER'S WORLDLY PHILOSOPHY

Another short quotation may serve to show the author presenting ideas, of which throughout the book he is delightfully prodigal.

Death destroys a man; the idea of Death saves him. Behind the coffins and the skeletons that stay the vulgar mind lies something so immense that all that is great in us responds to it. Men of the world may recoil from the charnel-house that they will one day enter, but Love knows better. Death is his foe, but his peer, and in their age-long struggle the thews of Love have been strengthened, and his vision cleared, until there is no one who can stand against him.

"Howards End" is packed full of good things. It stands out head and shoulders above the great mass of fiction now claiming a hearing. The autumn season has brought us some good novels, but this is, so far, the best of them.

Review by Archibald Marshall (1866–1934), prolific minor novelist and the author of *Peter Binnet, Undergraduate* (1899), *The House of Merrilees* (1905), *Exton Manor* (1907), and more.